SCORCHED SHADOWS

By Steve McHugh

SCORCHED SHADOWS

STEVE McHUGH

47NORTH

Text copyright © 2017 by Steve McHugh
All rights reserved.

Published by 47North, Seattle

www.apub.com

Amazon, the Amazon logo, and 47North are trademarks of Amazon.com, Inc., or its affiliates.

ISBN-13: 9781542046602
ISBN-10: 1542046602

Cover design by @blacksheep-uk.com

Cover illustration by Larry Rostant

Printed in the United States of America

For my readers.
Thank you.

LIST OF CHARACTERS

Nathan (Nate) Garrett: Sorcerer. Once worked for Merlin as the shadowy figure Hellequin. Partner to Selene.

Erebus (Nightmare): The living embodiment of Nate's magic.

Mordred: Sorcerer. Once nemesis of Nate, now friends.

Selene: Dragon-kin. Partner to Nate. Sister of Helios. Daughter to the Titan Hyperion.

Tommy, Friends, and Employees

Thomas (Tommy) Carpenter: Werewolf. Nate's best friend. Partner to Olivia. Father of Kasey.

Diana: Half-werebear. Works for Tommy's security firm.

Zamek Merla: Dwarven warrior commander. Works for Tommy's security firm.

Remy Roax: British son of a French aristocrat. Turned into a fox-human hybrid by a witch coven.

Irkalla: Necromancer. Mesopotamian goddess of the underworld.

Nabu: Och. Mesopotamian god of wisdom.

Grayson: Unknown species. Doctor.

Avalon Members

Arthur Pendragon: Sorcerer. Recently woken from coma. Head of Avalon.

Merlin: Sorcerer. Onetime mentor to Nate. Obsessed with keeping Arthur alive.

Elaine Garlot: Sorcerer. Mentor to Nate. Aunt of Mordred. Once acting ruler of Avalon.

Gawain: Sorcerer. Brother to Mordred. Head of Merlin's security force, the paladins.

Olivia Green: Water elemental. Director of southern England branch of LOA (Law of Avalon). Partner to Tommy. Mother of Kasey.

Fiona Daly: Conjurer. Agent of Avalon. Answers to Elaine. Married to Alan.

Alan Daly: Summoned. Reformed thief. Married to Fiona.

Manannán mac Lir (Mac): Water elemental.

Hades's Family, Friends, and Employees

Hades: Necromancer of incredible power. Husband to Persephone and adopted father to Sky.

Persephone: Earth elemental. Wife to Hades and adopted mother to Sky.

Sky (Mapiya): Necromancer. Half Native American. Birth parents murdered when she was a child. Adopted by Hades and Persephone.

Cerberus: Werewolf. Controls the Tartarus compound when Hades isn't there.

Tartarus Inhabitants

Lorin: Griffin. One of the guards of Tartarus.

Charon: Ferryman for Tartarus. Member of the Titans.

Atlas: Siphon. Member of the Titans.

Hyperion: Dragon-kin. Father to Selene and Helios.

Shadow Falls Inhabitants

Galahad: Alchemist. Father to Caitlin. King of Shadow Falls.

Caitlin: Alchemist. Daughter to Galahad. Onetime FBI agent.

Rebecca Dean: Guardian. Runs The Mill bar in Portland, Maine.

Harrison: Alchemist. Head of Shadow Falls security.

Leonardo: Alchemist. Partner of Antonio. Tinkerer and inventor.

Antonio: Alchemist. Partner of Leonardo. Leonardo's assistant.

Miscellaneous

Deimos: Negative empath. Son of Ares.

Ares: Negative empath. Son of Hera. Husband to Aphrodite.

Mara Range: Coven member. Mother to Chloe.

Helios: Dragon-kin. Brother to Selene, son of Hyperion.

Chao Wei: Huli jing. Friend of Diana's.

Polina: Head of Russian LOA task force.

CHAPTER 1

Mordred

Manhattan, New York, USA

By the time Mordred reached the front of the queue in the coffee shop, he'd read their winter menu a dozen times and discounted each of the drinks available as either too sweet or something he'd only drink under torture. Coffee, he decided, should not have sprinkles in it, on it, or close to the cup.

"Large Americano, please," Mordred said with a smile to the young man standing behind the counter.

The server looked vaguely disappointed that it was something so simple but rang up the order. "Your name?" he asked, poised to write it on the side of the cup.

"Mordred."

The young man was ready to write but instead looked back up at Mordred. "Seriously?"

"Who would possibly make up that name for themselves?" Mordred asked. "Yes, my name is Mordred."

The young man wrote something that was at best barely legible on the cup and passed it over to a second young man, who made Mordred's drink.

Mordred began to hum the theme tune to *The Legend of Zelda*, gaining a few strange looks from people, which he promptly ignored.

A minute later Mordred was passed his drink, and he walked off up a set of stairs to find a comfortable seat on the floor above.

The red leather couch he found was exactly what he'd been looking for, and he sat down with a slight sigh and looked out a large window beside him at the street below. He placed his drink on the pale wooden table in front of him and shrugged off his jacket. He was in Manhattan to meet Elaine Garlot. Elaine had been the ruler of Avalon before Arthur woke up and everyone assumed he would take control. She was also Mordred's aunt, and someone he had a genuine affection for.

Over a decade ago Mordred had been shot in the head, and instead of finding himself very much in the land of the dead, he woke up sans bullet hole. There had been a few benefits to being shot, a fact in and of itself he found strange, but the main one was that after over a thousand years of wanting to murder people, he was finally free from his homicidal desires. He was finally able to start putting things right.

It had been nearly three years since he'd revealed to Nate Garrett that he was alive, something Nate had been at first unhappy about considering he'd been the one to shoot Mordred in the first place. Gradually Nate began to trust Mordred, and now they were both in a place where they could be friendly, each man not having to worry about the other trying to kill him. Well, mostly, anyway.

It had been foretold by the Fates that Mordred had to kill Nate, because otherwise Nate would go crazy and murder everyone. Nate was, understandably, upset by this news, but the very idea of killing his friend made Mordred feel queasy. He'd spent the better part of twelve hundred years trying to kill him, but at last he was in a place where they could be friends again. Yet this specter of the future hung over them both. Mordred hoped they could find a way to avoid it; in fact he'd spent several months trying to figure out just that but hadn't come up with any ideas.

Concerned that he'd have to murder his friend to fulfill some prophecy he wanted no part of, Mordred avoided Nate for the better part of a year, trying all the while to find a way out of a future he was certain would come to pass.

Mordred took a drink of his coffee and thought about the many changes that had occurred in the three years since he and Nate had begun to re-form the bonds of friendship. Arthur Pendragon, once comatose by Mordred's own hands, had woken and taken charge of Avalon—the organization that secretly ran the world far from the gaze of humanity. Mordred hadn't seen Arthur since he'd reclaimed his position as the head of Avalon, and he had little interest in doing so. He was almost sure that Arthur would be in a much less forgiving mood than even Nate had been.

The enemies of Avalon had seemingly dropped off the face of the earth, too. Even Hera, who had claimed London as her own only months before Arthur had woken, had been quiet. Any trouble had seemingly been taken control of by Avalon as Arthur sought to regain control of an organization that had been trying to tear itself apart for too long.

The lack of people trying to kill him and his friends had made it easier for Mordred to walk away from that life and try to find answers. He'd traveled the world and eventually arrived in America so that he could talk to people there who were considerably older than even his own sixteen hundred years. Elaine had been around for thousands of years. She'd probably seen everything there was to see. If anyone had an answer, it would be her. Elaine had contacted him a month earlier to give a date, place, and time to meet. She told him she had information about the prophecy that he needed to hear.

One of the big problems with the Fates was that while they often saw *a* future, it was not necessarily *the* future, and frankly the whole thing made Mordred's head hurt. Just because the Fates saw something didn't mean it would happen, but they'd told Mordred that they had seen no other way forward for him and Nate.

He was still thinking about his reason for being in New York, and trying to stop whatever future lay before him, when someone cleared their throat. Mordred looked up at a woman on the other side of the table, standing next to one of two leather chairs.

"Is this seat taken?" she asked.

"Of course," Mordred said with a smile. "Sorry, I was miles away. Do you do miles? It's kilometers here, isn't it? I'm never all that sure which British words Americans understand."

The woman smiled. She had a nice smile, Mordred thought. In fact she was a very attractive woman. Her long hair had been dyed a mixture of greens, blues, and even a little red. Several strands of bright-green hair had been tucked behind her ear. She had a multitude of hoops in both ears, and a dragon tattoo on one arm that started on her wrist and vanished up the sleeve of her blue T-shirt. The other arm had several different tattoos, but Mordred was only interested in the Mario and Princess Peach tattoo on her forearm.

"So, it's taken?" she asked.

"Sorry, I said of course, didn't I?" Mordred motioned toward the chair. "Please take a seat and ignore my inane ramblings."

She placed her drink on the table between them and sat down.

"Nice tattoos," Mordred said, pointing to her arm as he tried to decide whether she was human. Or whether she was an enemy.

"Thanks, I'm a big Mario fan. You play?"

Mordred smiled. "I've been known to annoy friends by humming the theme tune, so a little, yes."

The woman laughed. "I'm Cass, by the way."

"Mordred."

She offered him her hand, which he shook, and he noticed that on each of the nails on her hand was a Mario 1-Up mushroom. The small green image made Mordred chuckle.

Cass looked at her nails. "Yeah, I'm a bit obsessed. Zelda, too."

"A woman after my own heart," Mordred said. "I only recently got into playing video games. I had some things to work though, and they genuinely helped. *Wind Waker* was a special favorite of mine."

"Ah, that's a beautiful one. So, what do you do when you're not drinking coffee or playing Nintendo games?"

"Oh, not just Nintendo," Mordred said quickly. "*Final Fantasy, Metal Gear Solid . . .* and I just realized you weren't asking me about my video-game habit. Sorry."

Cass laughed. "It's okay. You're passionate about it."

"That is one way to put it. As for what I do, not much of anything at the moment. I'm in New York to see a friend of mine."

"King Arthur?"

Mordred shook his head. "I hope not."

"Were your parents big fans of the folk story?"

He quickly understood that he was being mocked, albeit with affection. Mordred decided she was human, after all. He was certain that anyone who knew of Avalon, Arthur, and Merlin wouldn't call it a folk story. "The Mordred thing. Yes, I'm afraid it's my real name. My parents gave it to me and everything, although I have no idea why. You get used to it."

"Well, you're the first Mordred I've ever met." She smiled and sat back in her chair, as if at ease in her surroundings. "And I've met a lot of people with unique names."

"So, what do you do, Cass?"

"Ex-army. Left two years ago, and now I work at a charity helping people like me readjust to normal life."

"A noble goal."

"Thanks. Sometimes it's hard going back to being a civilian. You see things—do things—that maybe others don't understand. Things you don't always want to talk about with anyone who wasn't there."

"No, I get that."

"You military? You have that look."

Mordred's smile was tinged with sadness. "I guess you could say that, yes. I've certainly seen and done things that a lot of people wouldn't understand. Done things for my government that maybe I'm not proud of but at the time I thought were the right things to do."

"You're from England, right?"

"Yes," Mordred eventually said after realizing he hadn't replied for several seconds. "Born and mostly raised. Where are you from?"

"Texas. Dallas to be exact. Dad was an army ranger, and Mom was a teacher. And there was no way I was going to follow in my mom's footsteps. Other people's children make me twitch."

Mordred laughed. "Don't they say you should never work with children and animals?"

"I think that's for acting."

"Yeah, it would be a bit restrictive otherwise, I guess."

Cass chuckled. She had a nice laugh that went with her smile. Mordred hadn't come to New York intending to meet someone, but it was always nice to have a new friend, and if he was being honest, friends weren't something Mordred had in abundance anyway. People who knew of his past were always worried he was going to kill them.

"So, how long are you in New York for?" Cass asked after a while.

"A few weeks, maybe. I'm not a hundred percent sure."

"Would you like to get together again for another drink?" Her smile was somewhere between flirting and being coy.

"I'd like that very much." While Cass was attractive, and more importantly interesting, romance wasn't something Mordred had either the time or inclination to engage in. Still, it was nice to be able to talk to someone who didn't know his background, who didn't know exactly who he was.

Cass removed a card from her pocket and passed it over to Mordred. He stared at it intently, memorizing the phone number and email address without even thinking about it. Old habits were hard to break.

"Call me," she said. "It was lovely meeting you, Mordred." She stood up, and Mordred followed. He offered her a handshake, and she accepted before leaning over and kissing him on the cheek. "I'll see you soon."

Mordred watched Cass walk toward the stairs with a mixture of sadness at being alone again and happiness at how he'd met someone like Cass. He hoped he'd be able to do it again.

He was about to settle back for a few hours of doing nothing when he noticed that she'd left her wallet behind. The small blue leather object must have fallen out of her handbag, or pocket. It shimmered slightly as he turned his head to look at it from a different angle. Mordred shook his head; he was beginning to fixate on something pointless again. He reached over and grabbed the wallet, placing it on the table beside his cup, before sending a message to Cass to inform her that he had it. Hopefully she wouldn't be worried about it.

"Mordred," a man said from the foot of the table.

Mordred looked up, surprised that someone would use his name in such an angry tone. The man was just over six feet tall, and thin, with a small, dark beard and shaved head. His stare was completely neutral, as if he cared neither one way nor the other about being there.

"Yes, how can I help?"

"I have a message for you." The man had an American accent, although Mordred couldn't quite place it with any degree of certainty. Somewhere in the South maybe—he wasn't great at placing accents at the best of times.

"Okay, is it from Elaine?"

"It's from My Liege." The man tore open his shirt, releasing a mixture of glyphs painted there, before he raised his hands and shouted, "For My Liege!"

Power blasted out of him, forcing Mordred to put up a shield of magical air to stop being torn in half, and even then he was thrown back through the window behind him. Before he'd hit the ground, a second blast tore through the ground floor of the coffee shop, slamming him into a taxi with enough force to tip him up over it and into the road. He quickly rolled to the side, avoiding whatever might be coming, and pushed himself up against the side of the taxi.

The sound of the blasts had been deafening, but Mordred's magic allowed him to heal much quicker than anything human. Within seconds he was back on his feet, wishing his hearing was still broken. Screams and cries permeated the air, people begging for help, people weeping. Mordred ignored them—forced himself to ignore them—and entered the coffee shop through what remained of the front door.

The inside of the shop was littered with the charred and broken bodies of innocent victims. The closer Mordred got to where the detonations had been, the more the bodies had been turned into piles of ash. Chairs and tables had been vaporized, and the previously blue-and-white-tiled wall had been partially melted by the magical inferno. The ceiling had been destroyed in places, with a portion of the above floor collapsing, merging the bodies and destruction into one giant mess. Mordred looked up at the holes in the ceiling and noticed that part of the roof was missing.

Both magical explosions had been superheated, but they'd been unlike any fire magic Mordred had ever seen. It was almost as if it were just pure energy. He stepped over remains, hoping to find someone alive, but the devastation had been total.

Mordred used his air magic to put out any fires, smothering them until they were no longer a threat, before he walked up the nearly destroyed staircase to the floor above. More dead littered the floor, and near where Mordred had sat was the body of the man who had caused it. He was dead, which was a shame, because Mordred had wanted to kill him. The skin on the man's chest, where Mordred had seen the glyphs, was nothing but ash. Mordred wondered how the man had managed to stay mostly intact when everything around him was destroyed. Maybe the magic that allowed him to create such devastation had been designed to keep him relatively intact, despite killing him. Mordred turned in a circle as he surveyed the building. The magic had pushed out from the murderer to everything surrounding him. Maybe whoever sent him wanted people to know who had been the killer, or maybe whatever had allowed him to commit such a horrific act hadn't worked properly. Too many questions, not enough answers.

Mordred hadn't been able to find a second body on the floor below in any kind of state to prove conclusively that there had been two attackers, but he assumed whatever had allowed the body of the attacker above to remain intact had in fact incinerated the attacker below. Either that, or they were buried under mounds of innocent victims and pieces of the building. Either way, Mordred had no desire to go digging around for answers. One killer or two didn't matter in the scheme of things. Mordred sighed out of a combination of sadness and frustration. He walked back down the stairs, leaving the coffee shop, where strangers hurried to help the injured.

A young boy of no more than five or six lay on the ground, his leg twisted and badly broken. Apart from the leg and a small cut on his forehead, he appeared to be okay. Mordred could use his magic to heal him. Could use his magic to do a lot of things, but then Avalon would be angry that he'd done so. Magic was not allowed to be shown to humans. Oh, humans could discover Avalon on their own—the Internet had made sure of that—but it wasn't considered good form to use magic on humans to heal them. Or kill them.

Fuck it.

"I can help," Mordred told the woman beside the boy, who he guessed was his mother.

"You're a doctor?" she asked, hopeful.

Mordred just nodded and placed his hands on the boy's leg, and yellow glyphs lit up over his arms. The boy cried out in pain for an instant before he realized the pain was gone.

"How'd you do that?" a familiar voice asked from behind Mordred.

Mordred knew who the voice belonged to, and knew that his actions would cause more questions than he was comfortable answering. "Hi, Cass."

"I came back for my wallet. I saw what happened. I don't *understand* what happened here. I don't understand why you can heal people. What's going on?"

Mordred stood, ignoring the look of disbelief from the boy's mother beside him.

"An angel," the woman said.

Mordred snapped around to the mother, anger in his eyes. "Don't be so fucking stupid. Get your son somewhere safe. Preferably to a hospital. I healed the leg, but they'd best check for anything else."

The mother nodded hurriedly, picked up her son, and ran toward an ambulance that had pulled up just down the street.

"I'm not human," Mordred told Cass. "The people who did this are not human. I will find who is responsible, and I will bring them to justice."

Cass stood, mouth open, and then cracked a slight smile. "You can heal these people."

Mordred stared at Cass for a heartbeat, unsure if she was mocking him. Unsure if she was human, after all. He nodded anyway. Whether she was human or not, it didn't matter at that moment. "Some, but not all. I'm not a damn angel, or anything else like one. My kind has been confused with gods and goddesses for long enough—we don't need to add angels to the bloody mix."

Mordred expected questions, or at least some disbelief, but instead all Cass said was "Can I help?"

Mordred wanted to find out if Cass was human, but now wasn't the time. "Find those in desperate need of healing. I'll see what I can do."

For the next hour, Cass and Mordred went around the wounded, under the guise of Mordred being a doctor, and he helped heal a dozen people who would have otherwise died. Eventually, though, he'd used so much magic that exhaustion was beginning to set in, and he was unable to continue. He walked away from the scene, merging with the onlookers to duck down an alley.

"Just going to run off?" Cass said from behind him.

Mordred patted his pockets and removed Cass's wallet. "Sorry, I forgot. This is yours."

"What are you?"

"A sorcerer."

"Are you really Mordred? Like *the* Mordred?"

Mordred nodded. "King Arthur and all that? Yep, that's me."

Cass took her wallet and stared at Mordred for several seconds. She opened her mouth, and Mordred thought she was going to say something, but instead she turned around and walked away, soon vanishing into the sea of people.

Probably for the best.

Mordred removed his mobile phone from his pocket and dialed a number.

"You're in New York, aren't you?" Olivia Green said the moment she answered. Pleasantries could be done some other time.

"I was in a coffee shop that blew up," Mordred told her. "Now I'm about a half a mile away from that shop. He said 'For My Liege' before he killed himself."

"Just the one attacker?"

"Two, I think. I assume the glyphs were meant to turn them into ash, but for some reason they didn't quite do the job to the guy who attacked me."

"The news is saying that thirty-six people are dead."

"At least. This is the start, Olivia."

"You need to come back to England, Mordred."

"Not yet. There's something I need to do first."

"You're a target, Mordred. Things have gotten worse since you left."

"I've always been a target. You get used to it. Worse how?"

"It's Elaine Garlot. She's missing, has been for a few weeks now, from what I can tell."

"Define 'missing.' She contacted me a month ago and told me to meet her here in New York today."

"Have you heard from her since?"

"No, I didn't expect to, though."

"Avalon are saying she's just taking some time to herself. But that's bullshit. I know Elaine; she's not the type. And she would return her calls. I need you to go find her."

"Does Nate know?"

"Not yet. He'll run off after her without a second thought."

"Where was she last seen?"

"At her place in Scotland. We sent a team after her, and they vanished. Manannán mac Lir was a part of that team."

"Mac? Damn it. I'll be at Elaine's tomorrow. I need a team, people you trust. We'll find Elaine, Mac, and anyone else with her. And once we're done, we'll find out who this My Liege is and make him eat his own fucking hands."

Olivia paused for a second before continuing. "You okay?"

"No, Olivia. I just saw innocent people die. I am the exact fucking opposite of okay." Mordred hung up. The fact that he'd had a meeting with Elaine about the prophecy just before she'd vanished was far more of a coincidence than Mordred liked. Even if Elaine hadn't been his aunt, finding her was now at the top of his list of things to do. He glanced back at the end of the alleyway before continuing on. Whoever the people behind My Liege were, they were now happy to kill humans by the dozen, and do it in the open, in a busy city. Mordred could be certain of one thing: things were going to get a lot worse before they got better.

CHAPTER 2

Nate Garrett

New Forest, England

I woke to the smell of cooking and smiled. It was rare that someone cooked for me, rarer still that it was breakfast. I pushed the quilt aside and stood, stretching and making various parts of me click with the effort. The blackout curtains allowed almost zero light into the room, but the clock on the bedside table told me it was just after 8:00 a.m. I'd slept for five hours, which for a sorcerer was about as long as we ever needed, and for me practically a blasted miracle.

I opened the dark-blue curtains, letting in the gloomy sunshine. December in the UK is a mixture of cold, wet, and those weird days when it's sunny but it feels like the weather is just trying to lull you into a false sense of security. Today was apparently going to be overcast and drizzly. A combination either you got used to, or that made you move.

My bedroom window overlooked the large garden at the rear of my four-bedroom house in the middle of New Forest. At a point a few hundred feet from my bedroom window, my garden became New Forest, and then there were hundreds of square miles of woodland, heathland, and grassland. It was a beautiful place to live, and more importantly a quiet one.

My house was built in the late eighteenth century, although it has been modified and modernized over the years. A new two-story addition was built onto the side of the property, and I'd made a few arrangements to the interior so that I could call it home. One of the four bedrooms housed an extensive collection of weaponry and armor I'd acquired over my sixteen hundred years of life, and I'd made sure to install security detectors that covered the multiacre property.

I felt safe there. Secure. Somewhere in the distance, under the darkness of the forest, I built a small one-bedroom building. It was new and housed Remy—a good friend of mine who happened to be a fox-human hybrid. Turned out pissing off witches was a bad idea. Something he probably should have known before they used a ritual to turn him into said fox. Fortunately for Remy, they were also incompetent and ended up killing themselves and giving him their life force. Hence the fox-human hybrid. He did well with what life had dealt him, and it was nice to see a friendly face when I went outside.

A memory of Remy's friendly way with people flashed into my head. Well, usually friendly . . . Okay, sometimes friendly.

I grabbed a black dressing gown from the en suite bathroom door and put it on, covering the fact that I was only wearing black boxer shorts. I might have been able to conjure magical fire to warm myself, but sometimes it was just easier and safer to add an extra layer of clothing.

I walked downstairs, my mouth watering at the smell of cooking meat, and eventually entered the kitchen.

"Morning," Selene said from in front of the oven. Several pans were on top, all of which contained some type of food. "English breakfast okay with you?"

I smiled. "That sounds like a plan. Also, wasn't aware you'd learned to cook."

Selene looked back at me, a grin on her face. "I watched some Internet videos. And did some practice runs at home. Black pudding?"

I nodded. "Only if it's cooked. Cold black pudding is just weird."

Selene was one of the few women in my life I could say with certainty that I had fallen in love with. We'd been together for a few decades back in the early twentieth century, but Hera and her cronies had blackmailed her into leaving me and marrying Ares's son. A nasty little wankpuffin by the name of Deimos, who was about as pleasant and charming as rabies. The last time we'd met, he'd used his power to get inside my head and make me relive one of my worst days over and over again. It hadn't gone well for him, and when I'd last seen him, he'd been curled up in a ball on the floor after wetting himself.

Selene was just over five-four and was frankly the most beautiful woman I'd ever met. The top half of her hair was black, while the bottom, which was currently tied in a ponytail, was silver. Her eyes were an incredible green color and held both amazing warmth and a wicked temper that I'd been the target of several times.

As she cooked a fried breakfast, she wore one of my old black T-shirts that stretched down to her thighs. She turned back to me and winked. "I hope you're hungry," she said, putting down a plate in front of me. It was covered in sausages, bacon, poached eggs, french toast, black pudding, beans, and mushrooms. There were also several slices of regular toast and a full pot of tea. With this much food, there was a good chance I wouldn't need to eat anything else for a week.

Selene had even more food than me, with at least an entire pack of bacon and sausages just for herself. Dragon-kin, like most nonhuman species, ate a lot and often. The fact that Selene and I hadn't left the bedroom except to shower in the better part of a day meant we were both hungry.

I took a bite of food, and a happy noise left my mouth involuntarily.

"Nice?"

"Mmmm," I managed through a mouthful of bacon and french toast.

Selene chuckled. It was a beautiful sound.

"I'm glad you're here," I told her when I was capable of speech again.

"Me, too," she said with a sly grin.

After Selene left her husband, she'd needed time to herself, to figure out what she wanted to do with her life and the freedom she finally found she had. I told her I'd always be there for her if she decided that she wanted me in that life. Two months ago she had asked me to meet her in Munich. I was in the city a few hours later, and since then we'd gotten together on a regular basis. It wasn't quite what we had back in the early 1900s, but the best things evolve over time. You can never go back to what you had with someone, and it's pointless wishing for it.

"I want to talk to you about something," Selene said. "I'm thinking of moving to the UK. On a more permanent basis. Tommy offered me a job working at his security firm."

Tommy, or Thomas Carpenter, was my best friend, and an exceptionally powerful werewolf. He was also the head of a security firm that had, over the years, become the place to go if you needed help but didn't want to use Avalon. A lot of people didn't trust Avalon, often for very good reasons.

"Sounds good to me," I said, placing a forkful of egg in my mouth to ensure I couldn't say anything else.

"Yeah, well, yeah . . ." Selene breathed out. "This shouldn't be hard. I'm over four thousand years old. I'm the daughter of a Titan." She sighed. "I want our relationship to move forward."

I swallowed the food. "You mean making it public and the like?"

"Yes . . . no . . . no, not really. I mean move in together."

That was unexpected. I put my forkful of bacon back on the plate. "Seriously?"

Selene nodded. "I love you, Nate. I've always loved you, even when I wasn't allowed to. Even when I was forced to be married to . . . well, you know. I still loved you. If there's one thing I learned in the last few years since I finally found my freedom from Hera and her people, it's that I want to be with you. I missed you. I don't want to miss you anymore. I don't want to try to make up for all the time we lost; I just want to make new time."

"Sounds good to me," I said, and ate the food on the fork.

Selene stared. "That's it? I was sort of expecting a little more, you know, excitement."

"Sounds good to me," I repeated, but this time I waved my arms in the air.

"You're an asshole, Nathaniel Garrett."

I smiled. "I love you, Selene. I've probably always loved you. Even when I thought I hated you, I still loved you. If you want to move in with me, then I'm good with that. But are you okay with living here?"

Selene reached across the table and took my hand, rubbing her thumb over the back of my index finger. "Yes, always."

"Then welcome to your new home, Selene."

Selene stood and walked around the table, kissing me on the cheek. "I stink," she whispered. "I need to shower."

"I wasn't going to say anything," I whispered back. "I didn't want to sleep on the sofa."

Selene laughed, which quickly turned into a weird coughing, choking fit that only stopped after she took a drink of water. "Who knew I'd find love with a man less than half my age."

"Does that mean I'm your boy toy?"

"No, because that's fucking stupid, and I don't want to have to hit you when you say it."

It was a fair point. I finished off my breakfast as Selene went to shower, and had placed my plate in the dishwasher when the alarm to the motion sensors sounded. I walked over to the screen that was fixed to the kitchen wall, one of three in the house, and pressed the button to activate it. A black BMW 5 Series sedan was driving up the winding road to my house. It looked like there were two people in the front, and the rear windows were blacked out, so it was impossible to say if anyone was in the back. I sighed—the morning had been going so well—and removed a Heckler and Koch VP9 from a nearby drawer.

I knew the pistol was loaded—I'd done it myself—but checked anyway. It was indeed loaded. While I could have always used magic against anything that might be considered a threat, not everything in the world of magic and monsters can be hurt with magic, and not everything can be hurt with a bullet to the head. But pretty much everything can be hurt by one of the two, so I knew with the gun at my side and my magic ready to go that anything turning up better be friendly, or better be ready for a hell of a fight.

The last three years, ever since Hera had taken control of London from Brutus, had been fairly quiet. No one had tried to kill me or rule the world, or been a problem that had required me killing a large number of people. Since getting back together with Selene, I'd told Tommy I was going to take a few months off. He'd agreed it was a good idea, and that Avalon and its people appeared to have everything under control. It looked like with Arthur back in the driver's seat people were behaving themselves, at least for a little while.

I walked through the lower level of my house until I reached the bottom of the stairs. "Selene, you out of the shower?"

"Unwanted guest?" she asked, and walked to the top of the stairs, looking down at me.

"Not sure yet."

The doorbell rang, and I activated the nearby screen, revealing who stood in front of the door. "Holy shit," I almost whispered.

"Yeah, I can see who that is. I'll stay up here, if that's okay?"

I nodded, waited until she'd walked off before placing the gun on top of a nearby table, and opened the front door, revealing Arthur. King Arthur. Arthur Pendragon. My friend. A man who I never thought I'd be able to see walking around again after Mordred put him in a coma all those centuries ago. A man who mysteriously got better, and took control of Avalon. A man whom I wanted to trust, wanted to believe was going to usher us all into a better age, but I just couldn't. It wasn't that I didn't trust him; I just didn't know where I stood with him. Besides, he was still working with Merlin, and Merlin was all kinds of nasty. He was someone I'd almost thought of as a father figure, but now he wanted me dead. It meant my time of visiting Avalon was past. Frankly, the whole thing made me more than a little weary.

"Nathaniel," he said. The BMW was parked behind him, and two large bodyguards stood beside it, trying very hard not to look like they were watching the exchange.

"Nate," I corrected.

"Nate," Arthur said with a smile. "Can I come in?"

"Sorry, of course," I almost stammered, pushing the door open and allowing King Arthur to enter my house.

Arthur removed his long black coat, revealing a gray and black business suit. He looked around for somewhere to put his coat.

"In there," I said to him, pointing to the cloakroom door.

Arthur placed his coat inside and ran his hand through his chestnut hair before offering an awkward smile. He motioned toward the gun. "You expecting company?"

"I'm never sure these days. Too many angry people want me dead."

"And they'd knock first?"

"I never said they were smart."

Arthur laughed, and his demeanor changed, revealing just how tightly wound up he'd been beforehand. "How long has it been?"

"I'm not sure if you think it's a little early for alcohol, but do you want a drink anyway?"

Arthur smiled. "Good Lord, yes."

I took Arthur through the lower floor of my house to my study, where I removed a bottle of Yamazaki eighteen-year-old whiskey and poured two glasses.

"Japanese whiskey?" Arthur said, lifting the glass and inspecting it. "I expected you to be a Scotch man."

"I'm a drink-what-tastes-nice man, and this is one of the best I've ever had. Certainly better than that swill we used to drink back when we were young."

Arthur was ten years older than me, but we grew up as friends along with Galahad, Mordred, and several others. It was a friendship that had been tested many times over the years, and not all the bonds that we'd formed had weathered those storms. Mordred had been expected to be the king of Avalon back then, before he was taken and turned into a monster. Before everything we'd been working toward had to change.

"How's being king again?"

"I'm not using that title," Arthur said. "Which is fortunate, because you never used to use it, either, something I noticed you continued when you opened the door."

I chuckled. "Force of habit."

"Yes, well, the title of king was always a little strange. King of Avalon isn't something that should exist. Avalon doesn't need a king. I never wanted to be king of Camelot, or Avalon, or anywhere else in the first place. That was Mordred's role. I was meant to follow in Merlin's footprints. Meant to be the man to help Mordred unite the various mythologies of the world and bring peace. Didn't quite work out how I'd imagined."

I necked the whiskey. I needed the courage to ask, "It's been three years since you woke from your coma. Why haven't you contacted me?" Part of me was saddened that he hadn't contacted me, and another part was both sad and maybe a little angry that he hadn't reached out. It had made me question whether or not we'd been as close as I remembered. I'd brushed the thoughts aside at the time, but they'd stuck around to bother me.

Arthur placed his glass on my desk and sighed. "Officially, I've been very busy. No time to contact anyone, even old friends."

"And unofficially?"

"I'm scared shitless that those people I trusted, and loved, and thought of as the best are no longer who I remembered. Too many people are all vying for their own little part of the Avalon pie, and playing politics to stop things from getting worse has been a full-time experience. I've been changing people in positions of power, trying to get those I trust to do a good job in places that they can help. Also, I knew you and Merlin had fallen out."

"That's a nice way of putting it."

"Yes, well, Merlin is part of the reason I'm here. And Mordred, and you, and about fifty other things." He rubbed his hands over his graying beard.

"That's new."

"The beard? I look distinguished."

"I think the word is 'old.'"

Arthur laughed. "Well, I feel old, so it fits." His expression was suddenly serious again. "Why did Merlin let everything fall apart? I know that Elaine and her people did the best they could, but Merlin didn't give them an inch of help. He could have worked with them, and Avalon would have been the place we'd always dreamed of. But now, we've got factions in Avalon working against other factions. Hera controls London, with Merlin's blessing, and after unleashing a bloody dragon on the city."

"Yeah, it wasn't a fun night." A lot of people died, and a lot more were hurt in Tiamat's attack. An attack that only stopped because my friends and I managed to kill her.

"I'm sorry I wasn't there."

"You were in a coma. You're forgiven."

"Speaking of which, have you seen Mordred recently? Tale has it he's reformed, although many don't believe it."

"He was taken by blood elves and Baldr and tortured for the better part of a century. They made him think that we were his enemy and that he should kill us all. He's still got issues, but he's working through them."

"You trust him?"

I nodded. "Without question."

Arthur absentmindedly touched his chest where Mordred's blade had punctured it. "I think it would be best for us to meet at a later date. To me, I was only attacked three years ago. After finding you in bed with Morgan. I should apologize for the way I acted, by the way."

I shrugged. "Morgan and I stopped being anything close to a couple the day you were attacked. We're cordial now, but I doubt it'll go beyond that."

"Even though you trust Mordred."

"Mordred was driven insane by evil. Morgan just helped him, thinking that was the best thing to do. We're both very different people than we were back then."

"A thousand years in a coma. I dreamed, you know, of Merlin and the paladins who helped keep me alive. I dreamed of being in that damn tank, and I was never sure what was a dream and what wasn't. Didn't feel like a thousand years, though. And then I wake up and everyone expects me to click my fingers and make everything better. And I have no damned idea how that's supposed to work. I don't even know what 'better' is."

"Three years isn't long to catch up."

"No kidding. And Merlin seems to be withdrawing more and more. It's not exactly helping matters. But I guess if he's shut himself away in his tower, at least he's not trying to kill anyone because they offended him."

"You mean other than me?"

"Oh, you didn't hear? Merlin went full mad king on the council. Started to threaten to kill people who didn't follow my lead. Elaine and a dozen others had to have him subdued."

"I'm sure he didn't make it easy."

"We're remodeling the council chamber. That's how easy he made it."

"He'd been going down a slippery slope for a while."

"It seems my waking finally turned that slope into a cliff."

"You need help dealing with him?"

Arthur shook his head. "God, no. I've got people on it. Merlin can stay in that damn tower for as long as he likes, for all I care. Gives me time to deal with everything else."

"So, if you'll excuse my bluntness, why are you here?"

"You know Lucie Moser?"

I nodded. "We're not exactly friends, but I trust her. Why?"

"I've moved her from the head of the SOA and given her a position within the council."

"Good, she deserves it. She's done an excellent job."

"It means there's an opening as director of the SOA."

I couldn't believe what I was hearing. "Are you offering me a job?" The Shield of Avalon, or SOA, was one of three branches within Avalon. The SOA was a sort of combination of the MI5 and MI6. There were a number of reasons why I shouldn't work for Avalon again, the foremost being that I left because Merlin was using the souls of innocent people to keep Arthur alive, but mostly I just wasn't that person anymore.

Arthur shook his head. "No offense, but you're not exactly the first person I'd think of to take a director's job in Avalon."

I breathed a sigh of relief.

"Too many people remember Hellequin as the boogeyman of Avalon," Arthur continued. "And too many of those know that you and Hellequin are one and the same. It would make things difficult."

"'Impossible' is the word. Although I've been trying to change Hellequin from the boogeyman into something more positive."

"I heard. People are saying that Hellequin is on the side of the right. You always were; you just had awful PR."

I laughed. "Yes, PR, that was the problem. So, what do you want?"

Arthur took a deep breath, as if this were a conversation he'd rather not have. "I've heard mutterings. Concerns. Not quite accusations, and no one has come to me personally, but there are things being said."

"About me?"

"Oh no, not you. Galahad. Or more specifically, Shadow Falls."

I suddenly felt very uncomfortable. Shadow Falls was one of the few realms that had discarded Avalon rule and struck out alone. Galahad was their king, and from all accounts he was doing a splendid job. There were people in Avalon who felt that Shadow Falls' very existence was an affront to their honor, or some shit. "What about it?"

"There have been murmurs of them beginning to think they could take more of America for themselves."

"Galahad wants to take over America." It was all I could do not to laugh. "You've met Galahad, right?"

"Not for a thousand years, I haven't," Arthur snapped. "Sorry. Look, I want to know if you can go there and maybe convince him to talk to me. Just me and him. No, I don't think he's trying something, but if I could assure the council of that, maybe I could head off whoever is starting these rumors before they turn into something more."

I didn't even have to consider it. "Sure, I'll go to Shadow Falls and talk to Galahad. He is not going to be pleased that he's under suspicion, though. And you'd need to promise to meet on neutral ground outside of Shadow Falls' realm."

"I'm sure I can arrange that."

"I'll see what I can do."

"That's all I can ask. I'm trying to consolidate my power, but having rumors of Galahad using this time of flux to strike for himself makes things worse. I don't want to believe he, or his people, are doing anything untoward, and I know I can trust you to sort this without it going further."

Arthur stood and offered me his hand, which after standing myself I shook. He pulled me toward him and hugged me. Arthur was a large man, broad of shoulders and several inches taller than my own five-eight. The hug enveloped me, and when he released me, he stepped back and slapped me on the shoulder. "It's been a long time, Nate. I'm glad you're doing okay."

"It's good to see you again."

I walked Arthur to the front door, opening it while he retrieved his coat.

"I'll speak to you soon," he said as he left my house. "Take care of yourself, Nate. I get the feeling things are going to get more complicated the longer it's apparent that I'm not going anywhere."

"Glad to hear it," I told him, and closed the door after watching Arthur walk over to his bodyguards.

"So, that was weird," Selene said from the top of the stairs.

"He wants me to go to Shadow Falls and see Galahad."

Selene's expression of confusion and worry mimicked exactly how I felt. "Why?"

I explained everything we'd discussed.

"He's met Galahad, right?" Selene asked when I was done. "There's no way they're considering an expansion of territory. Why would they even bother? There's exactly zero benefit for them going to war to carve out a few more states."

"That's one way of putting it." We walked into my living room and switched the TV on.

"Are you going to go?" Selene asked.

"Yeah. I want to know what's going on. And if I don't go, someone else might take it upon themselves to get involved. Hera and her cronies have been quiet for a few years, and I wouldn't put it past them to start something so that Ares or one of the others could get a chance to grab his own realm. I'm going to sleep on it, though. I need to think about the best way to tell Galahad what's going on. I don't want to make this worse."

"And it's you, so that's a distinct possibility," Selene said with a smile.

I'd have argued, but to be honest she had a fair point. "It's not exactly the easiest situation to deal with. It's been a weird day, and it's not even noon."

"No kidding, Nate. A new girlfriend and a visit from the king in the same day. It's been quite eventful for you, hasn't it?"

I laughed and turned the TV on to the news channel, watching in horror as they discussed an explosion that had taken place in a New York coffee shop several hours earlier.

"What the hell is going on?" Selene said after we'd watched several minutes of footage.

"There was an angel," a woman said to a reporter. "He healed my son."

"An angel?" Selene asked.

"Mordred's in New York," I said. "You don't think . . ."

"That Mordred was there? It's a hell of a coincidence. Unless he was the target."

I picked up the phone to call Mordred just as the news cut back to the studio to report on a missing passenger plane and several other attacks around the globe. I put the phone down and listened to the reports of violence and death, with occasional cuts to various cities to talk to witnesses and journalists who were there.

"My Liege has finally made their move," I said, afraid of what the future now held.

"Whoever they are, they just declared war on Avalon," Selene said.

"Not just war on Avalon. From the sounds of things, they've declared open season on humanity."

CHAPTER 3

Nate Garrett

After five minutes of watching more of the mayhem and insanity that were spreading across the globe, my phone rang.

I picked it up, with one eye still on the TV, and someone spoke before I was able to: "Nate, that you?"

"Tommy?" I asked. "You watching the news?"

"Living it, mate. It's all gone a bit wrong. Mordred was in New York. He called Olivia, told her that the man claimed it was for 'My Liege' before blowing himself up."

"Wait, someone blew themselves up?"

"Two someones, from the sound of things. With their own magic."

That made me pause. "How?" I wasn't sure what else to ask, because I'd never heard of anyone ever being able to achieve death by killing themselves with their own magic.

"Not a clue. I'm hoping you can come over to Basingstoke so we can try and figure this out. Olivia is on her way, too. Shit has well and truly kicked off. Bring Selene and Remy with you. The more heads the better. These bastards are going after humans, Nate. Right now the death toll is four figures, and I only see it getting worse."

"I'll be there soon," I told him, and he ended the call.

"I assume we're off to Tommy's," Selene said.

I nodded. "I don't know what triggered this, but a lot of people are getting hurt because of it."

"What about Galahad?"

"There's no way he's involved in this."

"That's not what I meant. What are you going to do about seeing him?"

"It'll have to wait for now. I want to know what's going on with people committing mass acts of terrorism. I don't think Avalon is in any position to do this alone, especially if it's bad enough that Tommy's already involved. If we can help figure out how to stop it, we should."

"That why Olivia is coming to Tommy's?"

Sometimes I forget just how good a dragon-kin's hearing is. "I assume because she knows who she can trust there, and Tommy has probably the largest network of non-Avalon contacts I've ever seen. From what Arthur said, Avalon sounds like it's in some sort of free fall. That might be why My Liege has finally decided to launch their attack."

"Hera, Baldr, Nergal, and anyone else involved. That's a lot of power to go up against Avalon. I never thought I'd see Hera or her cronies go after humans like this. Not in the modern age, anyway. She has little care for humanity, but any pretense of keeping Avalon a secret is going to vanish if people keep using magic to kill humans in broad daylight."

"Maybe that's the point? Maybe they want to out us all, to make humans fear us. Humans fight back; whoever is involved in My Liege slaughters them and declares themselves rulers of Avalon."

"That's not a nice thought."

"No, it isn't. But it's one that needs considering." Selene took my hand in hers and kissed me on the mouth. "Go to Tommy. I'll go find Remy and meet you there."

"You sure? He might be out in the forest."

"And if that's the case, I'll be able to track him quicker than you. Remy has a distinctive odor."

Dragon-kins have considerably better senses than my own. I was about to ask if I had a distinctive odor when I changed my mind—there are some things I just didn't need to know.

I left the house, taking the keys to my Jaguar F-Type R in British racing green. It was a dark, sleek car that was probably about as sexy as a car could ever manage. The five-liter, almost six-hundred-brake-horsepower engine sounded beautiful and went like a rocket with a second rocket strapped to the side for added speed. Some people would say it was ostentatious, or too James Bond, but it made me smile, so I honestly didn't care.

I entered the garage and set the automatic outer door to open while I slid onto the comfortable leather driver's seat. I pushed the starter button, and the noise of the engine instantly made me smile. It was probably going to be an awful day, so any little pieces of joy would be welcomed. I took the car out into the driveway and drove sedately down to the edge of my property before pushing the accelerator, grinning from ear to ear the entire journey to Tommy's company, Enhanced Security.

Technically, Tommy's building was two buildings that were joined together by a walkway above the staff parking area. The smaller of the two buildings was three stories high and was the main entrance to the larger, twenty-five-story building behind it.

I entered the smaller of the two buildings and was immediately taken aback by the amount of extra security in place. Normally there would be a dozen or so guards patrolling the building, but I counted twelve just in the reception area itself. Behind the massive reception were six glass lifts that contained thermal imaging and a few special tricks so that the security could see who, and more importantly what, was about to head up to the main building.

At the reception desk I was greeted by a young man with a neatly trimmed, bright-purple goatee and short, dark hair. "Matias," I said with a smile. "The color is new."

"The color won't come off," he said with the returned smile of someone who had spoken about their facial hair a lot more than they were used to. "Was meant to be washable. Now I have a purple chin. Wanna guess how happy the boss was with my beard?"

"He pointed and laughed."

"That's exactly what he did, yes."

"Why don't you just shave it?"

"Because it's my beard, and it's a part of me. I'll dye it black before I shave it. I cannot have a naked chin."

I had to admire his dedication to his beard, even if he was being mocked for it. "Talk to human resources; tell them Tommy picked on you."

The large security guard standing beside Matias stifled a laugh.

"That's why I don't do that," Matias said. "I'm a water elemental. I've been placed here to give me a chance to deal with all kinds of people. What kind of employee would I be if I couldn't take a bit of gentle ribbing from my boss? I'm a hundred and nine years old; I know he's just trying to wind me up and get a reaction. It's not like he's being cruel or unpleasant. I sort of expected some mockery. I mean, my beard is bright purple."

"Even so, don't let him keep having a go. If he says anything again, you need to show him who's boss."

"He really shouldn't," Tommy said as he left the lift and walked toward me. "I'm a werewolf, remember? I can hear you."

"You were mean to your employee," I said, mocking him a little.

"I pointed and laughed at his bright-purple chin. It was funny."

I looked over at Matias. "He's got a point. It is funny."

Matias nodded. "I know."

Tommy looked serious for a moment. "You honestly upset that I mocked you?"

Matias shook his head.

"You sure? Because if you are, I'll apologize right here. My employees have the right to dye their hair any color they damn well choose. This isn't the military."

"I promise I'm fine," Matias assured Tommy while passing me a small wooden bead bracelet. There were magical runes written into the property's very skeleton, which meant the second I stepped into either building, and for my entire time inside, I lost all connection to my magic. It's an odd sensation to lose access to my magic, and feels a lot like when I wear a sorcerer's band, a small bracelet that stops the user from accessing their abilities or blows them up if they try to remove it. The bracelet that Tommy passed out to his employees was essentially the exact opposite of a sorcerer's band.

The bracelet's beads had been carved with runes that bypassed the security and allowed the wearer to access their abilities, be that magical or otherwise. They were custom-made for each person who worked here full-time, and I was fortunate enough to have had one made especially for me. Everyone who worked for Tommy wore a bracelet, even the humans. Tommy said that it was so everyone felt a connection to one another; no one was singled out as different, but I knew that it was so anyone attacking the place wouldn't be able to weed out the humans from the rest of the staff. It was a way to keep everyone safe. And I knew that the security of his employees was always Tommy's first concern.

"Why is it everywhere you go, you cause trouble, Nate?" Tommy asked me.

"Practice," I told him with a smile.

Tommy glared at me before turning back to Matias. "If I ever say something that upsets you, please tell me. Nate has no sense of keeping his opinions to himself, but I at least like to think I don't upset people on purpose."

I chuckled, and Tommy walked with me toward the glass lifts at the far end of the lobby. "Glad you came," he told me as the lift doors opened and we both stepped inside.

"It's been a weird day."

"In what way?"

"I'll explain when we get upstairs. Who else is there?"

"Olivia, Zamek, Diana, Irkalla, and Nabu."

"Mordred?"

Tommy paused. "He's on his way to Scotland. Elaine's there."

"Even without Mordred, that's some serious power. Olivia mentioned Mordred was there when one of these people killed themselves?"

Tommy nodded. "You ever heard of anything like this?"

"No. I didn't even know you could kill yourself with your own magic. I've never heard of anyone doing it. Not even rumors."

"Someone wants humanity to be afraid." The lift doors opened, and we both stepped out into the walkway beyond.

I glanced out of the windows that lined the walkway. We were several dozen feet above the ground, and the busy employee parking lot beneath the walkway was full.

"Everyone got their holiday canceled," Tommy said, clearly noticing what I was looking at.

We left the walkway by passing through a set of double doors, where two more security guards waited for us. Tommy nodded a greeting to them both, and I followed suit. I didn't recognize either of them, but I found it always paid to say hello to the people who were trying to protect you.

It took a few minutes of walking, and another lift ride, before we reached the top floor of the larger building, which was home to Tommy's office and very little else. There were a few meeting rooms, all of which appeared to be empty, but no one in the corridor, or guarding the entrance to Tommy's office. Tommy pushed open the door and beckoned me inside.

Tommy's office was massive. It was big enough to house a small family without any problem. Windows lined one side of the building, giving impressive views of the surrounding area, while the opposite side contained bookshelves and a door to a private bathroom.

Dozens of pieces of artwork sat on the walls, most of which were science fiction or fantasy based. More than one of them was of a *Star Wars* character or scene. A few were even signed by the actors. In one corner sat an exact replica of Darth Vader's costume.

"That's new," I told him as several of the occupants of the room turned toward us.

"Had it custom-made," Tommy told me as we approached the group seated around a large conference table.

"And it stays here," Olivia finished before kissing Tommy on the lips. "I have to put up with enough of his . . . quirks at home."

"I'm certain he wears it around the office," Diana said with a laugh. "I think he wants to chair board meetings while wearing it."

"That's a slight . . ." Tommy paused. "Okay, that would be really cool."

Diana hugged me, the scent of whatever fruit shampoo she used on her long, dark hair filling my nose. "It's good to see you, Nate. I've been busy with our new recruits and haven't had much chance for socializing."

"How are they coming along?" I asked.

"Well," Zamek said. "Kasey and Chloe were miles ahead of the others in the beginning, but the rest of the group is catching up. You should come see them again."

"I will," I promised him. Tommy had set up a small, covert team that consisted of Kasey, Chloe, and several others who were off Avalon's radar. Chloe had wanted nothing to do with Avalon after the death of her father and the subsequent arrest of her mother, Mara, but Tommy had asked her to do a job for him, and I hadn't seen her since. A few months ago Tommy asked me to come over and observe the new recruits, and I'd been impressed. I'd spent a few months helping out with the training, but the longer I was there, the more jeopardy they would be in, so I'd left them to it. I was glad to hear it was going well.

Zamek dropped down from the chair he was on and offered me his hand, which I shook. He was one of the Norse dwarves who had helped us escape from the realm of Nidavellir. Once a dwarven realm, and ally to Avalon, it was now ruled by blood elves, a species that lived to cause death and misery.

"How's the tablet translation going?" I asked. The tablet in question was one of the reasons we managed to escape from the blood elves. King Arthur's brother, Kay, had been using it to jump from the Earth realm to Nidavellir and back again. Unfortunately it only took its user from one exact spot in this realm to one exact spot in the other, and until we managed to figure out how to move the spot in Nidavellir away from the blood-elf stronghold, there was very little chance of rescuing the remaining dwarves holding out in Nidavellir.

Zamek shrugged. "I can't figure out how to change the teleport destination. I went back twice and ended up in the middle of the blood elves both times. It wasn't a fun experience. It's hard to translate, and even with Nabu helping, it's slow work. Three years of research and we still haven't managed to figure it out. We know how to get to Nidavellir, but not how to get the rest of the dwarves out of there without starting a war we might not be able to win."

"I'm sure they're okay."

"Oh, I know they are," Zamek said with a smile. "We left the blood elves something to think about, and I think they're going to be more concerned with their own problems than my people. We'll get to them eventually."

I placed a hand on his shoulder as an act of understanding. "Still wearing the leather armor, I see."

"And carrying these two axes," he said, meaning the battle-axe on his back and the one-handed axe that hung from his belt.

"It's taking him time to adjust to not having to fight every day," Tommy said.

Zamek took a deep breath. "It's a strange thing, not having to worry about blood elves attacking every day. Not having to go out and forage for supplies. Good, but strange."

"We will figure out the tablets eventually," Nabu told me as he shook my hand. At one point, Nabu had been considered the Mesopotamian god of wisdom, although in reality he was an och, a rare species and one of the few who were genuinely immortal. He was smart, and cunning, sometimes to his own detriment when he felt that keeping secrets worked better for him. Some of those secrets had come back to bite him on the ass. He was several inches taller than me, with long, dark hair that cascaded over his shoulders. His beard was neatly trimmed, and looked like he spent time and effort to achieve the effect. He wore an expensive gray suit that I was certain had cost a lot more than I would have felt comfortable spending on one item of clothing. I liked him, and I'd fought alongside him several times, but I wasn't certain I trusted him not to keep secrets again. He tended to work several moves in front of everyone else and thus expected people to know things he knew without having to tell anyone. It made for the occasional difficult moment when everyone really did catch up and wanted to know why he didn't mention anything.

"Hi, Nate. Care to join the meeting of the minds?" Irkalla said. She leaned against Tommy's wooden desk, a wry smile on her elegant face. She wore a simple pair of jeans, a red T-shirt, and black trainers, and still looked refined. Irkalla was a necromancer, and one of the most powerful I'd ever met, with maybe only Hades outclassing her, and even then I wasn't 100 percent certain she wouldn't be able to take him.

Irkalla walked over to me and hugged me tight. "It's good to see you again."

"You, too," I told her. "Selene will be along shortly with Remy."

A sparkle flickered in Irkalla's eyes. "Excellent, I haven't seen Remy in months."

The pair had become close friends in the last three years, something I never would have even considered if I hadn't seen it myself. Remy's natural ability to piss off anyone no matter how much more powerful they were than him was something Irkalla greatly admired.

"How are you doing, Nate?" Olivia asked as we walked over to the only remaining seated person at the long conference table, Fiona Daly.

"I'm good. Arthur came to see me earlier."

The room immediately fell silent.

"Why?" Fiona asked.

Fiona was a conjurer and was able to create illusions. It was a powerful ability, and she used it to great effect as an agent for the SOA. I'd known her for a few centuries and found her to be an excellent agent. She could be counted upon when the shit hit the proverbial fan, which happened a lot when dealing with Avalon. She was married to Alan Daly, who was . . . not . . . an SOA agent. For most of his life, Alan wasn't someone you could say was law-abiding. But since marrying Fiona, he'd become a changed man, and his lack of presence in the meeting was an odd one.

I explained about Arthur's visit and his request, as well as the information about Lucie Moser.

"This is news to me," Fiona replied. "Why would Lucie move jobs? She loves her job."

"News to me, too," Olivia said, making me feel nervous for the first time. It was rare that Olivia was unaware of something as momentous as the head of the SOA stepping down.

"Well, I'm just relaying information," I said, feeling their stares.

"What about Galahad?" Nabu asked. "You've shown no interest in working for Avalon and have in fact taken several steps over the years to stop people in Avalon from doing their jobs."

I shrugged. It was pretty much the only thing I could think of to do.

"Maybe that's why Arthur asked him?" Irkalla said. "Nate is friends with both Galahad and Arthur, yet he has no allegiance to Avalon or Shadow Falls. Do you think Galahad is involved with what's happening here?"

"No," I said instantly.

"I can't see it," Diana said. "It's Galahad. He's not the despot-murdering-innocent-people kind of person."

No one else had anything to say for several seconds.

"Do you want to wait for the rest of us to arrive?" Tommy asked.

"No, we need to get on with this," Fiona said, and I saw the irritation in her manner for the first time. She was usually excellent at keeping her emotions in check—it came with the territory when you worked for the SOA—but her control was slipping. I got the feeling she was dealing with something that I'd soon find out about, so I didn't bother to ask her what was going on.

"Anyone else coming can catch up," Fiona continued. "I had Tommy call everyone here for a reason."

"You did?" I asked. "So, I was the last to know?"

Tommy nodded. "We didn't want to include you until we knew what was happening."

"Why?"

"You'll see."

"So, does everyone else here already know what Fiona is about to say?" I asked, wanting to figure out exactly where I stood in terms of knowledge compared to the others.

"Selene and Remy wouldn't know," Olivia said. "Neither does Zamek, Nabu, or Irkalla. Only Tommy, Diana, and myself know what's happening."

"Can I start?" Fiona asked, her voice quaking slightly and a little anger leaking out, as if she were trying her best not to just explode and release whatever was bothering her.

"Sorry," I said, hoping to defuse some of that barely contained anger.

"Two weeks ago Elaine Garlot and a dozen of her bodyguards vanished. One of them was my husband, Alan."

"What?" I snapped.

"Nate," Tommy said softly. "Seriously, wait."

I opened my mouth to argue but immediately closed it. Despite my need to know what was happening right goddamned now, I had to swallow my outburst and wait for the information I knew was coming. I motioned for Fiona to continue.

"A week ago we sent a small group to try and find her. This group was made up of six people who were not officially tied to Avalon. None of them worked for Avalon or lived in Camelot. None of them were on any official list of employees. They went missing three days after looking into Elaine's disappearance. We don't know where they are, or what's happened to them. Manannán mac Lir was a part of the team."

"Mac," I whispered. "Does Mordred know?" Mordred and Mac had been close before Mordred's brain had been destroyed by a century of torture by Baldr and his allies. Since Mordred had become one of the good guys again, he'd reached out to find Mac, but I wasn't sure how that meeting had gone.

"He's aware of them both, yes," Olivia said. "He's gone straight to Scotland. She has a home there. Hopefully we can find some information about where she might have been taken from."

"Why were Mordred and Elaine meeting in New York?" I asked.

"It's something to do with the prophecy that Mordred will kill you," Nabu said.

"Damn it," I snapped. "I told him not to keep worrying about that."

"Which makes him worry more," Irkalla said. "You know he can't abide the idea that he has to kill you."

"I know, I just don't want him living his life constantly trying to avoid me." I turned to Olivia. "Why did you keep this from me? Elaine's disappearance, I mean, not the Mordred thing."

"Because of your reaction," Olivia said. "Tommy had no choice but to follow me on this."

"I'm not mad at you," I told her.

"Good, because we made the right call," Tommy said. "How much do you want to run off right now and find Elaine?"

"A lot."

"And that's why we didn't tell you. I'm sorry, Nate, but you would have cut your way through everyone in your path to find Elaine. If she's in danger, your brand of punch and destroy might get her hurt."

I nodded. It was one of the harder things I'd had to agree with in recent years. Irkalla, who sat beside me, placed her hand on mine, squeezing slightly.

"You are not always one to think with cold logic," she said. "It is both a great asset and terrible curse."

I nodded again. "Okay, so why tell me now?"

Fiona took a drink of water from the bottle in front of her before answering. "Because someone tried to kill Mordred in New York this morning, and it's no coincidence that Elaine vanished not long before she was meant to meet him. If she's been taken, and they found out about the meeting, they must really want Mordred dead. We think whoever this My Liege is, that they're just about to start their endgame. Removing Elaine and Mordred must have been a part of it."

"We know this My Liege character is in fact several people," Nabu said. "Baldr, Kay, Siris, and Hera; all of these were called 'My Liege' at some point. We know that all of these people are working together, presumably with Merlin's backing considering he allowed Hera to kill Brutus and take London. What we don't know is who the head of this . . . cabal is."

"And you think that this cabal—which is a good a name for them as any other—has taken Elaine and planned these acts of terrorism all across the world to destabilize Avalon even further than it already is?" I had to admit it sounded like a good plan—causing enough mayhem and murder across the globe, and removing those people who would be able to bring stability to an organization that is disorganized and under threat. Arthur could only do so much having been in charge for a few years. "Divide and conquer."

"That's our best guess, yes," Olivia said.

"Did you know about Merlin?" I asked. "That he's hidden himself away in his tower? That he tried to kill people at a council meeting?"

Olivia nodded. "It came up, yes. About three days before Elaine vanished."

"Arthur didn't mention Elaine going missing?" Irkalla asked.

I shook my head. "No. Maybe he thought the same as you, that I'd rush off to find her."

"We want you to find Elaine, though," Olivia said. "We'll deal with everything else regarding these attacks, and Merlin if need be. If he's helping, or orchestrating everything, we need to stop him. But in the meantime we want you and Mordred to search for Elaine and those we sent to find her. And we want you to do it covertly."

"Yeah, I get it. Who's coming with me?"

"Diana, Zamek, and I assume Selene and Remy," Fiona said. "And me, obviously. My husband is out there, and I intend to find him."

I was about to reply when the phone on Tommy's desk went off. Tommy got up and walked over to answer it.

"I'm in an important meeting," he said.

There was a pause while someone said something on the other end, but I didn't want to use my air magic to have the words carried over to me.

"No," Tommy said.

Another pause.

"Yes, okay, I'll be right down." He hung up the phone and turned back to us. "I need to see someone in reception apparently. There's someone there who is upset and will only speak to me. I'll be back momentarily."

"I'm coming with you," I told him, getting to my feet.

"Nate, you don't need to," Tommy said. "It's probably just a client who doesn't know anyone else here. It's fine."

"Someone tried to kill Mordred," I persevered. "I'm coming."

Tommy nodded, and as I turned around, I found Zamek behind me. "I'm coming, too. Don't fucking argue."

Diana got to her feet. "I'll keep you all safe."

"It's not a bloody outing," Tommy said. He sighed. "Fine, we'll be back in a moment."

The four of us left his office and made our way over the walkway to the first tower. We were about halfway across when I saw a huge articulated lorry barrel through the security post and crash into several parked cars. The occupants, all wearing body armor and carrying guns, spilled out of the back of the truck, shooting at anyone close by.

I was already sprinting before my brain caught up with my body, and reached the lift the same time as Tommy, Zamek, and Diana. I considered using my magic to blast the glass apart and jump out, but I wasn't certain my magic would be strong enough inside the building to do anything close to that, and before I thought to ask, I was already in one of the lifts going down toward the reception below.

Security inside the reception was already in response to the threat outside, and a low growl from beside me indicated that Tommy had turned into his werewolf beast form, before the lift stopped and the doors parted. Tommy and Diana were first out of the lift, with Diana turning into her werebear beast form within seconds and bounding out toward the exit.

Gunfire could be heard outside of the building, and several people were lying on the pavement. It was impossible to tell how many were injured and how many were dying or dead.

Tommy and Diana ran through the doors to the outside, engaging with the enemy while Zamek and I went over to Matias, who was talking to two guards flanking a large man with a black hoodie and shaved head.

"Matias, all okay?" I asked, eyeing the stranger.

Matias nodded.

"We're going to need weapons," I said, leaving no room for conversation on the subject. "We don't know who is what out there."

"I'll get them," he said, and turned away.

The tall man spun away from the reception and two guards beside him, sprinting toward the exit. I moved to intercept, but he quickly shrugged off his hoodie, dropping it to the floor, revealing glyphs tattooed all over his body. I was already creating a shield of air large and dense enough to try and wrap around the coming explosion when the man detonated. The shield kept the force contained, but it also managed to find a weakness, the point of origin—me. The shockwave tore through my shield of air hard enough to throw me back over the reception desk and into the wall behind me. I crashed to the ground, my vision darkening, and my head swimming while my magic quickly repaired my destroyed eardrums. When I could hear again, all that came to me were the sounds of fighting all around me.

CHAPTER 4

Nate Garrett

Nate, Nate, are you okay?"

I looked up at the face of Grayson, who was kneeling over me, an expression of concern on his face. Speckles of blood sat in his trimmed white beard, and judging from the lack of bleeding anywhere I could see on his face or bald head, I was sure the blood didn't belong to him.

"What happened?" I asked. The last I remembered was hearing gunshots and explosions before I was smashed into a brick wall.

"You tried to get up, fell back down again, and blacked out for a few seconds. You suffered a fairly serious wallop to the back of your skull, and you're lucky it wasn't worse."

"It was like every piece of magical power was leaving his body at the same time." I rolled onto my front and got back to a kneeling position. "Never seen anything like it."

I looked over at the fighting, which continued outside.

"This is bad," I said, grabbing hold of the remains of the reception desk and hoisting myself up.

"You should not be walking," Grayson said. "Or moving in any way. You're lucky you don't have a fractured skull."

"It's too dense to fracture," I said with a smile.

"You should know there's blood over your face, so you smiling is pretty damn awful."

I stopped smiling. "Sorry." My head continued to swim for a few seconds, and I wondered why my magic wasn't doing more to heal me. I looked down at my wrist and found that the bracelet was partially broken.

"Help me outside," I told Grayson.

"Have you lost your mind?"

"Not enough magic in here to heal me. I need to get outside to do it."

"People are trying to kill you out there."

"Me and everyone else. Beggars can't be choosers, and probably other useful sayings."

Grayson put my arm around his neck. "You hit your head again and you're going to sound like Mordred."

"Nah, I'll need someone to shoot me in the head first."

"There are people with guns outside. I'm sure they'll help you."

"How many are hurt?"

"We don't know." The pain in Grayson's voice was easy to hear even in my less-than-ideal state. "The fighting is still happening."

As we made our way through the room toward the exterior doors, several people who worked alongside Grayson as doctors and nurses helped the dozens of wounded.

"You need to get the security shut off," I told Grayson. "Too many people in here don't have the power to heal properly. The bracelets don't let enough power through."

Grayson barked an order to a nearby nurse, who ran off to do as he was told.

"You must be a fun boss to work for," I said, and swayed slightly as we reached the exit.

"There's a time for shouting, Nate."

I took two steps outside of the building and felt my magic wash over me, filling me, healing me. Grayson let go of me, and I dropped to my knees.

"Are you okay?" he asked.

I nodded. "Body is healing. It uses a lot of power, but I had some souls stored up."

"Won't that leave you vulnerable?"

I noticed he didn't ask who the souls had belonged to, nor how I'd come across them. At one point the idea of using my necromancy to take someone's soul to use as a makeshift battery for my magic would have been difficult to imagine, but now . . . well, now times were different. I didn't take souls lightly—it came with the unwanted gifts of living that person's life, of seeing every awful thing they'd ever taken part in. But sometimes that was necessary, and using my necromancy to power my magic was considerably more powerful than using my magic alone.

I looked around the chaos-strewn parking area where Tommy and his people were fighting for their lives. Several dead enemies lay on the ground, most missing parts of their bodies . . . fighting against a werewolf of Tommy's caliber often left his opponent with fewer limbs than when they'd started.

"Nate," Grayson said as I got back to my feet, feeling a lot more like my old self. "You're going to be vulnerable without a soul to boost your power."

Gray glyphs ignited over the backs of my hands and arms. "I won't be for long."

Grayson looked back into the reception area. "I need to go."

"Help people. I'll be fine." I turned to face the battle and heard the war cry of one of the assailants as he ran toward me, a machete raised high above his head.

I flicked my hands toward him, and the shadows closest to him tore out of the ground, enveloping him as he screamed in fear. Several of the attackers closest to me stopped for a moment, and I noticed the fear on their faces. "I'll be right back for the rest of you," I told them, and sank into the shadows beneath my feet.

I ended up in my shadow realm. Every sorcerer who could use shadow magic had their own personal realm which they were able to move into and out of with ease. Once in the realm, I knew where nearby shadows back on the Earth realm were, and could move between them easily—essentially allowing me to teleport between shadows. Unfortunately it wore me out quickly, so I wasn't able to do it for long distances, but it was useful in a pinch.

Also, as my would-be attacker discovered, I was able to drag people who couldn't use magic into the shadow realm. He threw the machete at me, but the shadows around me leapt up, picking it out of the air where it vanished into the darkness around us.

"You can't hurt me here," I told him. I motioned to the tiny pockets of light, the locations of the Earth-realm shadows. The closest ray of light moved toward us in an instant. "That's your way out."

The man was terrified and clearly wanted out of the predicament I'd placed him in.

"Who sent you?" I asked.

"My Liege," he said.

"Why are you here?"

"My Liege," he snapped, seemingly angry.

"Is that all you can say?"

"My Liege, My Liege, My Liege!" He screamed the last word and sank to his knees. "My Liege, My Liege, My Liege."

I sighed. "Someone broke your mind."

He looked up at me.

"You were sent here to die. If you were ever captured, your mind would snap like a twig; you'd be able to say nothing but whatever they needed you to say. Blood magic did this. Very powerful blood magic." I walked over to him and crouched. "I'm going to undo your shirt. I need to see if you have any marks."

He tore his shirt open, the buttons making no sound as they hit the floor. A large blood-magic curse mark sat on his chest. It was different than the marks I'd seen on the man who had exploded in the reception area. The attacker kneeling beside me was never meant to take his own life. He hadn't been a sorcerer, so had been given a different, but no less fatal, job.

I stood and pulled up my T-shirt. "Do you see the mark on my stomach?"

The man looked up and nodded as he saw the dark mark. I'd lost one a year ago, which had given me a further boost in magical power. Five down, two to go. The last mark was invisible and had been placed on my mind to ensure I remembered nothing of the first eight years of my life. I hadn't even known of the final mark's existence until a few years ago, and its discovery was still somewhat of a sore point.

"Someone put that mark there, and more like them. Someone cast a blood-magic curse on me so powerful hundreds had to die to fuel it. Do you remember anything about the person who did this to you?"

He shook his head. "My Liege, My Liege." He tried to stop himself from saying it a third time. "My Liege." He struck the floor beside him.

"You were told to come here, to kill and hurt, and in return you'd be given something. Power, money?"

He shook his head.

"Freedom?"

He looked up at me and nodded slightly.

"Freedom from what, though? You were in someone's servitude?"

He shook his head.

"A prisoner?"

A nod.

I walked away as sounds began to gather in the darkness around us.

"It's nothing to fear," I told the man.

That was a lie, and it was an exceptionally big one. Somewhere out in the darkness was a wraith. All sorcerers who used shadow magic had one. They fed on anyone sent to the shadow realm. While I was here, the man was safe, but the second I left, the wraith would pounce, devouring the man to make me stronger.

"Ordinarily I might take your soul and see the information I need, but with your mind broken, I'm unlikely to see anything useful."

The man stared at me.

"You shouldn't have come here. You shouldn't have tried to kill my friends. Did you see this My Liege person?"

He nodded.

"Just one person?"

He nodded again.

"A man?"

Another nod.

"Did you see his face?"

He shook his head.

Ordinarily I wouldn't have believed someone in his position, but he appeared to be so angry about his brain being fractured by the blood-magic curse that I was certain he was being honest. The expression on his face told me that he knew he'd been betrayed. Yet I felt little sympathy for him. He'd come here to kill and maim innocent people.

I took a step toward the light. "Thank you for the information. I'm going to find this My Liege character, and I'm going to kill him."

The man laughed and started shaking his head.

"Enjoy the last seconds of your life," I told him, and stepped into the light, vanishing from the shadow realm and reappearing in the shadows of an overturned car.

The fighting had continued to rage while I was in the shadow realm, with many of the attackers lying dead on the floor. The group I'd been with in Tommy's office were fighting their own battles all around me. A second truck had arrived, increasing the number of attackers. But Tommy's people outnumbered those who would hurt them by a considerable margin. The fight wouldn't take long. I got the impression that wasn't the point.

One of the attackers aimed a gun in my direction, and a slither of shadow jumped out at him, knocking the gun aside and dragging him down into the shadow realm. I wasn't sure how many the wraith could feed on at once, but I knew having the boost of two people was better than one. A few seconds later the familiar tingle of power spread through my body, followed closely by a second one. The two men were now gone forever; no traces of them would ever be discovered. I felt no horror or unpleasantness at that thought. Their fates were sealed the second they decided to come after the people I cared about.

A blast of air magic threw another attacker into a car near where Diana stood. She grabbed him with one massive, paw-like hand and punched him in the chest so hard that I heard bones snapping. She released him, and he fell to the floor like a bag of cement. She placed a foot on his head and pushed down, the noise forcing me to look away. Death and blood were staples of my world, but seeing a man's head crushed like a grape was a step over even my own considerably high threshold of violence.

It didn't take long until the last of the attackers were mopped up, but as I looked around to find Tommy I heard a roar behind me. I turned as two huge cave trolls tore through the back of one of the two trucks, flinging pieces of metal about and causing several people to dive for cover.

"Where did they come from?" Zamek asked from beside me. He was covered in blood, and the blades of his two axes were drenched in it.

"We've got the one on the left," I shouted to Diana, and tore off toward the smaller of the two cave trolls, although "smaller" is a relative term. It was still nearly eight feet tall and about the width of a tank—which, considering the amount of metal armor that adorned its torso, wasn't that far off.

Cave trolls are mean and nasty, and enjoy murdering people so that they can feast on their remains. They can also take an incredible amount of punishment before going down. The day wasn't going to be a fun one.

"I've killed cave trolls before," Zamek told me as we stopped beside a car close to the troll. "We need to get above it. They have a weak spot just behind the neck. If you can keep it occupied, I can get up there."

"I think I can do that." I stepped out from behind the car and threw a ball of fire at the troll's head. It roared in anger and took a ground-shaking step toward me. "That's right, you big bastard. Come fight me."

It took another step and roared again, the stink of decay on its breath now able to reach me. I ran to the side, forcing the troll to turn its back on Zamek. I walked back, throwing the occasional ball of fire at the troll to keep the attention on me while Zamek climbed on top of a nearby van and launched himself toward the troll.

For a second I thought that Zamek was going to make it, but the troll must have sensed the dwarf, as it moved quicker than I thought a troll could move, swatting Zamek out of the air and sending him crashing into a nearby wall. The troll turned back to me with rage in its eyes.

Dozens of shadows tore out of the ground, wrapping themselves around the troll, who roared in defiance and continued to walk toward me. I tried wrapping the shadows tighter and tighter, but with every step he made, one of the shadows snapped, forcing me to re-create it. My magic was not an infinite source of power, and even with the boost I'd had from the wraith, I wouldn't be able to keep up the newly re-formed shadows indefinitely.

I removed the shadows in one go, causing the troll to stagger forward, where I hit it with a blast of air powerful enough to knock the off-balance troll to the ground with an almighty crash. I ran toward the troll, my fist wrapped in dense air, and struck the beast in the side of the head, darting aside a moment later to avoid the swipe of its arm.

The troll climbed back to its feet, and I readied a sphere of spinning air in the palm of one hand, using my fingers to spin the ball faster and faster, until it was a blur of magical power. Only then did I pour my fire magic into the sphere, mixing it with the air and creating a ball of pure magical lightning. It crackled, and air around my hand became superheated as the sphere moved at an incredible speed.

When the troll was up on one knee, I sprinted forward, dodging the poorly swung punch, and drove the sphere into the troll's chest, where I released the magic it contained. The metal armor that adorned its body did nothing to stop the furious power I'd unleashed. But when it was all over and the magic had dissipated, the troll remained on its feet, albeit unsteadily.

"What do I have to do to kill you?" I said, feeling frustrated. If I used all the magic at my disposal, I was likely to kill the troll but could possibly hurt people who were already injured and being tended to by Grayson's team of medics.

I cracked my knuckles and raised a hand to the heavens as the clouds above me darkened. There was a clap of thunder. I was about to call down real lightning and mix it with my own magic, creating a power so vast that it caused me physical pain to do it, when Tommy smashed into the troll, taking the creature off its feet. Tommy was still in his werebeast form, and while he was shorter and considerably less bulky than the troll, he was also faster and probably not far off in terms of strength.

The troll tried to push Tommy away, but Tommy avoided the creature's massive hands and launched himself up at its head, sinking his razor-sharp claws into the flesh and skin of the troll. For a second I thought that Tommy was going to try and rip the creature's face off, but with a howl born of rage and anger, he tore the troll's head clean off its shoulders, ripping the skull in two. Tommy breathed heavily for several seconds, and for just a moment I thought the beast had finally won. I wondered whether or not my best friend was still in control.

"Tommy," I said, using my air magic to carry my words. I didn't want to get too close. If the beast inside of Tommy had indeed won out, he would try to kill me just as quickly as he'd killed the troll.

"I'm okay," Tommy said softly without looking back at me. He dropped the halves of the troll's head onto the ground, and they made an awful wet sound. I wasn't sure I'd ever seen anything like what Tommy had done. I'd certainly never seen a werewolf tear a troll's head in half before. I didn't even know that *could* happen.

I looked over at where I'd last seen the other troll and noticed the huge spikes of ice sticking out of its torso. Olivia was not a woman to piss off if you liked the idea of remaining in one piece. She looked over at me and nodded, and I made a motion toward Tommy. She looked his way and ran toward him. I took a step away and went to check on Zamek.

I found him sitting on the ground next to a large hole in the wall. He was rubbing his head and cursing a lot in dwarven. I'm not entirely sure that any species I'd ever met was as good at cursing and swearing as dwarves were. It was as if it was an intrinsic part of who they were as a people. Zamek didn't do it often, but he certainly made it count when he did.

"You okay?" I asked him as he got to his feet.

"Bastard troll."

"It's dead."

"Good." He looked past me. "Tommy kill it?"

I glanced over at my friend and found Olivia beside him. "Yep."

"He trying to control the beast inside of him?"

"That's my guess, yes."

"Never piss off a were of any kind. That's my mantra for getting through life. I forget that he's not even a millennium old."

"He'll be fine."

Zamek nodded. "I know." He looked around at the bodies that littered the ground. "A lot of bad guys died here today."

It was my turn to nod, but I didn't take my eyes off Tommy and Olivia. It wasn't that I thought Tommy's beast—something all weres had inside of them, ready to take control and kill with impunity—would suddenly cause Tommy to snap and kill Olivia. I knew him better than that. But I wanted to make sure he was okay. Tommy was rarely so emotional that his beast had any chance of being set free, but an attack on those he cared about—employees and friends alike—was always going to cause emotions to run high.

I walked toward Tommy, who changed back into his human form. His naked body was covered in the blood of those who had fought him and died. He looked down at himself and sighed.

"I'm sorry," he said to me as I got close enough to hear him.

"For what?"

"I should have guessed this would happen."

"Don't be daft," Zamek said from beside me. "You can't guess that crazed assholes were going to try and kill us all."

"I don't think that's what happened," I said, fully aware of the shock on people's faces, as they waited for me to explain what I meant.

I was about to say more when a black car came toward us. We all readied for more fighting, until I realized it was a Mercedes S-Class AMG—one of my cars. I motioned for people to stand down as the car screeched to a halt, the driver-side door opening before it had fully stopped. Selene stepped out, her clothes singed and her arms and face covered with soot. She ran around the front of the car, and then I noticed the blood.

I ran toward the car, getting there as Selene opened the passenger-side door and brought Remy out in her arms. "Helios attacked," she said to me. "Remy . . . Remy . . . he . . . he . . ." She looked down at the broken body of our friend. "He saved my life."

Remy's chest moved slightly, and I turned back to the crowd and spotted Grayson running toward us.

"Lay him on the ground," the doctor demanded, and Selene did as she was told.

"What happened?" Grayson asked. "What did Helios do?"

"Helios arrived, and I went outside to talk to him. He attacked me, almost killed me." Selene sounded shocked that her brother would ever do such a thing. "Remy attacked him, but Helios stabbed him in the stomach and hit him so hard I think it broke most of the bones in his chest. I heard them snap. Helios blew up your house, Nate."

"Will Remy live?" I asked. Remy had at last count nine lives left from the original twelve witches who had cursed him. If he died, Remy would just come back, minus one life.

"Remy's healing is similar to a human's," Grayson said. "This will take him months to heal from, if not longer." He removed a knife from his belt and passed it to me.

I knelt beside Remy. "You there?" I asked.

Remy opened one eye, the other too swollen. "Hurts," he managed, although the pain to even say one word was etched on his face.

"You know what I have to do, yes?"

Remy made the tiniest of nods.

"You're going to kill him?" Selene asked.

"Oh, you don't know about Remy's power?" Diana said. "He'll be back in a few minutes if he dies."

"I thought he was going to die. Like, for good. I cried over his broken body."

I placed the tip of the knife against Remy's chest and pushed, puncturing his heart and killing him almost instantly. I sat back on the ground and rubbed my eyes.

"You okay?" Tommy asked me, placing a hand on my shoulder. Thankfully someone had given him a pair of shorts to wear.

"I know he'll come back, but I still had to take his life. It's not exactly a fun thing to do."

A few minutes later Remy coughed and rolled onto his side, spitting blood onto the floor. "That fucking hurt," he snapped. "Fuck, fuck, fuck, fucking, fucker, piece of goddamn shitting fuckhead."

"You done?" Grayson asked, getting to his feet.

"Cock biscuit." Remy sat up. "Now I'm done."

Selene hugged him. "You saved my life. Thank you for that."

Remy shrugged and got to his feet. "Aw shucks, I'm just a great person all round."

Diana laughed, placing a hand over her mouth to stop it.

"You genuinely think Helios would have killed you?" I asked Selene.

She nodded. "I saw nothing but hate in his eyes. He said he was going to leave you a message. And then he blew up your house."

"This can all wait," Grayson said. "Right now we have people to help. I need all of you to pitch in."

"Okay, people," Tommy said. "Let's help the injured and make sure any of these assholes who aren't dead aren't in a position to cause more harm."

"If you find any of them able to talk, I'd like to have a few words," Olivia told us all.

"I don't think you're going to be that lucky," I told her. "These people were sent here with one purpose."

"To kill us all?" Zamek asked.

I shook my head. "They were sent here to die."

CHAPTER 5

Nate Garrett

It took several hours to get everyone seen to, and by the end time we'd had thirty-six injured, three dead on our side, and sixty-one dead on theirs. I knew we'd been lucky not to suffer more casualties, but I also knew that wasn't how Tommy would see it. One death was one too many, and he would want to ensure nothing like this happened again. I also knew that he wanted me to explain how our attackers had been sent here to die, but we were too busy to talk.

To my surprise, Mordred arrived just as it was beginning to get dark. He had Morgan with him, and they chipped in to help even though they were tired from their trip. Mordred said he had information of his own to give, but waited until after we'd helped Grayson and his staff move the injured to the medical facilities several levels below the ground floor and dispose of the corpses. Then we showered and changed into clean clothes and all gathered in an office at the rear of the reception area. Dozens of armed guards patrolled the entire compound. Tommy was going to make certain there would never be another attack against his people.

"So, we've all had a pretty shit day," Mordred began after everyone had piled into the room. Along with those who had attended the original meeting, Remy, Morgan, Mordred, Selene, and Grayson had joined the group.

"You get out of New York okay?" Olivia asked.

"Yes, thanks to Hades firing up the jet for me. The human authorities had shut down the airports. It's standard procedure, so I was repeatedly told."

"I thought you were going straight to Scotland," Fiona said. "To find my husband."

"Your husband is missing, too?" Mordred asked.

"We'll fill you in on the rest," Irkalla told him. "Why come here?"

"I tried to contact Tommy on the phone, and no one answered," Mordred said. "Figured you might be in trouble."

"I think you need to explain what you meant earlier," Tommy said to me.

"I took one of those attackers into the shadow realm and asked a few questions. Someone had tampered with his mind so that all he could say was 'My Liege.'"

"Like what happened at Wolf's Head?" Olivia asked, her arms crossed and a stern expression on her face. I wondered how far she was from losing her temper.

"What happened in Germany?" Mordred asked.

"A few years ago, a group of psychopaths attacked the Wolf's Head compound. It was their goal to get the Reavers to infiltrate the compound and get into Tartarus, where they could help Cronus escape. Lots of really awful stuff. We captured one of the attackers and found that he'd been programmed to say 'My Liege' instead of the person who sent them. That person turned out to be Hera."

"So, does this guy mean Hera, too?" Morgan asked.

I shook my head. "All I know is that whatever was done to this man was unlike anything I've ever seen. He couldn't say anything but those two words. Blood-magic cursed."

"That doesn't mean he was sent here to die," Remy said.

I placed a pistol on the table. "I took this from one of the attackers. It has normal bullets in it. No one in their right mind is going to send someone with normal bullets to attack this place and expect them to win."

"That could just be a coincidence. Or genuinely bad planning on their part," Mordred said. "That can't be the only reason you thought they were sent here to do something other than kill us and teabag our corpses."

Everyone looked at Mordred.

"I've been playing a lot of *Halo*," Mordred explained. "It's a thing. Honestly."

"I don't even want to know," Selene said with a slight shake of her head.

Tommy placed his head in his hands and tried not to laugh, while Diana and Remy didn't even bother hiding it.

"It's not like I do it in real life," Mordred explained. "It's a video-game thing. I don't go around doing it to people in actual life."

"You said that already," Remy pointed out after his bout of laughter.

"I know, I just want to reiterate. I don't teabag people in actual life. That would be weird."

"But in a game it's not weird?" Morgan asked.

Mordred remained silent for several seconds. "So these people who tried to kill us, Nate."

"Right, no, I didn't know about the bullets until I was cleaning up," I admitted, hopefully moving the conversation away from Mordred's pastimes. "But these people were sent here to make a statement of intent. You don't send people with broken minds and a complete lack of proper equipment if you want them to succeed. If any of our side died at the same time, then that was one less to worry about. I assume Helios was trying to take me out of the fight, which is why he blew up my house and tried to kill Selene and Remy."

"He sounded like he expected you to be there," Remy said. "He was angry you weren't. He lost it after that. It was as if you being there was the whole point of what he was doing."

"Helios is going to get what's coming to him," I said without looking at Selene. "But these attacks are just one more in a series of them across the globe. They're attacking humans, but they attacked here because they want us all off-balance."

"You think they attacked here so that Tommy and everyone get so angry they go storming after whoever was responsible?" Nabu asked.

I nodded. "Send a bunch of people to hit Tommy and those he cares about, but send cannon fodder. No one significant to the cause overall. The only sorcerer in the bunch was the one who killed himself. He had dwarven runes marked on his skin."

"What did they say?" Zamek asked.

"I only saw the one on his back. It was one of the original dwarven runes, and it said *contain*."

"Contain what?" Zamek asked.

I shrugged. "I'd like to see the body if possible," I told Grayson.

"The body is still in one piece?" Mordred asked. "In New York, the bodies burned up to ash. Or at least one of them did. The other one only turned to ash where the runes had been placed."

Grayson dropped in front of me several photos of the body of the sorcerer. "I printed these off. I thought they'd be helpful."

I flicked through them, each picture showing the glyphs on the dead man.

"I think your magic stopped the power from consuming him," Irkalla said as she picked up one of the photos. "Do you know what they say?"

I placed the photos in an order in front of me, showing each of the glyphs on the front and back of the man's body. A glyph sat on his chest, one on each wrist, and one on his throat. They were mirrored on his back, the backs of his wrists, and the base of his skull.

"*Power, contain, release*," I said, tapping each photo in turn. "Those on his wrists mean 'release.' I assume there's more of them because of how much power is pushed out."

"What does that mean?" Fiona asked.

The original dwarven runes had been lost in translation for thousands of years, known only to a handful of people. Even the majority of dwarves themselves were no longer capable of reading them. For some reason, when I was a child someone put the knowledge of them in my head. I got the feeling it wasn't done so I could show off and look clever.

"It means he was turned into a bomb," Zamek said. "A walking magical explosion. The magic was built up inside of him and contained before a trigger was used to release it. My guess was his touching one of the runes with his hands did it. I have never seen anything like this before, didn't even know it was possible."

"So, someone out there knows these runes just as well as Nate," Nabu said. "And they're using that knowledge to create people who explode with enough power to destroy buildings."

"Only sorcerers," I said. "I don't think it would work with anyone else. Maybe elementals at a push, but their power is different and this isn't an element—it's just pure magical power. I think whatever magic these sorcerers know is changed into pure energy and then detonated. Whoever did this is not someone we want running around. Those dwarven runes were hidden for a reason."

"Even from their own people," Zamek said without any hint of annoyance. "I only knew a few of them, and I don't know of anyone besides Nate who knows them all. And it wasn't like he sat down and studied them. They were forced into his head by a blood-magic curse."

"The one I took into the shadow realm was a prisoner of some kind. He must have agreed to attack us in exchange for his freedom. I got him to communicate without needing to speak, before anyone asks how I did it. I'm wondering if any of his friends were of a similar background."

"I'll check for any kind of prison escape," Olivia said, getting to her feet with haste. "Helios must have escaped from The Hole. If he managed it, there's no telling how many more prisoners went with him.

That's bad news for everyone." She sat behind a desk at the rear of the office, and picked up the phone.

"How do you even escape from that place?" Morgan asked. "It's an underground prison on an island in the North Atlantic. Even if you got out of the prison, it's at least an hour's flight from there to the nearest country."

"And after the trouble we had when we were there last, the security was meant to increase," Remy said.

"Shit, shit, shit," Olivia said, the phone handset cradled between her shoulder and ear as she wrote something down on paper in front of her. "This is not good news, people."

"I'm going to the morgue," Irkalla said. "I want to look at the blood-curse marks on the dead bodies. If someone has screwed with the minds, maybe my necromancy can try and use their spirits to piece things back together. Or at least the spirits might be able to give us something else to go on."

"Be careful," Morgan said. "There's no telling what was done to their minds."

"I'll be fine," Irkalla said with a gentle smile. Although many thousands of years older than Morgan, Irkalla never got annoyed with people giving advice.

"I'll join you," Grayson said. "Just in case."

Irkalla and Grayson left the room, and Nabu sat in the newly empty seat beside me. "This isn't over, Nate."

"Not by a long shot. But Elaine is missing, someone is attacking humans, and now they're attacking us."

"Speaking of Elaine, what's happening with that?" Mordred asked. "Do we have more information than her last whereabouts?"

"No," Fiona admitted.

"She knew that people within Avalon were working against them," Mordred said. "She's known that for a long time. Maybe she got a little too close to who those people were."

"You were meeting her because of the prophecy, yes?" I asked.

Mordred nodded. "I know you don't think I should be trying to stop something that might not happen, but I need to, Nate. I need to do something."

I nodded. I understood completely—I just wasn't sure it was going to do any good. "Take Morgan, Remy, Fiona, and Diana with you."

"I'll go, too," Nabu said. "We have no way of knowing where Elaine is."

"Where was the rescue team last seen?" Morgan asked.

"My husband was last seen in Moscow," Fiona said. "That was his last communication. All it said was he believed they were being watched, and would keep us informed. Then nothing."

"A trip to Russia?" Mordred asked. "Haven't been there for a while. I know a few people who might be able to help if Elaine is in Russia. We'll still go to her house first, though, and have a look, just in case someone missed something the first time around."

"I assume you'll be going after Helios?" Selene asked me as Olivia's mobile rang and she excused herself from the room.

I shook my head. "He needs to be stopped, but it's clear that whatever he's up to, at least part of it is to try and keep us occupied. If I were Hera or Baldr or any of the others in this cabal and I was launching attacks on humanity, I'd want the people who would try to stop it as preoccupied as possible. Helios is meant to keep me preoccupied. Burn my house down, attack my friends—he wants me after him. I assume the people he works for want that, too. Otherwise why break him out of prison? And we all know if he got free, he didn't do it alone, so instead of playing their game, I'm going to completely ignore him. I'm going to call Sky and see if there's been any activity where she is. This cabal attacked Tommy, so they might try to attack Hades, too. But first I'm going to go home and see if I can salvage anything I might need, and then I'm going to need a plane."

"I'm going with you," Selene said.

"Me, too," Zamek told us. "No arguments."

I looked over at Tommy. "Before you say anything, you need to stay here."

Tommy nodded. "If they attack again . . ."

"I know."

"I want to help, Nate."

"It's okay. You can help by making sure your people are okay. You're our eyes and ears on this one. We'll all need to be kept in the loop as to what's happening. If these attacks on humans escalate, the humans might start thinking they need to fight back. If Avalon loses control of the human leaders, then things are going to break down fast." I knew that given a choice, Tommy would be right beside me, storming off into whatever battle came my way, but as a director of a company, and one that was recently attacked, he had more pressing priorities.

Olivia entered the office, walked over to the desk, picked up the phone and threw it across the room, where it shattered as it hit the wall. "We have a problem," she said, her face ashen.

"We have a lot of them," Mordred said. "Sometimes I think we collect problems."

"If you compare our problems to any video games, I'm going to hit you." Morgan smiled while she spoke, but I was certain she meant every word.

"There has been no contact with The Hole for three days," Olivia said.

"No one thought to check?" Tommy asked.

"Apparently not, no." Olivia picked up a cup and threw it at the dent in the wall she'd just made with the phone.

"You want to stop throwing things?" Tommy asked.

"Not really," Olivia said. "Damn it. The Hole has been compromised. I'm sending people up there to check, but I'd take it as given there was a mass breakout."

"That would explain the numbers," I said. "And why they sent people here to die. Most of the prisoners wouldn't have been considered useful for anything but causing chaos. And sending them to die is a good way of getting rid of deadweight, while still sending a message of terror. Two birds, one stone and all that."

"You think the sorcerers who have been turned into bombs didn't know what was happening?" Tommy asked me.

"If someone can break a mind so that they can only say one thing over and over, it stands to reason that they can force them to blow themselves up. We won't know more until we capture someone alive."

"You think we're going to get the chance?" Nabu asked.

I nodded. "Almost certainly. These attacks aren't done. Even if a tiny portion of the attacks are carried out by these prisoners, there still seem to be plenty of people who are more than willing to die for the cause. Whoever is in charge of this cabal sure knows how to inspire loyalty."

"You sound impressed," Morgan said.

"Afraid more than impressed. I don't know if this cabal is achieving that loyalty through fear, the promise of a better life, or money, but something is making people work for them. Hera is one of the most powerful people on the planet in terms of sheer manpower and monetary wealth, and she did that despite being a raving psychopath. As a rule, people—human or otherwise—don't think of themselves as the bad guy. They rationalize, and create a narrative where what they're doing is just fine. Everyone says they have a line they won't cross, but when everyone around you is crossing it and making a new line further and further into the distance, it takes a strong person to say no and walk away."

"So, what happens now?" Remy asked.

"Now we all get ready to go do what we need to do," Zamek said.

"We get ready to fight," Tommy said.

"Just us?" Morgan asked. "Because I don't think we're going to be able to go up against Hera by herself, let alone anyone she's working with. Speaking of which, why isn't Arthur going after Hera or her allies? We know she's working with this cabal. Why doesn't Arthur stop her?"

"He can't," Olivia said. "If Avalon officially goes after Hera, who is entrenched in London, she'll turn that city into a war zone overnight. Hera and her allies have so much power, so much pull inside of Avalon, that it would start a civil war. All we know is that Hera, Helios, Baldr, Nergal, Siris, and Kay were working together. Kay is dead, so that leaves those five. We have no idea where Nergal and Siris are, Baldr is trapped in another realm, and Helios was in prison. I imagine that we'll be seeing more of these cabal members in the near future, but until we know who we're fighting, we're limited in our response. Arthur's power to deal with them is cut off at the knees until one of them does something brazen."

"And Arthur's trying to bring all of Avalon together," I said. "He's trying to find out who is and isn't his ally. He needs information before he can strike against Hera and the cabal. Otherwise he'll get stabbed in the back the first chance someone gets."

"I'm going to contact my other branches in New York and Tokyo," Tommy said, getting to his feet. "I want to make sure none of them are having similar problems."

He left the room, and I wanted to go after him to make sure he was okay.

"Olivia, how long before we can get transport ready?" I asked.

"A few hours. I need to make some calls. I'm keeping this out of Avalon's view for as long as I can. I spent a long time finding the traitors inside of Avalon, but I'm not convinced I found them all. So, I'll be using as many of Tommy's contacts as possible. At least until I can get ahold of Lucie and find out what she knows. It's nearly midnight, so give me until dawn."

I stood. "Then everyone has six hours to get some rest and prepare for what's next. I'm going to contact Sky and Hades and go see my ruin of a home. That should keep me busy."

"Nate," Mordred called after me as he followed me out of the room.

I stopped and waited.

"What you said about some of those people being sent here to die. That might be right, but the guy who blew himself up next to me in New York—he was a fanatic. I saw the look in his eyes. I saw the hatred. He *wanted* to be there. I just wanted you to know. They might be using prisoners as expendable help, but some of those people chose to die for their cause."

"Yeah, I figured."

"What if Hera is the head of the cabal? Or Merlin?"

"We both know it's not Hera," I said.

Mordred nodded. "Yeah . . . but it could be Merlin. Arthur has been back for three years, and everything is even worse now than it was back then. What if Arthur didn't exactly live up to Merlin's ideal, and Merlin finally gave up the pretense of helping?"

"I can't see why he'd take so much time and effort to keep Arthur alive, just to throw that away by attacking Avalon."

"Maybe that's why he kept Arthur alive? He thinks that after all these years he's finally twisted Arthur to his way of thinking, but Arthur wakes up and wants to make Avalon better. Not turn it into whatever Merlin wants. Merlin's sidelined, finally loses that last shred of being a good person, and—"

"Murders a whole bunch of people," I finished for him. "It's possible. If it's Merlin, we're going to have to confront him at some point. Arthur's appointing people he trusts, people who would push Merlin further away from power. He snaps. There's merit there."

"Nate, there's something else. About the prophecy."

"Mordred, you aren't going to kill me. You're not going to need to stop me from going full Darth Vader, or whatever Tommy would call it. Don't worry."

"But I am. I've stayed away from you for a year, because I thought distance was the answer. It isn't. I'm going to find out how we beat this prophecy, but I'm done pushing my friends away to achieve it. I'm sorry about that."

I placed a hand on his shoulder. "Don't be. I get it. I do. But the Fates have been wrong before, and they'll be wrong again."

Tommy burst out of a nearby meeting room door. "Nate, you need to see this. Now."

Mordred and I followed him back into the office. He grabbed the TV remote from the table and pointed it toward the large TV on the wall, switching it on. The screen came to life, showing a female news reporter sitting in a studio. Tommy paused the TV and began rewinding for several seconds, until the screen changed to a man in a mask. The mask was black, except for a white streak that moved down across one of the darkened eyeholes, stopping just above where the mouth would have been.

"I had a call from one of my people downstairs. You need to watch this," Tommy told me, and pressed play.

"I am responsible for the terror that has spread across the globe. Before I am done, you will bow down to me and my kind as your rightful rulers. My name is Hellequin."

CHAPTER 6

Nate Garrett

I didn't bother watching the rest of the video and left the office a few seconds later. No one tried to stop me or try to ask if I was okay; the expression on my face probably told them all they needed to know. I walked out of the reception area and into the night, where spotlights had been installed so that a cleanup crew could get rid of debris and bodies. I wasn't sure if Olivia had called in some of her LOA—the Law of Avalon, who were essentially Avalon's police force—people, or if this crew worked for Tommy, but either way they had a job I didn't envy.

I found a secluded spot at the rear of the building next to a small pond. I sat on the wooden bench and watched two ducks swim across the water, seemingly oblivious to what had happened here. Tommy eventually found me and sat beside me without a word. We stayed like that for some time before he said anything.

"So, this has been a really bad day."

I nodded. "You don't have to humor me, Tommy. I'm not going to do anything stupid."

He turned to look at me, the shadows around his face hiding his expression. "You always do something stupid when you're angry. You run after those responsible for revenge, or justice, or whatever reason it is. It's in your makeup. See problem, punch problem, be the baddest.

You don't always have to be the baddest, Nate. You're better than just using brute strength."

I turned away and watched the ducks again. "They used my name, Tommy. They went after me, my house, my friends, and my name."

"We'll find out who it is."

"Yes, we will," I said, my voice hard as iron.

"You know the attackers today . . . They didn't come here because of you, right? I know you're popular and all."

"I know. They were going to attack here no matter what. You help people who don't want to go to Avalon, and with your connection to Olivia, and people like Diana here, you were always going to be a target. I imagine that Hera has wanted to send people to kill Diana ever since she refused to work for her."

"They want you angry and not thinking clearly."

"Pretty much. You were right about me needing to use more than my brawn, Tommy. I've spent a long chunk of my life just running in without thinking. I'm going to do something else this time. I'm going to do the same thing I did with Kay when he wanted me to run after him, and I stopped myself and changed direction."

"You're going to cut his head off?"

"Well . . . yes, actually. Eventually I'm going to kill Helios, or whoever he's working for or with. But first I'm going to use my brain and try to stop these attacks. A lot of people are going to be scared . . . A lot of those will be human."

"A lot of human terrorist organizations have taken responsibility for the attacks."

"I figured they would. Most terrorist organizations would claim responsibility for starting anything that created some fear. This is too good of a chance to pass up."

"Hey," Diana said, running toward us. "You guys need to hear this." She looked worried, an expression that I wasn't used to seeing on her face.

"What's wrong?" I asked.

"Olivia just got off the phone with some people in Avalon. As of now there have been two hundred and nine attacks. Untold thousands are dead the world over. Olivia has her people trying to run down leads, but there are about a hundred different human government agencies with her people working in them that are currently freaking out. There was no warning for this, no intelligence that anything was about to go down. It literally just happened all at once."

"Shit," I whispered.

"Some countries are deploying martial law," Diana continued. "This just got a whole lot worse. Fiona has been recalled to Camelot. She refused. I genuinely don't know what happens now. Whoever was wearing that mask must have a problem with you personally, Nate. Or at least a problem with Hellequin."

"They could have been using the Hellequin name because they heard it," Tommy suggested.

I shook my head. "No, that was deliberate. I'd put money on it. I genuinely don't know where to start. It wasn't Helios on the film—I know that much. Whoever it was is stockier than he is. On the other hand, we know that Helios is involved." I rubbed my eyes. "Maybe I should reconsider my stance on being smart and go after him anyway?"

"You know that's what they want," Diana said. "If you're right about them coming for you, then they're making this personal. Which means they want you angry, they want you not thinking, and they know you'll go running after them all the first chance you get."

"I know. I just want to hit someone."

"So, are you honestly okay?" Tommy asked me.

I nodded. "I'll be fine." I stood and stretched, spotting Fiona and Olivia jogging toward us. "I want to go see Irkalla. Hopefully we can figure out where we're going from there. We have company."

Tommy looked around. "I hear you refused to go to Camelot?" Tommy asked Fiona when they both reached us.

Fiona nodded. Olivia kissed Tommy on the lips and sat beside him. "Not sure what Avalon is going to do next, but I think it's safe to say that they're no longer going to be helping Fiona find her husband."

"It wasn't even a choice," Fiona said.

Olivia hugged me. "Don't do anything stupid. And you can't go back to your old house. There are human police and fire-brigade people there. I might be able to keep you from having to talk to the human police, but it's time and effort that could be better spent elsewhere. I'm sorry."

I nodded. I'd expected to have to forgo seeing my house, but the thought of just leaving it all there for people I didn't know to go through still stung. I waited until she was out of earshot before saying anything. "Stupid? Me?"

Tommy laughed.

"How're Kasey, Chloe, and the others?" I asked him.

"I checked, and they're all good. Nothing to report. But then only a handful of people here know where they are anyway. They're safe."

"Good. What about Tokyo and New York?"

"Both offices are good," Olivia said. "No reports of attacks, but both are going to be on high alert."

That was some good news, at least. "Hellequin is dead after this."

Tommy nodded. "Yeah, I figured you'd say that. For good this time?"

"Someone just announced to the world that Hellequin is responsible for thousands of innocent deaths. Even if I managed to prove otherwise, the Hellequin name would never be the same. Better for everyone that it goes away and stays there. This isn't about clearing the name of Hellequin; it's about stopping these bastards before they kill and hurt more people."

Tommy sniffed the air. "Mordred wants to talk to you."

"That's weird and creepy!" Mordred shouted from somewhere in the shadows beyond. He stepped into the light and walked toward us. "Can I have a few minutes with Nate, please?"

Tommy got to his feet. "I'll see you both inside when you're finished. We'll make the final preparations once we've heard from Irkalla and Grayson."

Mordred sat on the bench as everyone else walked away. "I should have brought some bread for the ducks."

"I think they'll be okay," I told him.

"You ever consider that ducks think about more than just the pond they're in? You think they worry about how the ducks in the next pond over are doing?"

"Never considered it, but if they had that level of consciousness, I'd feel uncomfortable eating them."

Mordred nodded but didn't say anything for several seconds.

"What's up?" I asked eventually.

"You know that a lot of people in Avalon are aware that Hellequin and Nate Garrett are one and the same. And a lot of those people will have seen that video. Now, most of them who know you will know you're not a terrorist, but some of them . . ." He stopped talking for a second, leaving the sentence unfinished.

"Some of them will have decided I'm behind all of this and come after me? The thought had crossed my mind. Maybe that was their intent all along, to get people to see me as some sort of bounty to claim. Or at least to make my life more difficult." I rubbed my eyes with the heels of my hands. "This has been an exceptionally shitty day."

"You could go to Arthur, tell him the truth."

"I imagine he already knows it wasn't me. He's not stupid. And I can't go back to Camelot. Not while Merlin and his people are there waiting for me to show up. That would just start a fight and make things a thousand times more complicated. Besides, I don't trust Avalon. I don't know who is and isn't involved. They took Elaine—they can damn well take anyone else they like."

"It's not over yet."

"Well, aren't you just a ray of sunshine," I said with a slight laugh.

"Do you have any ideas who the head of this cabal is?"

I nodded. "I have my suspicions, yes."

"You feel like sharing them?"

"I'm mulling over your idea that it's Merlin. It makes sense. There are still things I don't get, though. Too many questions, not enough answers. Story of my life."

"These last three years have been the happiest I've ever had. And it feels like someone is trying to take that away from me. I know that's selfish, I know that how all of this affects *me* isn't exactly the point, but I don't care. I finally found a place for myself in the world, I finally found friends and allies I care about, and who care about me in return, and I finally feel like I could genuinely do some good. I'm not fighting with my own mind anymore; I'm not consumed with the need to kill people just because Baldr and his people decided they needed a puppet to murder for them. I'm going to fight for this, Nate. If that means I have to be front and center when the enemy march toward us, then so be it. No one is going to take this life from me, not while I draw breath."

"If anyone had told me a century ago, or hell, even five years ago, that I'd come to not only respect you, but like you, I'd have told them they were insane. I never thought we'd get anything close to a friendship back after so long at each other's throats. I'm glad it worked out this way, though. And I don't plan on allowing these people to destroy the lives we all have."

"Nate, there's something else. The whole I-have-to-kill-you thing."

"I thought we literally just agreed that just because the Fates told us we had to go down a road, it didn't mean we have to actually do it."

"I know, and I know that just because they said so doesn't mean you're going to turn into some kind of monster, murdering everyone in your path. I'm fully aware of all of that, but just hear me out—there's something I've just considered."

I motioned for him to continue.

"What if no matter what we do, it moves us closer to the future the Fates saw? What if they're right on this occasion? I know they see one possibility, but they told me that every permutation of the future showed me killing you, or you killing so many people. But what if that doesn't happen for a thousand years? I've spent the better part of three years trying to find a way to get around the Fates' premonitions and found nothing. And we both know that while what the Fates say doesn't *necessarily* have to happen, that doesn't mean it won't."

"That's incredibly vague."

"Okay, what if you going after this fake Hellequin is what leads you down a path of darkness? I'm concerned that the My Liege attacks are what kicks this all off for you. If people you love die, you go through people. I heard about Mary, your wife. I heard what you did to those responsible. I heard about America."

"What did you hear?" I asked. I wasn't thrilled that he'd brought it up, but now that he had, I might as well discover exactly what he knew.

"You went to America. Murdered people who you considered to be evil. Considered to be unworthy of living in a world where your wife had died. That it took Tommy coming over to stop you."

"That about sums it up. I'm not going back to that time. The Fates are tricky at best. It's a shame they stayed in the dwarven realm. Maybe we've already done something to change the future we were told about."

Mordred thought about that for a second before nodding slowly. "I didn't consider that. How would we know?"

"We wouldn't. But, Mordred, we can't live our lives based on the premise that possibly, maybe you might need to stop me from going full—"

"Sephiroth?"

I stared blankly at him.

"*Final Fantasy Seven* villain. He tries to destroy the world, was once a good guy, kills Aeris, or Aerith depending on how you consider her name is spelled."

"You're literally speaking a foreign language to me."

"Sephiroth bad. Aeris good. That about sums it up."

"Glad we cleared that up."

"Anyway, I guess we just have to see what happens from now on."

"You need to relax a little. You're going to drive yourself insane if you're constantly trying to look out for ways to stop something that might not happen. That's not a basis to be happy, Mordred. And you deserve some happiness."

"Maybe finding Elaine will keep me occupied from thinking about prophecies. Silver lining and all that."

I was about to agree with him when Tommy sprinted over to us. "You need to come to the medical bay. Now."

He didn't have to ask twice, and Mordred and I ran after him, through the reception and into the lift, going underground several floors to the medical facility. We followed Tommy down a hospital-like corridor and into a room at the far end. The first thing I saw was Grayson standing over a crumpled Irkalla.

"What the hell happened?" I asked, and took a second to look around the room. There were three tables in the center of a large morgue, but only the middle one was occupied. The body on the table belonged to one of the attackers. The skin of his arms and chest had been clawed open, and there was a hole where his heart should have been.

Remy and Nabu stood against the far side of the room with Selene and Zamek beside the table. Morgan sat on a chair next to the row of a dozen drawers that had been built into one wall. Each drawer was made of silver and had various runes etched into it. Sometimes things went in them that wanted to come out.

I focused on Irkalla, who was still unconscious on the floor. "What happened?" I asked, crouching beside them.

"We don't know," Selene said.

"We don't have any other necromancers on staff," Grayson told me. "I need you to figure out what's going on."

I stood and glanced between Irkalla and the dead man. I hadn't used my necromancy much except to take souls to charge my magic. It allowed me to become incredibly powerful, but it only worked on people who had died in battle, and I couldn't use that power to do a lot of the smaller, more power-demanding feats that people like Irkalla and Hades could.

I found out a few years ago that Mother had been a Valkyrie by the name of Brynhildr. From my research into the species, I discovered that they were able to channel their necromancy to make them faster, stronger, quicker at healing, all things I, too, was capable of. I could also create soul weapons—physical manifestations of my power, which when used against someone destroyed their soul, not their physical body. None of which was even remotely useful in the current circumstance.

I activated my necromancy and reached out for the spirit of the deceased attacker and immediately stopped when I felt my power tugged between both the dead man and Irkalla. My vision changed, and I saw Irkalla's spirit as it reached out and touched the darkness surrounding the dead attacker. I reached out with my necromancy to touch the darkness, but the second it made contact, a wave of power crashed over me. "Oh shit," I said, switching off my power as I fell to the floor. I rolled to the side and vomited into a nearby bin.

"What is it?" Nabu asked.

"I've never seen anything like this." I wiped my mouth with the back of my hand and lay back on the cool floor. I tried to get the image I'd seen right in my head so I could explain it. When I no longer felt nauseous, I sat up. "Irkalla's spirit is trapped. She reached out to the corpse, trying to get a read on his spirit, but it was a trap, and the second her power touched his spirit, it snapped shut like a bear trap. She struggled, and it began to tear out her spirit, forcing it partly into the darkness that now surrounds the body. I don't even understand what that is. I don't know how it was done, or how to stop it."

"There has to be a way," Morgan said.

"Maybe, but it's far beyond the power I have. I can try to take the darkness into myself, I can try to absorb whatever remains of his spirit, but doing so might mean taking Irkalla's spirit, too. I don't know if I can untangle them. I don't even know if trying will kill her. We need Sky or Hades—both of them are vastly more experienced than I am."

"And both are unable to help," Nabu said, kneeling beside me. "You're here, Nate. You're all we have. Hades is in Canada, and Sky is trying to make sure Tartarus isn't a target. Neither will get here soon enough."

I shook my head. "I'm not sure I have the . . ." I stopped and sighed. "I'm going to pass out for a few minutes. I'd really appreciate it if no one panics."

A few people in the room shared nervous glances. "You're going to pass out?" Zamek asked. "On purpose?"

"Are you sure?" Remy asked. He was leaning up against the far wall, his arms crossed over his chest, his eyes fixed firmly on the floor. "This isn't a great idea."

"Do you know what he's going to do?" Morgan asked Selene.

Selene stared at me. "You're going to talk to your nightmare, aren't you?"

I nodded.

"Have you lost your mind?" Zamek asked. "Nightmares are bad. They take control of sorcerers, and they kill people. They kill the sorcerer."

"Not quite," Mordred corrected. "I don't believe that's true. Mine certainly didn't kill me; it protected me. I think we've been lied to for a long time about what they do."

Zamek looked between me and Mordred. "You're both nuts."

"They're telling the truth," Grayson said. "Nightmares aren't a threat. Their default behavior is to protect the sorcerer. It's why so many of them attack; they lash out because they feel threatened, or the sorcerer was scared when the nightmare took control. If Nate remains calm, there's no reason for the nightmare to do anything other than help. It's Nate's power amplified. The nightmare taps into that potential and, in theory, could make Nate powerful enough to do this."

"Or he could go crazy and try to kill us all," Zamek said.

I shared a glance with Mordred. Was this the moment the Fates were talking about? Was this the moment the Fates warned us of?

"Mordred," I started. "I want you to—"

"I know," he interrupted. "If this is the Fates' prophecy, I'll make sure to stop it before it starts."

Tommy's growl echoed around the room. "You will not kill him," he said slowly.

"Tommy," I said, my voice calm and soft. "If we're wrong and this nightmare becomes a concern, it needs to be stopped."

"Are you certain the nightmare isn't a threat?" Tommy asked Grayson.

"I was there when the pact was made to keep it secret from the world," Grayson said. "I was there when Cronus, Rhea, Amaterasu, Tsukuyomi, Susanoo, Odin, Nergal, Ra, Seth, and a dozen more made the decision; any sorcerer accepting their nightmare was to be considered a danger to all living things and delivered a death sentence. A few discovered how to accept their nightmare, to control it. Most hid this information from the world around them, escaping their death sentences. Zeus, Hera, Merlin, and a few others managed to accept their nightmares, but most sorcerers who accepted their nightmares were hunted down and executed."

"Why?" Zamek asked.

"It was a way to manage the power levels of sorcerers," Grayson said. "It was a way to ensure that no one could activate their nightmare without the proper training. If you break a sorcerer's mind before allowing the nightmare to take control, you have a monster on your hands. A monster that does not recognize friend from foe. Some people discovered that they could manipulate a nightmare to turn it into a weapon to be used against their enemies. A lot of people died before that pact was made. A lot more died after, too, but it was deemed an acceptable loss. The law was flawed. Not all nightmares are evil."

"So, nightmares are good, so long as the sorcerer is of sound mind?" Zamek asked.

"That about sums it up, yes," Grayson said. "Otherwise you have a death machine on your hands."

"And everyone who signed this accord knew that?" I asked Nabu.

Nabu shook his head. "Sorcery was rare when we were considered deities. Nergal proclaimed that nightmares were the harbingers of all things evil, and considering I'm not a sorcerer, I had no way of countering that argument. My ability to know things, to understand things, doesn't work on nightmares. I tried once and felt like I'd been set alight. I decided that Nergal and the others must have been right in their thinking."

"If that's true," I said, "then you were smart to fear nightmares. Those sorcerers who became corrupted by power, or twisted in some way, needed to be hunted down. But instead of declaring nightmares a risk in totality, why not educate and help?"

"Those who were hunted down and killed for being out of control, they needed to die," Grayson said. "But even if the nightmare gave control back to the sorcerer, the person would be twisted, corrupt. There are a lot of things I haven't told anyone. Things I've kept to myself for thousands of years. Talk to your nightmare, Nate. It's safe—I promise you. When you're back, and Irkalla is safe, we'll talk more."

"What if I can't separate her from the trap?" I asked.

"Then she'll die."

My anger vanished in an instant, and I allowed myself to immediately connect with the nightmare inside me. I closed my eyes, and the world around me faded away.

CHAPTER 7

Nate Garrett

I found myself sat on the wet lawn of an old thatched cottage. The door had been painted white at some point, although it was now peeling, as if the elements had been battering it for so long it had given up the pretense of perfection.

I appeared to be in the middle of nowhere. Apart from a small stream that ran beside the house, and snowcapped mountains in the distance, everything as far as I could see was empty heathland.

A man who looked just like me opened the cottage door and stepped outside. "It's been a while," Erebus said. "I thought that maybe you'd forgotten I was here."

"I'm stronger," I told him. "It takes more for me to come to see you now."

"I know, I was just making conversation. Only one mark to go. Well, two marks, yes, but only one I can see. Who knows what's behind that door?"

"I need your help."

"I know. I'm you, remember."

"Still weird. Even after all these years, it's still weird."

"I imagine it is, yes."

"I need you to take control of me and use my necromancy to separate Irkalla from this other spirit. There's a . . . darkness that has snared Irkalla's spirit."

"And you can't do this by yourself?"

"I'm stronger, but not strong enough."

"Even with the fifth blood-curse mark's disappearance? That boosted your power by a considerable amount."

"Yes, my sorcery, but my necromancy isn't as powerful. I assume if I accept you and you take control of my body, that knowledge will be unlocked, but as I can't do that until all of the marks have vanished, I need your help."

"You've finally accepted that I am not the enemy?"

I sighed and nodded. Since time was different here, there was no need to hurry. However long the conversation with Erebus lasted, only a few seconds would have passed in the real world. Yet another thing that takes some getting used to.

"Yes. I don't know how nightmares genuinely work. I don't understand why you're here, or if you're unusual. Are all nightmares like you? Do all of them take the form of the host and have chats with them? There's literally an entire ocean of knowledge I don't have, but Grayson says you're safe, and Mordred has been telling me that his nightmare saved his life, so I'm having a little faith. Over the last decade I've realized nightmares are not the monsters we were warned against. I don't think you're the creature we should fear. I think you're something sorcerers are meant to accept to move onto another level of power."

"Took you long enough," Erebus said with a sly smile.

"Yes, well, when someone tells the world for thousands of years that something is bad, I tend to trust that information."

"And you think I can take control of your body and use your necromancy to help Irkalla?"

"I hope so. Because if you can't, and I can't figure out a way to do it, she'll die. She can't stay trapped like that indefinitely, and I have no knowledge about what it is that's trapped her."

"Yes, you do. You know exactly what it is. You know how it's created. You forget that there's knowledge in your head you don't have access to."

"I don't understand. I thought the only knowledge trapped in my head was about the first eight years of my life. Why would an eight-year-old know about complex necromancy?"

"Not like that. You honestly want to know what I am? It's the only way you're going to save Irkalla."

I didn't hesitate: "Yes."

He walked over to me and pushed his hand against my chest. I gasped and dropped to my knees, fighting for breath. I looked up at Erebus and noticed the arm he'd used to touch me was faded, almost transparent.

"What the hell?" I managed.

"The nightmare is knowledge and power. We give the knowledge and power to the sorcerer when they're ready. Your blood-curse marks stop me from passing on the knowledge and power, but every time you lose a part, you get a little more of them both inside of you. And I gain access to a little bit more of the information placed inside your head, information I can give you. And when you're finally ready for all of what I am, I'll vanish and you'll be whole."

"Your arm."

Erebus glanced where his arm used to be and shrugged. "You now have part of the knowledge contained inside of me. Eventually I will fade away. All nightmares operate in this way, but I am unlike almost any other nightmare in existence. There are others who have nightmares like me, but not many."

"Mordred?"

"I can't say for certain—I'm not in his head—but based on the knowledge in your mind, I'd say it's likely."

I got back to my feet. "So how long before I know whatever you just unlocked in my head?"

"A few moments. I don't think it's going to work like you believe it does."

"Just be straight with me. For once. You've unlocked stuff in my head, but you clearly must already know that information, so just tell me what it is."

Erebus smiled. "This is like when you learned how to mix your elemental magic. You're the one who has to learn it, and once you do, we can talk about it."

"And what do I have to learn?"

Erebus began to fade, and I reached out for him, but he'd already turned to mist.

"Hello, Nathanial," a female voice behind me said.

I turned and found myself unable to speak as my mum stood before me. She had long chestnut hair, pale skin, and blue eyes that were a similar shade to my own. She was shorter than me by several inches and wore a simple green dress that stretched down to her bare feet. Several gold and silver rings sat on the fingers of each hand, and a tattoo of a serpent stretched from her left shoulder, down her naked arm, stopping just above her wrist. The other arm had several runes tattooed onto it. A few years ago I unlocked the first memory I had of my mother. Of her leaving me to have the blood-curse marks placed on my body, before I was taken to Camelot.

"Nathanial, I assume you have questions."

"What the fuck is this?"

My mother paused. "I am a mental construct. A message left when you were born and Erebus was created inside of you. Your father left a similar message but . . ." She paused for a few seconds. "You don't have access to that information, so I can tell you no more about him. He did love you, though. We both did. We weren't meant to, but we did."

"What the hell does that even mean?"

"This is a message based on responses to questions I assumed you'd ask, as well as information about various aspects of your life that you might need answers to. I can't tell you anything I didn't know when you were born, and I can't give you access to information that Erebus doesn't have access to. I'm here because your father and I wanted to leave something for you to remember us. Because we wanted you to understand why we did what we did, and why you were never given the life you deserved."

"I understand exactly nothing that's going on." Irritation had started to creep into my voice, but I forced it aside. "Start at the beginning, and work forward."

"You are my son, Nathanial Garrett." She paused again. "You are unaware of your last name."

"I'm what?"

She took a step forward and smiled, reaching out for my hands. "My boy. My son. There's so much I want to tell you, but I've been informed that this information doesn't work like that. So, I get to put something personal in here before the information is relayed to you. I love you. I want you to know that. I have no way of telling how old you are, or what you've become, but I love you. I always loved you, and even though I had to give you up to Merlin, I still loved you."

She placed her hand against the side of my cheek, and I felt a lump catch in my throat.

"This isn't real," I said. "Not really. This is essentially a mental hologram. The magical equivalent of a computer program. Even so, I have a lot of questions for you. Can you answer any of them?"

"Some, maybe," she told me, removing her hand. "Mostly I'm just here to tell you what I can. And then I'm gone."

"Forever?"

She nodded. "This is a onetime-only deal. Once I've imparted this information, I'm no longer needed."

"I'm not sure that's the phrase I'd use."

I stared at my mother for several seconds. It was strange; my head should have been filled with questions fighting for the same space. I couldn't think of a single thing to say. I took a deep breath and exhaled slowly. One question remained in the front of my mind. "Why was I created?"

"You were created in a similar ritual as that used to create the seven devils."

"The what?"

"Thousands of years before you were born, seven people were created. I'm unsure exactly how it happened, or why, but they were called the seven devils. Weapons of war to use against the enemies of their creator."

"I was born to be a weapon?"

My mother nodded. "That was the original plan, yes. But unlike the seven devils, you were to be brought up by your parents. Unfortunately things changed and you had to go to Merlin."

"There was a war?"

"When you were born, we all knew that a Norse pantheon civil war was on the horizon. I made a pact with Merlin that once the war began he would keep you safe. I was concerned that you'd be dragged into it. You were sent to Merlin to be hidden and trained. Those marks were placed on you to ensure you didn't access power you had no hope to control. You were meant to unlock them as needed."

"It took me sixteen hundred years to unlock the first one."

"That was not the intention. Something must have gone wrong with the process. I'm sorry."

Despite how sad and sympathetic she sounded, I forced myself to remember that the woman in front of me was merely a construct and only had clinical answers to questions. Even so, having my mother sound dismissive about what had happened to me stung a little. "So, what else do you have to tell me?"

"A lot," she said. "I was a Valkyrie, and like all of my kind, I could use the spirits of those who had died in battle. Spirit weapons are used by all necromancers, but Valkyrie can channel the spirits we take to increase our physical attributes. We can also manipulate those spirits in other ways."

"Are you saying a Valkyrie put a"—a phrase popped into my head— "spirit snare on Irkalla?"

"Not necessarily a Valkyrie, but you know the term—that is good. It means the information is bleeding into your mind. We cannot place traps, which would have been done by a truly powerful necromancer. But we can manipulate the spirits of those who died in battle, and not just absorb them."

"I can try to remove the snare?"

"It would take a great deal of power on your part, but you could absorb both souls into yourself and then try to untangle them. I've done it myself. A word of warning, though: if you get it wrong, you will kill your friend."

"And if I do nothing, she'll die anyway."

"Yes. It is not an easy decision to make."

"Anything else?"

My mother's eyes softened again, and a smile spread over her lips. "My son, I assume all of the information I was to give you is currently being absorbed by your brain. I wish I could teach you so much, I wish I could stay here and tell you everything about who you are, and who you were born to be, but I can't. Do not trust Hera—she is a snake, the same with her people."

"Yeah, I got that one already."

"I hope that I'm still alive out there somewhere, and that one day we'll meet. You should know that the Valkyrie weren't a species; we're just necromancers with an unusual power quirk that makes us both incredibly powerful, and limited. Odin used the Valkyries to lay waste to his enemies. He was a great ruler, but I have no way of knowing if the war that threatened to consume the Norse gods is still raging on. And I have no way of knowing if any of my sisters are still alive, but if you can find them, they will help you. And if I'm alive, they will help you find me."

She began to fade, and I took a step toward her. "I will find you," I promised, and she vanished a moment later.

I stood and stared at the spot where my mother had been as Erebus appeared beside me. "A lot to take in?"

"She told me things I didn't know, about you. All sorcerers have nightmares—that's well known—but people like Mordred and I aren't normal sorcerers. Aren't normal anything. So, you're not a normal nightmare. Were you created as a separate entity and placed inside of me? Did you merge with the nightmare who was already there?"

"Sort of."

"Explain."

"Later. You need to save your friend. Time isn't infinite here, and sooner or later you'll be forced back into your world."

"Are you going to take control of me? Use my power better than I can?"

"No, you can do this without my intervention. We both know that. You're down to your last physical mark, so I'm not sure whether asking me to take control is a good idea. Once a nightmare takes full control, you're going to be out of it for a long time, and if I do this now, you'll be of no use to anyone. You can't risk the mark vanishing as I take control. Not now."

It wasn't the response I'd been expecting. "Who are the seven devils? My mother mentioned I was created in the same way, but I've never heard of them."

Erebus laughed. "You always were persistent. Of course you have. Everyone with even a passing knowledge of pop culture will know of them. There are a thousand movies, films, video games, TV shows, and books about them. They're everywhere. You probably know them better as the seven Princes of Hell."

I was about to say something else when I was dumped out of my mind and back to reality. Everyone stared at me as I blinked several times before trying to sit up.

"How long was I gone?" I asked.

"You fell to the floor about four seconds ago," Remy said. "What happened?"

I got back to my feet. "Long story, but I think I know how to separate Irkalla from whoever this guy is. I'm going to need power. A lot of power. I'm also going to need all of you to leave."

There were some odd looks exchanged around the room. "You sure?" Grayson asked.

I nodded.

"You okay?" Remy asked. "I've got to go help Mordred find Elaine while you lie about on the floor. Tommy, Nabu, Zamek, and Morgan left to go help with the injured. I stayed behind to make sure you didn't blow up or something."

I smiled. "Thanks for the vote of confidence. Be careful. Don't go losing any more lives."

Remy chuckled. "Thanks for killing me, by the way. Probably saved me months of pain and suffering. I know it must have been hard to do."

"It's everyone's dream."

Remy laughed. "Fuck you, Nate. Be careful out there. I don't want to have to console Tommy; he's weepy enough as it is."

It was my turn to laugh as Remy left the room, and I found myself alone with Irkalla, Grayson, and Selene.

"You two need to go," I said.

Selene came over and kissed me on the lips. "Don't do anything too stupid."

"Would I?"

"Every single day," she said with a slight grin. "Bring Irkalla back to us."

I watched her leave and started opening the silver freezer drawers, pulling out each of the trays as I went, revealing the dead they contained. I was three drawers in when I noticed that Grayson was still in the room.

"We need to have a chat when we're done here," I told him. "I want to know why you knew about the nightmares and never said anything. I'd also like to know how you were around in what I assume was at least ten thousand years ago."

"I'll tell you everything you want to know, but not now. We can't have distractions while people are getting hurt."

"Okay, but soon."

He helped me to open the rest of the freezers and drag the bodies out on their trays.

"You should go," I said.

He patted me on the back, and I watched him leave before activating my shadow magic. Tendrils of shadow shot up from the floor, wrapping around the dead bodies and dragging them into the now-shadow-covered floor. The effect took mere seconds as burst after burst of power flooded my body.

I placed a hand on the nearby wall to steady myself as power coursed through me. It took me a few seconds, but when I was settled, I reached out with my necromancy and saw Irkalla's spirit trapped in the spirit snare once again. But this time instead of the usual brightness I saw in most spirits, Irkalla's was a beautiful orange and golden color. I reached out for Irkalla's spirit, but when I tried to pull it away, the dark-red and black mass tightened its grip.

I released my power from Irkalla and reached out to the snare. Despite the newfound level of knowledge about my necromancy, knowing something and being able to actually do it are two different things. Magic isn't a science—it's about power, patience, and sheer will. And when it came right down to it, necromancy was just a different form of magic, albeit one that most sorcerers were incapable of wielding.

I stepped toward the body of the attacker and pushed my hands out in front of me. My spirit began to leave my body, and for a split second I panicked and the light-blue and purple spirit almost rushed back into me before it made contact with the snare, but I managed to catch my emotions and forge onward.

Being in control of both my body and spirit at the same time was a strange sensation, a bit like rubbing your head while patting your belly, or the other way around. There was a steep learning curve to this type of power use, and I didn't have time to practice. I either got it right the first time, or Irkalla, and possibly I, would die. No pressure or anything.

My spirit was still tethered to my body when it touched the snare, and I felt a jolt of pain, as if I'd hit a sword on stone and felt the vibrations run up my body. I pushed it aside, and my spirit began to expand. Blue and purple light wrapped around the snare as Irkalla's own spirit cascaded over mine, mixing together.

Memories flashed into my head. Irkalla discovering that her friend had been murdered by Siris, finding her friend's body, along with those of her friend's family. The rage that followed was something to truly fear, as Irkalla destroyed anyone who got between her and the target of her vengeance. She'd told me that Siris had murdered someone she'd cared for, but the depth of pain and suffering Irkalla had gone through felt like a shotgun blast to my heart.

Other images, of Nergal and Gilgamesh—the latter now dead, and the former now an enemy—and of Nanshe, an old friend to us both, came to me quickly without pause, until the second my spirit had completely encompassed the snare, and then there was nothing but darkness.

There were no memories in the man, no hopes or fears, no feels, no nothing. Whatever had once been there had been replaced with a void. But somewhere inside there was a voice. It was small and barely audible, but I pushed my spirit further, crushing the snare and pushing it further and further away from Irkalla's spirit, forcing the two apart.

The voice began to come through louder and louder, but it was muffled and I couldn't quite hear what it was shouting. I continued on, desperate to snuff the snare from existence. Smothering it seemed like the only way to remove Irkalla from its grasp, but the constant muffled cry was beginning to feel like I had a jackhammer going inside of my skull.

A wave of nausea hit me, and I crashed to my knees, fighting against the snare as it tried to stop me from destroying it. The muffled voice became louder and louder until I screamed in pure incandescent rage as I fought against the snare. And then, without warning, the snare vanished. I fell to the floor, panting and sweating from near exhaustion.

I looked over at Irkalla and willed her to move. For several seconds I was certain I was too late, until her eyes opened and she stared at me. "That wasn't fun," she said, her voice low and full of pain.

I nodded. I couldn't find any words to use.

"Did you hear it?" she asked me.

I nodded again. "The voice," I managed.

"I couldn't make out what it was saying. It was the man's memory, his one final memory that couldn't quite be destroyed by what had been done to him. Do you know what the memory said?"

Right at the end I'd heard the voice clear as day. It had been one word screamed into my skull. "Abaddon."

CHAPTER 8

Nate Garrett

"You okay?" Tommy asked me as he entered the morgue with Selene and Grayson.

"That was not a fun experience," I told him as I got back to my feet. "How's your head, Irkalla?"

"I wish to crush something so I can feel better," she said from beside me.

"Abaddon," I said. "That was the name I got from the snare."

I looked between Selene and Tommy, who both had an expression of pure shock on their faces.

"Wait, the devil guy from the Bible?" Tommy asked.

"Woman," Irkalla corrected. "Devil woman."

"As to whether she's from the Bible, yes and no," Grayson said. "It's a lot more complicated than that."

"She's older than I am," Irkalla said. "If you thought that Tiamat was trouble, Abaddon is just in another league. I never met her, but I heard stories from those who did. She's not a woman to mess with."

"So, we might be dealing with someone who may, or may not, be the actual devil?"

I shrugged. "That about sums it up, I guess."

"I'm hoping it isn't the devil. If it is, a lot of the music I like is going to be ruined for me."

"What, you mean if the devil is really just an asshole?"

Tommy chuckled slightly. "Yeah, I always thought he'd be cool. Or she. I'm completely open to a devil of either sex."

"Or both sexes at once."

"That, too."

I paused for a second. "You know I'm an atheist, right?"

"Yeah, I figured as much. What with you having shown no belief in any religion for the centuries I've known you." He made it sound as if I'd just said something incredibly stupid.

The urge to swear at him was great, but I pushed it aside. "I spent my whole life meeting people who, at one time or another, others thought were actual gods. I don't put a lot of stock in religion as a whole."

"But what if this woman genuinely is the devil? That's going to throw a spanner in your entire ideology. You worried?"

"No, because I'm an atheist. It's not the devil; the devil doesn't exist. Not Lucifer, not angels, demons, or any other part of the whole story."

Tommy stared at me for a heartbeat, his expression completely neutral. "You hope."

I smiled. "Fuck off."

Tommy laughed. "Nice comeback, very mature."

"Fuck off, my good man?"

"That's better. At least make it sound genteel."

"You two done?" Grayson asked with just a flicker of irritation.

I was about to make a rebuttal when something caught in my mind. "Erebus said something about the seven devils. Isn't Abaddon one of them? He said I was created in a similar way as the seven devils."

Grayson nodded. "Abaddon was one of the seven devils, yes."

"What do you mean, created?" Selene asked me.

I shrugged. "I don't really know. Erebus just said that I was created to be a weapon. Like Mordred."

"You all talk, and I'll go make sure everything is prepared," Tommy said. "Which means I'd quite like to know where you're going."

"My father has spoken about her before," Selene said. "She scared him."

"Hyperion was scared of her?" I asked, more than a little surprised. Hyperion was one of the most powerful beings I'd ever met; I couldn't imagine the number of people that scared him to be very high.

Selene nodded. "Not just her, but those she worked with. Those she answered to. If Abaddon is involved in this, we need the advice of people who have dealt with her before."

"What about Hades, and the like. Won't they have dealt with her?"

Selene shook her head. "The seven devils had vanished before the Titan war, so before the ascendency of Zeus and the Olympians. Mostly they'll only know stories and rumors, or they might have met one or two of the devils, but it's unlikely they've really *dealt* with them as a unit."

"So, Tartarus it is, then," I said, trying to figure out just how powerful someone would be to make a Titan afraid. "At least we can check on Sky and those who work there. Maybe some of the Titans can help us."

"I don't think Hades is going to be in any hurry to let any of them out," Irkalla said. "They might not be on the side of whoever this cabal is, but they have no love for Avalon, either."

"See, a nice chat with Hyperion will sort all of this out," I said, feeling very little confidence in my words.

"If I step away, are you going to be able to stand upright?" Tommy asked.

"I'm grand, just tired. I'll be fine."

Tommy watched me for a few seconds to make sure I wasn't about to fall over, and then left the room.

After checking that Irkalla wasn't about to collapse, too, Selene walked over to kiss me on the lips. "I was worried about you. Don't do anything stupid, I said. I'm pretty sure what you did classifies as stupid."

"Well, yeah, but it's always nice to be the hero, so they go hand in hand."

Selene shared my smile before kissing me again. "It's a good thing you're handsome, because you're not too good at the smarts."

"Ah, how sweet, thanks."

Grayson sighed, although I didn't know if it was out of a desire to not see the public display of affection, or because it had been a long day. "I'm glad you're both okay. I need to go deal with a few things, but I'll be seeing you all later."

"We're still on for that chat," I told him.

Grayson nodded. "I promise you, I'll explain it all. I just need to find out a few things for myself before we talk. I'll see you at Tartarus, and I'll explain everything. But know this: Abaddon is to be feared. She is unlike anyone you've ever faced."

"What is she?" Irkalla asked.

"A necromancer. Maybe the most powerful in all existence. She used to use snares like the one that grabbed Irkalla—she might well have been the person to invent them. Abaddon, like you, Nate, was created to be a weapon. But over time she became cruel, vicious, and full of rage at those around her. If she contacts you in any way, do not engage her in a fight." He strode toward me and took hold of my face in his cold hands. "Promise me, Nate. Promise me you won't fight her. She will kill you."

I nodded. "I have no intention of fighting her. But if she comes for me, I'll throw everything I have at her."

Grayson appeared to be relieved. "Wait for me in Tartarus. I'll come with answers." He turned and walked toward the door.

"How do you know her?" Selene asked before he could leave.

Grayson paused at the door and looked back at us. "She was my friend."

He left the room, leaving us with questions we would have to wait to hear the answers for.

"Road trip," Irkalla said after several seconds of silence. She steadied herself. "Just so we're clear, I've never seen one of those damn snares before, you?"

I shook my head. "No, I haven't. And you're not coming on this trip. We can't be certain that you're a hundred percent. I'd rather you stayed here and helped Olivia and Tommy. I'm concerned that whoever did this will try again."

Irkalla looked annoyed for a second before nodding. "Yeah, I'm fine here. I could use the rest, I guess. Make sure whatever happened to me is absolutely gone. I'm almost sure the snare was able to grab me because I'd never seen one like it before. I just didn't know what I was meant to do to get around it. The more I fought, the tighter it grasped. Not the most fun thing I've ever done." Irkalla sat back on a nearby chair. "I think I'm just going to take a moment to rest, if that's okay."

"I saw my mother," I said softly. "She told me that Valkyrie weren't a species. That they're necromancers who specialize in a very specific form of necromancy. The fact that this man died in battle meant I could screw with the snare. I'm not sure I could have done it otherwise."

"You saw your mother?" Selene repeated, concerned.

I nodded. "She put a construct of herself in my head when I was born. My father did the same, but I still have no idea who he is, so I don't get to see that one. She said I need to find the Valkyrie if they're still alive. That they'll help me find her."

"We'll find her," Selene said.

"I know, but that's for another day. Right now this is more important. Erebus, the nightmare inside of me, is a construct, too. My parents did something to give him the kind of personality he has; he didn't explain more. The more I learn, the less I know."

Selene, Irkalla, and I left the morgue and made our way back up to the ground floor, where we found Zamek and Tommy in deep conversation. The cleanup crew was pretty much finished, but a lot of people were bringing in family members to stay under Tommy's protection while this whole thing continued. No one was sure who the enemy was, and while that continued, so would the uncertainty over exactly how safe and secure everyone was.

Irkalla wished us all luck and went off to get some rest. She probably wasn't very happy about not being a part of what we were doing, but it was for the best.

"The jet is ready to go to Tartarus," Tommy said. "It's the one Hades loaned to Mordred and Morgan, so try not to break it."

"Take care of yourself, you hear me?" I said, hugging him.

"You, too. Try not to get into too much trouble." He stared at me for a second before laughing. "Sorry, I almost said it with a straight face."

I smiled. "I would hate to work for you."

"I'm an awesome boss, and everyone loves me. I bring them cake every Friday—how can they not love me?"

I left the building and got into a black SUV and found Zamek inside. "I wondered where you'd gone," I said.

He picked up the battle-axe from the seat beside him. "Needed to go sharpen my axe. I get the feeling it's going to get a lot of use."

Selene entered the SUV, and we were taken to a nearby airfield, where we boarded the jet. There was a time, in the not-too-distant past, when flying terrified me. Since then I'd jumped out of two helicopters to wage war on my enemies. Flying was never going to be my favorite mode of transport, but until someone finally invented a teleport that worked without risk of disintegration, flying was the best I had.

So, I gritted my teeth and spent the journey drinking whiskey and trying very hard to get some rest. I had the feeling I was going to need it. At some point I must have fallen asleep, because the next thing I knew I was jolted awake from the landing at the private airport in Mittenwald.

It was a short drive from there to the Wolf's Head compound near Lake Ferchensee. The security at the gate let us in the second they saw that it was me, with most of them saying hi and asking how I was before we drove in. The last time I'd been at the compound, they'd been attacked, and I helped defend the place. I really hoped it wasn't going to come to that again, and judging by the number of armed guards patrolling the area, anyone trying had better come armed for a long, protracted battle.

Selene parked the Range Rover we'd been given at the airport, and we all got out into the wintry south-German air. There was plenty of snow on the ground, and it crunched underfoot as we were motioned by one of the guards to move toward the command building at the far end of the compound. I was grateful for the warm clothing and new boots that Sky had supplied when we'd reached Germany, and hoped that those who had gone off to find Elaine weren't having too much trouble. The second the thought entered my mind, I became fully aware that it was the pot calling the kettle black, but the point still stood.

Sky walked out of the command building before we'd even reached it, and smiled. Sky had been born to a Native American father and a European mother who had been murdered when she was a young child. Hades and Persephone had taken her in and raised her as one of their own. She walked over and hugged Selene and me before introducing herself to Zamek.

"I've never met a dwarf before," she said.

"They're not all as great as I am," Zamek replied, shaking Sky's hand.

Sky laughed. "I'll keep that in mind if I ever meet more. Olivia told me you were on the way. You want access to Tartarus, is that right?"

"We need to see my father," Selene said. Her tone was solemn, and I knew she wasn't exactly thrilled to be here under such unpleasant circumstances.

As the four of us walked through the compound, heading down toward the realm gate room, we explained to Sky what had happened back in England, and how we believed that Abaddon was involved.

"My father spoke of her once or twice," Sky said. "He told me she was not someone to cross. My mother thinks she's about as evil as anyone has ever been. I think they both met her once or twice, although by that point the Olympians were in total control, so I'm not sure how much power or influence Abaddon actually had. Even so, my mother grew up with Hera in her life, so if there's one thing she knows, it's evil. If Abaddon is involved in these attacks, what's to say the other six devils aren't involved, too?"

"That's what we need to talk to Hyperion about. We need to know how likely that is, and why they would attack now," I told her.

"How are you doing, Nate?" Sky asked with some concern.

"I'm as okay as possible, thanks," I told her.

"Good, and you, Selene?"

Selene shrugged. "My brother, Helios, is involved in all of this. I don't think I can protect him any further. This will be his last time to hurt those I care about. I am both saddened and angry about that fact. He is my brother, after all."

I reached out and took her hand in mine, squeezing it slightly. She squeezed back.

"And you, Zamek?" Sky asked.

"I'd like to go home, back to my own realm. I'd like to see my friends again. I'd like to save my people. I'd like to kill every single blood elf I can find. But I can't do those just yet, so I'll just keep on fighting whoever needs to be fought."

"I'm sorry about your friends," Sky said as the group entered a lift, and she pressed a button on the control pad to take it down to the realm gate room. "I'm sure you'll see them again."

"Oh, I know I will."

The lift doors opened, and we were greeted by several heavily armed personnel. After the compound had been attacked a few years earlier, Hades and his people performed a complete overhaul of the security. It meant a lot more guards. The realm gate room had been a target during the last attack, so Sky and Cerberus had made it their mission to ensure anyone trying again would have a hell of a time.

Sky said hello to the four guards, who all nodded toward the rest of us without comment. They wore specially designed body armor that stopped magical power from having too much of an effect, and helms that combated psychic abilities. I wasn't sure who had designed the items, but whoever had done it would be in high demand with every Avalon office on the planet.

"So, you've made this place a lot more formidable," I said to Sky as we walked down the ramp to a lower level, where a guard at a second checkpoint waved us through.

"Only people who don't get searched are Cerberus, my parents, and my siblings, and even those get checked if they haven't been here within the last three months." Sky sounded proud of what she'd achieved at the compound.

We entered the realm gate room, and Cerberus walked over toward us as I started to look around. The last time I'd been here, I was in a fight for my life against two assailants and had pretty much totaled the place. It had been completely rebuilt since then with new computers and workstations for everyone monitoring the comings and goings through the realm gate that sat at the end of the room.

"Good to see you, Nate," Cerberus said. Cerberus was a werewolf of exceptional power. Over six feet tall, and more than 280 pounds of pure muscle, he was not a man to cross if you liked keeping the use of your body parts. He didn't carry a gun—one of the few in the compound along with Sky who didn't need one. I'd once seen him throw a car at someone. A gun on his hip would have looked kind of silly after that.

"You shaved your head," I said.

He ran his massive hand over his baldness. "I felt it was time."

"You kept the beard, though."

He stroked the graying, chest-length facial hair and smiled. "Of course."

I left Cerberus with Sky and Selene and walked over to the realm gate, where Zamek stood.

"Magnificent structure, isn't it?" Zamek said from beside me. "Thousands of years old, maybe tens of thousands. Who knows? The ancient dwarves weren't exactly forthcoming with dates and information about their creations."

The gate itself was a large archway with dark-green runes etched all around the side facing us that sprang to life when activated. While the colors differed depending on the gate, each of them looked similar in design. Realm gates were all made from a mixture of wood, rock, and metal, although no one really knew *how* the realm gates had been made, nor how it was that they managed to repair themselves from damage.

"So, you want to go to Tartarus?" Cerberus said as he walked toward them. He spoke to a middle-aged woman beside him. "Meet Rhianna—she's one of our guardians."

Guardians were the only ones who could activate a realm gate. They were immortal so long as they stayed within a certain distance from the gate, and were imbued with magical tattoos that adorned their bodies, linking them to one specific gate.

Rhianna shook my hand. "It's a pleasure to meet you," she said with an accent placing her from the US South, although I couldn't identify the exact region.

"You, too," I said. I stepped away while Rhianna spoke to Zamek, and found Sky and Selene in deep conversation. "You two good?"

"We're discussing her father," Sky said. "He can't come out of Tartarus. You know that, right?"

"It's come up before, yeah," I said. "We just need him to tell us about Abaddon."

"We're ready when you are," Cerberus said.

The realm gate activated, and we stepped through into Tartarus.

CHAPTER 9

Mordred

Basingstoke, England

The helicopter lifted off from the roof of Tommy's building with Morgan, Diana, Fiona, Remy, Nabu, and Mordred aboard. They sat three opposite one another, and no one said anything for several minutes. Mordred knew that everyone was worried about Nate and Irkalla.

It was twenty minutes into the flight when his phone vibrated in his pocket. It was a message from Tommy: *Nate and Irkalla are good. Stay safe.* Mordred showed it to everyone inside the helicopter's cabin, and he felt the mood ease almost immediately.

"Does anyone have any idea what we're meant to find here?" Remy asked. Everyone in the helicopter was wearing a headset that allowed them to communicate. Without one, the sound of the wind would be far too much to hear anything.

"This is where Elaine went just before someone grabbed her," Fiona said. "That's pretty much all we know. We went to check the house out but found the place ransacked."

"So, we're meant to find something that the people who trashed the house couldn't find?" Morgan asked.

"Look, we might as well investigate, and if we find nothing, we'll move on to Moscow," Fiona said, her voice clearly holding back the frustration and emotion she felt at the lack of information about the disappearance of Elaine and her husband, Alan. "I don't plan on leaving a single stone unturned until we find them."

"We'll find something," Remy said. "There's always something to find. You just have to know what you're looking for."

"And what are we looking for?" Diana asked.

"Hopefully something really big and obvious with a map and excellent directions."

Diana laughed. "You ever found something like that before, Remy?"

Remy smiled. "There's always a first time."

Mordred looked out of the window as they sped past everything far below. He wondered whether or not this mission was going to lead to something he'd rather not take part in. He wondered whether everyone in the helicopter with him would be okay if things didn't go well. He pushed the thoughts aside; negative thinking would do little to help in the current circumstances. He felt a hand reach out and take hold of his, squeezing it slightly. He looked back at Morgan, who mouthed *Are you okay?* Mordred nodded and squeezed her hand to hopefully prove it. After the talk with Nate, he genuinely felt good within himself, although somewhere in the back of his mind he wondered how long that was going to last. There were a lot of people he'd purposefully avoided since regaining full use of his faculties, and he knew that at some point in the future he was going to have to meet up with some of them. It felt to him like an inevitability. He just hoped he could keep everything together when that happened. He didn't want any of those people to think they could affect him anymore.

He let go of Morgan's hand and went back to looking out of the window. Eventually there was an announcement in his headset that they were going to begin landing, and he sighed, cracking his knuckles and mentally preparing himself for what was coming. He started to hum the *Mario* theme tune and got an evil look from Morgan for it, but he ignored it and carried on. He found that humming the tune calmed him, although he'd discovered some time ago that the busier he was, the fewer tangents his mind went on.

There was a slight bump as the helicopter landed, and Fiona pulled open the door, allowing everyone to exit. Mordred walked away from the helicopter and stretched, taking in the scenery. Apart from a large house with a hole where the front door used to be, there was nothing for miles. Mountains sat in the distance, but between him and there were just open plains and a stream. Remote Scotland was as harsh and beautiful a place as anywhere Mordred had ever been, but he found the solitude to be tranquil.

As the helicopter's engines died down, Fiona brought everyone together. "An LOA team went through here just after Elaine went missing, but seeing how we're not exactly trusting Avalon at the moment, you should still be careful."

"When did they leave?" Diana asked.

"A few days ago. This place has sat like this since then."

"Well then, let's go search the mansion," Remy said, and set off toward the building.

Mordred held back and watched the rest of the group enter the massive house. He had no way of knowing when Elaine had the place built, but it looked to be a hundred years old, at least.

"Five bedrooms, four bathrooms, two receptions, a dining room, lounge, kitchen, and no garden," Nabu said from beside Mordred. "And it's been ransacked. Both by whoever came and looked for Elaine first, and then the LOA."

"Maybe they're one and the same."

"That's an unfortunate possibility. I believe she was taken from here, although the lack of magical damage suggests otherwise. Maybe she was taken in Moscow and they wanted to ensure she hadn't left anything here that might lead us to them."

"You know, Elaine isn't stupid. She knew about the cabal; she knew that several of its key players are members of Avalon. She knew that

Hera was at least partly behind it all, and that Merlin is quite probably helping. Yet she came up here, to the middle of nowhere, with her guards, who are nowhere to be found, for what? A bit of a holiday?"

Nabu thought about it for a few seconds. "It is suspicious, isn't it?"

Mordred nodded. "There's no way Elaine would leave Avalon to crack on with everything while she swans off on her holidays."

"Crack on?" Nabu raised an eyebrow in question.

"It means get on with it."

"And swans off?"

"Storm off in a huff. Admittedly she's not the storming-off-in-a-huff kind of person, but I wasn't being literal."

"So, you believe she came here for another reason?"

Mordred nodded. "She was meant to come see me in New York. She said she had info on the prophecy about me and Nate. So, why come here two weeks beforehand? Why bother to leave Camelot? Why come all this way to do"—he waved his arms around him—"fuck all? There's nothing here. That's the beauty of this part of the world: there's fuck all bastards to ruin it."

Remy left the house and walked toward Mordred and Nabu. "You two planning on helping? Because at the moment you're just standing there like a couple of scarecrows with even less dress sense."

"That's not as good as your usual insults," Mordred said. "I feel kinda bad for you."

"Less swearing than usual, too," Nabu said. "Maybe his earlier death has given him much to ponder."

Remy raised his middle finger. "Ponder this."

"Have you found anything?" Mordred asked.

"No, because you two are out here with your thumbs up your asses."

"That was better," Nabu said.

"Remy, I need your nose," Mordred said.

"You what?"

"Nose, Remy, nose."

"I heard you, Mordred. I just don't know why."

"Did I not say that bit?" Mordred asked, wondering what he had and hadn't said aloud.

Remy shook his head. "I find it helps, though."

"Right, yeah, sure. Anyway, she has a secret stash. She uses it for information, not drugs."

"Why would we think it was drugs?" Remy asked, and turned a full circle. "There's nothing here."

"Kind of why I need your nose."

"You want me to pick up her scent? Because any tiny parts that are left are mixed with about fifty other scents. You'd be better off asking me to turn back into a human, because that might be easier."

"Isn't that impossible for you to do?" Mordred asked.

"Kind of my point there. Your brain gone weird again?"

Mordred shook his head. "About the same as it ever is. But in this instance, no, I don't need you to track her scent out here."

Remy remained silent.

"On the way over here, I checked on my phone and there's a cave system over to the north. People go climbing in it . . . 'Spelunking,' that's the word, right? Anyway, I'm not much of a spelunker, never really saw the point of it. You know? I know that Elaine likes to go climbing. She's a big fan, always has been. Again, it's a bit weird. Only reason to climb is to get away from something, in my opinion. Yes, I know I'm rambling, but my point is while she likes to climb, anyone who knows her will also know that. But going underground? Well, that might not be the first thing people think of."

"Mordred?" Nabu asked in a tone that suggested Mordred was rambling.

"Ah, yes, sorry."

"You think she's hidden important information in the cave?" Remy said. "Do you know the kinds of things that hide in caves?"

"Trolls, monsters of various shapes and sizes. It's going to be a blast. You'd probably better get Diana, though, just in case we need something torn in half." Mordred watched Remy run off and turned toward Nabu. "Useful skill to have around, tearing people in half. Never know when it's going to come in handy."

Nabu stared at Mordred for several seconds. "You okay?"

"My brain is moving very quickly. It happens every now and again when I feel stressed or concerned about something. Doesn't help that I'm impatient to get going, and my brain doesn't like it."

"I thought you were all better. Thought you'd managed to keep your manic side under control."

Mordred smiled. "That's a very subjective term. Compared to being a drooling wreck who wants to eat someone's face, I'm goddamned dandy. Compared to someone who doesn't sing 'Mario' fifty times a day, I might be slightly unhinged. But one man's unhinged is another man's sane."

"That's one way of looking at it."

Mordred's smile vanished. "I've spent a long time being damaged. I'm not going to be that anymore. I might be quirky, I might be strange, but I'm me."

"I never wanted to suggest otherwise."

"I know. I know you're just looking out for me. Everyone is always just looking out for me. Sometimes I think they do it because they're expecting me to revert to my old evil ways."

"I don't think that," Nabu assured him.

"Every day is a battle not to let my past actions crush me. Every day I tell myself that today I'm good, that today will be a good day. And for the last decade or so, I've been right."

Nabu remained silent.

"You're wondering what happens if one day I'm wrong?"

"The thought did cross my mind," Nabu admitted.

"Then one of two things will happen. Either I murder those I love, or they kill me before I get the chance. Neither appeals. I tolerate my slight brain farts because to do anything else might drive me even more insane than how I was before Nate shot me."

"Every day is a battle for many of us, my friend," Nabu said, resting his hand on Mordred's shoulder. "You are not alone in this, I promise."

Mordred turned to Nabu and smiled. "I know. And that helps me think I can do better. Can make amends for those I wronged."

"Is that why you're here?"

Mordred turned to watch as the rest of the group left the house. "No. I'm here to find a way to stop me from having to kill Nate. I'm here because Elaine is missing and she's pretty much the only member of my family who gives a shit about me. And I'm here because I want to find the people behind all of this and crush them into paste. They're killing innocent people, Nabu. And that shit won't stand."

"Remy says you have an extremely stupid idea," Morgan said. "I cleaned up his words a little." She paused. "A lot, actually. Damn, that fox-man can swear like a sailor."

"Thank you," Remy said.

"You want to go spelunking?" Fiona asked.

"Do people just like saying that word?" Mordred asked. "Spelunking. It is quite fun, I guess."

"Mordred," Fiona snapped.

Diana rested a hand on her shoulder. "Easy, my friend. He's not the enemy."

Fiona shrugged off the hand and took a deep breath. "I'm sorry."

Mordred shrugged, as if it were no big thing, although he wondered just how tightly wound Fiona was, and whether she might snap if she wasn't careful. "Not specifically, no. I came here a few years ago to talk to Elaine, and she told me about a cave system. She made a really big deal about telling me of this system. Pointed me in the right direction and everything. I promise you, she hasn't hidden anything in that house. Anything anyone found was of no real importance."

"And if you're wrong?" Fiona asked.

"We waste an hour and know I was wrong. I'll even let you sing a song about how wrong I was." He paused and held Fiona's gaze. "I'm not, though."

"A hidden cache of some kind?" Diana asked.

"Yes," Mordred said. "It's in those caves over there. I've never been down there myself, and I don't really know *exactly* where she would have hidden anything, but we won't find anything here."

The group set off across the plains, making good time as the morning sun warmed the cold just enough to make it bearable. They reached the cave entrance, and Mordred peered inside, expecting to see something of interest, but it was far too dark, and far too deep.

"There's a thirty-foot drop," Remy said. "I can smell the insects inside. Lots of them. Also, something else. A scent. Two scents. The first is Elaine, no doubt about it, but the second is—"

"Perfume," Diana finished, and took a sniff of a nearby rock. "I think Elaine dabbed perfume on these stones. It masks her scent, but more importantly it gives us something to track."

"What if the people who came here searching knew about this?" Fiona asked.

"No other scents," Remy confirmed.

"Remy and I will go first," Diana said. "The rest of you, keep back, and try not to get hurt."

"Have I ever told you how much I love your motivational speeches?" Remy asked. "They inspire such confidence."

"I can throw you down the hole, if you'd prefer."

Remy winked and darted into the darkness beyond, vanishing from sight within seconds. Diana followed soon after, leaving the rest at the mouth of the cave peering in.

"You see anything?" Morgan shouted.

"I can see all," Nabu said, and stepped into the cave.

Morgan and Mordred shared a look of surprise. "What is he?" Morgan asked.

"An och," Mordred said. "To be honest, I'm not exactly sure what he can and can't do. He doesn't talk much about himself."

"Are you all coming down here?" Diana shouted from somewhere inside the cave.

Mordred walked into the cave with Morgan and Fiona beside him and used his air magic to gently lower all three of them to the ground, then immediately wished he'd brought a torch.

The light from Morgan's phone illuminated a massive cavern. Several things moved on the walls, and Mordred was sure he didn't want to get too close to them. There weren't a lot of animals in the UK that would kill you, but that didn't mean they couldn't give a bite, and Mordred knew for a fact that some of those bites hurt like hell.

"So, any idea where she went?" Fiona asked.

"The perfume is still fairly strong in here," Diana said, sniffing the air. "It's maybe a week old."

"How long does the scent last?" Morgan asked.

"Two weeks and it's gone," Diana said. "Before then it depends on the air, moisture, other scents. But down here, there are insects, bat shit, and the perfume. It's easy to pick out the one I want. Elaine's scent is here, too, but it's too faint to be really useful."

"I found something," Remy said from the darkness. Fiona removed her phone and turned it toward his voice, the phone's torch moving over Remy. "Yeah, blind me, that's a good idea."

Fiona moved the light slightly but didn't apologize. "Better?" she asked, her tone hard.

"Sorry," Remy said to Fiona, seemingly remembering why she was there. "But you guys need to see this."

"So, you do notice when you piss people off?" Mordred asked as he followed Remy through a large crack in the cavern and down what appeared to be steps.

"Elaine made this," Remy said. "Or had someone else with earth magic do it. These steps aren't a natural formation. And neither is this."

Remy was pointing toward a small stone hut at the far end of another large cavern. There was no door or windows on the small stone building, but it was obvious what it had been created to be: a place to hide, or hide something important.

Water trickled down the walls, and stalactites had formed throughout the cavern, bisecting the entire place. Some of the stalactites were so long that anyone over six feet high would have to duck down to get under them, making it difficult to get to the hut on the other side.

"I think they had some help, too," Morgan said as she joined them.

Fiona walked over to the stalactites and was about to touch one when she stopped herself. "They're sharp—I can tell even from a distance. These aren't made by nature."

"So, how do we get past them?" Diana asked.

"I'll go," Remy said, and dropped to all fours, darting under the stalactites and into the hut.

Remy emerged several seconds later—although to Mordred it felt much longer—with a small metal box in his mouth. He made the trip back over to the group and dropped the box on the ground.

"Any chance that Elaine booby-trapped this?" Morgan asked.

Everyone stared at the small gray box. It was six inches long, and five wide, with a small handle on top. It was three inches deep, so whatever was inside wasn't large, but a booby trap didn't need to take up much space.

"Let's take it outside and open it," Diana asked.

There was a crunching sound, and Morgan flashed her phone's light toward it and discovered Remy chewing on something.

"Food," Remy said. "I'm part fox, remember? Foxes eat pretty much anything you give them, and bugs are a good source of protein." He bent down and picked up a dark beetle, popping it in his mouth.

"I need to leave now," Morgan said, and took the lead as the group left the cavern.

It didn't take long to get everyone up out of the cave, with Morgan using her earth magic to create a set of stairs that allowed the group to just climb out with ease.

"Why didn't you do that in the first place?" Fiona snapped when back outside.

"I didn't know what was below," Morgan said. "Can't start moving things around when I can't see what I'm moving."

"You could have moved those stalactites, though," Remy pointed out.

"You didn't give me a chance to do anything." Morgan turned to Fiona. "Look, I get that you miss your husband. That you're worried. But if you're going to keep snapping at people, you can go back to Tommy and wait."

Fiona took a step forward. "You're welcome to try and make me."

"I can't believe I'm the one saying this," Remy started. "But grow the fuck up, both of you. Fiona, you're pissing off everyone with your attitude. I know you're scared, but we are trying to help, and you're being a—"

"Bitch," Morgan finished.

"And you're not helping," Mordred said. "Fiona, if you can't deal with this, you really should go back home."

"I can't," Fiona almost whispered. "I can't just sit there and do nothing. I'm sorry for snapping."

Diana picked up the box, turning it over in her hands. "I don't see anything dangerous." She grew one nail until it was long enough to pry the lid off the box. There was a moment of concern followed by curiosity when the box didn't explode or start spewing noxious gas.

"We're not dead, right?" Remy asked. "I feel okay."

"All of those bugs probably saved you," Morgan said.

"So, what's in the box?" Mordred asked.

"There's a USB stick, a folded piece of paper, and a second piece of paper with a map on it. I think it was printed off." Diana removed the contents, dropping the box on the dirt. She passed the folded paper to Morgan, the map to Nabu, and held the flash drive in her hands, turning it over as if looking for something special about it.

"Is there a computer on the helicopter?" Morgan asked.

"Let's go find out."

"What does the paper say?" Mordred asked as Morgan read it.

"I love you, little nephew," Morgan told him.

"So we know this is Elaine's," Mordred said. "She called me that on occasion. She thought it was funny."

Mordred took the note and carefully folded it up before placing it in his pocket. "So, what about this map?"

Nabu passed it to him. "I have no idea what it is."

Mordred recognized it instantly. "It's a satellite image of a small town that doesn't exist."

"What do you mean it doesn't exist?" Morgan asked. "There are houses, and there's a car—it's red. There's a black X on part of it, though. I don't get that bit. Are we meant to go there?"

"The town doesn't officially exist," Mordred clarified. "It's on no official maps and has no official name. It's to the east of St. Petersburg, north of Sviritsa. It's called the Hamlet. Not named after Shakespeare, before anyone asks."

"It's Avalon-run?" Diana asked.

Mordred nodded. "That X is where a hundred years ago I tore off a man's arm, killed his best friend, and burned his home to the ground. When the ashes were cold, I salted the earth. I mean that literally."

"So, we need to go to this small village?" Fiona asked.

Mordred shook his head. "No. When I last spoke to her, she mentioned that the man I almost killed now lives in Moscow. I thought it weird at the time. I wondered what possible connection he could have to the prophecy, but she told me to leave it alone until she confirmed things. Looks like he's where we need to go."

"And Moscow is where my husband went missing," Fiona said.

"Yeah, looks like we're going to get even colder," Mordred said with a sigh. "And this might get a lot messier."

CHAPTER 10

Mordred

The flight to Moscow didn't take a long time, but it was long enough to make Mordred concerned about the reception he might receive. The last time he'd gone to Russia, he'd been more interested in hurting Avalon than helping anyone. Hopefully the fact that Mordred was with people like Nabu and Diana would make people think twice about attacking, because he was sure that no one was going to believe that he'd turned over a new leaf. Hell, he wouldn't believe that if someone had told him, and it had taken him several years to make those he sat with trust him. He pushed the thought aside and sighed—too late to worry about it now.

He picked up the USB stick from beside him and looked at it. There hadn't been a computer on board the helicopter, so it would have to wait until they got to Moscow, and hopefully someone there could help them. Presumably after trying to kill them, as was seemingly the more likely of the two actions.

Mordred placed the flash drive back beside him, keeping a hand on top of it.

"It's okay, you know," Morgan said. "We'll find out what's on it."

Mordred nodded and looked over at Fiona, who had the manner of someone filled with an exceptional level of anxiety. He looked around and found a small screw on the metal floor of the helicopter. Mordred's first thought was *Where the hell did this come from, and is it needed to fly the helicopter?* but he quickly told himself that it was probably nothing, and picked it up, throwing it across the cabin toward Fiona, who looked up at him.

You okay? Mordred mouthed.

"I'm fine," Fiona said through the headset, making everyone else in the group aware of their conversation.

"Just checking," Mordred told her.

"Well, don't. Not you, not ever."

Mordred felt the gaze of several of the helicopter's occupants on him. "Ah, I assume the man I used to be wronged you."

"Wronged me?" Fiona snapped, turning toward Mordred with fury in her eyes. "You murdered, you tortured, you did unspeakable things to innocent people because they were your enemy, or they were in the way, or just because you damn well felt like it."

"Your husband aided me on occasion. So, are you angry at me for what I did, or angry at him for his aid?"

Fiona reacted as if it took every ounce of self-control not to launch herself at Mordred. "You murdered a friend of mine in Berlin over a century ago. An LOA agent. You tortured him for days for what I can only assume was fun on your part. Do you even remember his name through the hundreds of bodies you left in your wake?"

Mordred took a deep breath.

"He doesn't have to explain anything to you," Morgan snapped. "He was out of his mind when he did those things. He was broken by Baldr and the people we now hunt. They took him, and for a century they tore him apart, let him heal, and then did it all over again."

Mordred leaned over to Morgan and placed a hand on hers. "It's okay." He looked over to Fiona. "I'm sorry about your friend. I remember all of them. Every single person I killed because I thought it was necessary. Every one of them. Your friend would have been . . . Eugene Lord, yes?"

Fiona nodded curtly.

"He died because he was sent to try and kill me, and I thought he might know where Merlin or Nate were. I killed him because I thought he needed to die. I was wrong. I was wrong about a lot of things, and I'm trying to make up for all the horror I inflicted over the years. Just like your husband, Alan, did after he married you. I heard about that, by the way. Alan told me about two years ago. I assume he didn't tell you that he'd been to see me."

Fiona shook her head.

"Nate set it up at my request. I wanted to apologize for my past, and I knew that he would want to ensure I wasn't playing games. I think he left satisfied with the answers he received. I wish I could take back every evil thing I did. But wishes don't mean shit, so instead I'm trying to make things better. I'm trying to ensure that Baldr and those who helped him create me are never able to do it again.

"Morgan and those who helped her keep me prisoner did the best they could, but I always escaped, and then the race was on to try and stop me before I did something awful. I'm truly sorry for your friend, and for many friends and loved ones I hurt over the centuries. Maybe one day you can look at me and not see the murderer who inhabited my mind for so many years. But then again, maybe not. I know I still have trouble every time I look in the mirror."

"I don't want to hate you," Fiona said. "Everyone says you're different. Everyone says you should be judged based on the person you are, not the monster you were forced to become. It's not that easy."

"Nor should it be," Nabu said. "I dealt with Mordred when he was crazed, and I've dealt with him now. They are not the same person. As hard as it is to reconcile the man who shares our quest with the one who would have done anything to destroy it, it's important that you allow yourself to believe in Mordred. If you do not, if we do not trust one another, this cabal will tear us apart."

"And it's that easy, is it?" Fiona snapped.

Nabu shook his head. "No. Wisdom is never easy. That's the point of obtaining it. If it were easy, we'd all be wise, and we'd all do the right thing all the time."

Fiona looked out of the window for a few seconds before speaking. "I'm here to find my husband, Elaine, and everyone else who was taken. Doesn't mean I have to trust Mordred." She turned to face Mordred. "If you step out of line, I will end you. And there's no one who will stop me."

Mordred bit back his reply and sighed. "You do what you have to do. And I'll do what I have to do, and hopefully it's the same thing. Right now, for example, I'm going to sit here with you people and hum 'Super Mario.' You're all welcome to join in." He started humming but caught the smile on Morgan's face as Fiona switched off her headset.

"You really need to get some new tunes," Remy said.

"From video games? I know *Zelda*, and a few *Final Fantasy* ones. You pick it, I'll hum it."

Remy laughed. "Let me think on it."

No one spoke for the rest of the journey, although they did switch off their headphones after several minutes of humming from Mordred.

Eventually the helicopter landed in a small private airfield just outside of Moscow. The moment the helicopter door was opened, and the freezing air rushed inside, Mordred wished he'd brought a much bigger coat.

The group moved outside, where they were greeted by a tall woman wearing a very thick and comfortable-looking orange jacket, the hood of which was pulled up, allowing very little of her face to be seen as fresh snow continued to fall.

She motioned for the group to follow her. There was little point in trying to have a conversation next to a helicopter, especially when the winds were beginning to pick up, so the group followed her off the runway and into a small building nearby.

The woman removed her coat and draped it over a counter while everyone else took a seat on the metal folding chairs provided.

"My name is Polina," the Russian woman said, running a hand through her blond hair and shaking off bits of snow. "I work with the LOA in Moscow. I received a call from Olivia telling me to expect you. She did not, however, explain *why* you are here."

"We're looking for Elaine Garlot," Diana said. "She vanished several weeks ago, and the team sent to find her was last seen in Moscow. We have a lead that suggests someone here might know what happened."

"And that lead?" Polina asked. "Do they have a name?"

Diana glanced over at Mordred. "We're not sure yet," she continued. "We need time to look around and hopefully figure out where we need to be."

Polina looked between Diana and Mordred before nodding. She was obviously unhappy with being kept in the dark. "If you need something, come to me first. Lots of people in Moscow who work for Avalon aren't always working with Avalon's best interests at heart."

"That seems to be the norm everywhere these days," Fiona said with a touch of anger in her voice.

"Yes, well, you should still be aware."

"We're looking for Viktor Egorov," Mordred said. "There, now you know why we're here, and now I know who to come looking for should anything happen to us or him before we find him."

Polina's expression remained neutral, but the anger in her eyes wasn't so easily concealed. "I am loyal to Elaine. I have always been loyal to Elaine, and I will not allow anyone to suggest otherwise."

"I'm not suggesting anything," Mordred said as he got to his feet. "I'm just making sure we're all on the same page. Do you know where Viktor is?"

"Probably in his home."

"And where's that?" Remy asked.

"I can take you." Polina held Mordred's gaze. "I promise not to put any bullets in your head before we get there."

Diana chuckled, and Mordred smiled. "Sounds fair," he said. "Is it a long ride?"

Polina shook her head. "Not really. We're not far outside of Moscow, but is he going to be happy to see you?"

"Judging from what Mordred told us about him, not even slightly," Morgan said.

Polina smiled. "Excellent. He's an annoying shit. I'll make sure to capture this moment on film."

She put her coat back on and escorted the group from the small building to two waiting Mercedes SUVs. Fiona, Morgan, and Nabu got into the rear one while Polina, Remy, Diana, and Mordred got into the front car, where several coats, scarves, and hats waited for them.

"Olivia said you'd need warm clothes," Polina said from the front passenger seat as the car started.

"You are a beautiful person," Remy said, putting on one of the dark-gray coats and making a sighing noise.

"You're furry," Diana pointed out as she put on her own coat before buckling the seat belt.

"Furry doesn't really make much difference when it's minus twenty and parts of me have frozen. Besides, I can talk. I'm sure if all foxes could talk, they'd tell you they were bloody well cold, too."

"Why don't you like Viktor?" Mordred asked Polina, not really expecting an answer.

"He used to be a big shot with Avalon, but things changed and he didn't take his fall from up high all that well."

Mordred relaxed a little. Maybe this wouldn't be the mess he was expecting. "Any chance he doesn't mention me by name as he's cursing people?"

"He stopped cursing you a long time ago, Mordred," Polina said. "Mostly he just curses Avalon, and the Kremlin, and anyone else who he feels let him down."

Mordred looked out of the car window. He was hoping that what he'd done to Viktor hadn't set him on a path of self-destruction and anger, but maybe it was all his fault. The number of acts he knew he had to make up for seemed to multiply by the day.

"If it helps," Polina said, "I have no reason to hate you, Mordred. Elaine told me you were a changed man. Her word carries a lot here."

"Do you know where she is?" Diana asked. "She was taken from a house in Scotland and presumably brought here."

"I haven't spoken to her in a few months. Last I heard she was looking into a place in Siberia. She wanted me to find information on an old gulag there."

"What did you pass her?" Diana asked.

"Just maps, details of who was kept prisoner. Nothing that I'd have thought was reason enough to get her grabbed."

"Can you get us those details?"

Polina nodded. "It'll take me a few hours, but yes. I did it for Elaine in an unofficial capacity, so I didn't exactly keep copies."

"That would be excellent, thank you," Mordred said. He hadn't been sure whether or not to trust Polina. He couldn't say for certain that she wasn't involved with My Liege, but seeing how Elaine trusted her, he would, too. He'd lived his life never trusting anyone, always expecting to be screwed over. It took a lot of effort to get rid of that mindset; he didn't want to go back to it.

"What does Viktor do now?" Remy asked. "Apart from seethe."

"He's an antiques dealer. And one with more ties to certain underground criminal enterprises than would usually be considered healthy."

"Criminal enterprises?" Remy asked. "You mean the mob?"

"Not the human one, no. Avalon doesn't have a lot of issues with them, but the human and nonhuman criminal element often work together. We believe that Viktor is involved with a local werewolf pack who owns a nightclub."

Mordred's eyes lit up. "Oh, we've got to go there."

"Why?" Diana asked.

"A fight in a nightclub? I've never done that, have you? I bet it's awesome. All *John Wick*, or some other film with an awesome nightclub scene in it."

"Why would there be a fight?" Diana asked. "Scratch that—if you and Remy go in there, it's almost a certainty that a fight will break out."

"We're classy like that," Remy said.

"You do not want to go starting a fight in their nightclub," Polina said. "People who start trouble in there don't ever come out. We've tried to infiltrate their group several times, and not once has anyone lasted more than a few days. They don't trust anyone who isn't known to them, and word has it the underground levels of the club are used to hunt the people who cross them."

"Does Olivia know?" Diana asked.

Polina nodded. "She thinks they have ties to this shadowy group who are working against Avalon. She found out they were involved with a group called the Reavers, who we all pretty much managed to destroy, but those Reavers were working for several people, like Hera. And we think the werewolves and Hera are in bed together."

"And Viktor works with these people?" Diana asked.

Polina nodded. "That's our thought, yes. He appears to be a money guy. Helping the rich get richer, knowing the right people to do the right job, that sort of thing. It seems to be a lucrative business for him."

"Viktor gets rich helping rich people stay rich by screwing over the poor?" Remy said.

"That's about the size of things, yes."

"Sounds like a dream."

"He's smart, and he's useful to the right people, so he's untouchable."

"Useful how?" Mordred asked.

"He keeps us informed when some of the more violent criminals come his way. He'll help some rich banker move his money around, but he's not too keen on helping some assassin asshole hide a million dollars in blood money. He has his limits. Doesn't mean I have to like him. And I certainly don't trust him, but you squeeze him every now and again and he gives up something worth knowing."

"Like who is the leader of this cabal, this My Liege character?" Diana asked.

Polina shook her head. "I doubt it. He's not the kind of person I'd trust with that knowledge. If this werewolf pack is involved with any cabal, they're not exactly on the inner circle, and Viktor isn't the kind of man you'd want to bring into that circle."

The two cars stopped a short time later outside of a large, white-bricked building with a long, curved driveway that led up to a set of steps, at the top of which was a wooden front door. On the side of the house sat a massive garage, which was easily big enough to keep four cars side by side. There were no trees on either side of the house, although Mordred spotted some at the rear of the property. Presumably Viktor wasn't a fan of not being able to see who was walking up to his front door. The lights on the top floor were on, but other than that it was bathed in darkness.

"How many entrances and exits?" Mordred asked.

"Is he going to run?" Polina asked.

Mordred shrugged. "People tend to run when they see me. It's something I'm used to."

Polina stared at Mordred for a few seconds. "One back, one front. He could leap from the windows, but that's not his style. He'll wait to be grabbed. We've done this dance a few times. He never puts up any resistance.

"The building is two stories above, and two below. Vault in the bottom level. It's all custom designed, and the first floor underground contains a safe room. This is his home, so there's not a lot of collector stuff here—that'll be in his workplace. Four bedrooms, although he lives alone, so don't expect much in the way of other people. He has at least three different girlfriends that we can tell, all of whom like to stay over on occasion. Sometimes more than one at a time. The downstairs has a large kitchen, two reception rooms, and a lockable door to his office. I know that because I kicked it in the last time I was here and he refused to open it. It was empty. He likes to play games."

"I'm just going to knock on the front door and see what happens," Mordred said. "I'd rather not give him any excuse to not work with us. We need his help."

"Why?" Polina asked. "What does he know that's so important?"

"I have no idea," Mordred said, opening the car door. "I'm hoping he can tell us that." He stepped outside into the cold and walked over to the steps, bounding up them as quickly as possible before pushing the doorbell.

The rest of the group soon joined him as footsteps inside the house could be heard.

"Step to the side," Nabu said to Mordred. "If he sees you first, he might run."

"Then we chase him," Mordred said, but he did as Nabu asked and moved aside so that when Viktor looked through the eyehole he saw only Diana and Nabu.

After unlocking it Viktor opened the door, beckoning everyone inside to the foyer of the house. Viktor was a tall, slim man, with a bald head. Several tattoos adorned his arms and hairy chest, and he wore purple silk pajama trousers with no shirt.

Viktor ran his hand over several days' worth of stubble growth and sighed. "Mordred."

There was an icy silence for a few seconds, and Mordred watched as several of his group tensed up, prepared for a fight.

Mordred stepped forward. "Viktor. It's been a long time."

"I always swore I would kill you when I saw you next." Viktor looked down at where his arm had once been. It now ended just after the elbow. "I wear a state-of-the-art prosthesis now. It moves to the commands of my brain. An alchemist designed it. Very expensive, very unique. Much stronger than my old arm ever was. But even so, I wanted you dead."

"If you want to try to kill me, I'm right here. Go ahead so we can get this over with."

Viktor grinned and clasped a hand on Mordred's shoulder. "I'm not going to try to kill you, Mordred. I'm going to go one better. I'm going to give you everything you ever needed, and then when you go off to find Elaine, the people who took her will kill you. They will torture you horribly for a long time, and when you finally die at their hand, I'll know. And on that day I'm going to sleep like it's the best day ever. I don't need to kill you; I just need to point you in the direction of the people who will."

"Point away, Viktor," Mordred said, smiling the whole time. "I know I did awful things to you, and I'm sorry about that. I really am. But if you screw with us, and I survive—and I'm excellent when it comes to surviving, just so you know—I'm going to come back here, remove your other arm, and I'm going to beat you to death with it."

CHAPTER 11

Mordred

Elaine told me you would turn up at some point," Viktor said after everyone had calmed down.

He took the group into his office at the rear of the property, which, for a reason Mordred couldn't quite grasp, had a bar in it. He poured himself a large glass of red wine and sat behind his desk, as if Viktor were in some sort of completely normal business meeting.

"What did she say?" Mordred asked.

"That you'd turn up and I was meant to help you. You have the USB drive, yes?"

Mordred removed it from his jacket pocket and placed the little blue and silver device on the desk.

"What's on it?" Remy asked.

"Documents and software," Viktor said with seemingly no interest in explaining further.

"Yeah, we're gonna need more than that," Morgan said. "I doubt very much that drive is full of Excel spreadsheets and the occasional PowerPoint presentation."

"We'll have to go into my safe room to access the drive. It's the only place in the house with a secure server. I don't trust a lot of people."

"Me, neither," Mordred said. "But on one hand, they only have to betray that trust once."

Viktor paused before getting to his feet. "Your thinly veiled threats mean little to me, Mordred. You took my arm. You killed my friends, and you burned my home to the ground."

"Don't say there's nothing I can do to you," Mordred said. "It's clichéd, and you live in a fucking mansion. There's about a million things I can do to you, and half of them still allow you to remain in use of your other limbs. Look, I'm tired. It's been a long day. Can we just get on with it?"

Viktor sighed and took the group down a set of stairs, where they stopped on a landing. There was another set of stairs, leading down into the level below, and a set of large metal doors. Viktor punched in a number on the keypad and scanned his hand before there was a hiss of air and the doors slowly opened.

"That is not what I expected from a safe room," Remy said.

"It's more of a safe flat," Fiona said. "It's huge."

"It looks like a penthouse suite," Nabu said.

"Just because I have to stay here to be safe doesn't mean I can't be comfortable," Viktor said.

The floor was all open plan, with a reception area just behind the doors, next to a kitchen and dining area to the right. Viktor led everyone to the right of those, under an archway into a massive living area, complete with oversized TV, and couch big enough to fit a football team comfortably. There was a bar, and pool table, and it looked more like the sort of place you'd go to hang out with friends than somewhere you'd go because something awful was happening and you wanted to be safe.

"The bedrooms and bathroom are just over there," Viktor said, pointing through a second archway to a hall beyond.

"Have you ever used this before?" Diana asked.

"All the time," Viktor told her. "Like I said, I like to feel safe. I also like to keep people guessing. I don't bring guests down here very often, though."

"Now I feel special," Remy said.

Viktor ignored him and walked over to a computer on a desk at the far side of the room. He tapped the mouse, and the computer screen lit up. "I keep it on at all times," Viktor said. "It's not like I can't afford the electricity."

"I tell you what, I'm not sure how you've managed to stay single for so long," Morgan said with as much sarcasm as she could manage. "Because dropping how much money you have into a conversation—that's sexy."

"I'm not ashamed of how much money I make," Viktor said.

"How about how you make it?" Fiona asked.

"Not that, either. We all have to eat."

"Yeah, this is barely getting by," Fiona said.

Viktor sat at the computer and plugged the USB drive in. "You know, Elaine didn't tell me you'd all be giving me so much shit for what I do for a living."

"I imagine she thought you probably deserved it," Remy said. "What's on the drive?"

"That's an excellent question," Viktor said. "I don't honestly know what's on it. It's encrypted and will take a while to open."

"Why you?" Mordred asked. "Why did Elaine come to see you? There's literally no reason I can think of that she would put a USB drive in a box in a cave instead of sending it to Tommy, Olivia, or anyone else she trusts. And she certainly wouldn't have come to you to discuss things. Besides, you're not smart enough to be a computer guy. You're a gangster, through and through. Not a brave or smart one, but still, that's the life you lead."

"She trusted me," Viktor said.

"Bullshit," Mordred snapped. "I don't trust you, and I've actually had dealings with you. You work with whoever will offer you the most of what you want. Money, power, influence . . . Whoever gives you what you need at that time, that's who you work with. What did Elaine offer you? What do you get out of it? Money? Prestige? Please don't say women and drugs, because I'd have to feel really disappointed if you do."

Viktor turned in his chair to face everyone. "A new realm," Viktor said. "I get to take my wealth and leave this realm and everyone in it. I get to move to a realm of my choosing and live like a damn king."

"Why?" Remy asked.

"Because just maybe I backed the wrong horse," Viktor snapped. "And just maybe some people won't be that happy with it when it's discovered."

"Who did you back?" Nabu asked.

Viktor and Mordred held each other's gaze for several seconds. "Elaine."

"What are you talking about?" Fiona asked. "She never mentioned you at any point."

"You remember when you ripped my arm off, left me for dead, and destroyed my life?"

"You want me to remind you why I did those things?" Mordred snapped.

"No. But Elaine found me. Offered me a job working for her in secret. She'd pay for my new arm, my new life, make it look like I'd earned it, and from there I was meant to ingratiate myself with people who might not have Avalon's best interests at heart."

"Like Hera, by chance?" Diana asked.

Viktor nodded. "I did a few things for her people, yes. I fed back what I could and made some profit where I needed to, but I never betrayed Elaine. Not once. A few months ago she shows up, tells me she wants me to keep some computer equipment here. That there's software on it that's been engineered to unlock encrypted data. Told me to leave it on at all times and keep it safe. In exchange she'd get me out of the realm. She said that Hera and her people were starting to move pieces around, that sooner or later I'd be discovered."

"So, you sold Elaine to Hera or something?" Mordred asked.

"No, of course not. I did exactly what she asked." He turned back to the computer. "Look." He clicked on a few screens and opened some software, which immediately gave a satellite view of a building in Moscow. "That can't be right," he said.

"What is it?" Diana asked, her tone suggesting Viktor was exceptionally close to irritating her.

"Good news and bad news," Viktor said, and Mordred thought there was far too much happiness in his voice for his liking.

"Just tell us," Diana said.

"Part of the encryption was to stop anyone from seeing the tracking device she wore."

"And the rest of it?" Mordred asked.

"I don't know. It's still going through the software. Anyway, this device needs contact with a living person to continue to function. So she's either in that building right there"—he tapped an image on the screen—"or she's placed it on someone who is there so we can find them."

"What's that building right there?" Remy asked.

"The nightclub the werewolves own." Viktor almost tensed as if expecting someone to hit him, and when it didn't happen he looked around the room to check where everyone was.

"You didn't give Elaine up?" Mordred asked, his voice hard, the anger seeping out.

"No, I swear I didn't. Elaine was going to keep me alive. I'm not a saint, and I did awful things for money, but no one knew I worked for Elaine. If they had, I'd have been killed years ago."

"There's always time," Fiona said. "It has to be a trap. Someone could have easily removed the device and be using it to bring people in."

"No one else knew," Viktor said, almost shouting. "No one but me even knew she wore one. Not even her bodyguards knew—she told me that herself."

"So why have it?" Fiona asked. "Why wear a tracking device that no one can find unless you get the USB stick, find Viktor, and use it here?"

"She was going to plant it on someone," Viktor said, and then regretted it.

"Who?"

Viktor shook his head. "Don't know. I just know she needed to get close to someone to do it, but she vanished before she could."

"So, that building—it's the same psychotic werewolf pack you mentioned earlier?" Remy asked.

Viktor smiled. "The very same, and if Elaine is in there, you're going to need a mop and bucket."

Fiona moved, and in an instant a blade was pressed against Viktor's throat. "Did you send her in there?"

His eyes widened as a thin line of blood began to trickle down toward his neck. "I just told you I didn't. They're fucking animals in there. I hate Avalon—they abandoned me—but Elaine had promised me everything I ever wanted. I'd never jeopardize that just to get petty revenge."

Fiona removed the knife and stepped back. "I'm going upstairs for a drink."

"I'll come with you," Morgan said.

"Why don't the rest of you go get a drink, too?" Mordred asked. "I'd like to have a little chat with Viktor."

"Don't kill him," Nabu said.

"Wasn't planning on it," Mordred told him.

That appeared to be enough for Nabu, who left with the others.

"So, you're having a shit day," Mordred said, taking a seat on a nearby dark-brown leather chair. "I'm in your home, your only way out of all of this is in the den of a group of psychopaths, and you're coming with us to help find Elaine."

"The hell I am!" Viktor shouted. "If they find out I was working with Elaine, I'd need to be moved tonight. "

"Viktor, you're coming with us. That's not open to negotiation. You don't have to step foot in the club until it's safe, but you are coming. Because I don't trust you not to."

"Trust? You want to talk about trust?" Viktor laughed, a cruel, unpleasant sound. "What's your angle here?"

"My angle?"

"Yeah, you know what I mean. You *hate* Avalon; you *hate* the people who work for it. You've spent the better part of your life trying to kill everyone and anyone who works there. So, what are you doing here? You expect me to believe that you've turned over a new leaf and now you're friends with Avalon? I call bullshit on that. So, what's your angle? What are you really after? Are you using those upstairs to get close to Merlin, or is it Arthur? Are you after the big man himself? You want to finish the job after you missed last time?"

"Wow, you just keep talking, don't you?" Mordred yawned. "Sorry, you're one boring man. My angle is nothing. I'm helping people I care about. I've had a . . . I guess you could call it a change of perspective on those I used to call my enemies. I'm not here to kill Merlin, or Arthur, or anyone else except for those involved with Elaine's kidnapping. I'm also not here to be friends with you. You know why I took your arm, you know why I burned your house down, and you know why I killed your friend. You know exactly what you used to be, and I'm not entirely sure that Avalon would be as forgiving about your past exploits as I currently need to be. Honestly, it if were up to me, I'd tell Diana and Fiona and watch them turn you into a man-sized piñata. But we need you in one piece."

"And don't you forget it," he snapped. "I'm your shot at finding Elaine. Remember that. She trusted me."

"No, she didn't. She needed you—that's not the same thing." Mordred watched Viktor for several seconds until the Russian got to his feet and exited the safe room, leaving the computer running so that Mordred could watch the percentage of encryption that had been broken.

"Did you know I was here?" Fiona asked from the other side of the room.

"No," Mordred said, trying not to show his surprise at her suddenly appearing from nowhere.

"I can make fairly powerful illusions."

"You left and came back, I assume."

Fiona nodded. "Needed to check you were on the level with us."

"You happy now?"

Fiona shook her head. "What are you keeping from us about Viktor?"

"Let me ask you a question, Fiona," Mordred said, getting to his feet and stretching his arms above his head. "Will it ever be enough? If I tell you everything, if I prove to you time and time again that I'm not the man I used to be, will it ever be enough?"

"I don't know."

"Well, at least you're honest. Viktor was a very bad man, who did very bad things. I was an amoral psychopath who wanted to butcher his way through Avalon, but I had my limits, I guess. Here's the thing, though: if I tell you, you're going to want to kill him. And doing that is certainly going to put this mission in jeopardy."

"You should still tell us," Diana said from the entrance to the safe room.

"She makes a point," Remy said from beside her. "We wondered where Fiona had walked off to. Wanted to make sure she wasn't trying to kill you. Which is a sentence I probably should never really have to say about an ally."

"Hey, any reason why Viktor was muttering about trust and then ran off out of the front door?" Morgan asked as she joined Remy and Diana at the front of the safe room. She looked around at everyone as they stared at Mordred. "This a standoff or something?"

"Fucking hell," Mordred whispered. "Where's Nabu?"

"Here," he said with a half-eaten sandwich in one hand and a bottle of beer in another. "I was just about to eat something, and everyone vanished."

Mordred walked over to the computer and moved the mouse to check that what he was seeing wasn't a screen saver. "Well, he hasn't fucked us over and run. He's just run."

"Who is he?" Fiona asked.

"Elaine trusted Viktor," Morgan said. "Maybe we should, too."

Mordred shook his head. "Elaine promised him she'd keep him safe if he helped her. She used him to run intel; she used him to keep an eye on people. He has a strange moral compass, but I genuinely believe he thinks Elaine was going to stand by him."

"Who. Is. Viktor?" Fiona asked without even trying to hide the anger she felt.

"Viktor was the leader of a small group of people. They lived in a small hamlet in the middle of nowhere, where Avalon personnel could go and rest and get information about new activities in the country. It was a clearinghouse where all of the information from Avalon's agencies went so it could be given out to their agents. There are a thousand of these small villages in the middle of fucking nowhere all over the world.

"Viktor used to take that information, which back when I last saw him was via physical mail, or astral projection, or telepathy—you know, the usual. Well, he took that information, and he sold it to the highest bidder, exposing Avalon agents, who they were working for, where they were, and who they answered to. I didn't really give a shit about this when I first found out, because I didn't give a shit about much, but two things changed my mind.

"Firstly, he sold information about me to someone who wanted me dead. Didn't work out so well, and I was mad about it, but I figured I'd get around to dealing with Viktor sooner or later. The second thing he did was sell information about me to Hera. At the time, I'd been hurt in a fight and was being healed by a young doctor in Finland. He'd just married his wife, and they had two children. They were kind to me when they had no reason to be and believed me when I told them that several Russian soldiers had shot me as I tried to stop them from killing a young boy who stole food."

"It was a lie?" Fiona asked.

Mordred nodded. "It was. But that small act of kindness was something I hadn't experienced much of, and considering I was near death, I was in no position to hurt them even if I'd wanted to. Except Hera found out exactly where I was, because the young doctor had spoken to someone in a nearby town about me. I stupidly used my real name when they found me, half-dead, delirious from silver poisoning. Hera sent her people to butcher that family. The things they did to them are not worth repeating, and I was still barely coherent when it happened, but I will always remember their screams. Always. The doctor hid me under a trapdoor in the house, and the men who came for me left empty-handed and decided to destroy the house as they left.

"I healed alone and in the darkness for a week until I managed to pull myself free from the wreckage. I found the dead family, and I buried them. I dug their graves myself, with shovel and hands, until all four were done. And then I went to Viktor. I threatened him, and he gave me the names of the people Hera sent. After that I killed his friend, burned down his home, and took his arm. I told him if he ever sold intel on people again I'd take one piece for every innocent it killed. And when I was done, I went after Hera's men."

Mordred paused and remembered their screams, their pleas for death as he'd tortured and ripped them to pieces, made them watch as he killed their loved ones, made them dig the graves of people they cared about. "I dealt with my grief and rage by doing the only thing I knew how. I allowed the monster inside of me to have free rein. From there I discovered intel that would later lead me to work for Mars Warfare and Ares. I could use my position to finally kill Hera, but she already knew I was working there and I hear found the whole thing quite entertaining, even if she hadn't told Ares any of this. In case you didn't know, Ares is an idiot."

When no one spoke for several seconds, Mordred started to hum. The humming relaxed him, and he felt incredibly uncomfortable with the silence that followed his confession.

"Viktor betrayed Avalon," Fiona said.

Mordred nodded. "Elaine knows this, by the way. I told her not long after it happened. I wanted her to know the kinds of people Avalon employed. It didn't work, because Elaine isn't a homicidal idiot, and I was. But I hadn't expected her to use him for her own gain. That was definitely not on the agenda."

"So, Viktor's run off to do what, hide?" Morgan asked.

"No, my guess is he's gone to whoever will offer him the best hope of survival," Mordred replied. "Elaine is missing, and I'm not exactly high on the list of people he trusts, so he's gone to someone who probably wants information on us."

"Hera?" Diana asked.

"A Hera proxy," Mordred said.

"The werewolves," Morgan said. "He's gone to tell them we're coming."

"That about sums it up, yes."

"We're still going to that nightclub, though, right?" Remy asked. "Because if so, we're going to need more weapons, and I've searched this house and found sweet fuck all. Unless you like the idea of going into battle with a potato peeler, which I have to admit would be kind of funny for about the first thirty seconds."

"Someone like Viktor is going to have weaponry," Mordred said.

"Why not screw with the computer before he ran away?" Fiona asked.

"No time. Either that or he wants to hedge his bets. If we make it through the nightclub, it's almost a certainty that he'll say he was helping us out by going to the werewolves as a diversion for us to assault the place."

"Doesn't deal with the lack-of-ordnance problem," Remy said.

"What's in the vault?" Diana asked. "Any chance he has weapons in there?"

Mordred nodded. "I don't see why not."

They all left the safe room and descended the staircase onto the floor below, only to be greeted by a single door with a numerical pad beside it.

Remy walked up to the door and tapped it with his knuckles, causing it to make a metallic sound. "Anyone know his code? Because I think this might be several inches of reinforced door."

Nabu placed his hand against the metal. "Reinforced titanium."

"How do you know that?" Fiona asked.

"My ability is to absorb information and understand it. But that doesn't necessarily have to be from books; it can also be from items. Things like computers or anything with multiple working parts takes me much longer to understand, but by using items I can figure things out quickly. While there are locks inside this door, the main problem is the runes that are designed to withstand magical force. I sense the number pad is the only way to get inside without serious time and effort on our part. And it's an eight-digit code, meaning there are millions of combinations."

Mordred walked over to the number pad, punched in eight digits, and the door slowly moved open.

"How'd you know that?" Nabu asked.

"The most important person in Viktor's life is Viktor. He used his date of birth."

"You know his date of birth?" Morgan asked.

"I studied people before I worked with them," Mordred said quickly, not adding that it gave him leverage over them if needed.

The vault was fifty feet long and thirty feet wide, and had rows of glass cabinets on either side. At the far end of the vault were ten metal cases, each one six feet high and three feet wide. Mordred ignored the glass cabinets and walked straight through to the cases, with Remy and Diana beside him.

"There's enough cash here to start your own country," Nabu said after opening one of the glass cabinets and going through the boxes it contained.

"Diamonds over here," Fiona said.

"Gold in this one," Morgan replied. "There's millions and millions of pounds' worth of gems and precious metals here. That's not including the cash."

Mordred pulled open the first case while Diana and Remy did the same with different ones.

"That's a lot of weapons," Remy said. "Rifles, handguns, shotguns."

"I've got some grenades," Diana said. "And by some, I mean a lot."

Mordred stared at the submachine guns and rifles that had been neatly hung in the case. Below it stacks of ammunition sat in their various calibers, each one in a different-colored box.

"Take what we need," Diana said. "Leave the money and gems—we don't need cash."

"No," Mordred said, and then realized he'd said it more forcefully than he meant to. He turned to Diana. "Sorry, I didn't mean to snap, but no. Take everything here, including money and gems, up to the front room of the house. Stack it all there."

"Why?" Diana asked.

"Because we might actually need cash to bribe people with, and diamonds and gold work better for people who don't like to be traced," Mordred lied.

"Anything else?" Fiona asked.

"Yeah, I really think having all the weapons out in the open gives us a better handle on how much we have and what we can use. And it's going to be damn funny when Viktor comes home, if he comes home, and finds his vault empty." That part was at least true.

When they were about halfway through clearing out Viktor's vault, Polina and her LOA agents entered the house. After a brief explanation of what was going on, they helped with the relocation effort. Polina in particular seemed to find the whole idea incredibly therapeutic.

It took a while to move everything out of the vault, up two flights of stairs, and into one of the living rooms, but when it was done, the room was almost completely full of enough riches and weapons to take over a small nation. Mordred had spent the time at the computer waiting for the files to decrypt. He didn't want to leave the USB drive running while they were away just in case, so despite his better judgment, he removed the drive and placed it in his pocket. Hopefully he'd get a chance to look through it again.

"So, now we need to go to the club," Remy said.

"Take Viktor's guns," Polina said. "No magic can be used in the public parts of the club."

"So, we need to stop their rune work," Fiona said.

"And you're going to have to fight your way through a lot of bad people," Polina said.

"Good," Mordred said, picking up a silver dagger and placing it in his belt. "I could use the stress relief."

CHAPTER 12

Nate Garrett

Tartarus wasn't exactly all fire and brimstone. It was somewhat dark and foreboding when you first entered, as a thick mist rolled over the nearby lake, blocking out a lot of the sunlight. After the mists, and the lake, the realm was quite beautiful, with rolling hills and stunning mountains. Some called it paradise, and some called it a prison—it very much depended on your point of view.

The inhabitants of Tartarus were guarded by griffins, who walk around on two feet, not the four of the stories, although the top half is still an eagle, and the bottom a lion. They're one of the few species I'd ever met that could fly, with their wingspan easily the size of two grown men. They're the top of the food chain in Tartarus, and few things—including the prisoners here—are stupid enough to try and fight them. Not the least because magic has exactly zero effect on them.

"Shouldn't there be a guard here?" I asked Sky as she walked through the realm gate.

"Yes, there should be," she said. "Let's go see if we can find Charon."

The four of us walked down toward the pier nearby, where Charon would hopefully be waiting with his boat. Unfortunately there was no one there.

"Okay, this is weird," I said. "There are a few empty boats there. How many does Charon have?"

"A few," Sky said. "We thought keeping one at both ends would be a good idea just in case we needed to get across in a hurry again."

"He's probably on the other side," Selene said. "Should we just take a boat and row over?"

"Sounds like a plan," Zamek said, rushing forward, but I put my arm out to stop him.

"Don't drink the water. Not even a mouthful—it ages you in seconds."

Zamek looked down at the black stillness of the waters all around us. "Don't drink the water. Got it."

"If you go for a swim in there, you're probably not coming out," Sky said.

"Water bad, boat good," Zamek said, eyeing the water with mistrust. "Poisonous water . . . This place isn't exactly the beautiful realm Sky said it would be."

"We're getting there," Sky assured him.

We climbed into one of several moored boats, which were easily big enough to seat us all comfortably. Selene took up the oars and began rowing. It didn't take long for the pier to become a distant blob on the horizon, and for the mists to begin to thin out, revealing the land.

"I don't see Charon," I said. I'd been quiet for most of the journey, as Tartarus takes some getting used to. The entire realm is a natural dampener, meaning that whatever my level of power back on the Earth realm, it was maybe a tenth of that here. On top of that, the longer you stayed, the longer it took for your power level to return to normal. So for those who have lived here thousands of years, it could be months or even years before they'd be back to normal. Even after a visit lasting only a day, it could be a few hours before you were back to full strength. Hopefully we wouldn't need to be in Tartarus for that long.

We soon reached the pier on the opposite side of the lake, where Selene secured the boat.

I walked toward Charon's two-story home. "Charon!" I shouted. "You about?" When there was no reply, I knocked on the door. Still no reply. I tried the door but found it locked.

"Maybe he's gone into town?" Sky suggested.

"Maybe," I said, not really sure I was convinced by that particular suggestion. I walked around the house and, after opening the wooden gate, found a sizeable garden at the rear of the property. Someone certainly loved their gardening, and it was full of flowers and vegetables, but no Charon.

"Nate!" Selene shouted, and I rushed back to the front of the house. "I smell blood inside."

Zamek unbuckled one of the battle-axes strapped to his back and prepared himself.

"Does he go everywhere with that axe?" Sky asked me.

"To the best of my knowledge, yes. I'm beginning to wish I'd brought something myself."

"We made an exception for Zamek, but I'm not sure the Titans would have been happy to see Hellequin turn up brandishing weapons."

The use of my old name stung. I'd pushed the terrorist out of my head for the last few hours, and now all those thoughts and anger rushed back in.

"Shit, Nate, I'm sorry," Sky said, placing her hand on my forearm. "You okay? I heard about the broadcast. I forgot."

"It's okay," I told her. "It's just one more thing I'm going to hurt the people behind this for."

"If you need to talk, you know I'm here."

I turned to look at Sky. There had been a point, over a century ago, where we might have been more than just friends, but that time had long since passed. "Thank you."

"You should talk to my dad, too. If there's anyone who knows about the power of people using your name for evil means, it's Hades."

Selene kicked the door to Charon's house, and it disintegrated from the impact. Dragon-kin were strong enough that even werecreatures thought twice about fighting one hand to hand. The fact that she'd managed to turn a door into a million pieces while the realm limited her power showed just how strong she really was.

She stepped inside the house, with Zamek close by. Sky and I followed soon after and stared at the chaos we found inside.

"Fucking hell," Sky whispered.

"How many bodies?" Zamek asked.

"Six," Selene said. "I can smell the blood."

"There looks like more," I said.

"It's the pieces," Selene said. "They were cut into pieces."

Immediately inside the front door was a set of stairs leading up to a landing above. Two figures lay on the stairs, their heads no longer attached to their bodies. The remaining four corpses were scattered over the living area in front of us. A couch was now so covered in blood that its original color was a mystery. All the corpses wore black leather armor, making it hard to identify much about them without getting closer.

"This was less of a fight, and more of a lesson in butchery," Zamek said, replacing his battle-axe on his back before moving from place to place, using his hands as if he were holding a sword. "It's artistry. Whoever did this moved like water."

"One person did this?" Sky asked.

Zamek nodded. "One exceptional warrior."

I walked closer to the bodies in the living area and picked up an evil-looking sword, all black metal and jagged edges. "This is a blood-elf sword." I tossed the sword aside and picked up one of the corpses, removing the helm to reveal a blood elf beneath it.

"How?" Selene asked. "This is impossible. How did blood elves get here?"

I looked over at Sky. "Any ideas?" I asked.

"I have no idea. Aren't the blood elves those things you fought in the dwarven realm?"

"You look here. I'll go check some of the other rooms on the left of the building," Selene said. "Just in case more of these bastards are hiding." She walked off without another word.

"They used to be shadow elves," Zamek said, removing the helm off a decapitated head before tossing both aside. "Then the magic twisted them into these monsters you see before you. They're made for murder and fighting, and that's it. They care for nothing else. And thankfully they're trapped back on my realm."

"So how the hell did they get here?" Sky asked.

"I've seen a few blood elves outside of your realm," I said. "Tommy had a run-in with some of them a while back. Something to do with Nergal. You'd have to ask him more about it. It didn't seem like Nergal had an infinite resource, though. Maybe they figured out a way to get some of them into our realm."

"Doesn't explain how they got into this realm," Sky said.

"There's only one realm gate," I said.

"That's true. After you found a second gate in Avalon, and in Shadow Falls, my father spent a long time trying to find one here, too. Nothing."

Zamek and I shared a horrified gaze. "The tablet," we said in unison.

"The tablet that lets you go between realms without a gate?" Sky asked. "I thought there was only one of them, and you have it. And doesn't it only go from the Earth realm to one very specific place in the dwarven realm? A place in the middle of the blood elves?"

"Maybe they made a second," Sky suggested.

"Let's find Charon," I said, looking around the room for signs of where he might have gone. "And get out of here. We need to talk to the Titans and let them know there could be more of these bastards running around."

"I'll go join Selene," Sky said, walking off in the direction Selene had gone a few moments earlier.

"Could Charon have done this?" Zamek asked when we were alone.

"He's an old man, albeit only outwardly." I saw the confusion on Zamek's face. "He drank the lake water a few thousand years ago. He's aged on the outside, but a young man still on the inside. Actually he's an old man on the inside, too, but he's not human, so it's hard to tell what is and isn't old for someone who's about five thousand at last count."

I turned toward a sound that came from the front door, igniting a blade of flame and waiting for more attackers as the door slowly moved open to reveal Grayson.

"What the hell are you doing here?" I asked.

"I arrived at the compound about a half hour after you. I had to row all the way here." He looked around the room. "What happened in here?"

"We don't know, but you're welcome to come help find Charon," Zamek said.

Grayson nodded, and joined Zamek and me as we searched the right side of the house, and it didn't take long before I found Charon in a bathroom at the far end of the house. He sat on the gray-and-white-tiled floor in a large pool of blood. A bloody dagger lay beside him. He looked pale and gave a weak smile when he saw me.

"In here!" I bellowed, and dropped to my knees beside him. "Hey."

"Nathan Garrett. It's good to see you, my friend." Charon's voice was weak, although he spoke with confidence and no hint of the danger his life was in. "Dagger is silver. Venom coated. Gorgon, I think. It's been a while. Thought they were all dead."

"Don't talk. You're pushing yourself too far," I told him, and moved his hands and tunic to look at the wound, which still trickled blood. "How long have you been here?"

"Hour or so. I killed them all. Still a young man at heart."

I smiled. "Yes, you are."

"One got me."

"I know. We'll get you patched up."

Charon coughed and winced as the pain of it wracked his body. "No. You'll go save the Titans. There will be more elves. Or whatever they are."

"Blood elves, long story." Zamek said as he entered the room with Grayson, who immediately went to Charon's side, moving me out of the way.

"I'm going to need to stitch this up and stop the bleeding," Grayson said, removing a small packet from his jacket. "I've got what I need to stitch, but it still has to be cauterized."

I ignited some fire magic on one of my fingers and poured power into it until the orange flame turned white hot. "This is going to hurt," I told Charon, and passed him a shoe to put in his mouth. "One, two . . ." I pushed my finger against the wound, and Charon screamed into the shoe and promptly passed out.

"I can smell the Gorgon venom," Selene said. "I've smelled it before."

"I can take it from here," Grayson said. "Go to the town; help these people. We won't be able to get anything from anyone if they're all dead. I can defend myself if I need to."

"Are you sure?" Zamek asked. "You're a doctor, not a warrior."

Grayson's expression hardened. "Go."

"I'll see you soon," I told both Charon and Grayson. Selene and I left the room, almost bumping into Sky.

"Will Charon be okay?" Sky asked.

"I hope so," I said. "Grayson is with him. I'll explain on the way. You coming to the town? I think there are going to be more of these things."

Sky and Selene nodded and walked with me and Zamek through the house. I picked up one of the blood elves' swords on the way. I was certain it was going to come in handy.

The second I stepped outside again I saw the thick black smoke in the distance. The run to the main town took only a few minutes, and even less until the view of large Roman-villa-like houses ablaze became all I could see in the distance.

The nearby beach was awash with people fighting, bodies littering the golden sands, staining it a mixture of black and red depending on the species.

The four of us ran under the archway leading into the town, and Zamek roared in anger as he saw several blood elves coming our way. He ran toward them, his battle-axe cleaving one in half before slicing the throat of a second. He spun, avoiding a spear jab from a third elf, before burying a dagger he'd removed from his belt into its heart. Three dead in less than ten seconds.

Zamek looked back at Selene, Sky, and me. "I'm going this way. I see more elves."

"I'll go with," Sky said, her soul weapons manifesting as a long dagger and a tomahawk. She ran off with Zamek to join the fray I could see further in the town.

"Selene, can you get some of those griffins free?" I pointed toward the fighting on the beach. "If you can get them to go back to the realm gate, one of them will hopefully know where the guardian is and should be able to open it."

"And what are you going to do?"

"Cronus and Rhea live up there. If there are Titans up there, we should be able to get their help. We don't have the numbers for an effective defense. And as much as I hate to admit it, the Titans are a lot more likely to listen to Cronus and Rhea than to me. With them on board, hopefully we can organize an effective counterattack against the blood elves."

"Stay safe," Selene said, and ran off toward the battle on the beach.

I watched her go for a few seconds before turning to find two blood elves stalking toward me, evidently hoping my attention had been elsewhere long enough for one of them to drive its sword into my back.

There was no point in trying to convince them to put down their weapons; it would have done no good, and I didn't have the time to waste.

A jet of flame tore through the ground beside me, forcing me to throw myself aside and put up a shield of air. I looked up at Helios in full dragon-kin form, his massive red and orange wings casting a shadow over part of the stone street. I watched as he floated softly to the ground, his golden-scaled skin gleaming in the sunlight, his reptilian eye full of nothing but hate for me. I'd taken the other one during one of his several attempts on my life. A metal bracelet hung about one wrist, and I wondered what it did.

"No one can save you now," Helios said, unhinging his jaw and unleashing a torrent of superheated flame at me.

I kept my shield up and dodged aside, trying to gain ground between the two of us while also trying not to get myself barbecued. When I got too close for comfort, he backed off, moving up the hill toward Cronus and Rhea's villa.

I managed to get within striking distance, but he swiped at me with deadly speed, his sharp claws forcing me back.

I wrapped air magic around his hand, pulling him toward me and smashing an air-wrapped elbow into his face, knocking him aside, but he caught me with a kick, sending me reeling.

"I was never sure if you were working with Hera, or if your goals just coincided," I said. "I assume she sprang you out of prison."

"She made me a good offer. I help her, and I get to kill you, my father, sisters, and anyone else I feel wronged me."

I threw a ball of fire at him, which he batted aside, laughing until I wrapped shadows around him, dragging him down to his knees.

"I learned a few things," I told him as he struggled.

He unleashed a torrent of flame, burning the shadows away and causing me to cry out in pain, but I threw a bolt of lightning at him, and he took off up the hill toward the villa as two blood elves sprang toward me. I darted forward, parrying the closest blood elf's attack, and knocked him off-balance. I spun around him, avoiding a slash from his friend before slicing his forearm. The blood elf screamed, losing his grip on his sword, which I caught and drove into his chest, then sliced the exposed throat of his friend. Two dead elves. I got the feeling there would be a lot more before we were done.

I ran up the hill toward the enormous villa at the far edge of town, fighting off several more blood elves who hoped to stop my advance. By the time I reached the outskirts of the villa, I was covered in elf blood.

Helios hovered just above the perfectly manicured lawn that made up a large part of the expansive gardens at the front of the villa. He roared fire at me, setting the ground aflame, and charged me. I created a blade of lightning and swiped up at him, but he dodged me, caught sight of his father, Hyperion, and flew up out of reach.

"See you again, sometime," he said, and took off toward the ocean, leaving me with the unpleasant thought of having to let him go so I could help stop the rest of the attackers.

I ran through the burning garden to the courtyard beyond, where pale stone bricks were now covered in elf blood as Hyperion fought off four elves with a sword and long spear. They were all dead before I could offer assistance. He spun his spear toward me before realizing who I was and lowering it.

"Cronus and Rhea," I said.

"In the villa," he told me, clearly surprised to see me. "I'm glad for the assistance. I don't know why Rhea and Cronus aren't out here fighting."

He pointed to the huge building behind him. Most of the horse-shoe-shaped villa was one story in height and made of white brick, with a red-tiled roof. It reminded me a lot of the old pictures of Roman villas, complete with pillars and large windows all looking down on the courtyard.

The sounds of blood elves rose from behind me, and I turned to see a dozen sprint toward us. "You go," Hyperion said. "I'll hold off the horde."

I didn't need to be told twice, and considering how much blood covered his golden armor, I was sure that Hyperion didn't need my assistance in fighting.

I ran up the steps to the front door, only to be greeted by a blood elf barreling out of it. The blood elf swung an axe at me, but I wrapped air around his wrist, pulling him off-balance, and drove my sword into his skull before he'd hit the floor. My magic was getting weaker the longer I stayed here, but it still had enough power if I really needed it. Hopefully I wouldn't really need it.

I walked through the villa without incident, although the further I went, the more damage there was to the structure, and the more bodies lay all around. Mostly blood elves, but more than a few were human in appearance. I recognized several of the bodies as being people who lived and worked in Tartarus, and at one point I even saw a griffin, his wings cut free and tossed aside. Several curse marks sat on the dead human attackers, and I recognized one of them from the last time I'd been in The Hole. The question of how everyone had gotten here could be answered later.

I continued on, and the second I stepped into the enormous open living area, I knew I was going to need every bit of magic I had. Cronus was pinned to the far wall in a crucifix pose. As I got closer, I saw that he'd been beaten and stabbed repeatedly before someone had slit his throat.

"And you are?" a woman asked as she entered the room through one of the two doors to the right of where I'd been standing.

She was of average height, with brown skin and long brown plaited hair that touched her waist. She wore dark leather armor, part of which had been cut through, revealing a deep wound that had bled profusely.

She carried a gleaming gladius in one hand and Rhea's head in the other. Blood dropped slowly onto the ground beside her. She placed Rhea's head on the floor by her foot and removed a small metal bracelet from her wrist that resembled the one Helios had worn, tossing it over her shoulder back into the room she'd just left.

"And you are?" she asked again, this time with a smirk.

"Ladies first?"

"Abaddon. Although I've had many names over the millennia."

I went to use my magic, and nothing happened.

Abaddon laughed. "Do you plan on telling me your name? I like to know the names of people I make scream and beg." She kicked Rhea's head aside with a laugh. "I always wanted to do that."

"What was the bracelet?" I asked. "The one you threw in the room?"

"Am I meant to tell you everything? You probably wouldn't understand even if I did. These two idiots certainly didn't, not until it was too late."

"You put dwarven runes in the villa? Or at least in this room. It's good. I didn't even feel the magic go away," I said as I backed up toward the row of windows overlooking the huge garden behind me.

I searched around me, trying not to take my gaze off Abaddon for too long. She must have had a tattoo that allowed her to bypass the dwarven runes and use her power. I just needed to figure out what word they'd used for the rune so I could counteract it. *Hopefully* counteract it. It was that or die horribly, and I've never really been one for the latter.

"It helps that I was there when they made them," Abaddon said. "You're an interesting one. On the one hand, you're clearly no one important because I'd have remembered you."

"Well, you've probably been away for a long time. Things have changed since the seven devils roamed the realms."

Abaddon laughed. "It's good you know that you are outclassed."

"Not sure about that. I got rid of one of your spirit snares."

Abaddon appeared to be impressed. "That doesn't mean you're going to live through the day."

I reached the windows and stopped and spotted the dwarven rune carved into the back of a nearby table. It was only about the size of a pound coin, but it glowed black. The amount of power that had been infused with the rune must have been immense.

Abaddon followed my gaze. "Do you really think you can counter the rune?"

I ran my finger through the blood on my clothes and drew a mark on my hand. Lightning crackled between my fingers. "Yeah, I think I can."

Abaddon's eyes widened in shock, but before I could throw magic at her, I heard the smash of glass and turned as Atlas grabbed hold of me, dragging me out of the house and throwing me across the garden as if I were a tennis ball. I wrapped myself in a shield of air to make sure I didn't die when I impacted with a stone hut thirty feet away.

"Nathan Garrett, you are mine," Atlas bellowed.

"Now is a *really* bad time!" I shouted back, standing up in the ruins of the shattered hut.

Abaddon rushed out of the house. "Stop it, you idiot," she snapped at Atlas. "Now isn't the time."

"I was told that Nathan was mine to kill," Atlas said. "And only mine."

Abaddon ignored his words and took a step toward me. "So, you're Nathan Garrett. I've heard a lot about you. I figured you'd be more fearsome, but you don't look like anything particularly special. Your use of lightning has made me curious, though. Was your father Zeus, by any chance?"

I shrugged. "No idea."

She placed a hand on Atlas's chest. "Now is not the time." She turned back to me as the clouds above us began to turn dark and thunder rumbled.

"I thought you'd like to see my lightning close up," I told her.

"Maybe later." Abaddon removed another bracelet from a pouch on her waist and placed it on her wrist. She removed another and passed it to Atlas, who put it on. Both tapped their bracelets and vanished. I turned toward a dozen blood elves who had heard the commotion and come to see what was happening, and called down the lightning. I pushed it through my body, mixing it with my magic, before throwing it out of my extended hand, which got badly burned as it went. The twelve elves vanished in a plume of gore as the magical lightning struck them, leaving a large crater in its wake.

I cradled my arm against my chest and hoped I had enough power left to heal it before we had to leave the realm. I walked back to the villa and stepped inside. Rhea and Cronus were dead, killed in their own home in a realm designed to keep them safe from harm. I picked up Rhea's head and took it back through the door Abaddon had used into a bedroom that had been the scene of a huge battle. Pieces of plaster and destroyed furniture littered the expansive room. The rest of Rhea's remains lay on the floor at the foot of the bed, where the final blow had been delivered. I placed the head next to the body and dropped a sheet over them before washing my hands in the en suite bathroom sink.

As I was leaving the bathroom, I saw writing on the back of the bedroom door I hadn't noticed before. I closed the door, and the feeling of dread intensified. Written in what I could only assume was Rhea's blood were the words *For Hellequin.*

CHAPTER 13

Nate Garrett

I considered removing the writing, but that wouldn't be good if someone discovered what I'd done. People would become suspicious, so I left it where it was and went to help with any blood elf or Hole prisoners who remained defiant and just wouldn't die.

It turned out I didn't need to worry: the fighting had already finished by the time I left the villa. Cerberus and a platoon of his people were mopping up the last of them. "Leave one alive," I said to the nearest soldier, who was about to kill a kneeling elf.

He looked at me as if I had lost my mind, but nodded and punched the elf in the face instead. To be fair, punching prisoners who want to eat your face isn't very upsetting. It's a bit like punching Nazis. I can't bring myself to be bothered about it. They're just inherently punchable.

I continued on and found Selene, Sky, and Zamek talking to Cerberus and Hyperion.

"They're dead, aren't they?" Hyperion asked.

I nodded. "I'm sorry. Abaddon was here. She had some help from Atlas."

"Son of a bitch," Sky said.

"I knew Atlas was unstable, but I didn't think he'd help murder his own people," Hyperion said.

"They vanished. I don't know how. Oh, and someone wrote *For Hellequin* in blood on Cronus and Rhea's bedroom door."

"They're really doubling down on the 'Hellequin is responsible for all of this,'" Selene said. "You okay?"

I shook my head. "Not really. Cronus was crucified and Rhea beheaded. I think Abaddon was in there for a while before all the fighting started out here."

I saw Grayson coming toward us, and I ran over. "How's Charon?"

"He'll be fine. I've left him with some of Cerberus's people. I think it's time we all had a chat."

We walked back over to the rest of the group.

"Lucifer, is that you?" Hyperion asked. "It's been a long time."

"Well, that deals with the 'How do you tell everyone who I really am?' part of the day," Grayson said, and shook Hyperion's hand. "It's been a long time."

"I'm sorry, I feel like we've overlooked something," Sky said. "He's Lucifer? As in the devil? The opposite of God? You know, the whole Bible thing?"

I stared at Grayson for several seconds. "Lucifer? You're real?"

"Let's go somewhere a little less crowded, and I'll explain," Grayson promised.

No one wanted to go into the villa, and as Hyperion already seemed to know that Grayson and Lucifer were one and the same, he went to deal with his friends' bodies. It was a task I didn't envy him for having.

The rest of us walked into a small nearby house, which, apart from having the contents trashed, was devoid of anyone living or dead.

"This was Atlas's house," Sky said, the anger radiating off her in waves. "Although now I guess it's the house of a traitor."

I picked up a wooden chair and sat down in it, crossing my arms and waiting for Grayson to tell us whatever it was he was about to say.

"I am Lucifer," he started. "A few things. I'm not a suave, womanizing nightclub owner. I'm not evil. I'm not the Prince of Darkness. I have never met God, or an angel, or demons. I've never been to hell. I have no idea if heaven and hell are real. I am not the Prince of Lies. My last name isn't Morningstar. I am not a dragon. I have not once accepted souls from someone at a crossroad in exchange for anything. Ever. I do not know anyone with the surname of Winchester. I am not the devil, or Crowley, or Satan, or any of the other dozen or so names that person possesses."

"Well, that summed up a lot of my questions," Sky said. "And all sarcastic questions, too."

"So, what are you?" Selene asked.

"Thousands of years before any of you were even born, when humanity was in its infancy, when warlords roamed this planet, and murder and destruction were all they cared about, there were those who wished only for conquest. These people would later become revered, worshipped by people who didn't know better. The gods before even the Mesopotamians, Egyptians, or Titans were anything but the future. Those people created us.

"Magic was dark and powerful back then. Sorcerers were rare, and many quickly discovered that blood magic was capable of feats of power that instilled fear in those who followed. I do not know whose idea it was to create me. I never met him."

"Why were you created?" I asked.

"There were seven of us. Each one conceived and born during a blood-magic ritual. The sorcerers discovered that taking the blood of various species and performing the magic with it had certain effects on the conception and birth. I don't know how many humans were used in these rituals. I know that those performing the rituals used as many different types of human as they could get hold of. They roamed the lands, looking for people to capture. I don't know if they tried it with people who weren't human, but I do know that the seven of us were born from different sets of human parents. Each of us gained some of the power from the ritual and the blood used, but it was power on a scale no one at the time could possibly imagine. I barely think anyone even now would be able to understand it."

"What happened to you after you were born?"

"We were sent to another realm to train and become warriors, but something happened and it took us a millennium to get back. In the meantime we conquered our new home, honing skills and slaughtering our enemies by the thousands.

"Eventually we managed to find a way back to the Earth realm, and by then people like Nergal, Cronus, and Ra had taken their seats of power. It would still be hundreds of years before the Olympians came to power, and thousands before Merlin and his Avalon. And we set about conquering this realm, like we had the last one. Unfortunately we didn't expect the resistance we received, and we were defeated. The pantheons of the age decided to take each of us to use as a sort of deterrent. We agreed to pledge ourselves individually to that pantheon, and in exchange we'd live like the gods."

"It was an ancient cold war," I said.

Grayson nodded. "No one made a move against the others, because each group had one of us. There was a kind of stalemate until our leader organized a rebellion. His name is Asmodeus, and he was the first and strongest of us, thus we made him our king."

"What is he?" Selene asked.

"A vampire. Possibly the first—we're not sure. We assumed there were vampires before him, because the blood magic must have used them to create one, but we were never able to find information one way or the other. Anyway, that doesn't matter. What matters is that he is a vampire in the same way that a space shuttle is a method of transport. He's so much more powerful than you can possibly imagine. He's essentially a sorcerer with the powers of a master vampire."

"What happened to him?" Zamek asked.

"Asmodeus's rebellion rose up and fought against the pantheons. They killed some, destroyed so much. Murdered so many that the streets of towns were slick with blood and death. The dwarves, elves, and pantheons of this world rose up to fight as one, and after much bloodshed, Asmodeus was driven into a realm. The gate was destroyed. Each devil who had taken part in the rebellion was sent through a different realm gate. Those who said no to his offer, who fought against Asmodeus, were spared under the promise we'd never contact the other devils again."

"How many were spared?" I asked.

"Two. I was one, and Beelzebub was the other. She hated me for not joining Asmodeus and hated herself for not joining him. I figured out too late that she'd been working as his spy, sowing discord along our ranks. She vanished from this realm not long after."

"And you never saw any of your kin again?" I asked. "Is 'kin' the right word?"

"We were not blood. Abaddon and Asmodeus were in a relationship for at least part of our lives together. They were a fearsome couple. If she's come back, it's either to bring Asmodeus with her, or because she knows where he is and wants to free him. Either of those options would result in the destruction of a large part of this world. Humanity has grown in numbers in the millennia since the last war, and even back then the casualties were high.

"As for your other question, yes, I saw one of them. Our powers are linked, so the use of our powers in the Earth realm is like a shining beacon to the others. I've purposefully not used my power at anywhere near full capacity for thousands of years. I used a little bit here and there, only enough to help out at the time. If the others knew I was alive, knew I was here on the Earth realm . . . they might all try to find a way back. Even so, I spent a long time hopeful that none of them would ever make it back here. One did. Sathanus. He was an incubus. A cruel, vile man with a taste for inflicting pain on people and making them enjoy it."

"You killed him, didn't you," I said. It wasn't a question.

Grayson nodded. "I did. I killed him and burned his body until it was ash. I saw him before he saw me, and I watched him. It was a thousand years ago in Eastern Europe. He used his power with impunity, reveling in the chaos and pain he caused. Every time he used his power, it drew me to him, and I killed him before he ever knew I was there. I regret a lot of things in my life, but not killing Sathanus. He was one of those who truly deserved to die for his crimes. For the evil acts I knew he'd performed over his life. If there is a hell, I really do hope he's burning in it."

"If you can tell when one of the devils is using their power, why couldn't you sense that Abaddon was here?" Sky asked.

"She's blocking me somehow. I don't know how."

"Dwarven runes," I told everyone. "She used them in the house. She could use those to block her power from being detected." A horrible thought came to my mind. "Or, like you, she hasn't used her full power yet."

"That is possible. She is exceptionally powerful, and I cannot imagine that her power has diminished over the years."

"So, could she be behind the My Liege cabal?" Zamek asked.

"That is also possible. I haven't seen any of them for several thousand years, so yes, maybe. But she was never the type to hide in the shadows for long. She likes to show off too much. She likes people to be afraid of her. If she's the one behind it all, I imagine she'll make a very large move soon."

"And if Asmodeus is back?" I asked.

"Then we will know soon. Asmodeus will lay waste to this realm in the pursuit of whatever he's after. Humanity is nothing but a nuisance to him, and Avalon will be little more than something to crush. He'll make it an example. Either way, they are not the kind of people who want to work *for* someone, not if previous experience is anything to go by. People do change, though, and it's been a very long time since I last spoke to them."

"How likely is it that Abaddon is here to bring the rest of the devils alongside Asmodeus?"

"Highly. There's something else you should know. The method they used to give us our power was used by the Olympians and other pantheons. Together they used this method to create the Four Horsemen of the Apocalypse. They were created, at least in part, in case we ever resurfaced. A weapon to counteract us. But it's said that the Horsemen were killed to stop their continued plague on humanity. They'd discovered their true origins and took it out on humanity, hoping to drag their creators into a war to stop them. They wanted to destroy humanity, make the world an example for their anger and hate."

"History repeating itself," I said. "You remember what I told you back in Basingstoke? Erebus said I was created to be the same thing. I was born to be a weapon. Did you know that?"

"Yes. But I only figured out after you told me about the dwarven realm and the vision of the pit of blood. I think they tried something new with you. Mordred, too. They tried to create you to be less unpredictable. I'm not sure it worked."

"So much has happened. I'd barely had time to sit and think about it, but we were experiments."

Selene reached out to hold my hand.

"My mother said she loved me, but we were creations of people who wanted to play God." I was sure I should have been furious at being conceived and born while a blood-magic ritual took place, but it just seemed like getting upset about it would achieve nothing. It happened, I couldn't have stopped it, and without the power it gave me, I probably would have been killed a hundred times over throughout my life.

"You okay?" Selene asked me.

"Yeah, oddly enough, I am. I'm not sure how I'm meant to feel at being told that I was created to be a weapon for someone, but calm wasn't what I'd expected. If my mother was a Valkyrie, does that mean my father was from the Norse pantheon, too?"

Grayson shrugged. "The ritual they used to create me was called From Burning Blood."

"Catchy," Zamek said.

"It was called that because those humans who did not manage to conceive were set alight, and their throats slit to allow more blood to pool."

"That is one of the most disturbing things I've been told recently," Sky said.

"So, when the pantheons created the Horsemen?" I asked. "They used that same ritual?"

Lucifer shook his head. "Over the centuries many people lusting for power used a version of the original ritual, but they rarely worked. And the few who did manage to survive the ritual did not go on to live long lives once we discovered their existence. As for the attempt made by the pantheons, they called it the Blood of Shadows. The original ritual has long since been destroyed. Trust me, I checked. Those who created us weren't in the habit of sharing information, and they were all killed as soon as we were able to kill them. No one knows how it truly worked."

"So, this second ritual was based on guesswork?" Zamek asked.

"Mostly, yes. I don't know the particulars, but I do know that it was decided not to use humans. Humans were too hit-and-miss in the original. Thousands had to die before it worked, and it took years to get there. The pantheons theorized that using people who weren't humans should speed it up. And it did just that. Unfortunately they hadn't taken into account the mental and physical suffering of having people born with a ready store of incredible power, and once they were told how they came to be, it broke the Horsemen."

"And me?" I asked.

"The ritual used was called Scorched Shadows. I don't know why exactly, except that the ritual called for various magical elements to surround the pit at all times. It was thought that maybe those elements would help contribute to the power given to the child. I know it was carried out on another realm, although I don't believe the original conception was carried out in the dwarven realm you visited. I think it was done elsewhere."

"I don't need to know where I was conceived," I said. "What else do you know?"

"Like you said, you were born to become a weapon. For what purpose, I do not know."

"That's why my mother took me to the dwarven realm, to limit my power. Mordred, too. We were never meant to have the level of power they'd given us at such a young age. We were a just-in-case scenario that they really hoped never happened."

"If it was anything like us, your power would have made you the most dangerous teenager on the face of the planet. The first time my magic activated, I leveled a house. They presumably put those marks on you so when your power activated, you wouldn't kill half a dozen people with a sneeze. If you were anything like we were, the power came through in a rush. It took us all a long time to learn how to control it, and we hurt people to get to that point."

"Is that why you became a doctor?" Sky asked. "Because of all the people you hurt?"

"Maybe," Lucifer said. "Mostly it was a desire to be far away from where my magic would be used. At least to be begin with. Over time I came to enjoy my job, and I became good at it. I liked being able to heal and not just destroy. Which is something I excelled at."

"So, Lucifer," I said, finding the name at odds with the person I'd known for so long as someone else. "Lucifer. What are you?"

"I'm a sorcerer. An exceptionally powerful one. I no longer have to use elemental or omega-level magic, at least not in a way you know them."

Omega magic was the second level of magic for any sorcerer. Sorcerers could learn two forms of omega magic, just like they could learn two elements. In my case it was shadow instead of light, but I didn't know what my second omega magic would be—or even if I'd ever discover a second one. The choices were mind or matter, and over the years I'd considered the positives and negatives of both."

"So, what do you have?" I asked.

"I can combine my magical forms into pure magic. It's a pure destructive force. There's no shield, or defensive use, for pure magic. It's what those prisoners who were turned into bombs use."

The memory of trying to contain that much magical power immediately came back to me, and I wondered just how powerful Lucifer really was. "Why can't people like Merlin or Zeus use it, then?"

Lucifer shrugged. "I'm not sure. We never did a lot of research into it. I believe it's the manner of my birth that allows me to use it, or at least allows me to use it before many sorcerers reach that level of competency. Other than that, I'm unsure just how many people are genuinely aware of its existence. Pure magic doesn't create glyphs on your arms and hands like normal magic, and the color is different from person to person. Mine is a light blue; Asmodeus's was purple. Pure magic isn't something taught to young sorcerers. It's something that is probably best left forgotten."

"But you know," I said, keeping my tone as neutral as possible.

"I understand your anger at the fact I kept that knowledge from you, but I have seen what sorcery unchecked does. I *am* sorcery unchecked. They created the story about nightmares being evil monsters who cause nothing but destruction, because sometimes they are just that. After centuries of everyone being told that nightmares were evil, telling the world what I knew would be quickly shot down by Merlin and Avalon, and it would reveal who I was. It's why I couldn't tell you, Nate. I couldn't reveal my true identity. Not without having to answer too many questions. I've spent thousands of years hidden from view, ensuring I stayed away from anything that might force me to use my power. Telling you who I really am would have put you all in great danger."

"You told Olivia," I said. "She knows who you are."

"Yes, she knows, although I didn't tell her. I worked for her predecessor, and when she took over the job as head of the Winchester LOA branch, I was already there. She didn't take the news brilliantly. Mostly because she'd heard the rumors about my past and it took me a while to convince her I was on her side."

"You could have told me," I said. "I'd have understood."

"I couldn't take that chance. Do you remember a few years ago, I went with you to Netley to see that old couple? The griffin that was there flew off, terrified?"

I nodded. "I remember."

"Pure magic has a certain scent that griffins can detect."

"Griffins can detect magic?" I asked. That was news to me.

"In small doses, yes. But with pure magic, there's no small dose. Even readying a small amount forces the power to come off you in waves. Griffins don't like pure magic—it triggers some deep-seated fear, because it's the only type of magic that can hurt them. It bypasses their natural defense. They tolerate me in Tartarus, but that's about as far as it'll ever go."

"Who else can use pure magic?" I asked. "Of the seven devils? I mean, if they're all back, what are we dealing with?"

"Asmodeus can. His vampire abilities include an affinity to pure magic. I'm not sure, but he seems to be the one person with the most varied abilities. Mammon is a dragon who can breathe a type of pure magic. He makes Tiamat look like someone's lovable pet."

"And the others?" Sky asked.

"Belphegor is an alchemist, Beelzebub is an empath who can manipulate feelings of hatred and anger, and you already know about Abaddon, the necromancer. She might be more powerful than even Hades. It's certainly too close to call. I don't think the others are here, not yet. We'd be seeing even more widespread carnage if they were."

"At least there are only six now," Sky said.

Lucifer nodded thoughtfully. "Like I said earlier, there were others who were created after us. Before the Horsemen. Some will be names familiar to you, but most wouldn't be. People have always lusted after power and will do anything to get it. That includes creating destructive and dangerous weapons they barely understand. They mistake their ability to control as their right, but most of the time that control isn't total and catastrophe happens."

"So, just to be clear, there could be more people born in the same way as you guys and Nate?" Sky asked. "Because that sounds like something we need to look into."

"Most were killed over the years," Lucifer said. "Merlin, Zeus, and the rest of the more powerful members of Avalon didn't really like the idea of people like myself running around. One in the sixteenth century called himself Satan. I think he thought it was a good idea, or maybe he thought he was clever. Zeus took his head. He did it personally—I saw it happen. Those beings born and conceived during blood-magic rituals can become incredibly powerful, but we're not immortal and that power is something we have to learn to use. I heard of no others until Nate and Mordred were born. And five others."

"Wait, there were seven of us?" I asked. "Where are the others?"

"I don't know. But they're out there somewhere. All born in similar times, in the same manner. I do not know why this was decided, or whether the children were meant to be the protectors of a pantheon, much like the seven devils did after our defeat. I only knew that you were born and you were out there. If I'm being honest, I didn't expect to meet you unless you tried to conquer the world. It's nice to see you skipped our mistakes."

"And made a whole new set," I pointed out. "Okay, so a few last questions."

"Sure."

"Did you know what I was?" I asked.

Lucifer shook his head. "I had no idea until a short time ago. I'd heard that the dwarves had helped various pantheons re-create the seven devils, but I had no idea where those children had been taken, or even who they were. Like I said earlier, I had no idea one was you, Nate, not until you told me about the memory of the pool of blood in the dwarven realm."

"How did Abaddon and her people get into this realm?"

"No idea."

I paused and thought of the last few seconds before she had vanished. "She touched Atlas while they both went. She had something on her wrist—she touched it. Could they have created a bracelet version of that tablet that Kay was using?" I turned to Zamek, who had been quiet for the majority of the time we'd spent in the house. "Is this possible?"

"In theory, I guess. I'm not an expert on the tablet. I've only been studying it for a few years, but if you could get someone to create those runes on a bracelet, it could be possible. The runes wouldn't last, though. Nabu said that they tried making the tablets with metal or wood and the runes would just vanish after being used. The stone was the only thing they could get to keep the runes for more than a few trips."

"What about Mara?" Selene asked. "She could do that. She made the tablet."

"She's locked up, isn't she?" I asked.

"So was my brother," Selene said.

"Okay, well, I don't know where Mara was imprisoned, but I'd really like to make sure she's still there. I need to contact Olivia about it."

"Did any of the bodies we searched have those bracelets?" Sky asked.

Zamek shook his head. "I don't know. I didn't look for them."

"We'll search the bodies," Lucifer said.

"I had the same idea Nate had," Sky said. "I was curious how so many had come here. There were hundreds of attackers in this realm. Unless they all held hands and had contact with this Abaddon woman, which I genuinely can't see happening, they came here some other way. A second realm gate would be the most logical explanation, but there isn't one. Which doesn't exactly leave us with a lot of options I can think of."

"A way to transport hundreds of people through realms at the same time?" Lucifer asked. "That's something we should be very afraid of."

"Considering the list of awful things we should be afraid of is already massive, I really don't want to start adding to it. If those bracelets allowed this to happen, we need to find out where they're being made and stop it."

"One last question," I said to Lucifer. "Why did you run off from Tommy's just before we left?"

"I needed to figure out what I was going to do next. I needed time to come to terms with the idea of having to confess everything I've been hiding for so long. I was never going to run, or not back you up, but I have notes at home about what the devils had done. Maps, drawings, writings about what we did. I needed to remind myself of exactly what we face if they're unleashed."

"I'd like to see that info," I said.

"When we're done here, it's all yours."

Before anyone could say anything else, Cerberus entered the house. "Not to interrupt or anything, but you're going to want to hear this."

"Hear what?" Sky asked.

"One of the prisoners we kept alive has been very chatty, but he can only say the same thing. Over and over again."

"My Liege?" I asked.

"No," Cerberus said, clearly unnerved by what he'd heard. "He's saying something else. Shadow Falls."

CHAPTER 14

Nate Garrett

I heard the bellows of the prisoner well before I ever got close to the beach, which was where he was being held. The cries of "Shadow Falls" appeared to be part anger and part frustration. Like the previous attacker, this one probably hadn't agreed to have his brain partially destroyed.

The prisoner was a slight man with a balding hairline and a mustache that had probably been in fashion in the 1970s. At some point his leather armor had been partially removed, and his shirt had been torn open, revealing several dark blood-curse marks on his chest. He screamed at a nearby griffin and received a punch in the mouth for his trouble, a blow that knocked out several of the man's teeth and caused him to spit blood all over the golden sands.

Cerberus stepped up to the griffin, who bowed her head slightly and stepped back.

"That is one angry female," Sky said as the griffin walked away.

"How can you tell?" Zamek asked.

"Females have red feathers on the tops of their skull. It's the only way I've ever been able to tell the difference."

"And no penis," Sky said. "But you have to get a bit closer to find that one out."

I turned to Sky, who smiled.

"Shadow Falls," the prisoner said to me.

"Agreed," I replied. It was not the time for jokes, but Sky always knew how to make me chuckle.

"Shadow Falls," the man said again, clawing at the sand.

"You're not grasping this, but you can't say anything other than 'Shadow Falls.' Your brain is fried. You were a prisoner of The Hole, you were freed, and then you went to work for someone who fucked your head up. Sound about right? Just nod or shake your head."

The man nodded.

"Abaddon, yes?"

He shook his head.

"Glad to hear she can't screw around with people who are alive. So, was it another woman who did this?"

A shake of the head.

"A man?"

A nod.

"That doesn't exactly narrow it down," Selene said.

I crouched beside the prisoner. "I have some news for you. Firstly, you're going to die in a few minutes. Not just because whatever they did to your brain is going to kill you, but also because you either die by my hand, or the griffins will kill you."

"Do you know how griffins deal with people like you?" Selene asked.

The man shook his head, his expression suggesting he was terrified about what was happening.

"They crucify them on a hill overlooking the lake. That's if they don't tear you into tiny pieces, slowly, while you beg for mercy, which you can't do because your brain no longer works."

The man looked at me, and I nodded to confirm she was telling the truth. "I have one last question. Did you know what you were signing up for? Did you know you were going to come here and kill people?"

He nodded.

"Did you know that you were going to come here to kill Cronus and Rhea?"

He shook his head, looked around, and went to pick up a dagger. I raised my hand to stop the griffin nearby from killing him. He placed the tip of the dagger in the sand and began writing, becoming more and more frustrated with himself when he wrote the word *shadow* and seemingly couldn't stop until he'd written *falls*.

"We're going to get nothing out of him," I said, standing. "I'd like to say I feel sorry for you, but I don't. Like all of your kind, you came here to murder."

One of the griffins took a step toward the prisoner, who sprang to his feet and sprinted into the lake. He continued wading deeper and deeper, until he was up to his waist before he dove in, resurfacing a dozen feet further up the shore. He looked back at me and cupped his hands in the water, taking a long drink. He did the same a second and third time, before he visibly aged in front of us.

"The water won't kill him," Cerberus said. "Just age him. He's only prolonging it."

"His armor," I said. "It's from Shadow Falls. It's identical to what the guards there wear."

"I noticed," Selene said. "That's not great news."

The female griffin who had stepped back earlier tested the weight of her spear and then launched it toward the prisoner. It caught him in the chest, flinging him back into the lake with a huge splash. She flicked her wings, taking off from the beach, and used the massive claws on her feet to grab hold of the prisoner, picking him up from the water and dropping him back onto the beach. No one moved toward the prisoner as she reclaimed her spear, turned, and walked away without a word.

"He deserved that," Zamek said. "The griffins don't mess about, do they?"

I didn't think a reply was particularly necessary. "We need to go back to the Earth realm. We need to figure out how Abaddon and these attackers got here, and we need to go to Shadow Falls."

"You're not seriously entertaining the idea that Galahad is behind all of this?" Cerberus asked. "We've had our issues over the years, but he's not the type."

"He did once get you to kill people for him by lying to you," Sky reminded me. "He's not always been the trustful, honest guy people seem to think he is."

She had a point. "I know, but I still can't believe that Galahad would be behind everything that's happening. It just doesn't seem like his style. And he would have to know that using my name as the person in charge of it all would just make it personal between us. The last time I saw him we left as friends. I'd like to believe that's still the case. Even so, Arthur asked me to go see Galahad because of rumors about some kind of Shadow Falls attack. I still don't think they're involved, and this cabal has used the name of an innocent person to get what they want, but we still need to see Galahad."

"We'll know soon enough," Selene said.

"I'll join you, if I may?" Lucifer asked. "Abaddon's involvement makes it necessary."

"Speaking of which, where's Hyperion? We came here to talk to him about Abaddon."

"He's in the villa," Selene said. "I'd tread carefully with him. I don't think he's in the best of mental places at the moment."

I promised not to piss off the exceptionally powerful dragon-kin and made my way back to the villa, walking past several groups of griffins and Cerberus's people, who were still helping tend to the injured or deal with the dead. I got the feeling that Tartarus was going to feel the blow of this attack for a lot longer than it took for the physical injuries to heal.

I found Hyperion in the same place where Cronus had been cruci-fied, although the old Titan's body had been removed. Hyperion stood before the wall where his friend had died and stared at it. I waited at the doorway, unsure of the best approach. We hadn't exactly had the best of relationships, especially when I'd believed that he'd been the one behind Selene's marriage to Ares's son, Deimos, a man for whom the phrase "creepy little bag of dicks" was probably invented.

"I did not think he could be killed," Hyperion said without turn-ing toward me. "Rhea, either, for that matter. I thought they would be as close to immortal as possible. I think for the first time ever, I wish I were human. I'm not sure I want to live another thousand years without Cronus and Rhea."

"I'm sorry," I said.

"You fought Cronus. He was genuinely shocked at how close you came to defeating him. Even in his weakened state, he said that you were a worthy foe. Do you think you can kill Abaddon?"

There was no point in being anything but 100 percent honest. "I have no idea."

Hyperion turned toward me, his eyes filled with tears that slowly cascaded down his face. He made no move to wipe them aside; he'd long since stopped caring about what anyone else might think of his show of sorrow. "I think that's the right answer. You're . . . courting, is that the right word? Courting my daughter, Selene?"

The rapid change of conversation threw me a little. "We're in a relationship again, yes."

"Do you love her?"

I nodded.

"I know she loves you, but I also know that Helios is involved in what's happening here. You fought him, didn't you? You're going to have to kill him if you have any hope of stopping him."

"I know."

"Are you prepared to be the murderer of my son, and Selene's brother?"

"I'm prepared to stop Helios from murdering more innocent people. If I have to take his life to do it, I will. I left him alive in the past because I love Selene and I wanted to give Helios a chance to consider his actions. That punishment, that incarceration, made him worse, not better. He tried to kill a friend of mine. He tried to, at the very least, incapacitate Selene. He came here to help Abaddon, and he'll come for me again, sooner or later, and then he'll die. I'm done giving him chances."

"And Atlas?"

"We were going to have to fight sooner or later."

"Your list of enemies grows larger by the day, it seems."

"Hera and her people, Helios, Baldr, Siris, Abaddon, Atlas, probably a few other people I've forgotten about. Yeah, I like to collect them. Everyone needs a hobby."

"And you believe you can beat them all?"

I shook my head. "Not even slightly. Doesn't mean I'm not going to fuck their day up by trying, though."

Hyperion laughed. "You sound like Zeus. He had a habit of enjoying the misery he caused his enemies. I guess Cronus and Rhea will never get the justice they wanted for his death. And yes, Zeus is dead— we all know it, so don't try to convince me otherwise."

"I had no intention of doing that. No one really knows what happened to him. Except Hera, and she's not exactly forthcoming about whatever awful stuff she decided to do."

"Why did you come here? To Tartarus? You couldn't have known about the attack. Not even Sky and her people knew."

"We found someone who had Abaddon's handiwork on them and thought it would be best to talk to the people who last dealt with her. I can't say it turned out well, but had we not come here, it might have been worse."

"Abaddon was someone who worked with the Titans. I knew her very well, possibly better than Lucifer himself, considering how long they were apart. She was part of our ranks for a thousand years at least, which made her betrayal to start a rebellion with Asmodeus all the more galling. Even worse was how soon after we defeated them, Zeus was born. And then when he was powerful enough to overthrow his father, he did. We made a lot of mistakes back then, mistakes that cost lives, which separated families. But the biggest was leaving Abaddon alive. We should never have taken in any of the devils. We should have just executed them all and been done with it. But we were younger, stupider, and the possibility of controlling that much power was hard for many to resist."

"Can she be killed?"

"Anything and anyone can be killed, but in Abaddon's case, I couldn't imagine how much power someone would have to wield to be able to do it. I'm not sure if Cronus and Rhea would have been able to defeat her with anything less than their full strength. And Asmodeus is considerably worse."

"That's what Lucifer said."

"Asmodeus is the closest thing I've ever met to an actual godlike being. He was placed with the Norse pantheon, and they used to burn through specially created sorcerer's bands. His power was just too difficult to contain. He needs blood to continue using it, though—that's his only downfall. Like all vampires, he has to feed to maintain power. And he feeds a lot."

"I'm going to do everything in my power to stop these people."

"And it won't be enough." Hyperion sighed. "I'll help deal with what happened here, and then I'll come help. Hades told me I can leave whenever I like, but my power will take too long to charge for it to be anywhere near a level that would be considered useful. Selene tells me that they're attacking humans in the Earth realm? That this cabal has finally shown itself, and they used your name to do it."

"That about sums it up, yes."

"Don't be drawn into a battle you can't win. Whoever is behind all of this is powerful enough to appeal to Abaddon for help. And it's not Asmodeus—he's not the shy type. It's someone who doesn't want to be known until they're ready. Until it has the most impact on whatever long-term game they're playing."

"This *game* has gone on long enough already. At least since they corrupted Mordred, and I presume even longer than that. I don't know why they finally decided to strike now, though."

"Abaddon has been trapped in another realm for thousands of years. My guess is her emergence from that realm has allowed these people to finally put their plan into action."

It made sense: you wait until most of your heavy hitters are in the same place before you destroy your enemies. "Baldr," I said aloud as my mind began to race.

"Baldr is not the leading type."

"No, Baldr and the blood elves were trapped in the dwarven realm. And Abaddon was trapped in some other realm. Now Abaddon is here, and she's brought blood elves. She can seemingly jump between realms with some sort of portable version of the old realm gate tablet we found." I walked toward the room where Rhea had been murdered, and Hyperion stepped in my way.

"No," he said.

"I need to look in the room."

"I won't have her property be thrown around while you search for something that may or may not be helpful." Hyperion didn't make it sound like he was going to leave me a lot of choice.

I really didn't want to get into a fight. "Look, when Abaddon left the room, she threw a bangle or something like it back inside. She put one on her wrist when she left the realm with Atlas, too. I need to find that bracelet. It's important."

"Rhea died in there, and you want to start rummaging around, desecrating her home even more than has already been done. What if it's nothing? What if it was just a piece of junk?"

"Then it'll have been eliminated as important."

"I couldn't save them," he almost shouted. "They were my friends, and they died because I wasn't here."

"And if you don't let me in there, a lot more could die."

Hyperion reacted as if he'd been slapped. He shoved me. "You *dare* lecture me about the consequences of my actions. I was ruling the piece-of-shit realm you call home before your parents gave even a second of thought to you."

"Move, or be moved. No more playing, Hyperion."

He took a step forward, and shadows tore out of the ground, wrapping themselves around him and dragging him to the floor. "I don't want to put you in my shadow realm," I said softly. "But if you push this, I will hurt you."

"You'll try," he said, changing into his golden dragon-kin form, and opening his mouth, burning away my shadows with molten flame, causing feedback that made me yell out in pain.

"Didn't know the shadows could hurt you, did you?"

Before Helios had managed to do the same thing earlier, I hadn't thought they could, no.

He stood to his full height and unfurled his massive wings, knocking over a vase beside him that crashed to the floor, scattering remains all around. He turned and looked at the vase, the anger on his face softening, and the dragon-kin form melted away, leaving only the man.

"I'm sorry," I said as Hyperion dropped to his knees and wept for his fallen friends.

"Do what you need to," he said to me without looking up.

I left him to his sorrow and walked into the bedroom where Rhea had been murdered. Her body had been removed already, but the blood remained, and nothing else appeared to have been touched. I moved several piles of belongings that had been discarded during the fight but found nothing. I used my air magic to push the bed several inches and spotted what I was looking for on the floor beside a bloodstained dagger.

I picked up the dagger and placed it on the bed. I didn't know whose blood it was, but Abaddon had been given a deep wound from what I'd seen, so it might have been hers. I picked up the copper bracelet and found it to be devoid of anything even close to a mark. There were several indentations on the top of the bracelet, but other than that it was completely smooth.

I left the room and found Hyperion sitting on one of the sofas, waiting for me. "I need to apologize. I'm sorry. I allowed my grief to override common sense."

"We've all done it," I told him. "And I found this." I passed the bracelet to him.

Hyperion turned the bracelet over in his hands. "It's just a copper bracelet. Nothing interesting. Not even a clasp. It looks like it's based on some old Roman design, maybe Greek." He looked up at me. "That's probably not important, though. I'm sort of grasping for straws."

"Abaddon threw it back into the room, and she put on another bracelet like this one before she vanished with Atlas." I remembered Zamek's words. "The runes vanish after being used."

"So, Abaddon has someone making these?"

"Yeah, but they probably take time to make—it's not a quick thing. I don't think they'll be bouncing around the realms or anything, but it depends on how long they've been stocking them. And how quickly they can be made. Both Abaddon and Atlas had to touch their bracelet to activate it. And if they'd been able to take more than just themselves, Abaddon wouldn't have needed to bring Atlas his own bracelet."

"We found bracelets on the other bodies. Only plain ones like that, though. So, everyone was given their own bracelet, but only one because they weren't meant to go back."

"That's what Lucifer and Zamek are confirming, but I don't think anyone who was left here was meant to survive the trip, though. They'd have had a return-home bracelet if they were."

"The attackers appeared from just outside of town."

"Where?"

"To the north, about a mile from here, closer to where Cronus dug his escape route the last time you were here. It's a massive field, big enough to house thousands of people. Hundreds of thousands. It's good that they didn't bring enough people to fit there."

"The tunnel was flooded and destroyed, though, yes?"

Hyperion nodded.

"I need to go back to the Earth realm. Hopefully we can figure out where Abaddon is by tracking the carnage she's liable to have caused. Can you search the area and report anything you find?"

"I'll get word to Hades or Sky if we discover anything, but I've never heard of so many people being transported through realms without a realm gate. If those bracelets are responsible, they could come back or go anywhere at any time."

"I never thought one of the seven devils was a friend of mine, or that I'd discover what happened to the dwarves. Life seems to be full of surprises these days. Besides, if they can jump from realm to realm as they wish, why aren't there a lot more blood elves, and where's Baldr?" I moved toward the nearby doorway.

"Nate," Hyperion called after me, making me pause and turn back. "Kill them. All of them. I don't care how, I don't care what you have to do to achieve it, but they all need to die for what they've done."

I left the room without a word and found Zamek running through the villa toward me. "Came to find you," he said. "The griffins said that we need to go back through the realm gate. Apparently it got worse while we were in here."

"Of course it did," I said, and passed him the bracelet. "This is how Abaddon got in here. I think you were right. The runes allowing her to travel through realms vanished after it was used."

Zamek turned it over in his hands, removing an identical one from his pocket and showing it to me. "Lucifer and I heard that these people had come from outside of town, so we went to take a look. There's a huge field there, and lots of these discarded across it. They've been made hastily. It's not exactly high craftsmanship. Monsters."

"Zamek, I'm not sure if this is the right time to be correcting their craftsmanship."

"Oh, right, force of habit. I think these were definitely used to bring the attackers here. You'd still need someone to get the words and runes right, though."

"Which means they got someone to learn how to do this from scratch."

"Which, considering how difficult it is, is not what I'd go with."

"Or they broke Mara out of prison, and Selene's earlier thoughts about her involvement are right."

"That's the easier of the two options."

"And it gives us another problem to deal with."

We both left the villa and jogged down the steps to several waiting griffins, Selene, Sky, Cerberus, and Lucifer. "So, how are we going to do this?" I asked, and then recognized Lorin, the griffin who had been guarding the realm gate when I'd last been to Tartarus. "Lorin, good to see you."

Lorin bowed his head slightly, the white feathers on his neck ruffling, which he quickly smoothed down with one taloned hand. "You, too, Nate. I wish we didn't always meet after something awful happened."

"When this is done, I'll come back and you can show me your realm without fear of some impending war."

Lorin laughed. It's a weird sound when a griffin does it. "That would be pleasant. As to your question, we're going to fly you over. It's quicker than a boat."

"You can do that?" I asked. "I always assumed you weren't able to."

"We can. We just don't like to. It's exhausting to carry someone that length, but on this occasion, we'll make an exception."

"And Charon?"

"Recovering. Angry. Belligerent. Not necessarily in that order."

The journey took less than half the time it would have by boat, but I spent most of it with hands firmly grasped around Lorin's legs. Being picked up by huge talons that could crush me or slice me into much smaller pieces and then flying high above water that could also put me close to death wasn't an experience I was comfortable with. When we finally touched down, I had an overwhelming urge to kiss the ground and tell it I was never leaving it again, but everyone else appeared to be okay, so I didn't want to make a scene.

"Best of luck in your hunt," Lorin said.

"Take care," I told him, and joined the others walking through the realm gate.

"I did not enjoy that," Zamek told me once we stepped back into the realm-gate room inside the Wolf's Head compound. "Dwarves were not made for flying in such a manner. I'm going to take a seat for a minute."

I pointed him toward one of the guards, who helped him walk to a seat. When Zamek didn't refuse help to walk, I knew he wasn't feeling good.

"Nate," Sky called. She'd been talking to one of the guards inside the control room.

"Zamek isn't feeling great," I explained. "What happened while we were gone?"

"You're going to need to come with us to the office next door," the female guard said.

We did as we were asked, and I requested that the guard tell Zamek where we were once she'd left us alone with a TV.

"It's the guy calling himself Hellequin again, isn't it?" I asked.

Sky nodded. "Apparently so." She switched on the TV. "This was thirty-seven minutes ago and appeared on every TV channel operating worldwide. Whoever these people are, they have some serious backing to do that."

"Just play it," I said.

The Hellequin character that came on screen sat in the same pose as before and appeared to be the same person. It was hard to tell with the mask and lack of lighting, but he spoke with the same voice as before. "We are the people who will put humanity in its place. We will take this world and make it better, make it in our own image, and all who stand in our way will be killed. To those of you who want to rise up, or disbelieve what we're saying, you'll soon see just how much power we have. Human, Avalon, or other, I no longer care. If you stand against us, you are our enemy, and you will be destroyed. My name is Hellequin, and we are Shadow Falls." He gestured behind him, and several people appeared, all wearing dark clothes with similarly styled masks: black with a white pattern of some kind.

The video stopped, and I realized I'd been holding my breath. "The prisoner said Shadow Falls. Arthur wanted me to check on Shadow Falls, and now everyone who watched that is going to think any rumors they might have heard are correct. This is bad. This is really bad."

"We need to get to Galahad," Selene said.

"We need to contact Olivia and find out if she can head this off in Camelot before Arthur decides to declare war on the people living in Shadow Falls," Lucifer said.

I stared at the screen, where a man using my name just threatened people I cared about, and felt the rage and hate course through me. I pushed it aside and picked up a phone that was on a nearby desk, then asked the man on the other end to patch me through to Olivia's number, before placing it on loudspeaker when she answered.

"Olivia, this fake Hellequin has declared war," Selene said. "Can you head this off at your end?"

"I'll do what I can," Olivia said. "Won't be easy, though. I'm starting to hear whispers of people who want to go to Shadow Falls and take it by force. At best, I might be able to convince Arthur to go alone, or give you a few days."

"With no concrete proof they were involved?" Zamek asked.

"Some people have been wanting to annex Shadow Falls for centuries. They just needed a reason to try."

"Anything you can do is good," I said. "Also, we think Mara is out of prison."

"I'll look into it," Olivia said. "Sounds like I'm being kept out of the loop on a few things. I'll call back soon."

She hung up, and we all waited while a jet was readied to take us to America. Before we were due to board twenty minutes later, Olivia called back. I answered and put it on speaker.

"I managed to get you two days," Olivia said. "I pulled a few favors with people who have Arthur's ear. And Arthur agreed to go to Shadow Falls with only a small contingent of bodyguards. That's the best I can do. Forty-eight hours, Nate—that's all we've got to figure out this Hellequin's true identity. After that Arthur is going to turn up, and when Galahad doesn't play ball, he's going to declare war on Shadow Falls and we won't be able to stop it. You know Galahad isn't going to just stand down and let Avalon troops into Shadow Falls. The east coast of North America is going to become a war zone.

"On top of that, Hera has walked away from Avalon and locked down London. The human news is calling it a terror drill and a high likelihood of an attack. She's sorting out her defenses for what's coming.

Oh, and Mara had been transferred to The Hole about six weeks ago. I, of course, was kept out of the loop."

"Who ordered the transfer?" I asked.

"Merlin."

"Shit," I said.

"Hera won't be the first to leave and show their true allegiance," Selene said with more than a little anger.

"Oh shit," Olivia said after several seconds of silence. "Oh, no, no, no, no."

"What's happening?" Selene asked.

"Olivia?" Lucifer said after waiting a short time.

"There's been another attack," Olivia said. "We don't know all of the details yet, but it looks like multiple magical detonations in North Carolina." She paused. "Nate, whatever you have to do, get it done soon. A lot more people are about to become casualties."

"Keep us informed," I told her, and hung up. "I know we don't number a lot, but we have to stop this. Or at least stop Arthur from making a huge mistake."

"What if these people are a part of Shadow Falls?" Lucifer asked. "What if Shadow Falls is about to have its own revolt?"

"Let's go ask." I turned to Sky. "We're going to need some things, if that's okay?"

"The jet is almost ready, but I'll speak to Cerberus. I'm coming with you. Galahad is going to need as many people as possible to convince him not to start a war he can't win."

CHAPTER 15

Mordred

Moscow, Russia

Mordred sat in the back of a van with Polina, Remy, Diana, and Fiona as the rest of the group sat in the back of a similar van in a parking lot around the corner. They were both well placed to watch the front of the nightclub and see who left and arrived. Mostly it was revelers, and with the time now after midnight, the majority of those leaving were a lot worse for wear.

"Police work sure is boring," Mordred said. "How about I just walk up to the club and go inside?"

"They'll know who you are," Fiona said. "We went through this."

"Doesn't make it any less dull," Mordred replied. They'd been watching the club for the better part of two hours, and he was beginning to feel the stress of staying in one place for a long time. "Also, calling your nightclub the Bear's Pelt seems to be really quite unpleasant to bears."

"A werebear used to own it," Polina said. "Legend has it they kept him in the dungeon for weeks, forcing him to stay in his werebear form."

"They skinned him, didn't they?" Diana asked, her voice a low rumble of anger.

"That's the legend, yes," Polina confirmed. "It's said that they keep the skin as a rug for an office."

"What you're saying is that the werewolves are bad people," Mordred said. "I'm going to go say hello."

"You are not," Fiona seethed.

"Listen, I get you think I'm evil still, but I'm not. I am, however, Mordred. People know me. People occasionally hate and fear me, but more importantly, people know me." He paused. "I said that already, didn't I?"

Diana nodded.

"Right, well, the point stands. I can go in there, and people are going to freak the fuck out. They might try to kill me, but probably not. Viktor probably told them we were coming." He turned to Polina. "Your people saw him enter the premises, yes?"

She nodded. "Alone and with a lot of looking around to ensure he wasn't followed."

"Excellent. He'll have told them I'm coming, so they'll be expecting us to storm the place in some covert operation. What they won't be expecting is me walking into the front with a mic in my ear so I can tell you what's happening. I'm sure that's something they're definitely not going to have planned for."

"You're just going to walk in and tell us what you see?" Polina asked.

"I like his plan," Remy said. "It's ballsy. And fun. And you know that after twenty minutes of being in there, Mordred will have started a fire or a fight. Possibly both."

"See, Remy thinks I can do it."

"Remy likes to blow things up," Fiona said.

"That makes me sound like a very one-note character," Remy said. "I have other hobbies. Old guns, old swords. The guitar."

"Really, the guitar?" Mordred asked.

"Yeah, I'm really getting used to doing some good solo work on it. I'll have to play you something."

"This is not the time," Fiona almost shouted before glaring at Remy. "You are not helping."

"Oh, I didn't realize I was meant to be, sorry."

Mordred rested a hand on Fiona's shoulder, removing it when she flinched to get away. "Fiona, I either go in and get killed, or I go in and help. Both are better than sitting in this cold van until someone makes a decision about what to do." He turned to Polina. "I know you want us to wait until the club is empty, but I'm sure I can sort that bit out."

Polina sighed, opened a small metal box beside her, and passed Mordred a small packet.

He opened the packet, removing the tiny mic inside, before placing it inside his ear. "So, you can hear me okay?"

Polina turned to a laptop and opened a piece of software on it. She plugged in a small speaker and activated it, which made a buzzing noise in Mordred's ear.

"That okay?" she asked.

The buzzing noise went away, and Mordred nodded. "I'll talk to you on the way to the club, and once I'm in I'll give details of what I see, but don't come in unless I give you the go order."

"You're going to blow something up, aren't you?" Diana asked.

"Now you've spoiled the surprise," Mordred said with a slight smile. "I'm not planning on it, but if that's my best option, then you'd best expect fireworks. Can you keep the human police away from here?"

"I'll be listening for any traffic from them coming our way," Polina said. "I'll do what I can to stop them, but try not to blow the whole building up. I'm sure they won't like that, what with the current world-wide attacks, or the fact that people don't like it when you blow up a part of their city."

Mordred opened the van door and stepped out into the cold night. "I'll do my best."

"That's what we're worried about," Diana said. "Don't get killed."

"Not planning on it." He shut the van door and set off toward the nightclub, where the line to get in had vanished to nothing, although the two large doormen remained outside. Both were over six feet tall, both were bald, and both had tattoos on their hands and skulls.

"Hi," Mordred said and waved.

The two men exchanged a confused glance, and Mordred guessed that they probably weren't used to people behaving around them in that manner.

"I'd like to get in," he continued, this time in Russian.

The men looked at Mordred in his jeans and thick, dark-gray coat made for keeping out the cold, but not really made for fashion. They looked down at his black boots, and then back up at Mordred. "Fuck off," they said in unison.

"How about this?" Mordred asked, continuing in Russian. "How about, you go tell your bosses that Mordred is out here in the freezing fucking cold, so they can either come out here and let me in, or they can come out here and remove your broken bodies from the street?"

Neither men liked Mordred's words, and the one closest to him threw a punch. Mordred avoided it easily, stepped around into the path of the second bouncer, and planted his foot right between his legs with enough force to send him to the cold pavement.

Mordred moved away, watching both men, as the first bouncer ignored his friend and threw another punch. Mordred blocked the punch and smashed his fist into the man's stomach, putting just enough magical power into the blow to ensure he made his point as succinctly as possible. The man crumpled to his knees, and Mordred drove his fist into the man's face, busting open his nose and dropping him unmoving to the ground.

The second man winced as he lay on the ground and tried to grab hold of Mordred's leg, but Mordred was too quick and kicked the man in the face, sending him into the same state of unconsciousness as his friend.

Mordred retrieved two guns from the bouncers, emptying both of their magazines and chambered rounds before dropping them back onto their owners. They'd used normal bullets, which was hardly surprising considering their bosses were werewolves, but it also meant that

Mordred wasn't about to be killed by a stray bullet. Besides, he'd left them alive as a warning—if they decided to come after him again, he'd reconsider his goodwill. He paused. He probably should have told them that. He glanced at the two men and was sure that when they woke up they'd figure it out on their own.

He pushed open the door to the club and blinked as the noise from inside washed over him. It was made even worse by the fact that the second he stepped into the club, his magic switched off. He took a deep breath, and while the loud music made him wish he could just turn around and leave, he took a few steps inside until he was more comfortable with it.

There were hundreds of people milling around the bar area at the far end of the floor or dancing near one of two sets of stairs that led up to the floor above. A large bouncer stood guard at the foot of the stairs, and across the floor, at the opposite side, was another bouncer guarding an identical staircase. The set of stairs furthest away from the dance floor was set back from any people. Presumably the guard there would be able to hear people a little easier than the one near the dance floor.

"Lots of armed guards," Mordred said. "Lots more innocent people. I presume they're innocent."

"Some people like to go to dangerous places," Diana said in his ear. "They like to feel as if they're close to the danger while being distant from it."

"Then these people must love being here," Mordred said, and looked up at the floor above, where he spotted more dancing. "More people on the floor above, and I can see those who are looking over the railings down on the people below."

"The third floor has the office," Polina said.

"Who's in charge of this group?" Mordred asked as he walked through the floor toward the bar, smiling at several women who looked his way.

"The alpha, and I hate that word, is called Alexi Popov. He's a bad guy, but his second in command is the one you really need to look out for. Her name is Daria Kozar. I'm almost certain she's ex-KGB."

"I thought there was no such thing," Mordred said. "Isn't that the phrase?"

"So I hear. But on this occasion, I don't think they'd really want her back."

"Vodka double, neat," Mordred said to the barman in Russian. "Sorry, go on."

"She killed her commanding officer over a disagreement. Escaped from jail, and at some point met Alexi, who turned her into a werewolf. That was in the nineteen sixties. She's said to be the one who skinned the werebear. She likes her knives."

"Sounds like my dream date," Mordred said, and thanked the barman for the vodka. He knocked it back in one shot and made a slight sigh of contentment. "They might be evil, but they serve good vodka." He placed the glass on the counter and walked over to the stairs the farthest from the dance floor while the bouncer there watched him with a cool detachment.

"Fuck off," the bouncer said when Mordred was close enough.

"I'd like to see Alexi."

"Fuck off."

"Oh, come on, I just want to go upstairs and talk to your boss."

"And I want you to fuck off." The bouncer placed his hand inside his jacket.

Mordred stepped forward, grabbing the bouncer's arm at the elbow with one hand and whispering into his ear. "I know I can't use my magic in here, but I can really hurt you. So, you either tell Alexi that Mordred is here, or I cut off your arm and bludgeon you with the wet end."

The bouncer held Mordred's gaze for several seconds.

"You've heard of me, I assume."

The bouncer nodded, and Mordred saw the fear in his eyes.

"Then you know I'm not screwing around here. I will *really* fuck your day up. I suggest not making me do that, by letting me see Alexi."

He nodded slightly and stepped aside. "Alexi is waiting for you."

Mordred walked up the first two stairs and paused. He turned back to the bouncer. "Just then, when you were scared. That wasn't because of me, was it? That was because Alexi was talking to you in your earpiece?"

The bouncer nodded.

"You a werewolf?"

He shook his head.

"You like working here?"

He shook his head again.

"Alexi really that scary?"

He nodded.

Mordred turned without another word and walked up the flight of stairs, where once he was at the top a second bouncer, this one female, met him and led him toward a nearby door. She punched in a number on a keypad and pushed the door open, motioning for him to go up the stairs.

He thanked the bouncer and began his ascension to the office above. Once the door behind him closed and locked, he was glad for the relative quiet the stairwell offered him. He reached the small landing at the top of the stairs and opened the door, revealing a spacious office.

Mordred stepped into the office, closing the door behind him. There was a large desk adjacent to him, opposite a row of windows that looked down on the main dance floor. A large leather couch sat near the window, with a drinks cabinet close by, its top made of glass, revealing several bottles of spirits behind it, while the bottom half of the cabinet was wooden. The two doors on the far wall across from the entrance that Mordred had used were closed, and in between them was a glass cabinet with several pistols and rifles.

The first door on the far wall opened, and a short, stocky man exited. He had blond hair tied back in a ponytail and wore an elegant black suit with a deep-red shirt, which Mordred guessed to be silk.

"You must be Mordred," the man said, walking over to him and offering his hand.

Mordred took it and was surprised to discover that the man didn't try to crush his hand. "You must be Alexi."

"That I am. Please take a seat." He motioned toward the leather couch, which Mordred thanked him for and took a seat.

"Drink?" Alexi asked.

"Vodka, neat."

"Good man," Alexi said, opening the drinks cabinet and revealing a small fridge-freezer in the bottom. Alexi removed the bottle of vodka and poured two glasses, passing one to Mordred. "I have this stuff shipped in from a small distillery in eastern Siberia. No one knows about it but a select few."

Mordred tasted the vodka. It was excellent. "Always nice to know of a good place to get vodka."

Alexi laughed. "Indeed it is."

"Nice office, too. I assume you have your own bathroom."

Alexi pushed open the closest door, revealing a spacious bathroom. "Only the best."

"What's the other door for?"

"I keep some important things in there. It's sort of my get-away-from-everything room."

"Sounds nice. I should really get me one of them."

"Viktor told me you were coming."

"Yes, I figured as much." Mordred knocked back the rest of the vodka and placed the glass on a coaster on the glass coffee table in front of him. "Good stuff. So, yes, I knew he would; it's why I didn't bother chasing after him. People like Viktor think of their own skin before anything else."

Alexi smiled. "We all know people like that. They put their own needs above the needs of anyone else. Capitalism at its finest."

"You're anticapitalist?"

"Not at all, I love money. I love the things it can buy, including power. No, I just don't like the desperation of those people who pretend to have my kind of wealth. It's unseemly."

"So, I assume you're going to try to kill me soon."

Alexi knocked back the rest of his vodka. "I was hoping you'd be persuaded to join our side."

"Your side? And what side is that?"

The smile on Alexi's face melted, revealing the true man behind it. "The side that'll win."

If Alexi thought that a slight sneer was going to scare Mordred, he clearly had no idea of the kinds of things Mordred had seen in his life. "So, if I say no, you'll kill me?"

"Eventually. First Daria will peel your skin from your body. She does so enjoy her work. You'll have to excuse her absence from this meeting—she's on the lower levels enjoying her time with a young man who tried to help Elaine Garlot. He's probably wishing she'd just kill him by this point. He's presumably feeling pain the likes of which you've never imagined. You come into my club with confidence and a swagger, but if you cross me, I assure you, we will teach you to be afraid."

Mordred stared at Alexi for several seconds before bursting out laughing. "Holy shit, you're an idiot."

Alexi's expression darkened.

"Seriously, you think telling me tales of some woman who likes to torture is going to make me afraid? Do you honestly know who I am? Do you have any idea of the shit I've done to people? Of the shit I've had done to me? I was kept alive and tortured every day for a century by people a lot badder and better at it than I'd hazard a guess your lovely friend is. Don't get me wrong—I'm sure she's very good at stabbing people with knives, but you think that's torture? True torture is making it so that you're broken every single day, until you begin to look forward to it, because your life without that pain and suffering is now meaningless. And then the day they leave you alone you scream at them to come for you, because all you've known for so long is the nightmare of having your mind destroyed in a way that never gets put back together.

"Try spending a few decades with a species for whom the word 'pain' is synonymous with the word 'life,' and see how you think being stabbed with a knife compares. So, while I'm sure your stabby little friend is very scary, she's not Baldr, she's not Hera, and she's not the dozens of people who took their turns on me for a hundred years. You think you know fear, Mr. Popov, well, let me assure you, you've never even glimpsed it. And if you threaten me again, I'll show you fear. I'll happily make the big bad wolf piss himself."

Mordred got up and walked over to the bottle of vodka, pouring himself a second glass and knocking it back. "Where's Viktor?"

A glass hit the wall beside Mordred, shattering. "How dare you speak to me in such a manner."

"I've killed kings and queens, Alexi. I've killed people with more guards than you have people in this club. I've gotten to people who prided themselves on being untouchable. You're just a mutt with the delusion you're someone important. And more importantly, you've trapped yourself in a room with me."

Alexi growled and began to transform into his werebeast wolf form, tearing off his suit as he did. Mordred drank some more vodka, removed the gun from the holster, and shot Alexi between the eyes. All in one fluid motion.

"No one searched me, you fucking idiot," Mordred said. "That's what happens when you buy into your own legend. You think you're immortal. I should know."

Mordred ejected the magazine and removed the bullet from the chamber of the Glock, placing them both in his jacket pocket, then took out a second magazine from another pocket and loaded it into the gun as Alexi groaned.

"Normal bullets," Mordred said. "Warning shot. Bet it hurts like hell, though."

"Gut you like a salmon," Alexi said.

"Actually I don't think you will. I now have silver bullets—these won't just hurt. I'm certain of that. I wanted to see if my theory about this room being soundproof was right. I figured you brought people up here for some alone time with you." Mordred walked over to the second door and kicked it open, splintering the wooden frame. Inside there was a computer on a desk, a king-sized bed, and a large-screen TV on the wall. The room smelled of sex.

"The runes to keep powers from working, where's the master one?" Mordred asked. "There's always a master one, and I'd really like it switched off."

"Not here," Alexi said.

Mordred removed a silver blade from the sheath on his hip and threw it at Alexi's leg. The werewolf screamed in pain as the blade bit into his thigh. "That will kill you eventually," Mordred said, walking over and pulling the knife free. Blood poured from the wound. "The silver is already in your blood. I can heal it with light magic. Can't do that without removing the runes, though. So, I'll ask again: Where is the master rune?"

"You'll die first," Alexi said, and started to laugh as the door leading to the stairs outside exploded in a hail of bullets.

Mordred threw himself through the open door and tapped his ear. "Diana, Polina, Remy—is anyone actually there? Because now would be a good time to storm the citadel."

"We're on our way," Diana said. "Just keep your head down. People are flooding out of the club, and until we can get through them, you're on your own."

Mordred risked a glance back into the office as two bouncers, one armed with a shotgun and another with a semiautomatic submachine gun, entered the room. He ducked back into the bedroom before anyone could fire another shot.

"If we have to come get you, we're going to make this hard," one of them said.

Mordred removed the gun from his holster and stood up against the wall. "That's funny, because I was going to say the same thing to you." Mordred reached into his pocket and produced a stun grenade. He pulled the pin, tossed it into the room, and turned away from the small explosion, and several shots fired blindly as the two bouncers were momentarily disoriented.

Mordred counted to three, stepped around the corner, and shot both men in the head. They dropped to the floor as Mordred walked over to Alexi and pointed the gun at his temple. "Where is the master rune? Now."

"Behind the gun cupboard. It's etched on the wall."

Mordred pushed the remains of the cupboard aside, revealing the large rune that had been carved there. It hummed with power, occasionally shimmering black. "Blood magic was used to create this," Mordred said. "You killed someone to make this." He knew that if destroyed the rune might backlash power against anyone nearby, so he walked over to the doorway and emptied the rest of the magazine of silver bullets into the wall.

With the rune destroyed, Mordred felt the magical power rush back into him. He walked toward Alexi and placed the Glock on the desk in front of him.

"Daria is going to kill you for this."

Mordred placed a hand on Alexi's arm, and his light magic went to work, healing the silver from the werewolf.

"Why?" he asked when Mordred was done and had stepped away from his reach. "What's to stop me from killing you?"

Mordred watched Alexi get back to his feet. "Because when I'm done, I'm going to come back here and you're going to tell me where Elaine Garlot is and what your involvement is in her disappearance. And if you're dead, you can't do that."

Alexi chuckled and took a step toward Mordred, flexing his fingers, ready to pounce.

White glyphs lit up over Mordred's arms and hands, and magical air smashed into Alexi, picking him up like he was nothing and throwing him against the far wall. Mordred flicked his hand, and tendrils of air slithered around Alexi. Another hand flick and the air dragged Alexi over to the windows in the room, pinning him against them.

Mordred used his magic to push Alexi against the glass as it began to crack under the pressure.

"She will kill you," Alexi seethed.

"She'll try," Mordred said, releasing the air magic from around Alexi, moving it around him in a shield. In an instant he used the blood of the two dead bouncers to power his blood magic and, mixing it with the air, smashed it into Alexi, sending him through the glass with ferocious force. Alexi bounced over the railing below and crashed into the empty dance floor as Diana and the rest of his friends entered the building. Alexi was breathing but was no longer going to be a problem. The LOA would deal with him. Now it was time for Mordred to hunt.

CHAPTER 16

Mordred

Mordred spent a few minutes going through Alexi's desk drawers but found nothing of any importance. He moved into the bedroom and almost stepped on the TV remote. He picked it up and threw it onto the bed, which caused the TV screen to come to life.

He was half expecting to see something unpleasant paused on there, ready for Alexi's return, but instead it was much worse. The picture was of a room with a concrete floor, and what appeared to be a drain close to the center. A short distance from it was a man in a chair with a blindfold on. The picture was in color, and Mordred could easily make out the wounds that covered the man's naked body. He was shivering, and Mordred was certain that it was as much as a by-product of the cold as of the horror he'd clearly endured.

"What did you find?" Nabu asked from the doorway.

"Torture porn," Mordred said, pointing to the TV.

"Is that live?"

"I assume so. There's nothing indicating otherwise." He picked up the remote and pressed the button to fast forward, but nothing happened. "Must be live."

"I've been hearing horror stories about what some of the people went through as captives here. A lot are never found again. Or at least not in their original state."

"Alexi isn't that strong. There's no way he's in charge of all this."

"You think the woman . . . Daria is in charge?"

Mordred nodded. "The whole pack alpha thing is something weres came up with as an easy way to say 'leader.' I get the feeling that Alexi was the leader because he had a good look, but he's not even on the scale of people like Tommy. If this werewolf pack is so scary, it isn't because of Alexi or those bouncers I kicked the shit out of. They were human. Where's the rest of the pack?"

"Waiting for us?"

"Or out hunting. Either way, Alexi is a figurehead, not the alpha, or whatever name they're using for it today."

"We have a werewolf pack of considerable power still active within this building."

"And they know we're here."

"That's not great news."

"Nothing about the last few days has been great news. Viktor is still here, too. I'd really like to find him before these werewolves cut their losses and remove his head for him."

"You think he knows where Elaine is?"

Mordred shrugged as he walked toward the door. "No idea, I just want to punch him in the face."

He left Nabu in the bedroom as Polina, Morgan, and Remy all entered the office.

"You really did a number on Alexi," Polina said.

"Did you know he wasn't the man in charge?" Mordred asked.

Polina licked her lips and looked irritated at the question, but her expression soon softened. "We suspected. No one we sent in was able to get word out about how the hierarchy in the pack works."

"You still think that Alexi created Daria?"

"Yes," Polina said without hesitation. "The power of a werewolf has no effect on the power of those they'll change. They're completely separate entities. There's every possibility that he still bit Daria and she just became more powerful than he is."

"That wouldn't be difficult."

"Nice bounce, by the way," Remy said from the hole where several windows used to be. "You got some really good air on crashing him through a reinforced window."

"My power is a little bit more impressive than it was before I regained my faculties," Mordred said. "We need to make sure this club is empty."

"The others are on it," Morgan told him. "We thought we'd best come and see how you were doing."

"I'm fine. Annoyed that I wasted a perfectly excellent vodka by drinking it with that asshole. Who, by the way, I'd like to see stick around for a bit."

"Why?" Polina asked. "We can take him in for questioning."

"Or you can leave him here, and he can watch as we dismantle the rest of his pack. I've seen it work before. Trust me on this. He's the type to fold when he has no option." Mordred looked out over the nightclub. "Any idea where the entrance to this underground complex is?"

"There's a lift in a hallway behind the level you entered on," Polina said. "Nice job not killing those two outside, by the way."

"I'm not an assassin," Mordred said. "Had Alexi just given me what I'd asked for, he'd still be sitting on his nice chair, drinking excellent vodka and pretending he was important."

"You know your demeanor changes when we do stuff like this," Remy said to Mordred. "You're less . . . flighty."

"Anger focuses me. Gives me something to consider and work toward. And after seeing the footage in his bedroom, and after him trying to kill me, I'm plenty angry. Daria seems to consider herself some kind of torture genius. I intend to show her otherwise."

Nabu left the bedroom. "There's a lot of older stuff in there, too. A USB stick was plugged into the TV. Alexi got his excitement from watching people get hurt—at least that's my guess."

"Hopefully the amount of pain he's in at the moment will have to suffice," Mordred said. "I assume you placed a sorcerer's band on him?"

Polina looked offended. "I know how to do my job, Mordred."

"I know, I just like to check these things. I mean no offense by it."

Her expression didn't change. "Yes, we put a sorcerer's band on him. It's not specifically designed for him, but it'll do. He won't be going anywhere, or hurting anyone else. Silver-laced cuffs, too, after he changed back into his human form. He won't be changing out of it while he's in them."

"Right, let's get the rest of the pack sorted, then," Mordred said. He left the room and jogged down the stairs, where he spotted several of Polina's people carrying out a search of the premises.

After making his way down to the bottom floor and through a set of double doors, he found himself in the corridor with the lift at one end. Diana stood in front of it, her arms crossed, while Fiona stood beside her. Fiona had acquired a rapier at some point, and it sat sheathed against her hip. Because she was a conjurer, her ability was based on creating traps and illusions. If she found herself in a fight, it was best done with weaponry.

"What's wrong?" Mordred asked.

"There's silver in the lift doors," Diana explained. "We can't open them. I try to pry them open and it burns my fingers."

"And we don't know the code for the numerical pad, either," Fiona said.

Mordred placed a hand against the lift doors and used his air magic to wedge it in between them. He slowly forced the doors apart, but the strain was too great and after only an inch the locking mechanism refused to budge and Mordred was forced to release it.

"You got any other ideas?" Fiona asked, her voice full of anxiety.

"One, yes," Mordred said, and placed his hand over the number pad. A cone of razor-sharp ice left Mordred's palm, smashing into the pad with incredible force, tearing it apart and causing several sparks. An alarm sounded all around him, and the lift doors remained closed.

"Good job," Diana said. "I could have just broken it myself."

The lights went off inside the club, bathing everyone in darkness for a short time before emergency lighting flickered on.

Diana sniffed the air. "Wolves."

"Go fight," Mordred said. "I'll figure out how to get down to the levels below. There has to be more entrances if they can get up here."

Gunfire could be heard from the main club area, and two wolves burst into the hallway from the door at the far end. They eyed Mordred, Diana, and Fiona before howling and charging.

Diana had changed into her werebear form before she took a step, charging into one of the werewolves, taking the massive beast off its feet and smashing it into the wall. Fiona removed a pistol from a holster and fired at the second wolf, who avoided the bullets with ease. She drew her rapier and moved to confront it, parrying the werewolf's claw strikes and catching it with a vicious cut across one eye, which burned as the silver content in the sword went to work.

A third werewolf appeared at the end of the hallway. His appearance caused Mordred to sigh, and he walked past Fiona and her opponent. The new werewolf growled and walked toward Mordred, who shot a two-foot-long blade of ice from his palm, which the werewolf smashed with a swipe of one huge paw.

Mordred cracked his knuckles and threw two more blades, which the werewolf destroyed once again as he got closer and closer. Mordred smiled and waited until the werewolf was close enough before unleashing a torrent of water from his hands. It crashed into the werewolf, who couldn't avoid it and was thrown back several feet.

Mordred moved his fingers slightly, and the water froze in place, pinning the werewolf's legs to the floor. He roared in anger and clawed at the ice, ripping off huge chunks that, with no magic controlling them, quickly vanished. Mordred sprinted forward, wrapping thick ice around his fist and driving it into the side of the werewolf's head.

The werewolf swiped back at Mordred, who blocked the blow with a shield of air and quickly countered by slamming a blade of ice into the werewolf's leg, pinning him to the ground. Mordred dodged a swipe and pinned the werewolf's arm to the wall with another blade of ice.

"Does that not hurt?" Mordred asked.

"Gut you," the werewolf said, frothing at the mouth.

"You're on something. Some sort of suppressant to stop pain? It'll wear off soon—that's one of the problems with having a healing ability as fast as yours. Also, those ice blades will stay there until I remove the magic, so you're not going anywhere." Mordred stepped around the werewolf, keeping his distance, and saw that both Fiona and Diana had killed their werewolves.

"You're all alone," Mordred said, and the werewolf turned as best as it could to look at him. "I'm going to be honest with you." Mordred raised his arm, and red glyphs ignited across his arms, moving over the blue ones for his water elemental magic. "This is mind magic. Do you know what that does?"

The werewolf said nothing but continued to stare at Mordred's arm.

"Right, well, basically it means I can turn your brain into a big puddle of mush. I can reach in there, grab everything I can, and shake it like there's no tomorrow, or I could . . ." Mordred paused, thinking for a second, before a smile spread across his lips and he clapped his hands together. "I'm going to make you think you're a poodle. No, a miniature poodle—that's perfect. I've never done this before, but if it works you're going to look lovely at next year's Crufts dog show. And if it doesn't work, you'll end up someone who really likes drooling while staring into space."

"What do you want?" the werewolf asked as Diana leaned up against the wall beside it, still in her werebear beast form.

"How'd you get up here?"

"There's a hidden door right inside the coatroom. There's a stairwell behind it."

"How many down there?"

"Four or five."

"Viktor?"

The werewolf nodded.

"What's your kill number?"

The werewolf paused, glancing between the three people watching him. "I forget."

"Bullshit. How many have you killed?"

"Forty-one."

Mordred drew the silver blade and slit the werewolf's throat in one smooth motion. "And that's where it ends."

The sounds of more gunfire came through the nearby door. "We need to go," Mordred said.

"Can you really do that?" Fiona asked, her anxiety still evident, but joined with more than a little fear. "Melt someone's brain?"

Mordred shook his head. "My mind magic is purely defensive. No telepathy, or telekinesis, or anything else that allows me to manipulate others. It's purely so that no one can mess with my mind or make me do anything I don't want to do. Magic isn't exactly an easy thing to research, but sometimes I think that the omega magic allows you to only do the things you really need to be able to do at the time of its activation."

The three ran back into the main area of the club, where several more werewolves were dead on the floor, with a couple more seriously wounded. Polina's men had taken casualties, too, with more than one unmoving on the floor.

Morgan and several of her golems threw two werewolves around as if they were bags of sugar while Nabu drove a sword into the heart of a werewolf, pulling the blade out and using it to remove the hand of another nearby attacker.

"We've got this," Diana said. "Go find Viktor."

"I'm coming with you," Fiona said.

"No, you can't," Mordred told her. "You're too close to this. Too emotional."

"My husband might be down there," she snapped.

"And if you go down there like this, what happens to you?" Mordred asked, keeping calm.

Fiona got in Mordred's face. "He's my husband."

"And that's why you're staying here."

"Mordred's right," Diana said. "You can't go down there. You won't be helping anyone. If Alan is there, Mordred will find him."

"If he's there, you'd best get him out alive," Fiona said.

Mordred ignored the threat in her voice and ran across the dance floor, using his air magic to fling one of the werewolves aside so that he could leap over the counter of the cloakroom and through the open door inside it. He took the stairs two at a time until he reached a door several dozen feet beneath the club area. He blasted the door apart with a gust of air magic, stepping through the remains and into a gray corridor that led off to the right and left. There were several doors down either side, and Mordred cursed the fact that it was going to take him forever to search everything.

He walked to the nearest door—a white door identical to all the others Mordred could see on the floor—and found it unlocked. He pushed it open and discovered three doors inside the dark-gray-tiled room. He went to each door in turn and found that two of them led into new, albeit identical, rooms, while the third door took him out into the opposite side of the hallway from where he'd started.

"They made a maze," Mordred said to himself. "Great, they're psychotic werewolf architects."

"Hello, Mordred," a voice sounded from hidden speakers around the floor. "You're probably wondering what's happening."

"I'm wondering why I don't just tear through this place like it's made of paper."

"We can hear you, just so you know."

"Good. Go fuck yourselves."

"Funny little sorcerer. This is my playpen. I bring humans down here and force them to run the maze. If they can get through it to where you stand, they can use the door you came through to escape. Want to guess how many escape?"

"They're just opening doors, so I'm going to guess all of them. Unless you pick people who are unable to open doors, but that's a really small population. Maybe you put key emblems on the doors like *Resident Evil*. You know if you do that, I'm going to find those keys and make you eat them. I hate those bloody puzzles."

"Do you ever shut up? I assure you it's not so easy to escape when one of my pack is chasing them."

"Ah, Daria, it is you. And you are in charge. You know I'm going to find you, and I'm going to be really annoyed if I have to run around this stupid maze. Just give me Viktor, and tell me where Elaine is, and I'm almost certain I'll let you live."

Daria laughed. "I've left you a surprise in the maze. Think you can find it?"

"I hate it when psychopaths think they're funny." Mordred opened a nearby door and walked into the room beyond. Another identical room, and another three doors. Mordred really wanted to punch someone.

He did this for a few minutes, leaving the doors he'd gone through open as he made his way into the maze, finding himself in a dead end on more than one occasion. He got fed up at one point and tried to destroy the walls and doors with air magic, but the air harmlessly dissipated. There were splatters of blood in more than one room, and claw marks in a few. The werewolves hunted in here. Mordred wondered if the enclosed fear that the victims must have been going through somehow made the hunt all the sweeter. The thought made Mordred feel even more anger toward the pack.

He eventually opened a door that led to a room identical to all the others, except for the man tied to a chair in the middle. He was bathed in blood, with dozens of cuts and wounds over his naked body. He whimpered slightly at the sound of the door opening.

"I'm not going to hurt you," Mordred said. "I'm going to try and get you out of here." Mordred moved around the man and used his air magic to cut through the plastic ties holding the man's limbs to the chair.

The man pulled up the blindfold and stared at Mordred.

Mordred had seen that expression more than once on people who just realized who he was. "Who are you?"

"My name is Gareth Borne. I came to Moscow with Elaine. I was one of her security team."

"Where's Elaine?"

"They took her. The tracking device was on her earring, and one of the werewolves tore it off her and threw it on the floor. I picked it up and . . . and took it."

"You swallowed it, didn't you?"

He nodded. "Not at first. At first they just left me in my cell, so I just held it in my mouth. It needs contact with a living person to work."

"They tortured you, you swallowed it, and now I'm here."

"Elaine said you'd come for her. She was going to use the tracking device to watch someone else."

"Yep, that's me, the happy guy who just traipsed across a continent to find someone who happened to be you. Where did they take Elaine?"

"Siberia."

Mordred put his head in his hands. "Are you shitting me? Siberia is a damn big place. Want to narrow it down a little?"

Gareth shook his head. "Sorry."

"Okay, what are you?"

"I'm a fire elemental. I'm four hundred years old, so I know what I'm doing."

"Why didn't you break free?"

"They forced me to swallow a small stone. It had a glyph on it. It was only about the size of a Tylenol tablet, but I can't access my power at all. They've forced me to take a new one every day for the week I've been here."

"Great, so you're useless until you take a shit. I'm not sure we have that long. You got any idea where the exit is?"

"No, but there's something you should know."

"And that is?"

The door behind Mordred slammed shut, followed by a hissing noise as the room became sealed. A second later a noise from above sounded like someone switching on the central heating, and soon Gareth started choking. Mordred immediately mixed his water and air magical glyphs, just before Gareth dropped to his knees. A second later he was unconscious on the floor.

"That's not going to work," Mordred called out. "Daria, this is pointless." He waited for a few seconds before raising his arms. "You don't know much about sorcerers, I assume. No? Well, a few of us can mix our elements. It's very exciting; fire and air makes lightning, water and earth makes these awesome little golem things, and earth and fire does magma. Amazing stuff really, but it's all very flashy. Air and water is a little less flashy, but sort of more useful in my current circumstances. It lets me breathe. Anywhere. In any situation. A gas-filled room, in water, in a vacuum—I can breathe and talk just like normal. Funny when you think about it. I'm sure you didn't know I could do that, but now you do, so you might want to forgo the gas, as it's basically just wasting money for you at this point."

Mordred glanced down at an unmoving Gareth. He took his pulse and found nothing. "You didn't need to do that," Mordred said.

"Funny, though, isn't it," Daria said. "Angry yet, Mordred?"

Mordred walked over to the far door and placed a hand on it. The dwarven runes on the door made it impossible for his magic to open it, but that just made him angrier. "Open the fucking door."

"Let's wait, shall we."

Mordred closed his eyes and resigned himself to what was going to happen next. He walked back to Gareth and placed his hand on his chest, allowing his light magic to try and heal him, but nothing happened. Mordred needed to be sure; he needed to be totally certain that Gareth was already dead.

"Isn't that just wasting *your* time?" Daria asked.

Mordred removed the dagger he'd kept with him and slit Gareth's throat, cutting through the artery and placing his hands on the fresh blood that spilled from it. Gareth was dead, so it didn't pump freely, but there was enough for it to meet his needs. He'd considered using his own blood, but using someone else's was more potent, and he didn't want to exhaust himself by using his own energy to power his magic.

When his hands were covered in Gareth's blood, Mordred walked back over to the door and used the blood to paint a rune on it. "Open it," he said. "Last chance."

"Do your worst, Mordred."

The fact that his magic was useless against the walls and doors suggested that the runes had been placed inside them, which, without knowing exactly where they were, and what rune was used, meant that it would have been impossible to use the correct dwarven rune to counteract whatever Daria and her people had placed there. But Nate had spent some time teaching Mordred some of the more rudimentary original dwarven runes. Specifically one to increase the power of whatever runes were close to it. It was a rune that absorbed magical energy, but pouring too much in caused both the original runes and any rune close to it to explode.

Mordred used the blood on his hands to power his own magic before using the blood to draw the rune on the door. Once done, he poured more and more into the rune he'd drawn until it flashed and exploded. Mordred wrapped himself in a dense shield of air, stopping the explosion as the entire wall and door separating him from the next room vanished. The shock wave picked Mordred off the ground and flung him back over the chair in the center of the room.

"What have you done?" Daria screamed.

The dust settled, and Mordred saw that several rooms beyond were now missing large parts of their walls. He got to his feet and cracked his knuckles, removing the shield and considering using his water magic to wash his hands but deciding against it.

"Daria, I see a metal door in there. Is that an exit from this place?"

"You've destroyed it all!" she continued to shriek.

"Daria, can you hear me?"

"Fuck you, Mordred. I'm going to rend the flesh from your bones."

Mordred smiled. "Excellent, it'll save me the bother of having to search for you."

CHAPTER 17

Mordred

Mordred kicked the door in and discovered that it led to a long corridor with a set of lift doors at one end, and a door to another stairwell halfway down. He descended the stairs and went through the door at the bottom, into another hallway—although one with black tiles and dark-red walls. It had only two doors along it, so Mordred opened the first, which led into another staircase, presumably one that went around the giant maze above. He wondered if he had time to go back to the club level and kill the werewolf for making him go through the maze but decided it could wait. Someone else needed to feel his ire first.

He opened the second door and stepped into a massive open room with several couches, and a pool table in the center. A TV larger than any Mordred had seen before hung on the far wall, and there were dozens of beanbag chairs dotted around, along with an even greater number of beer bottles. There were more doors along the wall opposite him, and adjacent to where he stood an open door showed a large kitchen.

A werewolf already in his beast form left the kitchen and growled.

"You all live down here, I guess," Mordred said. "I assume those doors lead to bedrooms and bathrooms, that kind of thing. It strikes me more as a club for parties than anything else."

The werewolf pounced but didn't make it half the distance before a whip of air struck it in the chest, wrapping itself around the werewolf's torso, crushing it. Mordred removed the air, walked over to him, and punched a blade of ice through the werewolf's throat, expanding the blade until he'd decapitated it.

Mordred checked the kitchen but, apart from a particularly vicious-looking potato peeler on the counter, found nothing of note. He tried the door closest to him, which led to another large room, although this one appeared to hold only bookshelves, computers, and large piles of cash. The next door along led to another hallway, while the third and fourth just opened to rooms full of pillows and beds.

"Because every werewolf pack needs a good orgy room," Daria said over the loudspeaker.

"Oh, for fuck's sake, are you still there?" Mordred asked, exasperated from having to put up with the disembodied voice.

"I want you to know that there's a gift coming for you. I hope you enjoy it. I know I will."

Mordred waited in the middle of the room for whatever was about to appear but after ten seconds wondered if there was anything, or if Daria was just trying to get inside his head. A few seconds later the door to the hallway opened. A young woman walked into the room. She wore leather armor with what appeared to be runes drawn on it. She was close to Mordred's height, with short gray hair. She carried a pair of daggers that she tapped almost absentmindedly against one another.

"Hello, Mordred," Daria said. "Surprise."

"So, I assume you're the boss fight?"

Daria nodded. "That's one way of putting it. If we'd met under other circumstances, I might feel bad about what I'm going to do to you."

"If we'd met under other circumstances, I'd have killed you already. Whereabouts in Siberia are Elaine and the rest of her people?"

"You mean those who came looking for her, or the ones she was with when we took her? The ones who were with Elaine when we took her died here. Those who came looking for her—we sent them to Siberia. Do you know how we grabbed her?"

"Viktor told you, I assume."

Daria smiled. "Not Elaine. Those I worked with grabbed her. They brought them all here for safekeeping, until they were ready to take Elaine to Siberia. But the people who came looking for her. Well, that's a different story, isn't it? Turns out that money can buy allegiance. At least where Viktor is concerned. And we were so worried that he was working with Elaine."

"Elaine was looking for the people who were working with this cabal against her and Avalon. I assume you know who those people are."

"I know a little. Elaine thought she was so smart. Her investigation wasn't as covert as she'd like to believe. She didn't feel so smart when we started killing her people."

"You weren't so smart for keeping them alive. Gareth, the one you killed earlier, had a tracker on him. You unknowingly set yourselves up for me to find. And now you're going to tell me exactly where Elaine is, and then you're going to die."

"So, what's my incentive to tell you anything?"

"If you tell me what I want to know, you won't die screaming."

Daria's expression darkened. She tapped the daggers again and charged Mordred, who threw a gale of wind at her, trying to knock her back. The magic had no effect, and Daria slashed at Mordred, who was forced to dart back away from the blades.

"Rune-scribed armor. Your magic has no effect on me," Daria said, sounding as smug as possible.

"But you can't transform, either, so I guess we're both at a disadvantage."

Daria grinned and raised her hand, showing it turning into a were-wolf hand with elongated fingers and bladelike nails.

Mordred winked.

Daria moved to dart forward, but Mordred stepped toward her, which, judging from the expression of shock on her face, wasn't what she'd expected. Mordred smashed his forearm into her nose, breaking the bone and causing blood to pour from the wound. She tried to catch Mordred with one of her blades, but Mordred grabbed her wrist, ducked under her arm, and shoved her away when he came up behind her.

Daria touched her nose and lunged at him again, the blade in her still-human hand moving with incredible speed, causing Mordred to try and track them both. She got close to him on more than one occasion, cutting his forearms and chest, drawing blood and pain, but nothing that would be considered lethal.

After a few seconds of this, Mordred left himself open to attack and grabbed Daria's arm as she swiped at him. He pushed her arm down, stepped toward her, and head-butted her as hard as he could. She blinked, and before she could recover, Mordred threw her over his shoulder onto the ground, keeping hold of her arm and locking it at the elbow.

Mordred knew that in a test of strength he had no chance against the vastly stronger werewolf, but he had speed on his side and used that to his advantage as he broke Daria's arm and stomped her head into the floor before darting back. He wasn't trying to beat her up; there was little point in it. He was, however, trying to make her really angry. Something Mordred considered himself a bit of a specialist at doing.

Daria growled and rolled to her feet, her arm healing itself with a sickening crunch, causing her to wince. "That wasn't very nice," she said.

Mordred shrugged and threw a bottle at her, causing it to smash against her raised arm. He picked up a second bottle and threw it, but Daria dodged aside, and the bottle harmlessly broke apart after hitting the wall behind her.

"Are you quite done?" she asked.

"I'm just wondering why you're not the public face of this werewolf pack. Why does that idiot upstairs have to be it? Because he's a bit shit, if I'm honest."

"He's better with people," Daria said. "And I like to leave people guessing."

Mordred threw another bottle, this one partially full, and Daria caught it. "You're just making it worse for yourself," she said, tossing the bottle aside.

Mordred shrugged, slowly moving around the room, throwing whichever bottles he could find, making Daria dodge on more than one occasion.

"I've had enough of this!" Daria shouted.

"I kind of expected you to be better at this," Mordred said. "You're just standing there doing nothing of any particular consequence. It's less frightening and more slightly boring."

She sprinted toward Mordred, swinging the daggers at him, but he was already moving aside, around her. He smacked her around the back of the head with the palm of his hand and jogged over to the opposite wall. Daria charged again, and Mordred was unable to dodge as she put herself in his way, so he stepped into the path of the blade, using his hand to push the top of it down, slicing through his palm as it moved.

The shock on Daria's face was as evident as the pain on Mordred's. He grabbed hold of Daria's wrist and twisted it as he moved around her, forcing her off her feet and headfirst into the wall. She released her grip on the blade, and Mordred caught it, using it to cut across the back of her armor before moving away as she spun around.

Mordred created a ball of air in his hand, pouring more and more magic into it as Daria turned to face him, blood trickling down a nasty cut on her forehead.

"That's not going to work," Daria said.

"Let's see," Mordred replied, and threw the ball of air at Daria, who arrogantly stood her ground until she was blasted back through the wall behind her.

"I think it worked," Mordred called after her as pieces of plaster and brick crumbled to the ground. He tested the cut on his hand and found that it was still bleeding, and sore. The silver in the dagger would make it more difficult for his magic to heal it, but he was in no danger of dying from it. He grabbed a discarded T-shirt from the floor and tore one of the arms off, wrapping the fabric around his hand and making a fist to keep pressure on the cut.

A low, rumbling growl emanated from the hole in the wall, followed by a werewolf's hand, claws raking along the undamaged part of the wall, tearing part of it away with ease. Daria stepped through the hole a moment later, nearly six and a half feet of black-haired werewolf towering over Mordred.

"You took your armor off," Mordred said. "Shame, I guess we get to do this again."

Mordred blasted a torrent of air at Daria, who sprinted through it as if he had only wafted a piece of paper in her direction. She grabbed his knife arm with one massive hand and squeezed until Mordred released the dagger. He created a blade of ice to swing at Daria, but she threw him across the room, and he landed on the unforgiving wooden floor with a splintering crash.

She was on Mordred in an instant, picking him off the floor and smashing him into the nearest wall.

Pain wracked Mordred's body, and for a second he thought about just killing her. It would be easier to fight Daria without having to take her alive. It would still be a difficult fight, but he wouldn't have to worry about having his arms torn off while he tried to subdue her.

Mordred pushed the thought aside and poured a torrent of water into Daria's face, freezing it solid. She dropped him to the ground, and he rolled away, using the frame of the kitchen door to pull himself back to his feet. Daria smashed her massive fists against the ice, using her claws to tear it apart in seconds.

She turned back to Mordred and took a step forward as Mordred pushed himself away from the door and rolled his shoulders. "I was being nice," he said. "Let's try something else." He threw a ball of magical light toward Daria, who turned aside in time to stop the explosion from blinding her, but that gave Mordred time to hit her with another blast of air.

She spun away, colliding with a nearby couch and spiraling over it, breathing heavily as she got back to her feet before she flung the couch at Mordred with ease.

Mordred used his air magic to knock the couch aside, sending it into a nearby wall with a loud crash as a second quickly followed. He followed the same defensive strategy with the second couch but couldn't create enough power to stop Daria from charging into him, picking him off the floor, and driving him back through the open door into the kitchen.

Mordred reached out and grabbed the potato peeler as they barreled past, stabbing it into Daria's ear. She released Mordred and screamed in pain as he surrounded his hands with air magic and clapped them across each ear, driving the potato peeler further into Daria's skull. It wasn't silver, so wouldn't kill her, but Mordred knew it would hurt like hell. Blood flowed freely across the peeler, causing it to quickly become slick, with the unpleasant side effect of it being too slippery for Daria's massive hands to take hold of and pull free.

"I asked nicely," Mordred said. "Now this is me being less nice." He wrapped air around the potato peeler and, twisting it slightly, caused Daria to scream and drop to her knees.

She immediately exploded up from her kneeling position, clawing across Mordred's chest just as he raised a shield of magical air to protect him. She punched through the shield as if it were nothing, grabbed him by the throat, and smashed his head into the ceiling above before throwing him back through the door behind her.

Mordred used his air magic to land softly but couldn't avoid Daria, who collided with him, raining down blows as he was forced to constantly restrengthen his air shield as she tested the limits of its ability to protect him.

She punched through the shield, grabbed hold of his wrist, and tore free the makeshift bandage he'd applied. She brought her other hand down onto Mordred's chest, knocking the wind out of him. Daria took a long sniff of the blood that trickled down the still-open cut on his palm.

"You smell like food," she said.

"Last chance to surrender," Mordred said.

Daria laughed. "I thought we were already at being not very nice. I'm beginning to wonder why people were ever scared of you."

Mordred placed a hand on top of hers, as if trying to pry her fingers from his wrist. She laughed until he clamped his bleeding hand on her wrist and activated his blood magic.

The screams that left Daria's throat were deafening as tendrils of blood magic wrapped around her arm. They snaked up to her neck and around her throat, tightening and silencing her. Helpless, she clawed at the agony-causing magic with her free hand.

"I don't use my blood magic very much," Mordred said. He got back to his feet and brushed himself off. "It's far too addictive, for one. But I did offer nicely, and it turns out you're strong enough to ignore my magic. If I started throwing really powerful elemental magic around, I'd probably bring this whole building down on us, so I'd rather not do that."

Daria thrashed on the ground, clawing the wooden floor to pieces around her.

"I don't want to do this. I don't want to be the person who causes agony. And I don't want you to think that I'm taking any enjoyment out of it. Because this is simply a necessity. It has nothing to do with your species, or sex, or anything else about you. But you're not going to come quietly, so I'm going to have to make you."

Mordred loosed the noose around her throat, and Daria screamed something incomprehensible.

Mordred removed the blood magic, and Daria began to pant from relief.

"I'd rather not do that too much," Mordred said.

"Fuck you," Daria said. "Fuck you, your friends, your family, and everyone you ever cared about. When you're dead, I'm going to find everyone you love, and I'm going to tear their faces off. I'm going to feast on their soft meat."

Mordred sighed. "That the best you've got?"

"Use your blood magic again. Let yourself go."

"I'm not going to do that. But I don't need to use my blood magic to get you to talk. I just have to give you to her." He pointed at Morgan, who stood in the doorway. "You took your time."

"Werewolves take a lot to kill," she said. "I assume this one doesn't want to talk."

"I've tried very hard not to kill her. I've tried very hard to be the better man, but I'm exceptionally close to doing very horrible things to gain the information we need."

"Things you'd prefer I did?"

Mordred shook his head. "We're meant to be better than torture. We're meant to be above it. It doesn't work to get information. Never has."

"So, what is she going to do?" Daria asked.

Morgan threw a sorcerer's band to Mordred, and he clamped it around Daria's wrist before she could stop him. Daria instantly changed back into human, cursing with every second.

"She's going to do whatever she needs to do. She's going to kill you, Daria. She's going to take her time doing it, and she's going to enjoy it. Morgan was never someone who helped me kill, but she's become quite adept over the years in keeping people alive as a punishment for their actions. You're going to scream a lot in the coming hours." Mordred picked up a silver blade and passed it to Morgan. "I'll see you upstairs."

Morgan smiled and shrugged off her jacket, placing it on the chair beside her. "Take your time. I know I will."

Mordred left the room and sat in the hallway. He removed his mobile phone from his pocket and set the timer for five minutes. After three and a half, Morgan left the room, and behind her Daria lay on the floor, abject fear etched on her face. Mordred had heard no screams, had heard no sounds of violence.

"You okay?" he asked Morgan.

"No," she said. "I do not appreciate being the one to do that. I am not someone who enjoys tearing someone's mind apart. Polina gave me the sorcerer's band because she figured that Daria might talk if she could no longer use her werewolf abilities. She was only partially correct."

"How broken is her mind?"

"It's not. She was physically strong, but making her compliant was easier than many I've had to break in the past."

Mordred nodded. He knew that Morgan hated delving into the minds of others to force them to cooperate. It was something that could only be done on someone who had no abilities to wield, and she couldn't drag the information from them. Instead, Morgan could twist enough parts of a person's mind to make them compliant.

Mordred stood and placed a hand on Morgan's shoulder, squeezing slightly. "Thank you for this."

"For Elaine, right?" Morgan looked away. "I'm going to go drink something strong. I'll tell the others where you are."

Mordred entered the room and picked up a chair and blanket, tossing the latter to a naked Daria and placing the chair close to her.

"I'm sorry," Mordred said. "I know how it feels to have your mind torn apart. I wanted this to be done differently."

"She made me see things," Daria said, her voice shaky and full of fear.

Mordred nodded. "It's part of her magic. She can make people compliant, but only through either breaking them by showing their worst memories or fears or by removing something that made them want to fight. The stronger the mind, the more she has to delve into, and the shorter the period of helpfulness after. It's not a nice power to have. She doesn't like using it. You are a cruel and vicious person, but doing this to someone makes her feel guilty. She was never cut out to be like I used to be."

"Elaine is in Siberia," Daria said.

"I'm going to need a lot more than that," Mordred said.

"About fifty miles southeast of Tiksi, there's a small village. It's long since been abandoned. She's there."

"What's the village called?"

"It doesn't have a name. It used to be called Work Camp Forty-Two."

"It was a gulag?"

She nodded. "A long time ago prisoners were sent there, yes. Long before Stalin. It's an Avalon work camp, not a human one."

"Why did they send her there?"

"Those we work for knew she was investigating them. She started to look into the pack, hoping to use our connection as a way to find out who our allies are. She just overstepped her ability to remain in the shadows."

"I'm going to find her, and if she's hurt in any way, I'm going to put aside my newly found moral compass, come back here, and use your knives to make myself a werewolf coat."

There was a knock on the door, and Polina walked in with two of her agents. "We're here to take Daria into custody."

"If you have questions, ask now. She's in a talkative mood."

Mordred stood.

"Viktor escaped," Polina said.

"That's okay. I know where he'll run off to."

"We did a good thing here today."

"Maybe," Mordred said. "Lots of people died here. These were-wolves, and Daria in particular, have done their bit to spread terror and fear through this city."

"They won't be able to do that again."

"Whatever you do with them, keep it secret from your bosses until this whole thing blows over. One way or another, you'll be putting sights on your back if you announce you've taken them."

Polina nodded. "You should know there have been more attacks around the world. Something big happened in America, and several other cities have declared martial law. I'm not sure how much help we'll be to you from here on in."

"I knew it would only get worse," Mordred said, saddened at what he was sure meant the deaths of so many innocent people. "They're not done yet. Be careful."

"Take care, Mordred."

Mordred left the room, and the club soon after, telling Fiona and Diana to meet him at Viktor's house, as he needed time to himself, which was partially true. He'd been close to losing his temper with Daria. It had taken a lot for him to stay calm enough not to kill her or continue to use his blood magic. The use of it felt sweet inside of him; it had almost sung to him, wanting him to give himself to it. A blood leech was a sorcerer who relied on blood magic to the exclusion of all other magic, and for a long time Mordred had been among their number. It had taken his death to stop his need to use blood magic, but its aftereffects lingered in his memory even after all this time.

It wasn't long before he found a cab and took it back to Viktor's house. He let himself in, prepared what he needed, sat on the comfortable couch, and waited. It thankfully didn't take long for Viktor to come home, slinking through the front door as if he were burgling his own home.

"Hi, Viktor," Mordred said, causing the traitorous man to gasp in surprise.

"Mordred," Viktor said, switching on the lights of the front room. "I didn't expect—"

"Yes, I know. You didn't expect to see me here. You betrayed us to the werewolves."

"No, I never."

"Don't lie to me, Viktor. You didn't betray Elaine—that's the only thing keeping you living right now. But you did betray the people who came for her. Alan, Mac, and the others. You gave them up to the werewolves."

"I had to. With Elaine gone, so was my chance of being safe. I had to hedge my bets."

"The same thing you did with us. Why didn't you tell them about the tracker?"

"I had to hold some things back, just in case Elaine turned up again."

"You were trying to play both sides. Shame you were so damn bad at it. You betrayed her people; you betrayed me and my friends. You got people killed. Horrifically butchered by a group of frankly evil bastards. I can't just let that go."

"You're going to kill me?"

Mordred shook his head. "Nope." He stood and walked over to Viktor. "That's too easy." He hit Viktor in the face with a fist wrapped in air, dropping him stunned to the ground. He removed a pair of handcuffs and put them on Viktor before dragging him out of the house and down the steps just as the rest of Mordred's group arrived.

Diana left the car first. "You want him dead?"

Mordred shook his head. "I have another plan." He removed a detonator from his pocket and pressed the trigger. The explosion inside the house blew out the windows downstairs and made the ground shake. "Okay, that was a bit bigger than I'd expected."

The fire took the house quicker than even Mordred had taken into consideration, and within seconds angry flames leapt from broken windows.

"Why?" Viktor almost screamed.

"You sold people when I first met you, and I burned your house to the ground and took your hand, but I still left you with enough to continue on. You had the others in the village; you had Avalon, who was unaware of your crimes. Now you have nothing. You have no money, no house, no friends, no allies, and the second Polina arrives, no hope of ever seeing natural light again."

Everyone stood and watched the flames consume the house until part of the structure collapsed in on itself. Polina and her people arrived soon after and took Viktor into custody.

"Why?" he screamed again as he was led away. "Why not kill me? That would have been easier. That would have been quicker than what will happen to me once I'm taken into custody. You've taken everything else, why not my life?"

Mordred walked over to Viktor. "Because this way you know I took *everything* from you. I've left you a broken man. You seem to be under the impression that because I'm no longer full of murderous hate that I'm one of the good guys. I'm not. I'm the man who people like you should be very afraid of. I didn't kill you for three reasons. One, it's too easy. Two, you're now officially a cautionary tale for those who would ever betray me and my new sensibilities. And three, I did this because it's the cruelest thing I could think to do to you. I want those flames to be etched into your mind for the rest of your miserable existence. I want you to know that I spared your life, not out of kindness, but out of a desire to watch you crumble."

Viktor was dragged away by Polina's people and almost thrown into the back of a car.

"We'll take care of him," Polina said, offering her hand, which Mordred shook. "You are not what I expected."

"Yeah, I get that a lot these days," Mordred said.

"I hope you find Elaine, all of you," Polina said. "Be careful in Siberia. There are places there where Avalon's law is considered the enemy. Try very hard not to come back to Moscow anytime soon. I'm not sure we can take the excitement you bring with you. Besides which, there are rumbles of Avalon declaring open season on anyone who isn't affiliated. I don't want to give people an excuse to go after you for your past transgressions."

Mordred watched Polina and her people drive away.

"I have a friend who lives near the Siberian-Chinese border," Diana said. "She might not be thrilled about helping Avalon, but then she's not thrilled about anyone these days. She'll know the area."

"My husband is in a Siberian gulag," Fiona said. "Damn it all to hell."

"We'll find him," Remy said. "Obviously, we'll find him without the use of all those weapons we discovered. Thanks for setting them all on fire, by the way, Mordred. Very helpful."

"I like to give you a challenge," Mordred said. "Also, I forgot all about them. I was a bit angry."

"It's a good thing we're awesome without them," Remy said.

Fiona walked away without another word.

"She's close to cracking," Diana said.

"Do we have transport to this place?" Remy asked.

"Already being arranged," Nabu said. "Another helicopter will take us as close as possible. We might have to hike some of the way, though."

"That's fine," Mordred said. "Let's just get going. I plan on finding these people before they can try to hide."

"Are you okay?" Morgan asked him as everyone else bundled into the car beside them.

"I should ask you the same thing."

"I'm fine," Morgan assured him.

"I'll be good once we're there. I just want this done. Elaine knew I'd come after her. She knew that if she didn't make our meeting in New York I'd track her down. I just hope we can get there before they decide she's too much hassle to keep alive."

"We'll find her," Morgan assured him. "Alive and well. She's too valuable to kill."

Mordred sat in the car without a word. He hoped that Elaine was too valuable to hurt. He needed to find her, not just because she was family, or because he cared, or even because she could help stop Avalon from falling into disarray, but because Nate's life depended on her information about the prophecy. Mordred would gamble with his own life—he was used to it—but not with the lives of his friends. He'd go through hell to keep them safe, especially after having done so much to hurt them over the centuries. On the other hand, he was certain that Alan and Mac were not valuable. And if their captors had murdered either of them, he was going to bury those responsible. That's the thing about Siberia: there's an awful lot of places to make people vanish so that they're never seen again.

CHAPTER 18

Nate Garrett

En route to America

We were over halfway from the Wolf's Head compound to America when more details of the atrocity of what had happened in North Carolina came through to us. Several sorcerers had assaulted those watching an American football game, killing several hundred as the human police tried to stop them.

I watched the news on the BBC as it unfolded, with more and more information coming in about the terrorist attack. "The humans aren't prepared for this," I said. "They're getting slaughtered."

"Olivia sent me a message," Selene said from the seat across the aisle from me. "Several off-duty LOA agents were in attendance and managed to stop the attack. If not for them, the death toll would be in the thousands, not hundreds."

I rubbed my eyes. It had been a long few days. "Even so, the humans will be less than happy at having Avalon involve themselves. We're meant to protect them—that's sort of the first thing about them not knowing we exist. Now they know we exist, know we can kill them, and can't do anything to stop us. I'm guessing they're going to be clamoring to do something about it."

"The human governments will calm things," Lucifer said. "They'll say the right things and let Avalon do its job."

"You hope," Zamek said, opening his eyes for the first time since we'd taken off.

"Avalon has to do something," Sky said. "Otherwise what's the point?"

"Not really sure how much worse it can get," I said. "I know, it can always get worse."

I looked out the jet window as time slowed and Erebus appeared sitting across from me.

He waved.

"Now?" I asked. "Seriously?"

"There are some things I mentioned you needed to know. Well, now is as good a time as any."

"Fine," I said, exasperated. "What is it?"

"You remember that your mother told you I was created by her and your father?"

"Yes. I remember asking you about it, and you dumping me back in normal time."

"Well, now is the time. The information that has been gathering in my head has had time to settle, and I need you to know some things. Some things that might be important in the coming future."

I looked over at Selene, who was seemingly frozen in place. "And what things are they?"

"The last mark on your body—it isn't what you think it is. The hidden one, the one on your soul, that's for another time, but that last mark needs unlocking. And it's going to happen soon."

"Why? Why now?"

"Because it is. Some things just happen when the time is right. And this is one of those things. I can feel the mark's power ebbing away. I can feel what's inside of me wanting to leave, wanting to join with you."

"And then you'll vanish?"

"Not for a while yet, no. You'll need to have your full power, and you won't have that at least until that last blood-curse mark on your psyche is gone."

"Okay, so what is this last physical mark?"

"It's what will unlock your last omega magic. But more than that, it contains information."

"About what?"

"A lot of things. Information that will slowly trickle into your mind over the coming months. Information about the past, about people, about different ways of using your magic. There's a lot in there, and it can't all come at once. You'll need to be patient."

"So if this last mark unlocks my last omega magic, and it contains info, what does the one on my psyche do?"

"Presumably it's the last mark that will give you full access to everything you should have as a sorcerer. You were born to be a weapon. A weapon so powerful and horrific that no one would ever want to use it. You were the nuclear option of the day. And Hera and her companions discovered this and forced a change in everything. They tried to have you killed, and then for some reason they stopped. I don't know why. I assume whoever they work for forced them to allow you to grow.

"Your parents created me. They wanted someone who would protect you, and they were aware of a nightmare's true identity. They came to me and asked for my help."

"To *you*?"

"Erebus. The actual Erebus."

"You're alive?"

"I was. I have no idea if I still am. I was a sorcerer. Like you I could use shadow magic, but I could also use mind magic. And when you were born, I agreed to place a piece of myself inside the nightmare that inhabited your body. Neither you nor the nightmare would be aware of it until you'd gained enough power that the nightmare was close to being able to take control and move you on to the next level. Your parents believed that by doing this they would help the transition from a normal sorcerer to a sorcerer on a level that you were destined to be. Unfortunately, instead of just leaving a piece of myself, I merged my entire mind with your nightmare. The level of power inside you was just too much to only give it a piece. So, I've been in here ever since, unable to know who I really am."

I stared at Erebus for several seconds. "I'm so sorry for what you've lost."

Erebus waved my words away.

"The Fates said I would turn into a monster who killed a lot of people," I said. "You think that Hera found out about that possibility and figured it would help her in the long term?"

"That is possible. On a happier note, it's a pleasure to finally meet you."

"And you couldn't tell me this earlier because my marks ensured you could only tell me a portion of what you knew?"

"You had to be ready."

"And what makes you think I'm ready now?"

"I don't get to decide that; your body does. And your body wants those marks gone. You're angry, and hurting, and you want someone to unleash that on. They're using *your* name to murder people, they're hunting you and your friends, and now these people are using Shadow Falls and Galahad to spread terror. I'm positive you're close to losing your temper."

I cracked my knuckles. "I can't afford to lose my temper."

"Why? You think that doing so will make things worse?"

"Is that what will remove my last mark, losing my temper? Because I've lost it plenty over the years and no marks vanished."

"I don't know exactly what will cause it to go; I just know that it's happening. I know how you're feeling, and I know that I needed to talk to you. Once the mark is gone, there will be one left, and I have no idea how you're going to lose it. It's not like the others; it's not affected by memories or power. It's something else. And I don't know what it will take to finally make yourself whole. But you'll figure it out. I have that faith in you."

"Do you know who my father is?"

"No. I believe that's locked behind whatever is in your head. Your mother loved you, Nate. I was there when you were born. She loved you so much. She left with you, moved to Constantinople to keep you safe. When this is over, you'll need to find her."

"If she's alive."

"I'm sure she is. She has your tenacity, and your stubbornness."

"So, we're not going to pretend that you're just me anymore?"

"No, I am Erebus, and I am a primordial god. Or was considered one."

"You kept the secrets of sorcery from people. Told them that nightmares were dangerous."

"I did. Or at least I helped. It was for the best, or we thought it was for the best. A lot of people turned into nightmares and couldn't handle it. They went insane, murdered, committed suicide, and other things that we needed to try and stop. Telling people that nightmares were a curse, were evil, was the best way to do it, even if it meant that a large number of sorcerers would never achieve their fullest potential."

"What happens to you when you vanish completely?"

"I have no idea. I imagine I'll fade from existence. I don't even know where my body is."

"If I can find your body, can I put you back in it?"

"Still unsure. Lots of questions still to be answered. For now, I remain. And now you know the truth about who I am, and how I came to be here. You have to fight, Nate. You have to fight everyone who would destroy everything your parents sacrificed to keep you safe."

"Merlin wasn't the best candidate to put me with."

"Merlin is not the man he once was. I do not know how or why he changed, but there is something dark inside of him that was never there before. I sensed it when you fought in Camelot. I didn't know how I sensed it, but with great power comes great sensory abilities. Isn't that how it goes?"

"No."

"Well, I can't be perfect. I've got a lot of your memories in here." Erebus tapped his head. "Tommy has said a lot of pop-culture references over the years. They jumble up a bit."

"I don't know if I can do this."

"Of course you can—you're Nathanial Garrett. Your mother was essentially the greatest warrior the Norse ever knew. I once saw her punch out a troll. She was the kind of person you didn't cross unless you'd decided that breathing was best done by other people. She terrified her enemies. And you did the same as Hellequin. You didn't have her power then, you didn't have her knowledge of so much, and yes, Hellequin is now forever dead to you, but that just means that people need to know who Nate Garrett is. Make your enemies tremble, Nate. Make them fear you."

Erebus stood and walked over to me. He bent down and kissed me on the forehead. "In a different time, I would have been called your godfather, I think. I would have loved you like a son. I am proud of you, and what you've become. Your parents would be, too. I think you're ready. Go forth and conquer, Nathanial Garrett."

Erebus vanished, and I gasped as pain wracked my body.

"Nate?" Selene asked. "Nate, are you okay?" She moved over to me as the pain subsided.

I pulled up my T-shirt and watched the last mark vanish. "We need to land," I said. "Really fast."

"We're a few hours from being able to do that," Sky said. "What's happening?"

"The last visible mark is gone," I said as my vision began to change. The world around me took on a purple haze, with dots of various sizes all over it. I looked down at the table in front of me and saw dozens of small dots. I instantly knew what they meant. They were weaknesses. The larger the dot, the larger the weakness. I placed a finger on one of the dots and pushed, but nothing happened.

"Nate?" Zamek asked, tapping me on the shoulder.

I turned to him and discovered that, unlike everything else, he had no purple haze or dots, and neither did Selene, Sky, or Grayson.

"Matter magic," Grayson said, looking at the purple glyphs that adorned my arms and hands. "What are you seeing?"

"Purple. Everything is purple."

"You okay?" Selene asked.

I nodded. "I'm sleepy. My brain has taken a lot in all at once. It's difficult to compute." I looked around the cabin. "I see weaknesses. Hundreds of them. Each one a way to break something if enough force is applied at that exact spot."

"Like this jet?" Sky asked.

I nodded. "Your father needs to have that hairline crack in the wall looked at. It's not dangerous, but even so. It looks like someone punched it."

Sky looked a little sheepish. "I had someone fix it."

"They did a bad job, then. Or a good job, and I can just see the imperfections. Not in you, though. None of you have any weaknesses. I think this magic only works on nonliving matter. And I can't tell how much force exactly will need to be applied to break it, just that it would break with enough force."

"You sound a bit out of it," Selene said. "Like you've been awake for a week."

"I feel like it, too," I told her, and closed my eyes. "Just wake me up when we get there. I'll try not to blow the jet up on the way."

"Can you do that?" Zamek asked. "Because that sounds like something we should be worried about."

There was a moment of silence.

"I have no idea," Sky said. "Doc, you're the sorcerer."

"I doubt he'll blow the plane up. He might break a few things by accident. We'll keep an eye on him."

I fell asleep soon after, and when I woke up I was in a large SUV outside a bar called the Mill. Selene was beside me with Zamek next to her. Grayson and Sky sat up front with the latter behind the wheel. I recognized the bar from my last visit to Portland, Maine, and figured we must have driven there from wherever the jet had landed.

"You okay?" Selene asked as I rubbed my eyes.

"I think so," I told her. "My vision is back to normal. Did you carry me into the car?"

"Didn't have much choice," Selene said. "We couldn't wake you."

"Thanks. Apparently I needed it." I opened the car door and stepped out into the cold air, using my fire magic to keep me warm.

"You feeling good, though, yes?" Selene asked after joining me outside. As a dragon-kin connected to the moon, and able to shoot ice out of her mouth, she rarely felt the cold in the same way as most people.

I nodded. "I feel good. Great, actually. Hungry, though."

Grayson passed me a bagful of sandwiches and chocolate. "We picked up a few on the way. I figured you might want some calories."

I hungrily devoured two chocolate bars, several bottles of water, and a packet of sandwiches before offering the bag around. With no takers, I placed it back in the car, but not before eating a third chocolate bar.

"Feel better?" Sky asked.

I opened another bottle of water and drank it in one go. "Pretty much."

We all entered the bar just as my phone went off. I checked the screen: it was Olivia. "You guys go. I'll catch up." I left the bar and answered the phone.

"Nate, we have big problems," she said before I could talk.

"I know, we're sort of living it right now," I told her.

"Well, allow me to add to your issues. Lucie is missing. Not officially, but I can't get hold of her, and no one I know has seen her in several days."

I pushed the anger I felt away. It would do little good to lose my temper. "First Elaine and now Lucie. Someone is going after Elaine's people."

"It gets worse, Nate."

"Go on," I said with a sigh of frustration. It *always* got worse.

"Officially, Lucie has put a bounty on your head. There's an arrest warrant out for you."

"How much?"

"Fifteen million dollars."

"Fucking hell," I almost shouted.

"Yeah, just make sure you keep an eye out for anyone who might want to cash that in."

"So, someone's using Lucie's name while she's missing. Great. What about you?"

"I'm fine. You don't need to worry about me."

"Stay that way."

"Yeah, that's the other reason I'm calling. I've been removed from my post as head of the LOA."

I leaned up against the nearest wall. "They can't get to you physically, so they're cutting your legs out from under you."

"That's my guess, too. I'm not in Camelot; Lucie was. We'll find her, Nate. Elaine, too."

"Speaking of, have you told Mordred about Lucie?"

"No, we can't get hold of anyone. Last I heard from Diana was they were heading to Siberia. Not a lot of phone reception in the middle of nowhere."

"Siberia? I guess if you're going to hide Elaine, you do it somewhere remote. Let me know if you find out anything else."

"Arthur's on his way to you. I've been informed he's upped the deadline. He'll be leaving first thing in the morning. You have about twelve hours. I think he's worried about people wanting to take control of Avalon for themselves. It's a bit of trial by fire."

"Hopefully I'll have convinced Galahad to speak to him by then. Any word on the attacks?"

"They're continuing at an alarming pace. Some countries are worse than others. There are a lot of people dead, Nate. And even more scared and worried. Making peace won't be easy once this is done. Humanity knows about us. That's not just going to go away."

"We'll figure that out when we've stopped My Liege from killing people. Stay safe."

"You, too."

I hung up and went back inside the bar, where I was greeted by Rebecca Dean.

She wore a black suit with deep-red high heels. Her hair, tied up in a bun, was dark brown and her eyes a deep blue. She was a few inches shorter than me, even with the heels on. "Nate Garrett, I wondered when you'd finally turn up." Her voice had a slight Irish tinge to it but otherwise could easily have placed her as from New York.

"Rebecca, I assume my companions have already been and gone."

Rebecca. She was a guardian, and an incredibly powerful one. Every now and again a guardian develops some alchemist-like powers, something Zamek confirmed to me had to do with the dwarven nature of the realm gate. Rebecca had not only developed those powers, but had also managed to wield them as if she were born with them. So long as she stayed within several miles of the realm gate, she'd retain those abilities and be next to invulnerable. Rebecca was in charge of one of two realm gates that linked the Earth realm to Shadow Falls. She also didn't like me very much, although the fact that I'd saved her king's life more than once brought me more than a little leeway on that matter. "There are people who are less than happy that you're here."

"Including you?"

Rebecca smiled. "Yes, including me. You're a magnet for trouble, and that's trouble my king doesn't need."

"Not 'my liege' anymore? I remember you calling him that. Now whoever is doing all of this wants people to think that Galahad and Shadow Falls are involved."

"I heard. I stopped using 'my liege' when it became apparent that certain forces outside of Shadow Falls were using it for less-than-stellar reasons. Much like Hellequin, I assume."

"Yeah, it's been a shit few days all around."

"It got worse. Have you heard anything from Avalon news? The head of the SOA, Lucie Moser, has put a fifteen-million-dollar bounty on your head."

"Yeah, I just heard. Lucie has been taken by the same people who took Elaine. Someone has hijacked her communications. They're using it to get the SOA to do things like take me into custody. I get the feeling that while Lucie and Olivia were hunting down the Reavers a few years ago, eliminating them from Avalon, this cabal was making sure its own people were in place."

"That seems about what I would expect from Avalon," Rebecca said. "But that doesn't mean you're going to be welcomed with open arms."

"You believe me, then?"

"Selene told me about Elaine. Her I believe."

"What else has Avalon said? I assume you have ways of hearing chatter."

Rebecca smiled again. It was a lot closer to sharklike than I was comfortable with. "I'm waiting for intel to come through. Until then we have only the official channels. And they're saying that Hellequin is murdering innocent humans the world over."

"You know it's not me."

"What I know and what I can prove are two different things. If the SOA has gone rogue, the intelligence services would be the first place to start spreading that corruption. Any ideas as to who might be causing these troubles?"

I thought about it for a second. "My guess is Hera has had Lucie removed from play. But as she's in London, and there's no way she'd give that up, I imagine it'll be one of her flunkies who's behind Lucie's vanishing. Can I go to Shadow Falls now? I'd really like to stop a war."

Rebecca motioned for me to follow her. "Sky and Selene said that Avalon has given you forty-eight hours to try and get Galahad to allow Avalon forces into Shadow Falls. He's never going to allow that."

"We have less than twelve hours to go," I said. "I just need to convince Galahad to talk to Arthur outside of Shadow Falls. If I can get them to talk, maybe we can get them to help one another."

"Arthur has been convinced that Shadow Falls is involved. Hell, a lot of people are probably convinced, especially considering these assholes have been writing the words *Shadow Falls* in the blood of their enemies. I assume you've been keeping an eye on the news. That's not something the human authorities have been releasing to the public."

"So, it's even worse than this Hellequin asshole spouting off about Shadow Falls. They're actively promoting their alliance."

"And Arthur is being led down the wrong path. He's coming here, and he's going to demand that Galahad come with him to answer for these accusations. And Galahad will refuse."

"Arthur swore to me that he'd arrive without his people, that he just wants to talk to Galahad and find the truth. I'm hoping Arthur demands nothing."

"You have faith in your friend. I have faith that Arthur can't take a whole army through a realm gate. He'd be slaughtered. The most we've ever sent through here is about forty people."

"What about the other gate?" The second realm gate had remained hidden for hundreds of years, known only to a few. Unfortunately one of those few had been a deposed king of Shadow Falls who wanted his crown back and was willing to align himself with a group of psychopaths to do it. A group of psychopaths who were, as it turned out, also aligned with the same group using the phrase "My Liege" a lot.

"The second gate has the entire town of Stratford around it. Arthur would need more than an army to get there."

"But the gate is larger there. You can take more people in."

"That's true, but that is sovereign Shadow Falls. The people there are trained warriors and won't hesitate to stop anyone from trying to access it without permission."

"I hope you're right," I said as we entered the realm-gate room.

CHAPTER 19

Nate Garrett

The Shadow Falls realm gate was made of similar materials as all the others, but the one in Portland glowed a dim purple. Getting from the bar area to the realm-gate room had consisted of going through several dozen guards and more than a few doors that required retina scans. Arthur might turn up here and demand to see Galahad, but this was Shadow Falls territory and if Arthur wasn't careful he could find himself in a fight that would last for months, if not longer. The levels below the bar had stockpiles of weapons and supplies to last a long time. And I doubted that Arthur would want to turn a major human city into rubble just to get to Galahad. But clearly there were people within Avalon who would stop at nothing to start this war.

Rebecca was one of half a dozen guardians who worked with the realm gate I was asking to use. Half a dozen almost-immortal warriors who would defend this place to the last, so long as they remained close to the gate. If Arthur tried to force his way through, he'd need to get the guardians to open the gate—which would never happen—or make his own. And that was a lengthy process. Either way, if Avalon did try to take Shadow Falls by force, it wasn't going to be a quick fight.

One of the guards in the realm-gate room activated the gate. "Harrison isn't going to be pleased to see you," Rebecca told me.

"He's never pleased to see me. The man lives and breathes to be as miserable as possible at all times." I stepped through the gate into Shadow Falls.

The realm-gate room in Shadow Falls was inside a temple on top of a hill just outside of the massive sprawling city by the name of Solomon. When I was last in the realm, a million people lived there, and from what I'd heard that number had increased over the years. Being a king suited Galahad a lot more than most people I'd met in the same position.

I stood in the realm-gate room as several guards and guardians watched me with a kind of concerned interest. I guessed that my friends had arrived and delivered the bad news. The realm gate shut off, and Harrison strode toward me as if he owned the place, which, because he was the head of Shadow Falls security, wasn't far off from the truth.

Harrison was huge. Imposingly so. He had the kind of physique that people only achieve after years of injecting themselves with large quantities of steroids. His ginger hair was still long, and tied back in a ponytail. In fact he didn't appear to have changed in any way since I'd last seen him several years earlier.

"I am not happy to see you," Harrison said, his voice deep and full of bass.

"Yeah, well the feeling is mutual."

He brandished a sorcerer's band and passed it to me. "You need to wear one of these. Don't argue. It's law. All sorcerers wear one. Your magic is unpredictable here, and after Leonardo figured out about microscopic pieces of magic being in the air, it's too dangerous to allow you to wander around without it."

Shadow Falls, much like Tartarus, had a strange effect on my magic. In the case of Shadow Falls, using my magic ignited the magic that existed all around Shadow Falls with devastating, spectacular results. Even a small amount of use would quickly become out of control. Strangely enough, the last time I was in the realm, Leonardo had told me that sorcerer's bands didn't work, something that Harrison was keen to explain.

"Leonardo makes them," he said. "They use a different type of rune than the bands on Earth realm. They'll let you still feel your magic, but not use it. It's thought of as being more humane."

I sighed and put the bracelet on, clicking it into a locked position.

"Now do something small with your magic to check," Harrison said.

"Fine." I tried to create a small flame in my hand, but no matter how much I concentrated, I couldn't make one. "Satisfied?"

"Excellent. Nathan Garrett, you will come with me to the prison, where you will be questioned as a possible spy for Avalon."

I thought it was just a really bad joke until I saw several guards place their hands on their swords. And then I just got really angry. "Have you lost your fucking mind? Haven't we been through this already? I figured you'd trust me after I saved your king's life on more than one occasion."

"That was then," Harrison said. "Come quietly, or I'll be forced to hurt you."

"You really are a dumb fucking idiot."

Harrison punched me in the mouth, knocking me to the ground, and my first reaction was to cleave him in half. I forced myself to calm and turned back to him. "Was that necessary?"

"In the last few days, a man calling himself Hellequin has claimed responsibility for countless acts of terrorism on the Earth realm. You used to go by that name. I'm not saying you're guilty, but we need to find out one way or the other. I can't allow someone to come into my realm if there's a shred of evidence that suggests they will cause problems. Not after the murders of the last few weeks. You'll be taken for questioning, and if I deem you to be uninvolved in these terrorist activities, then, and only then, will you be allowed to see Galahad."

"Wait, you think I'm involved with murders? What murders?"

"That's what the questioning you will undergo will determine. You will be placed in the prison, with your friends, until it's determined what kind of threat you pose to this realm. And if you resist . . ."

Harrison unhooked the massive hammer that hung from his back. He placed the head of the weapon on the ground beside me. "We'll find a more *permanent* solution to the problem."

I got back to my feet and allowed the guards to take me away. There was no point coming up with a witty remark, or threats—they wouldn't have done me any good. Harrison was stubborn and arrogant, and had been out to try and find some reason to validate his hatred of me for decades. I thought we'd moved past it when we'd fought side by side, but apparently I was wrong. I only hoped that we could sort all this out before Arthur and Avalon arrived and things became considerably worse.

I was led out of the temple and into a waiting horse-drawn carriage.

"So, there have been murders in the realm?" I asked the guard beside me.

"Yes. I'm not allowed to talk about it more than that."

"Okay, what are you allowed to talk about?" I looked around. "I see Leonardo didn't get the crystals to power vehicles."

"They kept blowing up," said one of the three guards who got in the back of the carriage with me.

Silence descended for the rest of the journey, until we reached the prison outside the city.

"Well, that's new," I said as I left the carriage, looking up at the huge building that had been built into the very mountain. The dark rock stood out against the green that surrounded us. I didn't even understand how we were going to get up there without a helicopter or something. It was hundreds of feet above where we stood.

"In there," the guard who'd spoken to me earlier said. He pointed to the mouth of a nearby cave next to a small fort.

Six guards took me into the cave and down a set of steps to a lift that was big enough to take a tank. Small purple crystals glowed in the gloom, and the guards took me onto the lift and pressed one of two buttons on the panel inside. The metal doors slowly closed, and we began to ascend.

"Glad to see the crystals were used for something," I said after a minute still ascending. "How long does this take?"

"Eight minutes," the guard said. "We created the prison when it was obvious that we needed a place to put people who didn't want to live by our rules. The palace dungeon was no longer deemed acceptable. We can't move the lift quickly, as our alchemists discovered that it makes the rock shake too much. We've been trying to figure out a way to get around it. Eight minutes each way is a long time."

We went back to silence after that for the remainder of the ride, until the lift stopped with a violent shake. The guard pressed the same button he had last time, and the doors began opening. The seven of us left the confines of the lift and walked down a long corridor that had been seemingly carved out of the mountain.

"Your dwarf friend," the guard said. "Zamek. He really a true dwarf?"

I nodded.

"He could teach us a lot about alchemy."

"He could, but you've imprisoned him, and he tends to take things like that personally."

"It's not like we're doing this out of spite."

I stopped and turned back to the guards, three of whom dropped their hands to their swords. "Oh, grow up. I'm not going to hurt you. And yes, this is personal. This is because Harrison is a complete fucking idiot who thinks with his biceps and wants to get one over on me."

"He is doing what he thinks is best for Shadow Falls," the guard replied. "And you haven't been here the last few months. Things happened."

"Those murders again?"

The guard looked away, clearly annoyed that he'd said anything. "Like I said, I've been ordered to remain quiet about it."

I tried to push down my frustrations, but part of them still bubbled over. "He's doing what he thinks is best for him. He's doing what he thinks is best to show everyone that he's in charge. Where is Galahad? What's he doing? Will he even be informed that we're here?"

"I don't know. That's not my job. My job is to protect my kingdom, and Harrison is my commander, so I do as he tells me."

I was about to argue but thought better of it. "Just show me to my cell."

It didn't take long before we'd reached the end of the hallway, where the guard knocked on part of the wall, which moved aside like a door and not solid rock. "We've got Nate Garrett," the guard said. "Harrison says he should be put with his friends. He'll need to be interrogated sooner rather than later. He seems to have important news he has to get to the king."

"Do I tell you how to do your job?" the thin, bald prison guard said. "No, no I don't. I'll decide when he gets interrogated, and Harrison has already asked that he be part of it."

"Of course he fucking did," I snapped.

The prison guard raised a small wooden club in my direction. "Did I ask you to speak?"

"You know that once Galahad knows I'm here, I'm going to get out," I said.

He thought about it for a second, and I could almost see the calculations in his head as he tried to figure out just how much trouble he would be in once I got out.

"You really want to piss me off more than I already am?" I asked, pointing him in what was hopefully the right direction.

"You behave, we won't have a problem," the guard said, lowering his club and shrugging as if he was in no way doing that because of what I'd said.

I turned to the guard who had spoken to me on the way to the prison. "Thank you for not being an asshole."

"I understand your anger at this situation, but we have to make sure you're not here to undermine or hurt us. I'm sure it'll be resolved soon."

"Hopefully before Avalon turns up with an army," I said, and walked through the hole in the wall, which closed behind me.

"You follow me," the prison guard said. "You behave, we won't have a problem."

"You said that already. I'm not here to cause issues. I'm here to talk to your king. As I have said more times than I care to remember."

The prison guard said nothing else as he and four others escorted me through the prison. Occasionally we'd come to a place in a wall where there was no way of going further, and one of the guards would use their alchemy to create a door for us. Eventually we reached what appeared to be a cellblock, where most of the cells appeared to be sealed with rock, with only a small, cat-flap-sized hole in each one. Each hole had several metal bars on it, making escape impossible for anyone over three inches wide.

After descending a set of stairs and moving through yet another wall, I found myself in a large room with four cells along the far wall. These cells had no rock covering the entrances and consisted of only the metal bars. The cells were large, easily the same size the lift had been, and most appeared to have a barred window.

Lucifer and Zamek were in one cell. Another held Sky and Selene. I was led toward the cell between them and told to go inside. One of the guards placed a hand on the bars, and they almost melted into the floor. I stepped inside, and the bars were quickly replaced.

"Behave," the prison guard said.

I ignored him and looked around at my new room. There was a bunk bed against one wall, with two comfortable-looking mattresses. A small desk and chair sat against the opposite wall, with paper and several pens on it. I assumed they weren't too worried about people using the pens to try and assault the guards. There was a toilet and sink next to the table. I walked over to the window and looked out over the city of Solomon far below.

"Nice view if nothing else," Zamek said from the cell beside me.

"So, we can hear one another," I said. "That's useful."

"Can't use my alchemy, though," Zamek said. "There are runes on the cell. I think they're written into the very rock of the prison. It's not an ideal venue for an impressive and bold breakout."

"There's nowhere to break out to," Sky said. "We're quite literally on top of a mountain. It's freezing outside, but nice and warm in here even though there are open holes in the side of the cell. That's some fairly serious rune work."

"Thank you," a voice said from the far end of the room outside the cells. "It took a lot of going back and forth to get it to work."

"Leonardo," I said as he walked into view. "It's been a while."

Leonardo had the appearance of a man who was in his mid- to late forties. He had a neatly trimmed white beard, which matched his hairstyle. "Nathaniel, it's good to see you. Not so good to see you in jail. We'd best be doing something about that."

"Yeah, how?" I asked.

"I'm just waiting for Antonio, and then we'll arrange everything."

"You're going to break us out of jail?" Lucifer asked. "Won't that make you an enemy of the state?"

"Probably, but there are more important things at play here."

"Leonardo, we're ready!" Antonio shouted as he entered the room through a newly formed hole in the wall.

"Hello, Antonio. What's going on?" I asked.

Antonio was taller than me by several inches, and barrel chested. He was bald and usually wore a smile no matter how stressful the situation.

He was the perfect antidote to Leonardo, who, for all of his intelligence, had a tendency to fixate on one thing at the expense of all others. "Nate. Essentially we know what's happening, and you need to see something."

"What?" I asked.

"A prison," Leonardo said.

"We're in prison," Selene pointed out.

"An older prison," Leonardo clarified. "Much older."

"And what does that have to do with anything?" I asked. Sometimes getting answers from Leonardo was hard work. It was difficult being the smartest man everywhere he went, and he tended to think everyone had the same level of knowledge that he did, which often made for confusing conversations.

"Ah, I've gotten ahead of myself. Essentially Galahad wasn't available, so when I heard that your friends had been captured, it was only a matter of time before I knew you'd be along. Then it was simply a matter of slowly using our alchemy to tunnel up and around the prison to get here, avoiding patrols and anything unpleasant. After all, I designed the place."

"So, who arranged all of this?" I asked.

"Caitlin," Antonio said. "Galahad's daughter."

"I know who she is," I said. "I brought her here. I introduced her to Galahad. I still don't understand why you're breaking us out. Why hasn't Caitlin gone to Galahad to get him to let us out?"

"No time. Galahad is off to the north, dealing with some unpleasantness."

"What does that mean?"

"I'll explain later. But right now we need to go."

Leonardo and Antonio placed their hands on the floor in front of our cells, and the bars melted, freeing us. They walked over to the far side of the room and touched the wall, creating a door to step into where purple light glowed beyond.

"Originally, I was just going to get you out of the prison. We have a problem, which Caitlin and I think you can help with. But seeing as he's with you, I think it would be best if you saw something."

"By 'he' you mean me?" Lucifer asked.

Leonardo nodded. "There's something inside the mountain I think you need to see."

"Yes, a prison. You already said," I told him.

Leonardo paused. "Yes, but it's not just the prison. There's something else."

"What?" Sky asked.

"Runes," Leonardo said. "Elven runes."

Now that I hadn't been expecting.

CHAPTER 20

Mordred

Siberia, Russia

The helicopter ride from Moscow to the middle of nowhere fifty miles southeast of Tiksi was about as unpleasant a journey as Mordred had ever taken. Not just because of the wind, and the snow, not just because of the freezing cold that seeped into the helicopter despite the heater being on, but because of the low mood that everyone felt. They'd discovered where Elaine was being held, or at least where she'd been taken to, but their time in Moscow had taken a heavy toll.

Morgan hadn't spoken to Mordred since they'd left the city, and he knew the signs that said she wanted to be left alone. If they'd been anywhere else, she'd probably have vanished for a few days, but instead she'd retreated inside her own mind. Mordred knew the effect using her mind magic to make people more compliant—or break their minds in more extreme cases—had on her. The fact that she couldn't use that magic without exceptional concentration didn't make it any easier. She had to purposely stop what she was doing and force herself into the psyche of another living being. Cruelty was not something she found easy. It was the thing that over the centuries he'd found most endearing about her. No matter what barbaric acts Mordred carried out, she never lowered herself to his level. She was better than him. And he admired and loved her for it.

"Landing in sixty seconds," the disembodied voice of their pilot said into their headsets.

Mordred gave a thumbs-up and tried to smile, but he didn't much feel like being all that celebratory, and it came out as more of a grimace, which made Diana laugh.

"Glad someone still has a sense of humor," Mordred said. "I think I left mine in Moscow."

"You haven't even made a *Mario* joke, or hummed that cursed tune," Remy said. "I'm beginning to wonder if you're feeling okay. I forgot to ask: How was your nightclub fight?"

"You know, you build these things up in your head and they're never quite as good in practice as they are in theory."

"Like threesomes," Diana said, making several of the group look at her. "I lived through ancient Rome. Yeah, there was the occasional orgy. It's not a big deal."

"The more I learn about you, the prouder I am of you," Remy said.

"Are you okay?" Fiona asked Mordred.

Mordred figured she was still worried that he was going to snap at any moment and try to butcher everyone. He doubted there was a lot he could do to change her mind about that. Didn't mean he wouldn't continue to try. For some reason changing people's perceptions of him from what he used to be to what he was now sat as an important thing to do in his mind. He wanted . . . no, needed people to understand that he had changed.

"I am fine, Fiona," Mordred told her. "I do not plan on any homicidal rages at the moment."

"You should make sure we know in advance," Nabu said. "I like to plan ahead."

"Was that a joke?" Mordred asked.

"Holy shit, Nabu made a joke," Remy said.

"Actually I really do like to plan ahead," Nabu said. "It's sort of my thing."

"Are you still joking?" Remy asked, clearly confused about the conversation. "I really don't know with you."

"I am one of life's little mysteries," Nabu said with a warm smile.

The helicopter touched down a few seconds later, and everyone waited for the engine to be turned off before getting out. Everyone in the group had several weapons and a backpack with supplies, all given to them by Polina, along with a gentle suggestion not to return to Moscow anytime in the near future.

Mordred opened his dark backpack and removed an energy bar, taking a bite as he pulled his fur-lined hat further over his ears.

"Well, this is desolate," he said, looking across the frozen landscape. The large open plain where they'd landed was covered in several inches of snow and was close to a forest. Mountains could be seen in the distance.

"How far to the abandoned village?" Nabu asked.

"A mile or so," Diana said. "I contacted my friend. She'll be there."

"Feel like telling us a little bit more about her?" Fiona asked.

"Her name is Chao Wei."

"She's Chinese?" Remy asked.

Diana nodded. "Yes, she settled here about a century ago. She isn't exactly full of social graces. She kind of likes her own company, and that's why she lives in the middle of nowhere."

"So, what is she?" Morgan asked.

"She's a huli jing."

Mordred was glad that based on the expressions on everyone's face, no one else seemed to know what that meant, either. "What's a huli jing?" he asked when it became evident that no one else was going to.

"Nine-tailed fox," Nabu said. "A being that can turn themselves from human to fox. They can sense anything around them for dozens of miles. Any change, anything out of the ordinary. They can make people forget things, or poison them, and generally they're just about screwing around with someone as much as possible. They're a rare, and dangerous, species."

"That sums Wei up pretty well," Diana said.

"How is it everyone you know is dangerous?" Remy asked.

"I'm just lucky," Diana said with a smile. "We'd better get moving."

The group made their way toward the nearby forest, where the snow was less abundant.

"Anyone worried about tigers?" Remy asked.

"I am now," Morgan said, looking around.

Diana sniffed the air. "There are no tigers within the vicinity. Trust me, you can smell them coming."

"Well, *you* can," Mordred said.

Remy sniffed the ground. "Bears, though."

"Let's get to the village," Diana said. "Bears consider werebears a threat. If we're in bear territory, it could see my presence out here as a challenge. We could do without the waste of time."

The rest of the trek was done in silence, and an hour later they walked over the crest of a hill and looked down on a village built close to a series of cliffs that led further up into the mountains behind it.

"That would be some good climbing," Nabu said. "That cliff face there must be a hundred feet high."

"There's a path that leads around it," Diana said, pointing to a barely perceivable pathway that led from the village up around the cliff.

"So, where's your friend going to meet us?"

"She's already here," Diana said. "About thirty feet to the left, closing in."

Remy sniffed the air. "I smell fox."

"I'll go meet her," Diana said, and walked off, leaving the rest of the group alone at the edge of the forest.

"You see that?" Nabu asked. He removed some binoculars from his backpack and looked through them before pointing to a large building at the side of the village. "What does that look like to you?"

"A prison," Morgan said almost immediately after being given the binoculars. "A small prison, but a prison nonetheless. The windows are barred. The door has some big locks on the exterior."

She passed the binoculars to Fiona, who took a look and passed them on to Mordred. "That's a very old building," she said.

"The structure is," Mordred said. "But the locks and bars look new. They've also painted over an old Soviet Union sickle and hammer. Did the humans use this place?" He took a moment to look around the rest of the village he could see. It was mostly just small huts, dozens of them, and a few larger buildings that looked considerably sturdier, and warmer. Presumably they were for the guards.

"They had prisoners mine up in the mountain," Diana said as she returned with Wei, who looked less than thrilled about being in the middle of Siberia in the winter.

She wore a white winter coat, and gray trousers that made Mordred think of something he'd once seen an artic explorer wear. She removed a dark-gray hat, and chestnut-brown hair fell over her shoulders.

"I'm Wei," she said.

"Thanks for coming," Fiona said.

"Don't thank me just yet. I'm not exactly an Avalon supporter."

"That's okay. Neither am I at the moment," Remy said, making Wei smile. "Between them and the humans, they keep trying to see who can fuck up the most."

"How's that working?" Wei asked.

"Too early to tell."

Fiona gave Remy a glare. "My husband and friends are down there somewhere."

Wei nodded. "Yes, I heard. Do you know what *there* is?"

"An old gulag being repurposed by people who'd like to kill a large number of very innocent people," Nabu said.

"There's a mine in the mountains," Wei explained. "Humans were used as prisoners here at one point a long time ago. Actually at several points. I don't know what they were looking for, but I had a friend from back in the day tell me and he didn't know, either. And he worked with Avalon during Soviet control. Whatever it is they're doing in there, they kept it secret."

"Who's they?" Remy asked.

"Avalon."

"So, not mining as such," Morgan said.

"If the mine was being used to produce something, it was something that never left this area," Wei explained. "It was something that even high-ranking members of the Soviet-era government had no idea about. This was a place where Avalon used to send its prisoners. It was disused for decades, but a few years ago it started up again. I tried to get into the mountain to see what they were doing, but there were too many guards at the time."

"Someone who works for Avalon," Mordred said. "Based on her previous form, it could be Hera."

"That's possible," Wei said. "I heard you swapped sides."

"Less swapped and more realized I wasn't exactly fighting the right people."

"And how's it working for you now?"

"About the same number of people want to kill me," Mordred said. "But on the other hand, most of those people probably deserve to die, so I don't feel so bad about venting my anger in their general direction."

"Are you going to help us, or what?" Fiona snapped.

Diana placed a comforting hand on Fiona's shoulder, but she shrugged it off. "My husband is in that hellhole, and I'm up here discussing niceties."

"Diana asked me here because I've been here before," Wei said. "It's nice to see another nine-tails here."

"Oh, I'm not a nine-tails," Remy said. "Just the one tail, see." He wiggled his tail to prove his point.

"Interesting," Wei said, staring at Remy for several seconds before looking back at Fiona. "I lived in a village close to here just before the Second World War was finally over. Fortunately the arrival of troops gave me the incentive to leave, but I came back a few years later when one of those in the village asked for my help. Avalon shut this place down just before the war, but it reopened in the fifties. Several people were abducted and forced to work here. Humans, I might add."

"Do you know the mines?" Fiona asked.

"I don't know too far down, as it was heavily guarded and I was only interested in finding those abducted. For some reason that mountain shields me from tracking people when you're inside it. I think it's got some sort of magical quality to it. I scouted the village a little before you arrived. I found nothing of note, apart from a few dozen armed guards patrolling the far end of the place." She pointed down toward the village. "You see the curve just there? The village opens out just behind there, but you can't see it from here because it goes around to the opposite side of the cliff. There's a building there that looks a lot like the one you were interested in. I saw guards going in and out, but I couldn't get closer. "

"Could people be held prisoner in it?" Fiona asked.

"Yes. I couldn't get inside to check, but I know for a fact that it's big enough. When I rescued the abducted humans, they were being held in there. Inside there's a set of stairs that leads down into the actual prison area. It's underground. When I checked earlier, though, I saw runes drawn on various places, although I don't know what they did. They're new."

"So, we've found our first destination," Nabu said.

"I'll go," Mordred said. "I just need a distraction."

"You sure?" Diana asked. "No offense, Mordred, but you're not exactly stealthy."

"I'll be fine. Besides, you're going to be better equipped at making enough noise to wake the dead."

"You're going in alone?" Fiona asked. "Because that's not happening."

"Fiona, whatever bullshit you think you know about me, push it aside. You want your husband back in one piece? Well, I've been sneaking in and out of places for hundreds of years. Normally to assassinate someone, but that's not exactly the point that's relevant at this point in time."

Fiona looked around for an ally and, finding none, resigned herself to the situation. "Fine, but if you do anything to put his life in jeopardy—"

"I don't plan on putting *anyone's* life in anything close to trouble. I plan on getting in, finding out what I can, and getting out. Or, should the need arise, getting in, killing everyone inside, and letting you guys come to me."

"You want us to take out everyone else in the village?" Morgan asked. "That wise?"

"It's necessary," Mordred replied. "If I get in there and someone can't leave under their own power, we need a clear line to escape."

"Or hunker down," Remy said. "This could turn into quite the protracted battle if anything goes wrong."

"Well, aren't you just a bundle of sunshine?" Diana said.

"Sunshine fucked off about two days ago," Remy told her. "Right now I'm a bundle of barely-held-together anxiety, rage, and just a smidge of sexual allure."

Everyone got a laugh out of that.

"That dreadful image aside," Morgan said, "we need to make this fast. We also need to figure out how we're going to get away from here. The chopper wasn't going to wait around for us."

"I brought a truck," Wei said. "A big truck. That should do the trick, yes?"

"It's better than walking," Diana said.

Five minutes later and Mordred had removed a sheathed dagger, which he hung from his belt, along with a holster, and Heckler and

Koch P30 .40 S&W. Thirteen rounds of hollow-point, silver-tipped bullets. He removed three more magazines and placed them in the pockets of his black hoodie. He didn't need a silencer—he could always use his air magic to try and make the noise less pronounced, but he was hoping he wouldn't have to use the gun at all. Knives are a lot quieter, and reusable, too. He tied the bag to a head-height tree branch and dropped his jacket over it. It kept him warm, but it was too bulky and obtrusive.

"Everyone ready?" he asked.

Everyone nodded.

"This isn't going to be fun," Nabu said. "Whoever these people are, whoever they work for, will have expected someone to come to free any hostages. And if Elaine is down there, you can be certain they'll want to keep her that way."

Mordred nodded.

"Be careful," Morgan told him. "I don't think you get to die twice."

"I'll be fine," he promised. "Keep safe."

"Mordred," Remy said, calling after him when he'd begun his descent toward the village.

Mordred stopped and turned back.

"Just don't die, okay?" Remy said. "We've had enough deaths. I can say from experience. We've all become somewhat fond, if sometimes through duress, of having you around. Stupid songs aside, we'd like to keep you in one piece. Besides, if you get killed here, Nate will never let any of us live it down."

Mordred smiled, turned, and continued down the side of the hill, keeping to the dense forest while he checked ahead for signs of enemy combatants. Mordred had told the rest of the group to count five minutes and then launch an attack on visible guards patrolling the furthest side of the village. He'd hoped that would be enough to draw away however many people were hidden from view. He didn't want to run around a corner into a battalion of heavily armed assholes.

Mordred reached the tree line and glanced back up at where his friends had been but saw nothing. The forest was too thick, and even so, he hoped they'd started to make a move. It was sixty feet across open ground to the first building in the village. If he got spotted, he was dead. It was that simple. He looked around, saw no one, and risked it.

He sprinted with everything he had, running toward the first building. As he got closer he saw that the door was ajar, and he slammed into it at full speed, rolling into the one-room building and coming to a stop by the far wall. The building had a bed, kitchen, and bathroom in one small space. It gave Mordred the impression of a jail cell more than somewhere someone might live. The kitchen consisted of a small stove and pans. There was a sink that had long since turned brown, an old mattress that Mordred wouldn't lie down on for all the money in the world, and several holes in the wooden floorboards.

Mordred placed a hand against the floor and pushed his air magic out, across the floor. The magical air seeped into the cracks between the floorboards, and when he'd used enough, he pulled the magic back toward him, tearing several boards free in an instant. He paused and looked out one of the grime-covered windows to ensure no one had heard. He could use his air magic to muffle sounds, but he couldn't have done that *and* used the magic to pull up the floor.

When he was certain he was okay, he dropped through the floor to the cold, hard ground beneath the small building. Like most of the buildings in the village, it had been built above the ground, leaving a gap big enough for him to crawl under. He'd thought about diving straight under the crawl space to begin with but wasn't sure what was under there, and diving headfirst into a dark crawl space was on his list of things he didn't want to do unless completely necessary.

Once under the hut he crawled to the edge of the building and pulled himself out of the crawl space so that he was between the hut he'd just broken and the one next to it. It was dark between the two buildings, and Mordred moved around the second hut, darting from cover to cover as he made his way through the village, thankful that the slope of the cliff became higher and higher until it cast a shadow over the huts. He'd moved past seven huts and was preparing to run to the eighth when he heard voices.

He stopped at the edge of the hut and peered around the corner. There were three guards twenty feet in front of him. All three of them huddled around a metal barrel, which had been used to start a fire. They wore dark-gray uniforms, sturdy boots, thick trousers, and thigh-length coats. And they weren't cheap clothes, either. Mordred couldn't remember the last time guards wore expensive coats and boots. None of them had any kind of insignia on their clothes, but all of them carried Sig SG 553s. He considered going out there, killing all three of them to take one of the assault rifles, but decided it wasn't worth the agro it would clearly cause.

He waited for several seconds, using his air magic to pick up what the men were talking about, but it became clear that it was mostly about how cold they were, how long they'd have to be here, and how they all really wanted to get drunk.

Mordred moved on, putting distance between him and the guards, but the further he moved around the cliff, the more guards were on patrol. Eventually he made it to a hut that allowed him a good visual of the large building at the end of the village. As Wei had said, it looked like a place to put prisoners. There were bars on the windows, and four guards stood outside the only entrance. If Elaine, or anyone else, was going to be held somewhere, it was in there.

Mordred took a step around the corner, almost directly into the path of an approaching guard, whose eyes widened in surprise. The man's hand dropped to his sidearm, but Mordred was too fast for him and used his air magic to wrap around the guard, pinning his arms in place, before dragging him back over. Mordred grabbed the man and threw him up against the rear of the hut he'd been hiding behind, slashed open the guard's throat with his dagger, and pushed him to the floor, rolling him under the hut.

Mordred cursed himself for moving too quickly and not checking for approaching guards. He looked around the corner and was thankful that none of the other five guards out in the clear had seen what had taken place. He wiped the blood off his dagger but kept it in his hand as he continued toward the edge of the hut just as an explosion rocked all around him.

CHAPTER 21

Mordred

Shouts and screams filled the air as Mordred's friends descended on the unaware guards. It didn't take long for the guards in front of the prison building to charge off, leaving only one concerned-looking guard to protect the entrance. These weren't Avalon agents, and they certainly weren't blood elves. Mordred would have guessed they were human mercenaries, hired to keep people in one place. But that left the uneasy question of the location of those who took Elaine and the others. There was zero chance that any of them were going to be taken out by a group of human thugs, no matter how nice their guns were.

Mordred looked up at the cliff behind the prison building. The dense forest covered a large part of it, and the mountains could clearly be seen behind it. A winding path had been carved into the cliff. It sat behind the prison building, and Mordred figured it for the best place to take the prisoners in their attempt to escape the village. Certainly better than running back through the firefight going on behind him.

He removed his pistol and fired two rounds into the guard's head, killing him, the gunfire muffled by Mordred's air magic. After searching his immediate surroundings and finding no guards, he ran over to the prison door and tried the handle, finding it locked. He searched the dead guard at his feet for a key and eventually found one in a pocket on his vest.

Mordred unlocked the door and pushed it open, revealing a set of stairs leading down into a dimly lit corridor beneath the ground. He descended the stairs slowly and about halfway down felt his magic vanish. He paused and looked around, but it was too dim to see any runes that might have been drawn on his surroundings. Instead, he removed the pistol from its holster and continued.

He checked the corridor and found nothing of concern before stepping out into it. There were five shut doors along each side of the corridor, and he tried the first, finding it unlocked, so he pushed it open, revealing a small cell. The smell of blood and death hung around the cell, and the floor was wet where it had been cleaned. A drain sat in the center of the room, and Mordred remembered the werewolf nightclub and Elaine's tortured guard he'd found there.

Mordred left the cell and tried the next door but found it locked. After the third locked door, be began to hear noises coming from one of the rooms at the far end of the corridor. He moved toward them, making sure to keep low and quiet, just in case the door suddenly opened and he had to react quickly.

It didn't take long for him to reach the cell door, which like the others was made of thick metal. He placed his ear to the door but heard nothing apart from the muffled sound of someone being repeatedly hit. With his pistol ready, Mordred pushed on the door a little until it revealed two men standing with their backs to him. A third man sat tied to a chair, although Mordred couldn't make out that man's face. He was clearly male, though, seeing how he was naked.

"Where are they?" the guard questioning the prisoner asked.

"I don't know," the man said, his speech slurred. They'd clearly done a number on him.

"Lies," the guard said, and punched the man in the face.

Mordred stood up and saw who was being tortured, and a cold rage filled him. With two steps he was behind the first guard. Mordred buried the dagger in the back of the guard's neck, killing him instantly.

He stepped around the falling guard, firing twice into the second guard's head. Both men were dead, and Mordred ran to the prisoner.

"Mac," he said, his voice soft. "Mac, you hear me in there?"

Mac mumbled something unintelligible. Mac was a water elemental, and without a supply of water, there was no way he was going to heal himself. The amount of cuts and bruises over his body suggested he'd been subjected to a prolonged beating.

Mordred looked around and found a pitcher of water on a nearby table. He picked it up and threw it over Mac, drenching the man before cutting the plastic ties that held his wrists together.

Mordred waited for a minute as the worst of the wounds on Mac's body healed, until his eyes were no longer puffy and closed. Mac blinked. "Mordred?"

Mordred nodded. "You up for walking?"

"They removed my toenails. Fingernails too. Broke my knees and let me heal. Point is, I hurt, but not enough to stop me from removing their spines."

Mordred helped Mac to his feet. "It's been a long time, old friend."

Mac smiled. "We're friends now? I thought you wanted to kill everyone."

"Yeah, we'll say that's a bad judgment call on my part."

"I'm naked, Mordred."

Mordred propped Mac up against the nearest wall and removed the clothes from the first guard, passing them to Mac. "You good to get dressed?" he asked.

"If I say no, will you hold it against me?" Mac asked after fumbling with a pair of trousers. "I think my hands haven't quite healed yet."

Mordred helped Mac into a pair of trousers, shoes, and a jacket. It wasn't going to be the most comfortable of clothes for him, and they were a little larger than he was probably used to, but Mordred figured too large was better than too small.

"Anyone else in these cells?"

"They killed the whole lot of them," Mac said. "Made us all watch as they killed them. Eight good people, dead."

"Where's Alan?" Mordred asked, feeling a ball of hurt inside him at the possibility of losing more people.

"He escaped into the mine. They took humans from some of the nearest villages and made them work in there."

"Doing what?"

"Whatever they needed. I don't really know. I don't understand why they'd go to all this trouble to dig around in a mountain. They thought I'd know where Alan escaped. Thought we'd made a pact to escape and I got caught."

"And?"

"We did make a pact, and I did get caught, but I don't know where Alan is apart from in the mountain. Although I can't say that for certain. He could be anywhere by now. Maybe he went for help. Is that why you're here?"

Mordred shook his head. "No, we came to find you all. Elaine, too."

"She's closer to the mountain. There's a camp up there. It was built by whoever these bastards are. I saw lorries driving up there on the road around the cliff. If Alan hasn't gone for help, he's up there."

"How long ago did he escape?"

"Few hours."

Mordred helped his friend up the stairs to be greeted by Diana and Wei, both in human form.

"Mac," Diana said, picking him up and carrying him out of the prison building.

"Everyone okay?" Mordred asked as Diana helped Mac lie in some nearby snow.

Mordred didn't bother asking Mac if his light magic would heal him; he already knew that it would have no effect on the water elemental.

"It's not exactly flowing water, but it's better than nothing," Diana told Mac before turning back to Mordred. "The others are mopping up.

These were almost entirely humans. I recognized a few more of those escaped prisoners from The Hole. What the hell is going on here?"

"Where's Alan?" Fiona asked after sprinting up to the group, with Remy and Morgan jogging behind her.

"Fiona," Mordred began, but Fiona shoved him aside and ran into the prison building.

For several minutes they all stood outside and waited, until Fiona re-emerged and saw Mac slowly getting to his feet. Apart from the dried blood on his face, he appeared almost normal.

"Where's Alan?" she snapped.

"He escaped a few hours ago," Mac said, and picked up a handful of snow, rubbing it over his face.

"Escaped? What the fuck does that mean?" Fiona asked.

"Fiona," Diana said softly.

"No," Fiona snapped, raising her hand in Diana's direction but not turning back to face her. "Where is my fucking husband, Mac?"

"I don't know," Mac said. "That's why they've been kicking the shit out of me. We were the last two left alive and decided to make a break for it. He'd stolen a key a few days ago, and we used it to get out of the cells, but we got grabbed. I held them off while he ran. Like I told Mordred, I think he'll have gone up to the mountain. It's where Elaine is."

Fiona looked around at everyone and nodded before walking off.

"Shit," Remy said. "So, we're not done here?"

"Since when have things ever been that easy?" Diana asked him. "Besides, I'd really like to find out exactly what is going on here."

"I'll come with you," Wei said. "I'd like to find out the truth, too. Besides, I think you're going to need all of the help you can get."

"Me, too," Mac said as he tried on the clothes of another dead guard. "I want some payback, and more than that, I just need to finish this mission. Elaine is up there. I was meant to help find her, and instead I got captured and tortured. I can't go home without knowing

I did everything possible to fix that." He picked up an SG 553 and checked the ammo. "Silver rounds. They might have been human, but they were armed to kill us."

"And what a wonderful job they did," Morgan said.

Mordred heard the gunshot almost immediately after Morgan dropped to her knees. Mordred felt like he was moving in slow motion as he ran toward Morgan, who was already on her back, her face pained, her eyes registering the shock of the bullet that had struck her.

Mordred covered Morgan's body with his own and created a shield of dense air, just as the second bullet struck it.

Diana was picking up Mac and running with him back into the prison building, where Remy and Fiona were already heading. Mordred picked up Morgan and with Wei's help followed the others. They descended the steps, and Mac opened one of the doors with keys he'd found in a guard's pocket.

"It's where they brought us to help heal," Mac said, helping Mordred place Morgan on a bed before using scissors to cut away her jacket, revealing the blood-soaked clothes beneath it. "Mordred, you need to step back. She's been hit in the chest."

Mordred placed his hands where the wound was, and his light magic ignited, but nothing happened.

"I don't understand," he said, feeling completely helpless.

"We'll figure it out, but I need to examine her first," Mac said.

"Save her," Mordred said, walking to the door.

"Where are you going?" Fiona asked.

"I'm going to find who did this and make them understand their mistake." He turned back toward her, and she almost recoiled.

"Your eyes," Diana said. "It's like Nate."

Mordred turned away.

"I'll join you," Wei said. "I know the forest around here."

Mordred nodded and left the room. He didn't care who joined him in his hunt, so long as they didn't get in the way. He wasn't good at waiting around and watching people die; he needed to be doing something. And that something meant spilling the blood of those involved. No matter how much he'd changed over the years, that was something that had remained inside of him.

"Mordred, wait," Diana called as he walked down the corridor toward the stairs.

Mordred paused. "Don't try to stop me."

"I'm not. I'm trying to tell you there was no scent from the forest above. If I'd have smelled something, no one would have gotten close enough to fire. So, they were either too far away for me to get a scent, which makes it an exceptionally good shot, or . . ."

"Or what?" Wei asked.

"Or, do you remember that Nate said something about a sniper killing people and leaving no scent behind?" Diana said. "A witch. The same witch Nate and Tommy said was working with Mara Range, you remember her?"

"The woman who made the tablet that let us into the dwarf realm, I remember," Mordred said. "You think the witches are here? That they're helping to keep Elaine prisoner?"

"Mara Range has more than a few links to Hera. And whoever took Elaine had to have a lot of power."

"No witch has that kind of power."

Diana nodded. "But Hera does."

"I don't care who's up there right now, Diana. I'm going to find who shot Morgan. If I have to go through Hera to get to them, so be it." He began to ascend the stairs again.

"Don't do anything to get yourself killed," Diana called after him as he continued to climb the stairs without listening to her. "Damn you, Mordred."

Mordred waited at the entrance to the prison. He was grateful that his magic returned to him halfway up the staircase. He poured air magic out of the prison, manipulating it to go up above the building toward the edge of the cliff, but it was too far and there was no way he could use his magic to reach where Diana had suspected the shot had come from.

"Let me," Wei said. She moved her hand, and a nine-tailed fox appeared on the ground just outside the prison. It ran over to where Morgan had been shot and then sprinted across the clearing to a building on the other side, close to where the path up the cliff face started.

Mordred wrapped himself in dense air and stepped outside. If the shooter had used a silver bullet, his magic wouldn't have stopped the second shot from hitting earlier. That meant the bullet that had hit Morgan might also have not been silver, which meant despite how bad the wound might be, and how much blood she'd lost, she had a good chance of making it. Mordred pushed the thoughts of Morgan's survival aside and had made it two paces when he extended the shield and looked up at the cliff face.

"They've gone," Wei said. "If Diana is correct, how do we hunt someone who leaves no scent?"

"I have no idea," Mordred admitted. He sprinted across the clearing toward the cliff, putting his back against the jagged rocks that made up its face. The run up the pathway was done as quickly as Mordred was able, using his air magic to increase his speed as much as he could as Wei kept up with seemingly little effort.

They reached the top of the cliff, and Wei sniffed the air. "They fired from over there," she said, pointing to a group of rocks a few feet back from the cliff edge.

Mordred walked over and searched the ground by the rocks. He picked up a shell casing and was looking at it when Wei knocked it out of his hand.

"Venom," she said by way of explanation.

"Any idea what kind?"

She licked the shell casing. "Gargoyle. I'm sorry."

Gargoyle venom was exceptionally potent and quick acting, but more than that it had an awful tendency to bypass any magic that might allow someone to heal. "Gargoyles are rare," Mordred said. "Most sorcerers aren't stupid enough to want to become one. Hell, not even I was that far gone."

"I never understood the appeal," Wei admitted. "Allowing your magic free rein to change your body, allowing blood-magic curses to tear you apart and put you back together in a new form. It's an act of someone as depraved as I could possibly imagine."

"I've met two gargoyles in my life. Killed one, Nate killed the other. Both deserved to die. If there's a gargoyle here, we need to kill it, and kill it quickly."

"First we need to find the shooter." Wei set off into the forest, with Mordred close behind.

CHAPTER 22

Mordred

Mordred and Wei had gone several hundred meters when Mordred thought he saw a shimmer of something up ahead. He immediately put up a shield of dense air and moved aside as a bullet tore into the tree beside him, causing it to rip apart as if it were paper.

Mordred kept running, changing direction and throwing the occasional blade of ice at where he thought the sniper would be hiding. Two more bullets hit trees close to where Mordred ran past, and a third struck a stone, showering tiny spikes of sharp rock across Mordred's side and arm, cutting open his hand. He dove for cover to take a look at his hand, which had a three-inch shard of rock protruding from it. He removed the shard and placed one hand over the other, using his light magic to heal the wound. In seconds it was as if nothing had ever happened, although the memory of the pain still lingered.

Mordred concentrated, allowing his mind magic to activate. While what he'd told Fiona was true—he couldn't use his mind magic except in defense—he could use it to see how many living people there were close by. It would only work over a few dozen feet, and he was forced to sit and concentrate, but it wasn't like he could go anywhere while someone with a rifle was firing shots at him. It took a few seconds, but when he opened his eyes he could feel two people close by. One was

Wei—that much was clear—but the other was a young woman he'd never met before. She was twenty feet to the left, trying to flank his position.

He waited until the last second before throwing a blast of water in the direction he knew she'd be. There was a scream of shock and pain, followed by a gunshot and then nothing. As he stood Mordred froze the water in place around a large tree. He walked over and picked up the rifle from the ground. It was the same make as the ones the humans had been using in the village.

Mordred moved the ice aside, revealing a young woman wearing a black balaclava and combat fatigues. "You feel like telling me your name?" Mordred asked.

"Emily Rowe," she said.

"You're English."

"Yes. I'm a witch. I live in England."

"You shot my friend."

"I'd have shot you, too, given the chance."

"Are you the same woman that Diana said knows Nate?"

At the mention of Nate's name, there was a tiny amount of recognition and some fear. "You're afraid of him?" Mordred asked.

"I've met him, so yes. He is incredibly powerful, and the last time we met he told me he'd kill me should our paths cross again."

"My name is Mordred. Have you heard of me?"

"Yes, everyone has. I was told to kill you and your friends. You aren't the scary person you used to be. Shame, I'd have liked to have met the old you."

Mordred laughed, although there was no humor in it. "No, you really wouldn't have. How'd you keep your scent masked?"

"Witch magic."

Mordred grabbed her arm and pulled up the sleeve, revealing the dozens of small tattoos that were there. "That's a lot of power for a witch. Trying to get yourself killed?"

"That's what sorcerers always say to a witch trying to unlock their potential. The more magic we use, the quicker we die."

"You don't believe it?"

"I'm not dead yet."

"An antidote for the venom. Now."

"I've got a better idea."

Mordred saw the shadow cast over him a second before he flung himself aside, dropping the SG 553 and narrowly avoiding the descending gargoyle. The creature stood to its full seven-foot height and stretched out its enormous wingspan. Its body was covered in gray armored stone plates, and it had a foot-long horn growing out of each temple. A long red tongue flicked out of its stony mouth. Venom dripped from its claws onto the soft snow.

"I think you have bigger problems," Emily said with a chuckle as Mordred took off at a full sprint into the forest. Gargoyles weren't great at flying, but they could move in a straight line with incredible speed, and Mordred wanted to put some trees between the two of them.

A fox ran into Mordred's path, turning into Wei a second later. "You get to kill another gargoyle," she said.

"You feel like helping?" Mordred asked, looking back at where Emily was and finding both her and the gargoyle gone.

"I can't puncture the stone plates. I can, however, keep Emily occupied. I promise I won't kill her, but I'll keep her and her rifle busy until you can join us. I assume you have questions."

"We need an antidote."

"And you think she has one?"

"I'm just hoping more than anything. It's that or make one from the venom of the gargoyle."

"There's another way," she said, but a rifle round smashed into a nearby tree, forcing Mordred and Wei to cut short their conversation.

Wei turned back into a fox and bounded off into the forest, vanishing from view.

The gargoyle roared and began to tear its way toward Mordred, who tried to remember how he'd managed to kill the last gargoyle he'd met. Luck, and a lot of cheating. He remembered Nate telling him about how he'd turned the air so cold that the plates on the gargoyle's chest had moved just enough for him to get to the flesh beneath.

He watched the gargoyle crash through the forest toward him, tearing apart trees, which Mordred decided was more about instilling fear than anything else.

Mordred started to hum the battle tune to *Final Fantasy IX* and readied two blades of ice in preparation for what was coming.

"You can't hide from me!" the gargoyle shouted. "No one can hide from me."

Wei stepped out from behind a tree, as if appearing from nowhere, directly between Mordred and the gargoyle.

"Where's Emily?" Mordred whispered.

"Busy hiding from me," Wei said. "I gave her a nice bit of poison to slow her down. She didn't have an antidote, by the way. I checked. She'll be preoccupied for a while as she tries not to throw up her lungs. "

"Classy."

The gargoyle laughed. "You're going to stop me?" he asked Wei.

Wei took a step forward and then vanished from view, leaving a trail of mist where she'd once stood.

The gargoyle looked around, trying to find her, until he'd turned in a complete circle and was staring at Mordred again. He looked confused.

Wei reappeared next to Mordred. "He's forgotten I was there," she said. "It's easier to do with simple people."

She sprinted toward the gargoyle and vanished again just before reaching him, causing the gargoyle to roar out in anger for a second before once again appearing to be incredibly confused.

"That has got to be winding you up," Mordred said, and his thoughts immediately went back to Morgan, who was dying not too far away. He blasted the gargoyle in the chest with ice, taking the large creature off its feet and smashing it through several trees.

"You want to hear my plan?" Wei asked as Mordred walked toward the gargoyle, who was pinned to the side of a tree with thick ice.

"Morgan needs help," Mordred said. "What's your plan?"

"My blood can be used to poison people," she said. "But if I'm infected with poison or venom, I can also use it to create an antidote."

"Which means you need the gargoyle's venom inside of you."

Wei nodded. "I'd rather not be sliced to ribbons by those claws, though, and Morgan doesn't have long enough to wait while we kill it."

The sound of shattering ice filled the air, followed quickly by a roar of anger as the gargoyle freed itself, dropping to the ground. It charged forward without a word, forcing Wei to vanish once again while Mordred threw himself aside, using his air magic to propel him further than his own strength would have managed. He threw a ball of light into the gargoyle's eyes, blinding it enough to send it careening into a huge, ancient tree, knocking it slightly askew. The gargoyle tore into the tree, cutting through it with ease, until he could smash it down onto the ground where Mordred had been.

Mordred wrapped air around the legs of the gargoyle and pulled, tripping the beast and forcing it headfirst into the tree trunk. The gargoyle roared in anger once again and leapt toward Mordred, who blasted it with jets of ice, freezing it in place. He continued to pile on the pressure as Wei reappeared next to the gargoyle.

"Leave one claw free," she called over to Mordred.

"Just do it so I can kill it already," he said.

Wei took hold of one finger of the gargoyle, the claw popping out into her palm. She yelled and stepped back as the ice began to crack once again.

"Go," Mordred said. "I've got this."

Wei nodded and turned into a fox, sprinting off through the forest to hopefully save Morgan's life. The brief lapse in concentration was all the gargoyle needed to tear his way out of the ice and move toward Mordred at frightening speed. He picked Mordred up in one hand, throwing him back into a nearby tree. Mordred's shield of air saved him from serious injury, but even then the wind was knocked out of him, and he fell awkwardly to the ground.

The gargoyle was upon him in seconds, forcing Mordred to block the attacks lest he be infected with the same venom that was killing his friend. His mind was on Morgan, not on the fight at hand, and that would get him killed.

Mordred blocked a swipe of the gargoyle's claws and blasted him in the chest with blinding light, allowing Mordred to escape and put some distance between the two of them. Whoever the sorcerer had been before turning into a gargoyle, he'd been incredibly powerful. Much more so than the gargoyle who Mordred had fought all those centuries ago.

"You're like a rat," the gargoyle bellowed. "I'm going to enjoy crushing the life out of you."

Mordred bit his tongue and kept quiet as he moved behind a large tree to figure out his next attack. Fighting head on wasn't getting him anywhere, and despite the cold of this part of the world, combined with his magical ice, he hadn't seen much movement in the plates that kept the gargoyle safe. If he was going to get through to the flesh under them, he needed a different strategy.

He glanced around him, trying to figure out if anything in his surroundings was going to help in the fight, and spotted Emily's rifle lying thirty feet away to the side. The gargoyle was close enough that if Mordred ran for it, he wouldn't have enough time to get to the rifle and use it before the gargoyle got to him. Mordred would have liked to have gotten hold of the SG 553 again—it had silver bullets and would have probably done some damage even to a gargoyle. He couldn't remember if silver could kill a gargoyle, but he was certain it couldn't hurt to find out.

"Where are you?" the gargoyle roared. "You coward. You sniveling little nothing."

"Aren't you just a joy?" Mordred asked, using his air magic to throw his voice fifty feet to the right of him, deeper into the forest.

"I'm not going to fall for that trick," the gargoyle said.

"You sure? You look exceptionally stupid."

Mordred felt a trickle of blood run down his scalp and touched it, rubbing the blood between his finger and thumb. "Damn you," he said. "I really don't want to be that person anymore."

"What are you talking about?" the gargoyle asked with a laugh. "You just gave your position away."

"I know."

Mordred stepped out, whipping a tendril of blood magic at the gargoyle, wrapping it around his arm.

The gargoyle laughed as he walked toward Mordred. "You can't hurt me if it doesn't touch my skin."

"I know," Mordred said, and launched a second, much thinner tendril from his other hand. It slammed into the open mouth of the gargoyle, muffling its screams as he pushed it further and further inside. The gargoyle thrashed and bucked, trying to swipe at Mordred, who remained just out of reach.

The use of so much blood magic made a smile tug at Mordred's lips, and he knew he could keep going. Just keep pouring more and more blood magic inside the gargoyle until there was enough to tear him in half from the inside out. Mordred stopped and switched the blood magic off as tears of blood fell from his eyes. "Not like this," he whispered.

The gargoyle was on his hands and knees, coughing up blood onto the snowy ground, as Mordred tried to push away the need to keep using the blood magic. It called to him, screamed at him to continue the assault on the gargoyle, to allow himself to give in, but he wouldn't. The desire to use blood magic would always be with him, and sometimes he had to give in to that to do what needed to be done, but to use so much all at once was inviting something back into his life he wanted no part of.

Mordred walked away from the gargoyle and picked up Emily's rifle. He went back to the gargoyle, who was still on his knees, and fired two shots into the creature's chest, knocking him back onto the ground and cracking one of the stone plates that covered his heart. Mordred ejected the magazine and, finding it empty, tossed the rifle aside.

The gargoyle rolled to his side as Mordred sprinted toward his target and smashed a ball of frozen air into the cracked plate, forcing the magic inside, tearing the plate apart.

The gargoyle screamed in pain before Mordred drove a blade of light into its chest. He poured more and more light magic into the body of the gargoyle, tearing the beast apart from the inside, and in one motion Mordred leapt back, dragging all the magic he'd put into the gargoyle out of it. The gargoyle was torn to pieces as the light magic left the body, turning everything around it into a crimson mess.

Dozens of small balls of light flickered around in the air, until one by one they vanished, leaving Mordred alone next to what used to be a living creature.

"Not enough of him to pick up," Wei said from behind Mordred.

"How long were you there?"

"Long enough to see you kill him, not long enough to help."

"Morgan?"

"They took my blood. She'll be okay, we hope."

"Hope?"

"It depends on how much venom was in her, and how strong she is."

"She'll be fine, then. Where's Emily?"

Mordred followed silently as Wei took him to find Emily, who was lying on her side, curled up next to a large pool of vomit. Wei touched her head, and Emily groaned, but after a few seconds she was no longer green.

"You here to kill me?" Emily asked.

"Yes," Mordred told her. "You tried to kill my friend. I won't have that."

"You should keep me alive. You need me. Why not just let the poison kill me?"

"Because the poison I inflict doesn't kill," Wei said. "It makes you wish you were dead, but it's not lethal. I'm not an assassin. Not anymore, anyway."

Emily sat up and wiped her mouth with the back of her hand. "So, this is you allowing me some dignity?"

Mordred shook his head. "Not really, I just wanted to ask you a question. How many are up at the mountain?"

"Few dozen blood elves."

"You got anything you'd like to say before you die?" Mordred asked.

"A confession?" Emily laughed. "Why bother?"

"Nate told me he was angry with you because he'd liked you. He felt betrayed. I kind of think he'd have liked you to die quick, with a clear conscience. Morgan is safe now, so I have a few minutes."

She thought for a second before sighing. "You know what? I liked Nate. He was a good guy, and it sucked that I had to play him like that.

I don't like Mara. She's helping Abaddon and her crew, by the way." Emily laughed. "Doesn't have a lot of fucking choice in the matter, though. Goddamn, it was funny to see her face when she realized she was a prisoner, not an ally. She's such a fucking asshole. If you kill her, make her suffer. I would."

"Anything else?" Wei asked. "Do we need to sit down for this? It sounds like you weren't a good person."

"I killed dozens for Hera, and that witches' coven. It was a shame I had to kill Gilgamesh, though, but he couldn't be trusted to keep his mouth shut. He was all about honor, and he knew too much. Still, a rifle round was never the way. He deserved to go out in combat, although at least he died after losing in combat, so there's that. Elaine's alive, by the way. She's in the mountain somewhere. I thought they'd kill her, but that Abaddon chick is really keen on keeping her alive for some reason."

"Abaddon?" Wei asked. "You mentioned her a moment ago. Is that the same Abaddon of old? One of the seven devils."

"You know her?" Emily asked.

"By reputation, yes." Wei looked over at Mordred. "If Abaddon is here, we're going to want to get Elaine, Alan, and anyone else you need, and we need to leave. Soon."

"She scary, I take it?" Mordred asked.

"She's going to kill you all," Emily said. "Like, all of you: your friends, family, their pets, the people who cut their hair. Literally anyone who knows you. She does not mess around." She stared at Mordred for a heartbeat. "You want to know how I used magic to mask my scent, don't you? I can tell. You keep me alive and maybe I'll tell you."

"No thanks, I'm good."

"I'll tell you all about real magic. The stuff you can't even comprehend."

Mordred created a thin blade of ice on the palm of his hand. He held it between two fingers. "Real magic. You don't know anything about real magic." He threw the blade of ice at Emily, catching her in the eye and piercing her brain. "And now you never will."

Wei drew a dagger and jammed it into the witch's heart. "I hear they can come back if you don't destroy the heart," she said.

A second later Mordred was running back to Morgan. He almost leapt down the cliff at one point, but thankfully his better judgment took over and he was soon back inside the prison and found Mac standing beside a still-unconscious Morgan.

"She'll make it," Mac told him. "She's strong. Stronger than most."

Mordred continued to look down at Morgan and smiled. "The strongest I know."

CHAPTER 23

Mordred

The twenty minutes that passed after Morgan had been given the anti-venom were some of the longest in Mordred's exceptionally lengthy life. Apart from Mac and Morgan, everyone was outside the prison building, sitting on the steps of a hut as Fiona paced up and down.

Two minutes after that, Fiona demanded that everyone get going. "We don't know what's going on up there," she said. "We need to get moving."

"We can't leave Morgan down here," Remy said. "And we can't exactly cart her up the bloody hill, either. She's not strong enough to be moved like that. And it's not like Mac is in fine fighting form, either. He needs a proper source of water to get healing. Lying in the snow is only a stopgap."

"How about using the truck I brought?" Wei asked.

"Could Morgan be moved to the truck?" Mordred asked. He understood Fiona's need to find her husband, but his thoughts were with Morgan, and he knew once up there he needed to ensure his attention wasn't split.

"You know what's strange?" Nabu asked. "There are no radios here. There is literally no way for these people to contact anyone up above."

"They're the sacrificial lambs," Diana said. "Left here to be the first casualties. I assume that's what the witch, Emily, was up there for."

"Waiting for us," Remy said. "I've looked around at some of the bodies here, and they're a mixture of human mercenaries and some of the prisoners from The Hole. No one with any real power or influence died here today."

Mordred looked his way. "Not yet, anyway."

"Morgan is going to be fine," Remy assured him. "She's not exactly the type to just pack it all in. She kept you under lock and key for over a thousand years, and every single time you escaped to go do whatever craziness you needed to do, she hunted you down. Doesn't strike me as the behavior of someone who gives up easily."

"I'm sure you're right."

"On the plus side, I found a lot of walkie-talkies. They're digital, and I can't pick up any chatter from anyone else, but we can use them to communicate between one another."

Mordred's heart sang a little as Mac and Nabu walked out of the prison with Morgan, who was leaning on Mac for support. Mordred rushed over.

"Easy there," Morgan said before Mordred could hug her. She looked pale and tired, and more than a little weak. "I'm not exactly healed."

"But you are alive?" He looked at Mac. "She's not a zombie or anything, right?"

"She'll be fine," Mac told her. "With rest."

"We don't exactly have a lot of time for resting up," Remy said.

"Well, Morgan will need to rest for several hours before she can use her magic. Doing so beforehand could cause the venom's damage to become irreversible."

"Gargoyle venom is potent," Nabu said. "But many people survive with an antivenom. I helped as best I could, but Mac has a much better bedside manner than me. There are some things it seems you can't learn."

"So, she needs to sit and rest," Mordred said. "Looks like you get to sit in the backseats of the truck."

"I have you to thank," Morgan said to Wei.

"Little old me?" Wei said. "Don't worry about it. Besides, the longer we stay here, the more likely it is that something unbelievably bad is happening up there, so let's get moving. Morgan and Mac can stay in the truck and keep their heads down. That okay with you?"

Morgan nodded. "I don't think I'm going to be doing much moving in the next few hours. I'm sorry, I should have been on the lookout for snipers."

"You couldn't have seen her," Mordred said. "She was invisible to any senses, and she hid herself behind some rocks up there."

"She's dead, though," Wei said. "Very dead actually. I made sure of it."

"How can you be very dead?" Remy asked. "Surely dead is dead?"

"Things sometimes come back. I've seen it happen. More than one witch has returned from an early grave."

The horn of a pickup truck sounded at the edge of the village, and everyone turned to see Fiona open the driver's door and motion to the dark-blue-and-black vehicle. It was big enough to seat five inside the cabin, with enough space in the open flatbed to seat a few more.

"That's a pickup truck," Remy said. "I was expecting, you know, a fucking great truck."

"You mean a lorry?" Diana asked.

"Yeah, a lorry. A big, building-crushing lorry."

"The Mitsubishi is the best I could get on short notice," Wei said. "You're welcome to walk, if you like."

"I didn't say I didn't like the pickup truck," Remy said. "I was just expecting something a little bigger. I call shotgun."

"No," Diana said as they all walked toward the pickup. "You don't get to call shotgun."

"I can see the vehicle; therefore I can call shotgun."

"Let him have it," Mac said as he and Mordred helped Morgan walk toward the pickup. "Morgan and I will sit in the back. Nabu, can you join us? Just in case we need some more medical expertise."

Nabu nodded.

"I guess that leaves Wei, Diana, and me in the flatbed," Mordred said.

"I'll be going up front," Wei said. "I move faster on my own." Without another word, she turned into a fox and sprinted up past the pickup, moving faster than any fox had a right to move.

"How does she do that?" Remy asked.

"Nine-tails sort of exist between realms," Diana said. "It means they can move in a way that no one else can, but only for short periods of time. Takes some getting used to."

Diana picked up two more Sig assault rifles and placed them in the back of the pickup. "Just in case."

"Can't hurt," Mordred said, helping Mac and Morgan into the rear of the cab. When he was certain Morgan was okay, Mordred climbed into the rear of the pickup and found that two small benches had been installed along with some straps to hold on to. He wrapped himself in tendrils of air, moving them around the rear of the pickup, anchoring himself in place.

"Feel better now?" Diana asked with a slight smirk.

"Not really," Mordred said. "But slightly safer."

Diana shook her head and banged on top of the Mitsubishi's roof, and the engine roared as Fiona took them all up the path toward the mountain above.

Mordred found the pickup to be surprisingly robust and more than capable of handling the off-road dirt-track-like path, as well as the increasingly thick snow. They used the tracks of previous vehicles to stay on the right.

"There's no one up there," Diana said as they drove closer to the settlement in the mountains.

"You sure?" Mordred asked. "That witch hid from you." Mordred removed the air tethering him to the pickup and banged on the roof of the pickup. Fiona slammed on the brakes, causing Mordred to fall down.

"Sorry, I thought you were banging because we were in trouble," Fiona called out.

Mordred dropped down over the side of the truck and walked to the driver's window. "I'm not sure yet. Diana can't smell anyone. And we're too far away for me to see anyone. Doesn't mean there's no one there."

"We stay and wait for Wei," Diana said. "She won't be long."

Fiona parked the pickup on the side of the trail. Once everyone besides Morgan and Mac were out, she placed her hands on the pickup and closed her eyes. The pickup vanished from view, as if it had never been there at all, and the new tracks that she'd created in the snow did the same, leaving no signs.

"It'll last a few hours," Fiona said. "It's not one of my best illusions, but you do what you can with the time you have to work with."

"Has anyone ever said how scary conjurers are?" Remy asked.

"My husband on a regular basis," Fiona said with a smile. She looked up the trail and breathed out slowly.

"We'll find him," Morgan said from inside the pickup.

"The disembodied voice is going to take some getting used to," Mordred said. "What happens to the illusion if they have to leave the truck?"

"It'll vanish fairly quickly. It's not designed to take many changes to its current state. They can move around inside as much as they like, but once a door opens that's it."

"You guys hear that?" Diana asked.

"Stay put, don't piss around," Mac said. "Yeah, we got it."

A fox came running down the hill toward them, turning into Wei midleap. "It's almost empty."

"The settlement above?"

She nodded. "I sense one woman. That's it. Whoever is digging up in the mountain carved a huge chunk of it out of the side of the rock up there. I got as close as I dared but couldn't see anyone. There's a notice board with a map of the mountain interior on it. It looks like the tunnels that go down into the mountain go much further than when I was last here."

Mordred passed a walkie-talkie to everyone. "I'll go up with Wei, Nabu, Diana, and Fiona. Remy, you stay here with Morgan and Mac, and if it's clear, we'll let you know and you can head on up."

No one had any issues with his idea, and they set off on the several-minute walk up an increasingly steep slope, until it plateaued after several hundred feet, opening up into the large settlement that Wei had visited.

"It's over there, the portable cabin near the cave entrance." Wei pointed to a blue-and-white building.

"Just one woman?"

"Unless there are dozens in here who all have the same markings as the witch, yes. I made a thorough check, and there are no signs that anyone has been here in the last few hours."

The group used the edge of the settlement for cover, moving between temporary buildings until they'd reached the cabin in question. Fiona walked over and tried the handle but found it locked.

Diana sniffed the air. "One person inside. We could kick it in, but I have no idea just what might be written on the other side."

"Time for me to work, I assume," Nabu said. He crouched down in front of the lock and placed his hands around it. He removed a small pouch from his pocket and opened it up, revealing several lockpicks. "It's a new hobby."

"It's something unexpected," Diana added.

"The windows on this building are blacked out," Fiona said. "It's like the prison down below."

A few seconds later Nabu stood and pushed the door open. "Now, *that* is unexpected."

He stepped into the building, followed quickly by everyone else. Mordred couldn't help but laugh when he saw Mara Range inside. She was chained to the floor by one ankle. The thick metal chain was just long enough for her to get around the small building, which to Mordred's mind was basically just a slightly bigger caravan.

"You're the one who made the tablets that got us stuck in the dwarven realm," Diana said, picking up part of the chain and immediately reacting as if it had stung her, dropping it to the floor. "Shit, there's silver in the chain."

"You're Chloe's mum," Fiona said. "The witch. How's siding with Hera and her people working out for you?"

"How does it look?" Mara snapped.

Nabu picked up one of several metal bracelets that sat on a nearby workbench, turning it over in his hands. "These are miniature realm gates, like the stone tablets. How did you do this?"

Mara looked away.

"Seriously?" Diana asked. "Now you're going to be a dick about it?"

"I can't imagine you like being chained up," Wei said. "I can't imagine this was how you thought it would work."

"Of course not," she snapped.

Wei crouched beside Mara and placed a hand on her arm. The witch visibly relaxed, and a few seconds later she looked close to falling asleep.

"Why don't you tell us all about it?" Wei suggested.

"Nice trick," Mordred said.

"It's not something I can do often," Wei said. "Or for long, so save the gratitude and ask questions."

"How do you make these?" Nabu asked.

"You can make them out of anything," Mara said sleepily. "But they only last one time each. It has to be made of stone for it to be permanent."

"Why are you chained up?" Diana asked.

"I demanded things from that bitch Abaddon. She said I was lucky to be alive. So they chained me in here. Looks like I need to learn to be nicer to people."

"Can't fault their logic there," Mordred said.

Nabu picked up the dozen bracelets there and dropped them into a nearby bag.

"Where are my husband and Elaine?" Fiona asked, her voice cracking a little.

"Elaine is inside the mountain. Alan, too. They found him about an hour ago. He was not looking his best when they dragged him past. As a water summoner with no water to summon from, he must feel quite impotent."

Fiona threw a punch at Mara's head, but Diana grabbed her wrist before it connected. "Not helping," she said, and Fiona turned and left the cabin.

"Where do those bracelets take you?" Nabu asked.

Mara mumbled something.

"Shit," Wei said, and removed her hand from Mara's leg. "I needed to stop. She's slipping too far into sleep. If I keep this up, you'll get nothing but one comatose witch."

"Still think Hera is the good guy?" Diana asked as Mara blinked, clearly angry. "You murdered your ex-husband and almost got your daughter killed. All because you wanted to crawl up Hera's ass. Now your daughter, Chloe, hates you. Do you remember that? Do you even care?"

"My daughter is a disappointment," Mara said, her voice beginning to sound more like her usual self. "She sided with you over her own family. I might have ended up in a less-than-ideal situation here, but once Demeter and Hera find out what those animals did to me, they'll release me."

"Can we take her with us?" Fiona called from the front door.

Nabu picked up the chain. "No. It would take too long to cut through the chain, and that much power would draw attention."

"We could cut her leg off," Mordred suggested.

"We're not cutting limbs off," Diana said.

"Just a thought. One quick cut, the leg is gone and she's a little easier to carry."

"Mordred, no dismemberment."

Mara's color was an unhealthy shade of green.

"Not the whole leg, just the bottom half," Mordred continued before smiling at Mara and drawing a pistol, aiming it at her head.

"You won't kill me," Mara snarled. "My daughter would hate you if you killed me. And she's more important to you than I am."

"That is true," Mordred said.

"But she'll get over it," Diana pointed out.

Mara moved aside her shirt, revealing the glyphs at the top of her shoulder. "You seen these before?"

"They're the same ones used on the magical bomb people," Mordred said.

"I leave this cabin, I go boom. My heart rate stops, I go boom. Either way, I take out myself, you, and anyone else in a few dozen feet. You want to make that much noise?"

"You're not a sorcerer," Nabu said. "How can they use that glyph on you?"

"I access the magic by using my own life force. They modified the glyph to work on me. It won't be as spectacular as when the sorcerers do it, but it'll be enough."

"Mordred, we need to go," Fiona called out. "We have trouble."

Diana punched Mara in the face, knocking her out, as everyone else piled out of the cabin and walked straight into a fight with several blood elves.

Mordred avoided the swipe of one blood-elf sword and used his own sword of ice to cleave his attacker in half before moving to a second blood elf. He threw three fist-sized balls of water at the blood elf, and as each one touched the elf, he froze them into thousands of tiny ice shards, killing the blood elf instantly.

The battle was quick, and brutal, and ended with the eight blood elves dead. Mordred froze the edges of Mara's cabin with thick ice, hoping it was enough in addition to the chains, to keep her there until everyone had escaped. He'd have liked to have gone back in and killed her, but he knew that she had been right about Chloe. He'd met Mara's daughter, Chloe, several times and had been there when Chloe's father had been murdered by blood elves. He liked Chloe. They'd fought side by side, and in some ways her presence forced Nate and him to come to terms that would later be a new friendship. He recalled the way she looked as she cradled her dying father. Mordred would have liked nothing more than to kill Mara once and for all, but magical bomb or not, he couldn't do that to Chloe.

The group ran to the mouth of a nearby cave and stopped.

"Runes," Nabu said, pointing just inside the mouth of the cave.

Mordred took a step into the cave and expected his magic to vanish, but it remained. "That's weird," he said as he stared at the bright-red runes.

"I can't smell you," Wei said. "Can't sense you in any way."

"Me, neither," Remy said as he joined the group. "I got bored, and once we saw you fight those blood elves, I figured it was best if we were all together. Turns out, Morgan and Mac are really stubborn."

"Yes, it's come up before," Mordred said. "Morgan, you can barely walk. Is this really the best idea you could come up with?"

"Yes, now shut up and help me stay upright. Mac is wobbling."

Nabu took Morgan's arm and dropped it around his neck. "I'll stay with you. We'll go find a cabin where it's warm. Mac, are you with us?"

Mac nodded. "Mordred, I don't know what's in there, but they went to a lot of effort to keep it secret."

"Everyone either is dead or ran away. I'm not sure that constitutes an effort."

"That's what worries me."

Mordred walked further into the cave, with Fiona, Remy, Diana, and Wei close behind him. "Can you smell anything?" he called back.

"No, nothing," Wei said.

"It's like my senses don't work in here," Diana said. "I've never felt anything like it."

"I'm really glad I have a gun," Remy said, tapping the Sig slung across his back. "I'd prefer a tank, but beggars can't be choosers and all that."

Dim lights had been placed along each wall, and every few dozen feet were wooden boards partially buried in the ground, allowing people to descend the steep slopes that led further down into the mountain. They walked for a few minutes before they came to a junction.

"Remy, Wei, you want to take left?" Mordred asked. "Fiona, Diana, and I will take right. If you find something, don't engage. Just come back and get us. Make sure you use the walkie-talkie and let the others know."

They split off, and it took only a short time before Mordred found a metal door built into the wall. He tried the door and found it locked, but there was a key hanging from a hook a few feet away. He took the large key and tested it in the lock, which clicked open. Mordred pushed the door open with a squeak, revealing Elaine on a bed with Alan on a wooden chair next to her.

"Alan," Fiona said, and ran to her husband, who kissed her.

"Is this real?" he asked.

"Yeah, we're here to rescue you," Mordred said, feeling his magic cut out on him again. "Well, I am. These two were just hanging around being lazy."

Elaine forced a smile. She looked tired and had some dried blood on her forehead but other than that appeared to be physically okay. Even so, Mordred had to check. "How are you?"

"It's been a long few days," Elaine said. "I think. I don't know anymore. They did things to my brain. Did things to my memory. I assume everything in Avalon has gone to shit."

"I think we're a few stages past shit," Remy said from the doorway.

"The prophecy, Mordred—it's a lie," Elaine said. "It's not real. It's a trick put there by . . ." Elaine dropped to her knees, clutching her head as she screamed in agony.

Mordred dropped beside her as Remy hurried off, presumably to get help. "Elaine, Elaine."

"I'm okay," she said, sounding weary. "They did something to my memories. I can't remember why I was looking into things. I can't remember who took my memories."

"When I arrived, she could barely remember me," Alan said from across the room. "Her memories are returning, but I don't know who took them."

"We'll find out," Mordred promised.

"Right now we have new issues," Remy said, reappearing at the door.

"What issues?"

"The dead appear to be rising from the grave and walking up the hill outside. Nabu, Mac, and Morgan just moved into the cave as quickly as possible."

"Abaddon," Elaine confirmed, getting back to her feet. "I haven't seen her in a few days. I was hoping she'd left for good. We'll have to go further into the mountain. There's a way out there."

Wei stood outside the cell with Morgan, Mac, and Nabu. "It's a big old army of dead people," Morgan said. "They look about as well as I feel."

"Mordred," came a female voice that filled the tunnel. "We installed a PA system inside the mountain. I know you can hear me. You have until the count of ten to leave the mountain before we come find you. You didn't really think you got to Elaine because you were that good, did you? You've managed to trap yourselves. Either you come out, or I assure you the alternative will be less than pleasant."

Nabu removed the bracelets from the bag he carried. "We can use these to escape."

"We don't know where they go," Fiona pointed out.

"Tartarus," Alan said. "They attacked it. They killed Rhea and Cronus. Ares told me, bragged about it as he beat on me. He was proud that Abaddon had removed Rhea's head."

Everyone was stunned into silence for several seconds. "How strong do you need to be to be able to kill both of them?" Remy asked.

"I'd really like to be elsewhere," Wei said.

"Tartarus is better than staying under a mountain fighting a godlike necromancer and her minions of the undead," Diana said.

"The moon would be better than that," Remy pointed out.

Mordred looked over at Alan, who was leaning on Fiona. "You okay?" he asked.

Alan nodded. "Just been a rough few days. Feels like my body has finally given up trying to work properly."

"Just lean on me," Fiona told him. "I'll get you out of here." She kissed him on the forehead, and Mordred looked away, not wishing to intrude on a tender moment.

"How do these bracelets work?" Mac asked.

"We really should have gotten that information from Mara," Diana pointed out.

"I've seen them used," Elaine said. "You put them on your wrist and tap them."

Mac placed one on his wrist, tapped it, and glanced around the group. "I'm not saying it's broken, but it's not exactly impressive, is it?"

"We need to go further into the mountain," Elaine said. "There are no runes down there. That's where they use the bracelets."

"How do you know this?" Mordred asked.

"Do you think I've just been waiting for them to come get me? I've escaped six times since they've had me here. I've killed four guards. The Hole has been destroyed; the prisoners escaped. They've been working for Abaddon and her people."

"Yeah, we met them," Remy said. "Some of them have a tendency to blow up."

"We met some on the way here," Morgan said. "They were working in the village below."

"They're a bit dead," Wei said. "I'm Wei, by the way. No one seemed to want to introduce me. Understandable considering the impending death and doom coming our way."

"This is Wei," Remy said. "She's full of sunshine and joy."

Wei laughed. "Touché."

The group was moving seconds later, slowly at first, then faster after Diana picked up Morgan, sprinting flat out through the tunnels, going deeper and deeper into the mountain. After several minutes of following Elaine and ignoring the majority of small tunnels that had been carved ant-nest-like into the mountain, they came to a cavern with writing all over the walls. It glowed slightly purple.

"What is this?" Morgan asked.

"I don't know," Elaine said. "I found it on my first escape. It's where Merlin caught me."

"Merlin is here?" Mordred asked.

Elaine nodded.

Mordred walked over to the metal structure in the center of the cavern. It had the appearance of a large dais that could have easily fitted a hundred people. More of the strange writing was on it, although it was colorless.

"What is this place?" Nabu asked as he joined Mordred. "I've never seen anything like this. My power doesn't work. I can't see what all of this is. It's quite infuriating."

"Welcome to the rest of the world," Elaine said. "We need to leave."

Everyone was given a bracelet.

"Let's go, people," Mordred said. "I'll go last, just in case you need cover."

People started vanishing one after the other until only Elaine, Diana, and Mordred remained. "I knew you weren't going to go until we all did," Diana said.

"I'll be right there. I just wanted to make sure I could collapse that tunnel. The fewer people being able to use this place, the better."

"Don't screw around, Mordred," Diana said, and touched her bracelet, disappearing.

"Mordred," Elaine said, pointing toward the entrance to the cavern that the group had taken. There stood a man with short white hair, and a short beard of the same color. Another man stood behind him, wearing gleaming golden armor.

"Gawain," Elaine said. "Merlin."

Merlin placed a hand on Gawain's armored arm, stopping the knight as his hand reached for the broadsword that hung at his hip. "Leave us," he said.

"Die painfully, little brother," Gawain said to Mordred.

"Eat shit," Mordred said cheerfully.

Gawain nodded to Merlin, turned, and walked out of sight.

"Elaine," Merlin said. "You can't run from me."

Elaine placed her hand over her bracelet and vanished.

Merlin screamed in rage and flung a block of earth at the place Elaine had been. He turned to Mordred. "It has been a very long time, Mordred. I assume you're going to run, too."

"I thought I'd kill you and save us a lot of trouble for later."

Merlin laughed. "You always did have a high opinion of yourself."

"And you always had a very low one of me."

"You should have stayed hidden away. You should have never involved yourself."

"Yes, well, that's the problem with people trying to kill you: you kind of have to be involved. But then you know all about people trying to kill me, don't you. So, did you have a hand in creating the prophecy where I kill Nate? I'm just wondering who I need to hunt down."

"I have no idea what you're talking about."

"So, are you My Liege, or just another asshole following him?"

Merlin laughed. "What do you think?"

"I think you were once a good man, and I'd hoped that there was still some of that left inside of you," Mordred said with a touch of sadness. "I'd hoped that if I'd managed to come back from the darkness, that you'd be able to as well. Guess I was wrong. Why are you doing this? Why are you going against Avalon?"

"I am Avalon," Merlin snapped, spitting.

"No one is so important that they can't be replaced. You taught me that as a child. You taught me that Avalon was only as good as those working for its benefit. So what's your plan here? Get people to fear you, get the humans to go to war for you? Did you have a hand in what Baldr and his people did to me? Did you know?"

"I never would have let you go if I'd known," Merlin said. "Never. You are my son, and at one point I loved you. But you were never the man I hoped you were. You were never good enough. And there are some things more important than love. Like my duty, and Avalon's need to be strong."

"You're My Liege, aren't you?"

"You have to die, Mordred, because you oppose me, and that can't be allowed to stand."

Magical power flowed out of Merlin, and Mordred reacted in an instant, throwing a torrent of powerful air magic at the top of the tunnel. Merlin screamed in rage as tons of rock and dirt fell in front of him, covering the exit to the tunnel.

A wicked smile appeared on Mordred's lips. "Stay buried, Dad. I don't think you're going to like what I do to your Avalon if you and your friends take back control." He placed his hand on the bracelet and vanished from view.

CHAPTER 24

Nate Garrett

Realm of Shadow Falls

Antonio and Leonardo took us through the mountain, creating new tunnels and stairs out of the sheer rock around us. They hadn't said much beyond the need to see a prison cell and some elven runes, and that they needed our help. It wasn't like Leonardo to remain silent for long, so whatever was going on was either really bad, or really, really bad. There were no good options when it came to a quiet Leonardo.

"We won't have long," Selene said from beside me. "Those prison guards are going to notice we've gone."

"And then they're going to come find us," Zamek said. "I don't relish trying to explain why we're escaping when we're not really sure ourselves."

"So who does this cell belong to?" Sky asked.

"Asmodeus," Leonardo said, to the surprise of everyone else.

"Asmodeus's prison was never meant to be in Shadow Falls," Lucifer said. After knowing him as Grayson for so long, I was finally coming around to using his original name.

"Where was it meant to be?" Sky asked.

"No one knew for sure. It was a secret. And not supposed to be anywhere near people."

"Leonardo, can you please tell us what's going on?" I asked. "In slightly more detail. Is Asmodeus still in his prison?"

"No, it's empty," Antonio said. "And Leonardo is not talking, because he's trying to shift the rock behind us to make it look like we went in another direction."

"He can do that?" Zamek asked. "That's incredibly powerful alchemy. Actually forget that. What he's doing is dwarf-level alchemy."

Leonardo stopped walking and turned back to face the rest of us. "Thank you for the compliment. I assure you, it took many years of practice. Also, I should inform you that those sorcerer's bands can be removed whenever you wish. I didn't put explosives in them like the Avalon ones. I tend not to want to put cruelty into my inventions anymore."

I pulled the sorcerer's band from my wrist and tossed it to the floor; the others did the same. My magic flooded back into me. "Thank you. I did wonder how long I had to wear that blasted thing."

"We're almost there," Leonardo said, completely ignoring me once again and walking off to move more rock.

"It'll be worth it," Antonio promised. "He's been excited and terrified in equal measure about this thing since we found it."

"If it's Asmodeus's prison," Lucifer said, "I'd be more terrified than excited."

"So, have you finally told everyone you're Lucifer?" Leonardo asked as he moved several tons of rock out of the way, creating a new passage.

"How long have you known?" Lucifer asked.

"I figured it out when I found the prison a year ago. You'll see why."

We were silent for the rest of the journey until Leonardo led us into a gigantic cavern. Purple writing glowed across the walls, and in the center was an empty dais that was big enough to put several dozen people. I walked over and found that it had similar writing to what was on the walls, although there was no color to it.

"What is this place?" I asked.

"What is this writing?" Selene asked at almost the exact same moment.

"There's no prison here," Sky said. "Unless it's invisible, which is a distinct possibility considering the weird shit I've seen in the last few days."

"It's further on," Leonardo said. "I just wanted you to see this, too."

"It's elvish," Lucifer said. "I can't read it, though."

"The only elvish I know is from blood elves," Zamek said. "And this isn't anything like that."

"I recognize this word here," Lucifer said, pointing to a long mass of swirling patterns. "It means 'moving,' or 'forward,' something like that. It's hard to explain, as elvish writing is a difficult thing to master. The elves kept their language a secret. There were no manuals, or people willing to teach it. What you learned you had to figure out on your own."

"We believe that Shadow Falls was once an elven kingdom," Leonardo said. "A shadow-elf kingdom to be exact."

"That would be quite the coincidence," Selene said.

"I think whoever came here first and named this place Shadow Falls knew it was always called that. I've found information that suggests this mountain was always known as Shadow's Peak. So, whoever first came here probably knew the history of the realm."

"So, if shadow elves lived here, it would have been before the elven civil war," Zamek said. "Long before."

"Thousands of years before, yes. There's evidence of old ruins to the north. I think it was an old city that was razed to the ground at some point. It's hard to say exactly when. I can't read all that much elvish. There's something you need to see, though."

Leonardo led us under an archway at the edge of the cavern, and down a long, winding slope to a second cavern, which made the first one look about the size of a matchbox. Dozens of crystals in the ceiling lit the room, casting a blue-and-pink glow over everything.

"You could fit an aircraft carrier in here," Sky said.

The cavern was the largest I'd ever seen outside of the dwarven realm, something Zamek appeared to think, too, considering the look on his face.

"You okay?" I asked him.

"It's like home. It's a lot to take in. Are you saying this isn't dwarven, Leonardo? Because elves aren't alchemists."

"No. These caves were probably made by dwarves. I have no way of confirming that one way or the other, though. Do you notice there's no writing?"

"What the fuck is that?" Sky asked, pointing to the center of the cavern.

In the center of the cavern was a cell. It resembled a huge bell with a metal door and several barred windows on what appeared to be two floors. Chains ran from the ceiling to the top and sides of the cell. Separating us was a twenty-foot-wide gap. I walked to the edge and looked down.

"Seven hundred feet deep by our last estimations," Leonardo said. "There's a bridge just there."

I looked where he'd pointed, and indeed there was a sturdy-looking metal bridge.

"It's the giant statues I'm more interested in," Selene said.

Four fifteen-foot-high stone elf statues stood around the cell, all looking down on the cell. Each held a sword and shield that were taller than most people, and if the idea was to intimidate whoever was inside the cell into behaving, someone had certainly gone to a lot of effort.

"We don't know what they are," a voice from behind us said.

I turned to see Caitlin, Galahad, and Harrison enter the cavern. "Glad to see you made it down here okay," Galahad said.

"Look, if you're here to fight—" I started.

"We have a lot of explaining to do," Harrison assured me.

"Those statues are one of the reasons we think that this was an elven realm," Leonardo continued, as if the three newcomers hadn't entered the room. "We've found plenty of items that we've taken from here showing drawings of elves, various pieces of writing. There's a lot we don't know, but we're almost certain Shadow Falls was an elven realm."

"What the hell is going on?" Sky asked.

"You might all want to sit down," Galahad said, pointing toward a nearby workbench. "There's a lot to go through."

Once we were all seated next to the lengthy workbench, Leonardo picked up an old leather-bound book, passing it to me.

I flicked open the first page and found a drawing of Lucifer. "You're in here," I told him, showing him the picture of someone who looked almost identical to him.

He took the book from me and flicked through several of the pages. "Abaddon," he said, showing me the picture of her. "And this is Asmodeus."

Asmodeus looked like the kind of suave, sophisticated vampire that people wrote books about. He was handsome and in any other walk of life would probably have graced the covers of modeling magazines or would've been a big-name actor. He didn't look threatening, or menacing. In fact there was a small smile tugging at the corners of his lips.

"He doesn't look like someone I should be scared of," Zamek said. "He looks like someone who enjoys preening in front of a mirror for hours on end."

"He's a monster," Lucifer said. "Let me assure you of that." He went through more pages. "The rest of the devils are in here, too. All seven of us. And then there are details on their positions in what realms. I can read the occasional word, so I'm only guessing, but I see the names of several realms here, and not all of the writing is in elvish. This book was used to keep an eye on us. It ends just after the rest of them were banished. This book is thousands of years old. I knew the elves did something to their paper to make it not age, but this is astonishing."

"The dwarves do the same thing," Zamek said. "Although we use our alchemy to do it."

"Okay, anytime someone wants to explain everything," Selene started.

"Yes, I think we're owed that much," Lucifer continued.

"We've had some problems over the last few weeks," Galahad began as he took a seat. He'd cut his dark hair since I'd last seen him, and grown a short beard. There was a small scar on his cheek that I didn't remember.

Caitlin sat beside him. She wore jeans and a T-shirt instead of the suit she'd worn as a member of the FBI. It was good to see her again, and I hoped that the last few years had been kind to her.

"A few weeks ago a man by the name of Lee O'Hara arrived in the city, claiming to be your friend," Harrison said to me. "I assume you know that name."

I nodded, feeling the shock of the name of an enemy for the first time in years. "He's the son of a crime boss in London. When I lost my memory, after Mordred's attack, I worked as a thief for the family. Lee was a monster. Human, but evil. He tried to have me killed, and almost got his sister killed in the process. His family had him exiled from the UK for it. He doesn't like me a whole lot."

"Well, he's not human anymore," Galahad said. "He's a vampire. A very powerful one."

"He murdered people," Caitlin said. "Left marks saying it was the work of Hellequin. He ran off to the forest at the north of the city. We sent people after him, but they didn't come back."

"And more than one person in the city defected to his cause," Harrison said.

"You had traitors in your midst again?" I asked.

"It would appear so," Harrison said between clenched teeth.

"How can Lee be so powerful after only a few years? Vampires take centuries to become powerful." I glanced at Lucifer. "Asmodeus, I presume?"

"Those he turns are abnormally strong," Lucifer said. "It's possible this Lee is one of his. And if that's the case, we have a problem. Wherever Lee is, Asmodeus will know about it. He can track his creations, but more than that I doubt very much Lee's arrival here is a coincidence. Asmodeus must have sent him."

"What does that have to do with us?" I asked.

"You are Hellequin," Galahad said. "And several of my council decided that if you arrived, you should be arrested and questioned. That demand only increased when someone calling themselves Hellequin starting murdering humans on Earth realm. So, I needed to make your arrest look good so that when you emerged from prison, everyone would be convinced that I'd discovered your innocence."

"Yes," Harrison said. "We had to arrest you all, unfortunately. It wouldn't have worked if we'd just taken you, Nate."

I noticed that Galahad hadn't apologized for what he'd done, although I wasn't about to hold a grudge about it. "Did you have to punch me, too?"

Harrison smiled. "No, that was just for fun."

"You're such a dick," I told him, and enjoyed seeing that smile falter.

"We don't have time for this," Galahad snapped. "We need to discuss what's happening."

"Well, Avalon is declaring war on you because someone using my name is murdering humans and attacking Tartarus," I started. "They killed Rhea and Cronus. They wrote *Shadow Falls* in blood near their bodies. Someone is doing an excellent job making people think that you and Shadow Falls are behind it all. In just over a day, Avalon will launch an offensive against you. They will expect you to hand yourself to them for questioning. They will expect you to allow their forces into Shadow Falls."

"Then they will be very disappointed," Galahad said. "You came here to do what, convince me to let it happen?"

"We came here because we hoped you'd be able to talk to them before this went any further," Sky said.

"If you can talk to Arthur and make him realize what's happening, a war might be averted," Selene said. "You need to let Arthur and some of his people into the realm to discuss what's going on."

"So they can try and take control?" Harrison asked. "Never going to happen."

"This isn't about taking control," I snapped. "This is about Avalon's war machine marching to your front gates. If you can't convince them of your innocence, they will try to force the issue."

"Then they will be upset," Galahad said. "They will not come into this realm. They will not be invaders."

"Then go talk to them," I said. "Arthur is coming alone. He'll be here in hours. I will go with you, to neutral ground. The pair of you can talk."

"I tried," Galahad snapped. "About a month ago I was given word that Avalon was looking for reasons to invade."

"A month ago?" I asked, looking over at Sky and Selene, who both shrugged.

"What can I say? Avalon already has ideas to take this realm for themselves."

"You really believe that Arthur would invade Shadow Falls without reason?" I asked. "He came to me before all of this death and told me that he'd heard rumors of a Shadow Falls expansion plan into America. He asked me to come here and find out what's going on. He doesn't want war with you, Galahad."

"I agree. I don't believe he wants war," Galahad admitted. "But that's not to say that people who want control of Avalon for themselves wouldn't move Avalon into a war with us. A war they could capitalize on."

"Hera?" Selene said. "That sounds an awful lot like her."

"Or Baldr, or Merlin, or any number of a dozen people who want what we have," Leonardo said.

"The crystals," Caitlin finished for him. "You remember those, yes? An unending source of energy. A weapon of immeasurable power, and a way in which Avalon could gain more and more control over all of the realms."

"They're unstable," I said.

"You think they'll care about that?" Galahad asked.

"Are these the same crystals that created the blood elves?" Zamek asked.

"Similar, yes," I said. "Less stable, and there have been no adverse effects of magic on people."

"Blood elves, they used to be the shadow elves, yes?" Leonardo asked. "Before the civil war with the sun elves? Before they lost and were sent to be watched over by the dwarfs?"

"Yes, that's them," Zamek said. "Before that, the elves and dwarves lived and worked side by side for hundreds of years, right up until the point they attacked us, killing thousands. You say the crystals here have had no effect? Well, we didn't think they affected the elves until they became crazed monsters."

"But the elves are the only species the crystals affected," Selene said. "And that was after hundreds and hundreds of years of exposure. Before then the humans worked with the crystals with no ill effects."

"That's true," Zamek said. "But who wants to bet that certain people in Avalon will want to experiment with those crystals? You really think that Hera won't try to create her own blood elves, but with a different species?"

"Zamek, can I discuss the crystals with you?" Leonardo asked.

Zamek nodded and walked off with Leonardo and Antonio.

"I've seen what those crystals do in the wrong hands," I said. "You had us all arrested to appease people in your government. What happens now, Galahad?"

"Now we make out that you were all questioned at length and you'll be helping with inquiries. I am their king, but I'm not all-powerful. I can't have my council and advisers fighting amongst themselves."

"So, why not just question us in the prison?" Sky asked.

"Because you needed to see this," Caitlin said. "Specifically, the cell over there."

"It's a very nice cell," Selene said. "Asmodeus isn't inside."

"No, it appears to be empty," Galahad said. "It was shut when Leonardo found it during an expedition into the mountain. And then, a month ago, we came here and it was open. Back in the room with all of the purple writing, there was one dead blood elf. That was the first time I'd ever seen one of their kind. It was a bit of a shock, and it took more than a few calls and favors to even figure out what it was."

"Okay, so it's quite possible that Asmodeus was inside and is now free," Selene said. "In fact it's probable considering that it appears someone turned this Lee guy into a powerful vampire."

"Couldn't another master vampire have turned him?" Sky said. "They can make powerful people quickly. It would have been within the last month, so that's a lot quicker than usual, but it's possible."

"It is, but it's also unlikely," Lucifer said. "I'd need to see Lee to be sure. Asmodeus's vampires had a very specific way about them. They were more bloodthirsty than most, capable of acts of depravity that shocked people. They murdered whole families just to bathe in their blood."

"He did that," Harrison said. "My men found him lying in a bathtub full of the blood of the family he'd slaughtered."

"Sounds like Asmodeus to me," Lucifer said.

"Have any of you been in the cell?" I asked as Leonardo rejoined us.

"Of course," Leonardo said.

"Is it safe?"

"It appears to be, why?"

I got up. "I'll be back in a minute."

"Did you know he was trying to make a realm gate?" Zamek asked me as I walked toward him.

"Who, Leonardo?" I replied.

"Yes, I'm trying to see if I can manipulate the crystals to make a larger realm gate," Leonardo said. "Essentially I want to operate one of the gates we have and then use the crystals to widen the gate. It should allow a lot more people in and out of a realm."

"Or blow up," Galahad said.

"That's why I haven't tried it yet," Leonardo said.

"That and they won't let you," Antonio sniped.

"Yes, and that," Leonardo replied.

I walked away, across the bridge, repeatedly telling myself not to look down. I took a moment to myself when I was over, and looked around at the four stone giants, trying to make it appear as though the walk over a narrow, old bridge wasn't something completely awful.

Writing I couldn't read had been carved into the legs of each of the giants. "I presume this is elvish?" I called back, and discovered that Leonardo had crossed the bridge and was closer than I'd expected. "Sorry, didn't mean to shout at you."

Leonardo smiled. "It's elvish, yes. And no, like everything else I have no idea what it says."

I walked to the door of the cell and looked up at the writing above the thick metal cell door. "That says *Asmodeus*, though."

"Yes. I've found his name in a few pieces of writing, but the elves didn't have an alphabet like we do, so translating an *A* in 'Asmodeus' isn't the same as an *A* in 'apple.' It's a . . . frustrating exercise."

"I can imagine." I pushed the door open fully and stepped into the cell. "Give me a minute. I have an idea." I took a deep breath, and in my head I called for Erebus.

"Hello, Nate," Erebus said. He sat on the bare floor of the cell, wearing a pair of black jeans and a white T-shirt. "I didn't expect to hear from you again so soon. This isn't back inside your head, by the way, so we're operating on real time here."

"You said the last mark would gift me with knowledge."

"Yes, your mother told me that."

"What knowledge?"

"Whatever it was decided you needed to know. Things about history, about the various players in the game of Avalon, all kinds of things."

"Elven writing?"

"Ah, not so much, no. Elven writing is a by-product of their magic. The elves had a very odd magical ability. Part nature magic, part blood magic. They could instinctively understand one another's writing. It was the intent of the word, not the word itself, that mattered. It makes it almost impossible for anyone to learn more than a word or two, and even then not everyone would have written that word the same way."

"Okay, so there's no way to know what any of this all meant?"

"Not unless you can absorb the spirit of an elf. And even then you might not be able to."

"And the elves here died thousands of years ago, so that's out." I thought about the problem for a few seconds. "Any chance *you* know any elvish?"

Erebus smiled. "No, unfortunately not."

"Any chance you could just pour all of the information that the mark held back into my head at once?"

"Only if you'd like to be turned into a vegetable for the next decade. My role now consists of giving you that information at a rate your brain can cope with. This has nothing to do with your power of a sorcerer, and everything to do with the fact that too much of this information at once will overload your synapses."

Okay, so that was out. "You know, it's weird you're Erebus, but you still look like me. Any chance you could . . . not?"

"No. I'm still essentially the nightmare in your body, so I get to look how your nightmare would. Most sorcerers don't even get a chatty nightmare. You could always use the elven magic echo."

"The what?"

"Elves wrote things down, but sometimes they could imbue their words with blood magic. Creating a magic echo. Essentially it records everything that happened in the few minutes after the magic was used. It was quite the interesting use of power. Also, it only works with words that glow."

I looked around at the words written on the walls of the cell. "None in here, but there are a lot of those back at the realm gate. I assume that is a realm gate?"

"Yes. Very few of us knew about them. The elven civil war was fought because the shadow elves wanted to tell the world about what they knew, and the sun elves refused. The realm gate requires blood to use, though. Quite a bit of it."

"A sacrifice."

"You can see why they weren't popular."

"The blood elf they found?"

"That would do it. If someone came here through a realm gate, they'd need a sacrifice to get back out again."

"So a month ago they come here, open the cell, drag Asmodeus out, kill a blood elf, and escape. We need to know exactly what happened. I need to go use one of these echoes. Thanks."

"Glad to have helped," Erebus said before vanishing.

"I have an idea," I said, running out of the cell to see that several of the group had made their way across the bridge. There was a rumble from beside me, and I had to throw myself aside just in time to avoid one of the massive swords of the now-moving stone giants.

Soon all four giants were moving, ready to destroy anyone close to the cell.

CHAPTER 25

Nate Garrett

Selene, Sky, and Zamek all dodged aside as two of the stone giants moved to attack them. One of them swiped with its massive shield, catching Lucifer in the chest, sending him flying into me.

I tried to catch him, but the force was too much, and we collided, throwing us back toward the edge of the island. I used my shadow magic to anchor both myself and Lucifer to the ground as I caught a glimpse of Zamek scaling one of the giants and using his alchemy to tear it apart with his bare hands as Galahad and Harrison removed its legs.

Lucifer was on his feet before me, and pure magic leapt from his fingers, smashing into the closest giant and taking it off its feet, making the ground shake from the force of the landing. Sky brought one stone giant to its knees so that Leonardo and Caitlin could place their hands on its head, turning it to dust, while Selene jumped up onto the last giant, turning into her dragon-kin form as she moved. Her strength and power tore into the giant with vigor, and it took only seconds for the fifteen-foot goliath to be turned into several tons of rubble.

I got to my feet and brushed myself clean.

"Glad you could help out!" Zamek shouted to me.

"You could have left me one," I said with a smile.

"Sorry, I guess I figured if you wanted to take part, you wouldn't have been lying on the floor."

I walked over to the nearest giant, which swiped at me with its one remaining arm. I darted back, activating my matter magic. Purple glyphs appeared over my hands and arms, and my world became a purple haze. I took a step toward the giant and focused all my power into my right hand, pouring as much matter magic as I could into it.

It took only a second for the punch to completely destroy the giant, showering everything around it with dirt and rubble. I stood there for several seconds as I removed my matter magic and my body got used to seeing normally again.

"How'd you do that?" Zamek asked. "That was crazy."

I shrugged. "Everyone okay?"

Everyone made it known that they were fine.

Selene took my hand in hers and kissed me on the cheek. "You okay?"

"Yeah, I am. I haven't used my matter magic like that before. I wasn't really sure how it worked until I switched it on, but I figured I'd give it a try. Erebus said he's drip feeding knowledge into my head. He told me about an elven magic echo."

Caitlin poked the destroyed giant and looked back at me, surprised at the devastation my punch had caused. "That's new."

"I've got a lot of new things since I saw you," I told her. "I don't know who set that trap, but I'm guessing it was done by whoever came here a month ago and removed Asmodeus."

"What's a magic echo?" Galahad asked.

I quickly explained what Erebus had told me.

"So, we need to go back to the realm gate?" Leonardo asked. "This is turning into an incredibly interesting day."

"Yeah, I'm not sure 'interesting' is how I'd put it," Galahad said. "I guess it at least breaks up the day's council meetings."

Everyone made their way back to the realm-gate cavern and stood around the outside of the cave, near different pieces of writing.

"So, how does this work?" Galahad asked from beside me. "Do we each have to bleed, or is this a one-off thing?"

I shrugged. "Leonardo assumed that the color changed because someone used the realm gate."

"I thought the same thing," said Lucifer.

"Maybe that's not what the color is for," I suggested. "Pass me your knife, will you?" I asked Harrison, who removed the dagger from his belt and gave it to me.

I used it to cut into the palm of my hand, then placed my hand against the purple writing. The effect was instantaneous as all the writing in the cavern turned a deep red and several figures started to appear on the dais in the middle of the cavern.

I took my hand away—my magic would heal it within moments—and watched the six figures flicker for several seconds until the picture settled.

"It's like they're holograms," Selene said. "Tommy would be comparing it to *Star Wars* about now."

To my mind it wasn't a bad comparison. The figures were all in light blue, and we couldn't hear sound, but we got the gist of what was going on. One man, his arms shackled behind his back, was kneeling on the floor.

"That's Asmodeus," Lucifer said. "It's weird seeing him like this. It's been so long since I had contact."

One of the elves around Asmodeus was talking to him, and after listening for several seconds the king of the devils started to laugh.

The two elves behind Asmodeus each took one arm and held him down while a third elf slit his throat, allowing the blood to pour into several vessels below the dais. The vessels were a few feet high and sat in front of Asmodeus and the two guards, who continued to hold Asmodeus until he had no strength left to fight. It was at that moment that I noticed a vase.

The elf who had slit his throat unsheathed a curved sword that sat at his hip and cut Asmodeus's head off. He picked it up by the hair and dropped it into one of the containers that was full of blood.

"That's not exactly what I was expecting," Galahad said.

I walked to the dais as the elves dragged Asmodeus's body away, toward the cell in the other cavern. The picture of the blood-filled containers and the vase remained for several seconds before they, too, vanished from view as the footage ended.

"Nate, you okay?" Selene asked.

"I've seen the markings on that vase before," I told her. "I saw them a long time ago. In London. Merlin had the Reavers collecting souls for him to feed to Arthur. They're called soul jars. The markings on this one here are the same as on the jars I saw in London. They killed Asmodeus and placed his soul in a jar and drained him of his blood. That's not a cell—it's a tomb."

No one spoke for several seconds until Leonardo broke the silence: "So, the elves killed Asmodeus. But you think he's involved with what's going on? That can't possibly be right."

"No, it can't," Selene said.

"Nate, soul jars are bad news," Sky said. "You don't think that someone out there has Asmodeus's soul jar? Because if they fed that soul to someone, like Merlin was feeding souls to Arthur, how long do you think it would take for that person to be completely taken over by the evil in Asmodeus's soul?"

"Not long," Lucifer said.

"Did you find anything with blood, or soul jars while you were poking around in there?" I asked.

"No," Leonardo said. "Just old drawings and pieces of paper. It's amazing how it's survived for so long with barely any degrading. Elven magic was impressive."

"That means someone broke in and stole his body, but nothing else," Lucifer said. "Why would someone want to steal Asmodeus's body?"

"Was his soul jar in the cell?" I asked.

"We didn't see it," Leonardo said.

"Could they have taken him and the jar to try and bring him back?" Antonio suggested. "Is that even possible? He is a vampire."

Lucifer didn't look convinced. "I honestly have no idea. He surprised a lot of us with the range of his power, so I never counted anything out when it came to dealing with him."

"Maybe Lee will have some of the answers we need," I suggested.

"This is all very theoretical," Harrison said. "You're all just guessing that someone has used his soul. We don't know that it's been used."

"That's true," Galahad said. "But what if Lee wasn't turned into a vampire by Asmodeus, but found the soul jar and opened it? How much work does it take for a soul to be transferred into a person?"

"A lot," Sky said. "The way Merlin used to do it required dwarven runes and a lot of magical power, but a soul as corrupt and evil as Asmodeus? It's possible you wouldn't need as much. Either way, you'd need to know the correct runes and glyphs and have magical ability. People can't just bleed on them and suddenly you've absorbed one."

"Okay, if this Lee is possessed by Asmodeus, just how powerful will he be?" Zamek asked. "I'm only asking because if you four go find Lee, and he is Asmodeus, or has part of that devil's soul in him, then it's going to take a lot more than the four of you to subdue him. I get that you're all very powerful, but are you powerful enough to bring down someone who absorbed even part of a god?"

"Either way, we need to find Lee," I said. "Whether he's involved with Asmodeus or not, he still murdered people and said it was Hellequin. Maybe he knows who this fake Hellequin is."

"I'll join you," Harrison said. "I'll bring some of my men with me. A few dozen soldiers should even the odds a bit."

"They can't know what we're going up against," Lucifer said. "It's one thing to go up against a powerful vampire, but to know you're about to fight the king of the devils, that's going to give people some pause. And we can't have any. Not today."

"Give us an hour," Galahad said. "We'll have to smuggle you out of the city to do this. Too many in the council would see you walking about as me putting our friendship before the safety of this realm. Hopefully, by the time you return, I'll have convinced the council that you're not here to set us up for your Avalon overlords' invasion."

"I have overlords now?"

"I never said it was a rational problem," Galahad said. "Just one that is yelled at high volume."

"I forgot to ask. Caitlin, is your mum still a guest of the prison?"

"Oh yes, she's still a joy unto all who meet her," Caitlin said. "Why, you think she's involved?"

"She has ties to people who have ties to whatever is behind all of this. I don't think she'll directly know anything because she's, well, she's nuts—no offense."

"None taken. She's a big box of frogs in the crazy department. But I'll go see her. You never know; it might be worthwhile. And at the very least she can call me a long list of names and threaten to hurt people I care about. You know, normal mother-daughter bonding."

"Your mother sounds evil," Selene said.

"She is. But it's the stupid kind of evil, not the try-and-take-over-the-world kind. She's a werewolf who is never leaving her prison cell. She murdered my stepfather in front of me, tried to murder my real father, and butchered her way across this realm and the Earth realm. She's a monster."

"You want company?" Sky asked. "I like pissing off evil people. Since meeting Nate it's sort of become my hobby."

"See, I bring people together," I said with a smile.

"To annoy people," Galahad said. "And trust me, he's been doing that for a long time."

We all got up to leave, except for Lucifer, who sat on the floor beside the dais. "I'll catch you up," I said to everyone. "I assume there's a way out of this place?"

"We closed it up after we found all of this," Leonardo said. "But I'll wait with Antonio for you outside."

"You will?" Antonio asked. "I was going to go home and sleep."

"You can sleep when you're dead," Leonardo said.

"Which, working with you, will be a lot quicker than I would doing something less dangerous."

"The only thing dangerous about working with me is that you run your mouth," Leonardo said with a grin as the two of them walked away.

"I'd hoped to see him again," Lucifer said. "I wanted to ask him why. I wanted to see if he'd changed. I wanted to see if he'd become the force for good he could have been if he wasn't so interested in making everyone bow to him. When he was first made, we were just children and he was kind and sweet. He helped people; he felt sadness and empathy for those who were weaker than him. Or maybe he didn't and it was all a game? I really don't know anymore.

"I know he was a cruel, vindictive tyrant, but he was my brother. And while we weren't of the same blood, we were the same in so many other ways. I know it sounds stupid, but I feel sorrow that he's gone. Not even Asmodeus could survive having his head cut off. They shackled him, bled him, and killed him, stuffing his soul in a jar. The elves aren't exactly the benevolent good guys from the stories, but I didn't expect his end to be like this. I thought he'd go out in a blaze of glory. I shouldn't be sad, but I am. I'm sad for all of the lost opportunities. It probably sounds strange."

"He was your brother. No matter how evil and cruel he was, he was still your brother. I understand completely. I felt the same about Mordred for the longest time. And it took him repeatedly trying to kill me for me to get over it."

"He knew I betrayed his cause. He knew I had no interest in a rebellion. I told him so myself, and he told me that the next time he saw me, he'd kill me. He'd have tried, too. I just wish I could have killed him myself all those years ago; it would have saved a lot of death and destruction."

"You can't think like that," I said. "You can't say that it would have changed anything. If Asmodeus hadn't been alive, maybe someone else would have come along to do the things he did. More than enough people have tried over the years, and at some point someone was going to achieve their goal of being a murderous bastard."

"If Asmodeus is dead, who is Abaddon taking orders from?"

"I did wonder that myself. I honestly have no idea. Who would Abaddon feel was above her?"

"No one. She answered to Asmodeus, and that was it. Even after the rebellion, she had to be sent away to an unpopulated realm because she refused to work with anyone else. She just doesn't think anyone but the most powerful should be in charge. Survival of the fittest in its purest form."

"Doesn't that mean Asmodeus wasn't fit enough?"

"Who knows? Abaddon isn't exactly what you'd call predictable. It's what makes her such a terrifying opponent. I haven't had to fight in centuries. And since you came into my life, I've had to almost fight on several occasions. And now I'm fighting again, using my magic again. They're going to know I'm here now. They're going to come here to find me. There's no going back to Grayson after this."

"Isn't this better? To be yourself, I mean?"

Lucifer shrugged. "Maybe. The jury is still out on that one." He got to his feet and looked over at me. "Once this is all done, if there's anything left of that jar, we need to find and destroy it. Asmodeus's soul is too powerful, too dangerous to just leave lying around."

"We will, but first things first. Let's find Lee and make sure he's not Asmodeus's reincarnation, or however that works."

"You know, if he is that, it means someone out there has access to his soul. A month ago someone broke in here, opened the tomb, and took Asmodeus's body. Leonardo said they hadn't seen a vase, but maybe he knows something else about it."

Lucifer and I walked through the mountain, meeting Leonardo and Antonio outside. We waited while they sealed the entrance.

"I'm curious: What if Lee's not forthcoming about the answers you need?" Antonio asked.

"If I remember Lee O'Hara well enough," I said, "he'll be tripping over himself to gloat about how smart he is."

The four of us began to walk back toward the city of Solomon. "Why is it that everyone who hates you is coming out of the woodwork?" Lucifer asked.

"I wondered that myself," I said. "I really wish I had an answer, but whatever it is, at some point they're going to start running out of people to send to kill me."

"Or they're going to get lucky," Leonardo said.

I looked over at Leonardo. "Thanks for that. Always nice to have friends standing behind you."

"Nate, if there's anyone who can overcome these odds it's you, but just once wouldn't you prefer it if you weren't in the middle of the storm?"

"I get the impression that's a fantasy, a dream that won't come true. Too many people want me dead. Too many people will go through my friends or innocents to achieve that goal. Maybe when we're done with all of this, we can hope for some semblance of peace and quiet."

"You'd get bored," Lucifer said.

"Yeah, but when people are after me, every day has to be my best day. That's the kind of thing that starts to exhaust after a while. Maybe I just need a few years off. A holiday. A nice long holiday in some remote little place where no one can find me."

"You'd still get bored," Lucifer said. "Or trouble would find you anyway. It seems to have that habit."

I smiled. He had a point: trouble and I did go arm in arm.

CHAPTER 26

Nate Garrett

The forest at the northern part of the city of Solomon was big enough that some Earth-realm cities could have been placed in the middle of it and lost forever. It took several days to get from one end to the other, but we didn't have that kind of time.

Fortunately Galahad's people had been tracking Lee since he fled after he'd commenced his killing spree. He'd murdered several guards in his escape from the city and had laughed the whole time he was tearing them apart. Lee was always unhinged—he once beat a man almost to death for bumping into him—but that was over the line even for him. With great power might come great responsibility, but for some people, with great power comes a need to use that power to hurt everyone. Lee definitely fell into the latter group.

"So, do you wish you'd just killed him?" Harrison asked me as we walked toward the destination where his recon troops had said they'd seen Lee.

"Yes," I replied, not really wanting to dwell on the subject. "How long before we find him?"

"It's about an hour away, apparently. My people say he's in some old ruins not too far from the city."

"Elven ruins?"

"Apparently so. At least that's what Leonardo says they are. He found the entrance about a year ago while trying to figure out if there was any more evidence for this place once being a shadow-elf realm."

I spotted several of Harrison's men off in the front. There were fifty of them, along with Lucifer, Zamek, and Selene. Selene had taken to the sky to try and track Lee from above, but she wasn't having a lot of luck, judging from the fact that she'd been up there an hour.

"So, I need to ask you something," I said to Harrison. "Are we good? I know you punched me, and you had me locked up, and that was all to make it look good, but are *we* good?"

"Sure, why not? I'm sure you're not involved with whatever is happening. And if you are, I'll kill you." Harrison walked away, leaving me alone, which was probably for the best considering how frustrating it was to deal with him.

"He really doesn't like you an awful lot, does he?" Selene said after landing beside me.

"He's not a fan, no."

"When this is over, however long that takes, I think we should go away somewhere remote and relax."

"Remote? Like a desert island in the middle of nowhere?"

"I was thinking like a realm in the middle of nowhere."

"I'm sure we can arrange something."

She took my hand in hers and squeezed slightly. "If it comes down to it, and you have to kill Helios, will you do it?"

I nodded. "He's had his chances. He's squandered them, and he has no interest in anything but killing and causing pain and suffering to others. He needs to be stopped, and he won't be taken alive."

"I know. I'd hoped otherwise, but I know. And I know that it's you he wants to hurt. I just wanted you to know that if you do have to kill him, I won't resent you for it. I know you've spared him for me in the past, but don't do that again. I don't want you to put yourself in harm's way just to keep him alive. You need to do what you need to do."

"I know." I paused. "Thanking you sounds weird, so I won't do that, but I'm glad you told me."

"Do you think you can beat him?"

"Yes," I said without a second thought. "I've done it before; I'll do it again."

"I'd very much rather you didn't die, Nathan Garrett."

"You and me both." I leaned over and kissed her. "I'll be fine. I've survived everything else that's been thrown at me over the years—what's one more thing?"

"Even if your enemy is more powerful than any you've faced before?"

"You know that as far as pep talks go, you suck at them."

Selene laughed. "Yeah, sorry about that. I can buy a cheerleader outfit if that would help."

I shrugged. "It might. I wouldn't want to commit to something until I'd seen it myself."

"Oh, you wouldn't want to commit? That's very kind of you."

"You'll just have to see how I react to you wearing one, and we'll go from there."

Selene stopped walking and pulled me back, kissing me on the lips. "Oh we will, will we?"

I winked. "I could wear the cheerleader outfit, if you'd prefer. I'm not sure I have the legs for it."

Selene laughed again. "I think you'd look sexy."

"Are you two done?" Harrison called. "Or do you need to get a room?"

"Do you have a room available?" I asked. "Just curious."

"We'll resume this conversation at a later date," Selene said. "In private."

"I look forward to it."

I kissed Selene and ran to catch up to Harrison. "You might not be taking this seriously, but my men sure as hell are," he snapped.

"Harrison, I take everything seriously when I hunt someone. But you know what? I don't think a little levity in a situation like this is a bad thing. I'm not a soldier, I'm not regimented and regulated, and we have some time until we reach the area you think Lee is hiding. But for you, I'll look somber and scowl a lot more."

"You want to know why I don't like you? It's because you don't take things seriously. You joke and mock. You don't show anyone the respect they're due."

"I show a lot of people the respect they're due, if I think they're due it. I respect Galahad. I mock him because we're friends."

"He's a king."

"Not my king. You don't have to like me, Harrison. I may joke and mock people, I may be sarcastic and a smart-ass, but when it comes down to it, I'm fairly sure you'd rather have me on your side than opposing you. The joking is just my way of dealing with everything, of allowing myself to not be consumed by the awfulness of everything happening around me. If you don't like that, tough, because I haven't changed for people I respect a lot more than you."

"I understand why you have so many people who want to line up to kill you," Harrison said through gritted teeth. "I just don't understand how you're not dead a hundred times over."

"Essentially it's because I'm stubborn. I'm just too stubborn to lie down and let death take me. And it won't be taking me today, either."

"Commander," one of Harrison's guards said.

"Yes, trooper," Harrison said to the young female guard.

"We've had a report from the recon team. The ruins are approximately twenty minutes' walk from here. There are no obvious guards there, and nothing to stop us from going inside."

"Excellent. Tell everyone that they're to maintain silence on the way there."

"No," I said. "I want you all to make as much noise as possible and move on beyond the ruins, as if you have no idea they're there."

"That's insane," Harrison said. "Why would we want to let Lee know we're coming?"

"Because you're not."

"Want to explain?" Selene said as she caught up with us.

"I'm going in alone," I said.

"That seems foolish," Lucifer said. "Even by the standards of stupid things you do."

"And there have been a lot of them," Zamek said. "And I haven't known you long."

"Okay, and thanks for that," I started. "But something has been bothering me about all of this. These people . . . Lee, Deimos, Helios, and Atlas. They're all people who have wanted me dead, and they're all working for this My Liege group. On top of that, they've all come out at the exact same time as someone pretending to be me. So, I want you to make a loop around the ruins and come in after I've had a few minutes to get inside and hopefully find Lee."

"You're seriously considering this?" Harrison asked. "This isn't time for a dick-measuring exercise."

"Actually that's exactly what it's time for," I said. "Lee is all about the dick measuring. That's the most important thing to him. Looking like the biggest, baddest asshole in the room. That's all he cares about, and when someone questions that, or makes him look weak, he goes after them. But he always wants people to know *why* he's gone after them. He always liked to explain to people why he's doing it."

"He's a James Bond villain," Lucifer said.

"Yeah, but even dumber. And I don't plan on getting killed by someone whose IQ is comparable to a wet sponge."

"And if you're wrong and he tries to kill you right off the bat?" Harrison asked.

"Then I kill him and bring out his corpse. Or most of his corpse, depending on how it goes."

"If he's a creation of Asmodeus, that won't be easy," Lucifer said.

"If he somehow got hold of Asmodeus's soul jar and absorbed a part of the soul, that means he has friends who got him the jar, got him the runes he needed to get the jar to work, and got him the ritual he needed to absorb part of the soul. He didn't trip and fall and absorb Asmodeus's soul."

"Okay, we'll do it your way," Harrison said. He turned to the trooper beside him. "Tell everyone we're going past the ruins. We're going to make a loop all the way around, and come back at it on the second pass. Officially it's so we can scout out for possible traps and allies of Lee. Do not tell anyone Nate's stupid plan. I'd really rather not have people think that stupidity is a good trait to have."

The trooper ran off.

"You believe in me—that's touching," I said to Harrison.

"You're an idiot, but you're a powerful idiot who I've seen fight. If this Lee asshole wants to fight you, I'd rather you were down there containing him than allow him to have full rein to go at my people. If you do get yourself killed, though, I'm going to laugh my ass off. Fair warning."

Harrison walked off, leaving me with Selene, Lucifer, and Zamek. "This is a stupid idea," Lucifer said. "But it's probably the least stupid idea we could have at the moment. You want someone to come with you?"

I shook my head. "I don't want him to realize that there's more than just me, and if fifty soldiers go down there, he might start trying to pick them off in the darkness."

"What if Lee has allies down there?" Zamek asked.

"He'll want me for himself," I said, feeling hopeful about being right.

"You have three minutes, and then we come in," Selene said. "If he has help, and they're ignoring you, that gives us something to do while you have Lee's attention."

"See, I'm all about delegating the hard work to everyone else," I said.

We stopped at the entrance to the ruins. "If you didn't know they were there, you'd walk right past," I said after crouching down behind a tree large enough to conceal a dozen people. The only part of the ruins that were visible were three large stone columns, and even they had been mostly consumed by vegetation.

"The entrance is behind the columns," Harrison said. "My people are already moving on around the back of the ruins. If anyone is watching for us, they're going to think we couldn't find them. Or at the very least that we're going to ambush them."

"I don't have to tell you to be careful, do I?" Selene asked.

"I've done this kind of thing before," I said.

"You've done this kind of thing before?" Zamek said. "You've gone up against a vampire who may or may not have at least part of the soul of an ancient vampiric devil inside of him?"

"Every Tuesday," I replied. "And twice on Fridays."

"You're so full of shit," Zamek said with a grin as he removed the battle-axe from his back and tested it for weight. Harrison had made sure the things taken from us when we were first arrested had been returned, and Leonardo had given us all any extra weapons we'd need. For a man who hated the idea of his inventions being used for war, he sure was good at creating them.

I unsheathed the silver broadsword that Leonardo had given me and walked around the tree toward the hidden ruins. As it turned out, they weren't so hidden when you got close, and while vegetation had grown all around the steps moving down into the ruins, it only made them difficult to see from a distance.

Small purple crystals lit the inside of the ruins. I'd been worried that I'd have to use my fire magic to let me see in the dark, a simple proposition in the Earth realm but one that was liable to start a forest fire in Shadow Falls.

I waited at the bottom of the long staircase into the ruins and allowed my vision to become accustomed to the new lighting before continuing. The plant life of the realm had long since overrun the ruins, and occasionally I'd hear something scurry around in the darkness, but I had no interest in finding out exactly what it was, so I hurried on.

The elven ruins would probably have been beautiful back in their day, and evidence of that beauty still existed in the ornate carvings on the walls, and pillars with stone that shone brightly as the light from the crystals touched it. After thousands of years of disuse, their work remained functional and impressive. Occasionally I saw something that interested me enough that I wished I'd the time to stay and examine it more, and it was easy to understand why Leonardo loved coming here to excavate. Elven culture was a mystery to most of us, and even to those who lived at the time it was something that had been kept largely secret, so to be able to wander around their achievements, even after millennia had passed, felt like how humans must have first felt when they'd finally discovered the Rosetta stone.

I occasionally stumbled over loose stone, which was neither stealthy nor particularly heroic, and I made sure to omit that detail from any epic storytelling I'd undertake about my descent into elven ruins to fight a master vampire.

"Nate, you came." The voice echoed all around me just before I entered a large room with several exits. The room had a high ceiling, where the crystals lit up the remains of the faded murals.

"I'm not doing this," I called out. "This isn't some bad-vampire-movie crap. I'm not doing the follow-the-disembodied-voice shit. You're not Christopher Lee, and this isn't a Hammer horror."

The voice laughed.

"My word, you're a dick," I said.

The laughter stopped. "Take the third path from the left. There are no traps. I want you to see me for who I am. I want you to witness my glory before you die."

"I want you to shut the fuck up, but that doesn't seem to be happening, either." I walked over to the exit Lee had told me to take and stepped inside. It wasn't going to be a trap—I was confident of that. Lee thought he was more powerful than I was—if he didn't, we wouldn't have been having the conversation—and I knew that Lee would fight fair if he thought he would win.

I followed the path to a second large room. At the far end of the room was a throne, upon which sat Lee. He'd changed a lot since I'd last seen him. He'd kept the goatee, proving he was in fact evil, but grown his red hair out so that it was long enough to touch his shoulders.

"You look like something out of a romance novel," I said. "I assume you swoon about, too."

Lee stood up, revealing the long coat and expensive suit.

I sighed. "Seriously, that's what you think you should wear as a vampire? Haven't we all moved on from the stereotypical bullshit?"

A flicker of anger moved across Lee's face before being replaced with a calm smile. "It's been a while, Nate."

"Not long enough. So, you're a vampire. How's that working out for you?"

"I was made an offer, and I just couldn't refuse it. Do you know what that offer was?"

"To look like you stalk young high-school girls? Did they teach you to talk with a really bad Eastern European accent, too? Say, 'I vant to suck your blood.' Make sure it's 'vant,' though, not 'want.' That's very important."

"You think you can mock me? With all the power I possess, I could snuff out your life in an instant."

"You are literally the least threatening vampire I've ever seen. The count from *Sesame Street* looks more badass."

"You think you can goad me into making a mistake."

"Mate, you made a mistake the second you got up and decided that was a good look."

Lee smiled. "You know the horror I inflicted in the city, yes?"

"Yeah, it came up. I'm beginning to think someone else did it, though. Because if you killed them looking like that, I'd think they were more embarrassed than anything."

More anger, this time staying for a few moments longer. "I murdered those people and bathed in their blood."

"It's good for the skin apparently."

Lee walked down the steps from the stone throne, standing only a dozen feet from me. "I killed my parents. You remember them, yes?"

I nodded. Mark and Lyn O'Hara had been in charge of a criminal gang back in London. Despite their profession, I'd liked them both. "How?"

"I went to them—they were so shocked to see me. And then I butchered everyone in the house. I would have killed Holly, but she lives with her new husband in Scotland, and frankly I didn't have time. Maybe later, though—I hear she had a kid. Did you know that I really don't care how old my victims are? The bloodlust is insatiable. I just need to feed, and prey is prey."

"So, how'd you get turned into a vampire?"

"Abaddon found me. Searched me out because she knew how valuable I was to the plans. She introduced me to this older guy, who had these containers of blood. I had to drink some. They told me it was the blood of a god, a vampire sorcerer. That it would change me. It certainly did that, and I became something better. A vampire the likes of which is rarely seen. And with that power, I was taught how to use it, how to be the man I needed to be."

"In a year?" I asked. "It takes decades."

"They hooked me up to a machine," Lee said. "They made me live my life in my mind, years of life all in the space of six months' real time. They called it—"

A shiver went up my spine. "The Harbinger trials," I finished for him.

"You heard about them," he said with a smile. "The man said you'd recognize it. He told me to tell you all of this. He wants you to know that you're going to watch your friends die. He wants to break you."

"Who is he?"

"Told me his name was My Liege. That was all he said. I dealt with Abaddon more than anyone else. She told me that you'd come. She said you'd arrive in Shadow Falls."

"She sent you here to cause fear and confusion."

Lee laughed. "And I'm not done yet. I knew you'd want to help the second you heard my name. You and Galahad are friends, after all. And he's the kind of person who puts trust in his friends. Much like you. You're going to take me to see Galahad."

"Are you about to invoke the Accords? Because I really don't have the time or effort to give two shits about them."

Lee laughed. "The Accords are as worthless as the paper they were written on. You know, I was told to keep you alive, but your blood, it smells so . . . nicccccce." His speech became almost a hiss as his spoke. "I can smell the power. It's smellssssss so good."

The torrent of fire that left my hands smashed into Lee the second he leapt toward me. Unlike on the Earth realm, the microscopic particles of the crystals in the air of Shadow Falls made my magic unpredictable. A small amount of fire could cause an inferno with ease. And down in the ruins, far away from anyone who might get hurt, I didn't hold back. The flame turned white hot in a second, and it took more than a little effort to switch my magic off before it started to adversely affect the stone supports.

The stone floor remained bright red for several seconds as Lee's smoldering body lay on the floor. His clothes had been burned away, along with his skin, and a large amount of muscle. White bone showed on what remained of his legs. A breath escaped his body.

"Still alive?" I asked.

He moaned in pain.

"Why were you down here?" I asked, looking around. "What were you doing?" I wasn't expecting an answer; I wasn't even sure he was capable of speech. I was mostly just talking to myself as I performed a circuit of the room, looking for hidden exits and trapdoors.

Zamek, Lucifer, and Selene rushed into the room. "We didn't hear fighting," Lucifer said. "We figured something must be wrong."

They all looked down at Lee. "Fucking hell," Zamek said. "Did you do that, Nate?"

"Yeah, he tried to kill me," I explained. "And I really didn't like the idea. He'll live and heal. It'll just take him a while."

"What about the answers we need?" Selene asked.

"He doesn't know anything. He was sent here by Abaddon to just cause trouble. But I don't think he was down here by accident."

"What are you looking for?" Selene asked as I started to tap on the walls.

"Something doesn't feel right. He let his bloodlust override his common sense, but he was meant to be captured." I looked at my friends. "I guess he got his wish."

Harrison and several troops arrived, making the room a little more crowded than it was when it was just me. "Holy shit, is that Lee?" Harrison asked.

"He wants to see the king," I said. "He wasn't very hospitable about it."

"Fuck him." Harrison stepped forward before anyone could stop him, and Lee moved slightly, causing at least one of the guards to jump.

"Don't let him bite you," I said. "Blood will heal him. And right now I'd rather he wasn't healed."

"How do we get him back to the castle?" Harrison asked. "He looks like he'll fall apart once someone touches him."

"Bring the prison cell here. I'm sure he was in these ruins for a reason. I think we need to search them—something doesn't feel right."

"Do you have any idea how far underground these ruins go?" Harrison asked. "Leonardo hasn't even finished mapping them. There could be miles and miles of tunnels that stretch as far as the realm allows."

"Then we'd better get searching, because he came here for a reason. He was going to allow himself to be taken, for a reason. He wants to see Galahad for a reason."

"Maybe he wants in the palace?" Lucifer asked.

"That's where he would have been taken," Harrison confirmed.

I was about to say more when a young guard ran into the room. She saw the charred living remains of Lee and blinked before looking up at Harrison. "King Galahad sent me, sir," she told him.

"What does our king want?" Harrison asked.

She pointed at me. "Nate needs to come back to the palace," she said. "Arthur has arrived."

CHAPTER 27

Nate Garrett

It took me an hour of jogging to get back to Solomon, where I found Galahad outside the palace waiting alone. "I heard Arthur arrived," I said, and accepted the pitcher of water that Galahad had brought for me.

"Feel better?" he asked as I downed the cool drink.

"You are a beautiful person for bringing this."

"Arthur is waiting at the Mill. I had word sent that I'd be a few hours, as I was waiting for you."

"And how was that received?"

"Arthur took the time to go have a nap."

"That doesn't really sound like the behavior of someone who wants to overthrow you and your government," I said as we entered the palace.

Galahad didn't bother to reply, instead allowing me to fill him in on what Lee had said and done. With that finished, and with Galahad seemingly lost in thought, we made our way through the palace and into the throne room. The high ceilings and ornate decoration were something that I knew Galahad was less than happy about. He'd never been into the grandiose side of things, but he'd once told me that being king meant an expectation of a certain level of pomp and ceremony, so he put up with it.

"Do you ever actually use the throne?" I asked him as we walked past it. Several people in the room bowed to Galahad, who waved and said hello before we continued.

"No," he admitted when we'd finally left the throne room. "Not often, anyway. It's uncomfortable, and gaudy. I'd rather just have a table."

"A round one?"

Galahad looked at me and shook his head. "Don't mock me."

"I'm not. I remember the table. It was very big. Not round, though. Never really got why that part was so important."

"It was so no one was better than the others."

"Galahad, I *understand* why Merlin said it; I just never understood why he felt the need to say it. He made it up—the table never existed. I just found it weird he made up a story about it instead of just, you know, making the table."

"Ah, sorry."

We continued through the palace, passing dozens of guards, until we arrived at the huge palace doors, which Galahad unlocked with a touch of his finger. He pushed one of the doors open, and we both stepped out onto the top of the steps looking over a large part of the city of Solomon and his kingdom of Shadow Falls.

"You were never one of the knights," Galahad said. "Why was that?"

"You know why. It wouldn't have been a good idea for someone in my line of work to be associated with all of you fine knights in your lovely shiny outfits."

"You're mocking me again."

"Always," I told him, looking over the ramparts to the city below.

"Can I tell you something?"

I looked back at him.

"No mocking," he continued.

I laughed. "I guess so, sure."

"I miss you. I miss you, me, Mordred, Morgan, Gawain, Mac, and the others. It was a time of camaraderie, and friendship, and I just miss it. I miss fighting back against the evil that infected the lands we lived in. I miss being heroic. I'm getting old."

"You're my age, and I don't feel old." I paused for a few seconds. "But I know what you mean. Things were easier."

"They were. And none of us had even hit our first century, and we thought we could take on the world. All of it. Our biggest problem was dealing with Kay and the assholes he was friends with."

"Kay isn't going to be an issue again."

"Mordred told me you killed him. That Kay killed your wife. I'm sorry for that. I wanted to reach out and ask how you were, but I wasn't sure how to put the words together. It's weird—we fight, we bleed, we stand side by side, but I can't figure out how to say I'm sorry you discovered someone we knew murdered your wife. How are you dealing with it?"

"I killed him, Galahad. I dealt with it well, considering."

"Nate, when she died, you went really dark. I saw the swath of pain and misery you cut across a continent. I saw that it took Tommy to bring you back from that brink of darkness and self-destruction. I know how hard Mary's death hit you, so I'm asking if you're feeling similar."

"No," I said. "Mary's dying changed me, but I put that behind me. I put the anger and hate I felt behind me. I killed Kay because he deserved it. Not just for Mary, but for so many people whose lives he ruined. I'm in a good place about everything. What about you? You seem to be doing well as a dad."

"It took some getting used to, yes. It took more than I'd have expected. I sometimes have to remind myself that she's a grown woman who managed for a long time without my interference. It's difficult to juggle the need to be protective with the need to let her remain independent. I never thought I'd have children. I certainly never thought I wouldn't find out about one until she was an adult, and that the mother would be a crazed psychopath."

"Surprise."

Galahad laughed. "Yeah, it really was. What about you and Selene?"

"I love her. I've always loved her. That's it. We decided to move in together."

"Marriage?"

I shrugged. "I have no idea. Neither of us has had good experiences in that department, so we haven't really talked about it."

Galahad hugged me for several seconds before saying anything. "I'm happy for you. Genuinely happy. I always wanted to see you in a good place again. And I was worried you'd never allow yourself to go back to that place, and the fact that you did it with Selene, again, is good to see. Don't ever piss her off, because she'll kick your ass."

I laughed. "Yeah, no kidding."

After that, conversation was kept to a minimum. I couldn't blame him—if I was in his shoes, I'd probably be nervous, too. Galahad and Arthur hadn't seen one another in centuries, and there was no telling how either man would receive the other. I knew both of them, and they were both capable of being more than a little stubborn.

We used a private version of the rail transport that linked the various parts of the city with the temple and palace, traveling in as close to silence as possible. I got the feeling that Galahad wasn't looking forward to seeing Arthur.

It didn't take long to reach the temple, and Galahad passed his sword to one of his guards. Galahad was possibly the finest swordsman I'd ever met, with very few exceptions, and rarely went anywhere without his sword. Maybe he was really trying to ensure that Arthur had no excuses to start something. I certainly hoped so.

"You got a second?" I asked as we walked through the temple to the realm gate. "There's something I need to tell you."

Galahad nodded.

"Lee went through the Harbinger trials," I told him. "Whoever Abaddon is working with, they have access to Avalon procedures."

"Didn't you go through those trials?"

"Yeah, something like that." In fact, whereas the Harbinger trials weren't officially to be performed on anyone under one hundred years of age, I'd only been a teenager when subjected to them. A fact that could have easily killed me. The Harbinger trials were designed to take someone who was already powerful and allow them to unleash their potential far more easily than they would normally. While unconscious they would live out everything happening to them, making it feel as though years had passed, when in reality it was only weeks or months.

"Okay, so what aren't you telling me?" Galahad asked.

"Merlin. Merlin has access to the Harbinger trials. He has the power and expertise to put someone through them without getting them killed."

"You think Merlin is this My Liege character?"

I nodded.

"It could be Abaddon," Galahad suggested.

"Agreed, it could be, but either way one of them is working for the other one. I don't know Abaddon well enough to say that she's the kind of person who would be okay with being the second in command, but I know that Merlin wouldn't be okay with it."

"Unless it was Arthur who was in charge."

"You don't think Arthur is My Liege, do you?" I asked.

Galahad shrugged. "I'm not counting anyone out until we have proof one way or the other. You don't, I suspect."

"I find it hard to believe that if Arthur is My Liege he would have asked me to come here and try to defuse the situation. Or promote Lucie. Or have Merlin placed under house arrest."

"You're trying to convince yourself that he can't be My Liege, but none of that proves anything."

"I know."

We both walked through the realm gate into the Mill, where we were greeted by Rebecca Dean. "Arthur has just finished eating," she told us.

"He's definitely alone?" Galahad asked.

"Yes, my lord. I sent people to check the surrounding area, and we've verified that he's alone."

"Is the meeting taking place here?" I asked.

Rebecca nodded. "My office, to be exact. We'll be able to keep people from interrupting you, but if you need us—"

"We won't," Galahad said. "He's not here to fight. He'd have brought an army if that was the case."

"Either way," Rebecca said. "We'll be close by."

Rebecca took us to her office—a large room that contained a pale-blue sofa, a desk, and three chairs, a large TV on the wall, and various pieces of electronics that allowed Rebecca to do her job running both the guardians and the establishment she'd created for herself. Arthur sat on the sofa, reading the paper, which he put down beside him as we walked in.

"Nice black suit," Galahad said. "You going to a funeral?"

"Nice armor," Arthur replied, standing. "You going to war?"

This wasn't getting off to the best start, and judging from the expression on Rebecca's face, there was a moment when I was sure she thought about asking for a guard to stand in the corner, before both men smiled and embraced.

"It's been a long time," Arthur said with a warm smile.

"It has, old friend," Galahad replied. "You'll have to excuse the armor. I didn't have time to change. I didn't want to leave you here all day waiting for me."

"That's okay, I had a nap. I have barely slept since I became king, so that was a nice change of pace. And Rebecca here made me some ribs." He turned to Rebecca. "You are a goddess of cooking."

Rebecca nodded her head as a thank-you and left the room.

"I make everyone nervous," Arthur said. "That wasn't my intention. It's why I came alone. Several on the council wanted me to bring an army, and they don't see the idea of invading Maine as an act of war."

"Thank you for not making things worse," Galahad said, and motioned for Arthur to sit.

They both sat on the sofa, turning so they could see one another, while I took a chair.

"Are you the mediator?" Arthur asked me.

"I'm the rational one . . . apparently," I said.

"That's a terrifying thought if nothing else," Galahad said with a laugh.

"Yes, I remember you being the rational one back in Camelot when someone tried to stab Mac with a knife for . . . inappropriate behavior toward the daughter of a visiting lord."

Galahad looked at me. "Mac did something he shouldn't have done? I am surprised."

I smiled. "Yeah, well, I had to step in. Otherwise the lord would have been soundly beaten. He was human and had no idea what Mac was. Apparently the lord believed that Mac and his daughter should be wed, despite neither of them being all that keen on the idea, but we're not here to reminisce."

"Indeed not," Arthur said. "I need to know if anyone in Shadow Falls could be involved in what's happening with this Hellequin and his murder spree."

"No," Galahad said. "My realm and its people are not involved."

"You can account for them all?" Arthur asked.

"Can you account for all of Avalon?"

"A fair point," Arthur said. "But Avalon isn't openly being accused of killing humans by the tens of thousands and allowing humanity to know of our existence. Shadow Falls is."

"I am, you mean."

"I'm not accusing you of anything, Galahad. I don't genuinely believe you would ever be involved in such an act, but these are dangerous times, and not everything can be solved with a simple no and a little bit of trust."

"How can I prove it to you so that your council will be happy?"

"Allow a small group of them to visit Shadow Falls. To look around, ask a few questions, and see for themselves that you are not a realm full of murderous despots."

"No," Galahad said. "I will not have my authority undermined by Avalon."

"I'm not trying to undermine your authority. I'm trying to stop people from throwing your name around in the same sentence as a murderer."

"You know that people on the council have wanted Avalon to annex Shadow Falls for centuries."

"Something you will allow to happen because you're too stubborn to let them see for themselves."

"I'm not about to let people who would betray my people into my realm just so they can be happy. Or as is more likely, so they can find evidence of a crime that no one committed."

"Be careful what you say, Galahad," Arthur warned.

"We both know that the council of Avalon is corrupt. We both know that if they came to Shadow Falls, they'd find evidence. Evidence they brought with them."

Arthur stood and walked over to the window at the far end of the room. "Galahad, whether or not there are councilors who undermine my authority, who are, as you say, corrupt, would it not be better for everyone if Shadow Falls and Avalon showed them a unified vision of what we could achieve? When they find nothing, we can move forward, together. We can strengthen ourselves and root out those who would seek to cause us harm."

"Those who seek to cause us harm are the same ones who want to find evidence of wrongdoing in my realm."

Arthur looked at me. "Talk some sense into him."

"I agree with him," I said. "We both know that whoever is throwing around these accusations is somewhat suspicious considering it wasn't long after that this Hellequin starting saying they were working with Shadow Falls."

"You're saying that the rumors were spread by councilors so that when Hellequin started killing people, those same councilors could say, I told you so?"

I nodded. "Abaddon, Baldr, Hera, all of her clan of assholes, and countless unknowns are working for this My Liege bag of dicks. I find it hard to believe that these rumors were a coincidence before Hellequin started spouting off about Shadow Falls."

"Agreed," Arthur said. "But the council wants to go to war, and I'm not sure I can stop them."

"You're the king," Galahad said.

Arthur sat on a chair next to the desk. "For now. Merlin has vanished, as has Elaine."

I was about to say that we were looking into the latter, but something stopped me. I didn't want Avalon to know everything I knew, because I wasn't sure who I could trust, and while I trusted Arthur, I didn't know who he would tell.

"You sacked Olivia," I said.

"She refused to return to Camelot. She forced my hand. Fiona, too."

"And put a fifteen-million-dollar bounty on my head," I continued. "Signed by Lucie."

"Not a chance," Arthur said. "Lucie did no such thing."

"I know. But Lucie has gone missing, too, and someone has taken her place."

Arthur looked shocked. "I spoke to her only a day ago. I can't believe that she'd vanish. She's under a lot of pressure."

"Maybe your own house needs looking at," Galahad said with no mocking or judgment in his tone.

Arthur nodded. "There are people on the council who want me out. There are whispers that I'm not living up to expectations."

"Hera's allies?" I asked.

"That's my guess. There is no proof that Hera and her people have ever acted against Avalon. At least nothing that will reach back to her personally. Merlin appeared to give her carte blanche to do whatever she wanted, and now that I'm trying to push back a little . . ."

"She wants you gone," I said.

Arthur nodded.

"You can't really expect me to let these people into my realm," Galahad said.

"No, I guess I couldn't. I'd hoped we'd be able to figure out a way to do this so that we could shut whoever is behind My Liege out of Avalon for good."

"That's why you wanted people in my realm?" Galahad asked, his tone slightly angry. "So you could find out who's working against you and grab them? You wanted to use my realm as bait."

"I wouldn't put it quite like that," Arthur said. "But it's not like I'm swimming in options here."

"These people would undermine me, Arthur. They would undermine everything my people have worked for."

Arthur sighed. "So, what do we do now? Because the councilors are still going to keep pushing their agenda, and this Hellequin guy is going to keep committing atrocities in the name of Shadow Falls. Do you know how many have been attacked since I left England to come here? Twenty-seven attacks in ten hours. Over ten thousand people worldwide dead in ten hours. Nearly a quarter of a million since all this shit started. Sorcerers are blowing themselves up; werewolves are running rampant; elementals are attacking people on their way to work. Cardiff, Berlin, Oslo, Tianjin, Cape Town, Lima, Salvador, Accra . . . I could keep going if you like. We need to stop this, and instead of enabling me to deal with it, the council is pressuring me to look into Shadow Falls because some of them have an agenda."

"They're using these attacks as a way to get what they want?" I asked.

"I've been in a coma for a thousand years. I get out and things are worse now than when I went in. How the fuck could Elaine and Merlin let this happen?"

"Elaine didn't let shit happen," I said, irritated that her name was dragged into the mud. "Merlin didn't let her do shit. Every time she tried, Merlin and his allies in the council would vote it down. She did everything she could just to stop Avalon from turning into a mess."

Arthur rubbed his eyes with the heels of his palms. "I know, I'm just . . . This whole thing is shit. And I don't see a way to make it better. If I go after the councilors who are against me, they will have me removed from power. Part of me thinks that's what they want. The days of the king's word being law were over before I was comatose. Over the centuries, the council has gained more and more power, but they were always fragmented, arguing amongst themselves. Shadow Falls has given half of them a focus for their rage and fear, and the other half are rubbing their hands with glee at the prospect."

I walked over to the window as Arthur sat back on the sofa. "What's your plan?" Galahad asked. "Because if we don't come up with something, it's going to get worse."

"I know," Arthur said. "And I don't know how to stop it."

I looked up at a clock on the wall, which read the time was midday, then looked out of the window to the city streets below. The block around The Mill usually began getting busy at this time of day, but maybe due to how cold it was outside, there were very few people on the streets. The few miles surrounding The Mill were used almost exclusively by Shadow Falls personnel so that if anyone like Arthur arrived, it would be easier to manage, easier to ensure the safety of all involved. But the lack of people made me wonder what was happening.

I stopped listening to Arthur and Galahad as I stared out of the window at the street below.

"You okay?" Galahad asked.

I nodded but didn't turn around. "I think we need a break. I'm getting paranoid."

Arthur glanced at the watch on his wrist. "A break sounds good."

"I'm going to get some air," I told them both, and left the room, walking past the three guards in the hallway outside and finding Rebecca downstairs in the bar.

"It's not going well, is it?" she asked.

"Define 'well,'" I said. "We're taking a few minutes to stretch our legs. At the moment, everyone seems to be at an impasse, and it's not going to be resolved by everyone just sitting around repeating the same argument."

"I'll go check on them," she said, and started off upstairs as I went to the entrance and stepped out into the cold air.

I ignited my fire magic to keep me warm and crossed the road. I wasn't sure what I was expecting to find, but something felt off, and I'd long since come to trust my gut feelings.

I walked a short distance down the road and was a hundred feet away from The Mill when I heard a rumble somewhere above me. In the distance I saw a helicopter flying at low altitude, and I turned and sprinted back toward The Mill, almost crashing through the door and barreling into Arthur.

"What's up?" he asked.

"I think we're about to be attacked," I said.

He looked skeptical as I turned and pointed to a helicopter that was no longer there. He looked a little concerned, but the concern soon vanished. "It was probably just a news chopper or something like that. I think it's a little bit much to think people are going to attack us with helicopters. From what we've seen of this Hellequin so far, it's all about using magic. Helicopter attack feels a little bit out of his usual bailiwick for destruction."

"I'm being paranoid," I said, still feeling a little on edge.

"I'm going outside for five minutes. You're welcome to join me."

"Without any guards?"

"My guards are in that building over there." He pointed to a three-story redbrick building. "I still brought guards with me. I just didn't want them in here."

"I'm going to go see Galahad," I told him.

Arthur left The Mill, and I went upstairs to find Galahad, who was on the sofa in Rebecca's office with a cup of tea. "We ended up shouting," Galahad admitted. "I'm not sure how this is going to work."

I was about to say something when I looked out the window and saw someone standing on top of the nearby roof, a little less than fifty meters away. He wore a black mask, and as I stepped toward the window, I saw the white slash across it. He picked something up off the roof and placed it on his shoulder.

"RPG!" I shouted as he fired the missile.

The missile hit the outside of the window, just above where I'd been standing before diving toward Galahad. I created a shield of air as the shrapnel from the explosion rained down through the room, tearing it apart. My ears rang, and I couldn't see through the smoke and fire that had consumed the office. Galahad lay beside me, his hands over his head.

"You okay?" I asked.

He nodded just as a second RPG round came through the window. The blast threw both Galahad and me into the nearest wall. We landed with enough force to knock the wind out of me as I concentrated on keeping the shield up. Two more explosions came in quick succession, and part of the building collapsed, causing the floor to give way. Galahad and I fell onto the front entrance of The Mill, spilling out into the street as a large part of the building fell onto us.

As the building covered us both, I heard gunfire, followed by the squealing of tires as a car sped away.

CHAPTER 28

Nate Garrett

This is officially the worst meeting ever," I said as several tons of building above me shifted slightly, forcing me to change my air-magic shield so Galahad and I wouldn't get crushed.

"I've had better," Galahad said. He had a nasty-looking cut above one eye, which had bled a lot, but otherwise he appeared to be uninjured.

"Any chance you can use your alchemy to get rid of this rock?"

Galahad looked around us. "I can try. You'll have to remove your air magic, though."

"It's not exactly giving us a lot of chances to get this right."

"No, one wrong move and we both get squashed."

"You are not making me feel better."

Galahad rolled onto his stomach as he searched for a way out. "Can you raise your shield just a few inches?"

"Probably, why?"

"If I can touch those bricks there, I can hopefully use them to connect to all of the weight bearing down on us. The thing is, if there is anything above the bricks that hasn't fallen yet, and I start moving stuff around, we might have a bit of a problem."

"Define 'problem.'"

"The rest of the building might fall on us."

"That's a bit worse than just a bit of a problem."

"Can you use your magic to blast the debris away?"

"I can, but I have no idea what I'm blasting the debris into."

"So, we're not in the best situation."

"We're alive—that's something," I said, trying to point out the only good thing I could think of. "I heard gunfire and saw that Hellequin dick."

"I heard the car leave in a hurry."

"Arthur was taken by Hellequin."

"They'll keep him alive," Galahad said. "Too valuable to kill. Either way, this Hellequin bloke has upped the stakes somewhat."

"King Galahad!" someone shouted from beyond the rubble around us.

"We're in here!" Galahad shouted back.

Parts of the rubble were quickly moved, revealing more and more daylight until Galahad and I were able to stand and I could remove my magical shield. Rebecca and several guards were still moving parts of the building when I looked up and saw that the entire front of the structure was gone. Everybody had multiple cuts of various sizes, and most had their clothing torn and were covered in dust.

"Those RPGs did a lot of damage," I said.

"Not just them," Rebecca said. "Two sorcerers ran into the building and detonated their magic. I've never seen anything like it. They just ran in and blew themselves up. Why would they do that?"

"Based on what I've seen so far, they either didn't have a lot of choice, or they're fanatical," I told her.

"Did you see where Arthur went?" Galahad asked.

Rebecca shook her head, sat at the remains of a nearby table, pulled a pair of sneakers out from under it, and put them on her bare feet. "There was a helicopter that took off soon after too. I'm guessing it was used to drop off some of the attackers."

"Did we lose anyone?"

"Eight are injured, three seriously enough that I had them taken down to the medical facility close to the realm gate. No one is going to die, though."

Galahad sighed with relief. "That's something at least."

"Any damage to the realm gate?" I asked.

"None of them got close enough," Rebecca said. "If that was their intention, I'm not sure why they'd have even bothered trying. But I think they were after Arthur. That masked Hellequin guy bundled him into a car. They opened fire on us. Two cars, both black SUVs, and enough firepower to make us pause."

"I'm thinking Galahad was their aim, too. They waited until almost the exact moment Arthur left the building to launch an attack, and there's no way it was a spur-of-the-moment thing. They'd been waiting for their chance for a while."

"That's my thought, too," Rebecca said.

"We need to get back to Shadow Falls," Galahad said.

The three of us ran through the remains of The Mill without stopping until we reached the realm gate. "Stay safe," Galahad told Rebecca. "Thank you for all you've done here."

"You, too," she told him, and we stepped through the realm gate back into Shadow Falls, where we were greeted by Harrison and several of his people.

"King Galahad, we heard you'd been attacked," Harrison said, clearly unnerved by what he'd been told.

"This Hellequin and his cohorts decided to kidnap Arthur and try to kill me," Galahad quickly explained. "Thankfully Nate was there to keep the building from falling on me. What's been happening here?"

"Lee escaped custody," Harrison said. "He attacked one of the guards who got too close, and tore his throat out. We'd used a huge amount of sedatives on him and thought it was safe to keep him in a locked room, but he managed to use some sort of shadow magic, and when the guard went to investigate, Lee killed him."

"Do you know where he's gone?" I asked.

"We had eyes on him as he ran back toward the ruins, but with the information that you'd been attacked, I didn't want to send a contingent of guards to retrieve him."

"I'll go," I said. "I never did figure out why those ruins were so damn important, and it gives me a chance to finally kill the bastard. No screwing around this time."

"Anything else?" Galahad asked.

"No, my lord," Harrison said. "Apart from that, it's been quiet. We followed security protocols and had both realm gates shut down until they were activated on the other end by a known ally. No one coming or going."

Galahad set off through the temple, with me and Harrison behind. "Thank you," Harrison said. "You saved his life again."

"He'd have saved himself if I hadn't been there. I didn't do anything special, I assure you."

"Even so. Thank you."

We reached the mouth of the temple and looked down over the city of Solomon. "Avalon will hear of Arthur's kidnapping, and they will come for us," Galahad said. "They will not listen to reason; they will want retribution."

"So, what are you going to do with a million people?" I asked.

Before Galahad could answer, explosions rocked the city, causing several buildings on the outskirts to topple. Clouds of smoke and dust were thrown into the air.

"What the hell was that?" Harrison asked as the temple shook so violently parts of it collapsed.

"We need to get down there, quickly," I said, and ran down to one of the closest three-coach trams that ferried people around the city. "Can you make this go faster?"

Harrison prized a panel off the front of the tram and flicked a few switches, causing the tram to speed up and throwing me onto the floor. The bullet-train-shaped tram now officially did bullet-train speed.

"Little warning!" I shouted out as we sped past the scenery far below.

"These can only be modified in an emergency," Harrison said. "I think this counts."

The trams followed the same pattern as the aqueducts that had been built around the town, meaning it took a little close to ninety minutes to get from the temple to the palace at normal speed. At the speed we went, it took us a little over twenty agonizing minutes, and in that time more explosions had gone off across the city.

"What is that?" one of the dozen guards who had accompanied us onto the tram asked as he pointed out the window.

I watched in horror as hundreds of blood elves attacked the people of Solomon, the plague of them crawling out of craters in the ground. "My Liege has made his move," I said. "Get your people ready, Harrison. You're about to go to war."

As the doors opened and we all piled out onto the platform, Harrison and his men sprinted off to fight the blood elves. "I'm going with them," Galahad said. "You're going after Lee still."

"Those blood elves came from the ground. Someone said there were mazes of tunnels under the city. If that's where Lee is, maybe My Liege is using it as a staging area."

"Go to the palace, get a horse—it'll be quicker than running. You armed?"

"Not yet."

He passed me his sword. "Just humor me," he said when I suggested he keep it. "I can always grab another one. If you use magic down there, you could bring the tunnels down, and probably most of whatever is above us. I'd rather not have a street vanish because you decided to throw some power around."

I took the sword harness and strapped it on my back. "I'll behave. Promise."

Galahad took off toward the trouble, taking a sword from an injured guard on the way.

I ran toward the palace, ignoring the sounds of fighting, and paused. The buildings had started to collapse nowhere near the ruins. I turned to the closest collapsed building and ran toward it, noticing the ragged tear in the ground that led down to darkness below. I looked around for anyone who might need medical attention but found no one. I grabbed some sturdy rope that I found on the street and anchored myself to a nearby metal post before abseiling into the dark chasm.

After about a minute I realized the gap I'd entered was deeper than I expected. I stopped and glanced down into the darkness. I couldn't use my fire magic, not even to give me night vision. Instead, I continued. I had no idea just how far beneath the ground I was when I finally touched the bottom, and I tried not to think about it. I didn't need distractions when I was hunting a powerful vampire.

The tunnel I found myself in was lit by dozens of purple crystals, giving my surroundings a strange, unearthly glow. After a few minutes of running, I found myself in a cavern. There was only one other tunnel leading from it, and after I had taken a few steps inside, there was an explosion behind me and several tons of rock fell into the tunnel mouth, blocking my escape.

"Those crystals are so volatile," Lee said from somewhere further up the tunnel, although I couldn't see him, even with the light of the crystals illuminating the darkness.

"You came down here to make this place a realm gate, didn't you?"

"I came here to make sure my allies could do what they needed to do. Thousands of blood elves are currently rampaging across the city, and even more will be coming up through the ruins as we speak. Attacking the enemy on two fronts."

"You can't possibly have enough people," I said, drawing my sword and moving forward, hoping to keep him talking.

"Not to take the realm, no," Lee admitted. "But to cause devastation and fear? We have more than enough for that. These tunnels link up to the mountain."

"Asmodeus's prison." A thought crossed my mind. "They've been bringing people down here for months, haven't they? They go into the elven realm gate and then climb down by the prison. That chasm takes you down here."

"Good guess," Lee said with a chuckle. "You burned me alive. I'm going to feast on you for that. All of your power will make me whole again. It'll feel so good."

"You talk a lot. Has anyone ever told you that?" I stopped by a large cluster of crystals. "You blew up the crystals down here to get the blood elves out. Dangerous gamble."

"Smart," he snapped.

I continued until I reached a second cavern, and in the center sat Lee, bathed in purple light. His face and arms were still a mass of burned flesh, although he looked considerably less horrific than before.

"Take me in for questioning again, Nate? Is that the idea?" He glanced at my sword. "Or are you here to kill me? That little pointy stick isn't going to get the job done."

Lee charged forward, and I moved as if to bring the sword down, which he anticipated, and moved to the side. I stepped away, bringing the sword down in an arc toward where Lee would end up. It caught him just above the hip, splattering blood against the stone wall.

Lee screamed in pain and turned into vapor, moving away from me. I held the sword with one hand, the point of the blade aimed at the floor, and stepped toward Lee.

"That hurt," he seethed after he re-formed.

"Come get some more, then," I told him, darting forward and bringing the sword up toward Lee's chest.

He moved quicker than I'd anticipated, turning into vapor and then re-forming around my arm so that he held my wrist in his hands.

A second later the sword clattered across the tunnel as he broke my wrist and punched me in the ribs hard enough for me to feel at least one of them buckle.

Lee was on me in an instant, a snarling rage with nothing close to humanity behind it. His clawlike fingers raked across my cheek as he tried to force my head to the side, exposing my neck.

"I think I might turn you," he said, licking the side of my neck with his elongated tongue. My neck numbed in an instant.

"Go fuck yourself," I told him, and drove a blade of lightning up into his chest, kicking him away from me.

Lee staggered back, his white shirt turned black from the wound on his chest. He used the crystal-lined tunnel wall to keep upright as lightning magic continued to flicker over him. I looked down at the blade, which was considerably larger than I'd been trying to form, and attempted to shut it off. Even this far underground, and this close to so many crystals, the particles in the air made my magic even more unpredictable and dangerous.

I concentrated on the magic until it finally vanished, but as the last remnants of it extinguished, a small spark leapt uncontrolled from my hand to a nearby crystal, causing it to explode. I wrapped myself in dense air as the blast tore through the tunnel, flinging me down it like a rag doll. Every blast ignited more crystals, until I was a hundred feet from the original blast. I was covered in dust and dirt and remained on my hands and knees in the center of another cavern as I tried to shut off my magical shield of air before I lost control of it.

Thankfully I remembered that the destruction of the crystals meant that the particles in the air were no longer volatile, and shutting it off became easier after the noise of the explosions stopped ringing in my ears. I wiped my face, finding it covered in blood, and tried to get back to my feet, but my ribs felt as if they were on fire. My wrist was broken, but even with the agony I was in, there was no time to use my magic to heal. I forced myself back to my feet just in time for Lee to barrel into me, smashing me against the nearest wall.

Thick black blood oozed from the dozens of cuts across his face. "It's not that easy," he snarled. "You don't get to win."

"There's no win or lose, Lee," I told him, and drove another blade of lightning into his chest. I removed the magic and watched him slump to the ground, blood pouring from the new wound.

"Your body can't keep up with all the healing," I said. The shadows around Lee moved up over him as he scrambled to try and escape. They wrapped themselves around his limbs and began to drag him into the shadow as Lee screamed in defiance, trying to change into a mist form, but the shadows blocked his escape, forming a dense shield around his body as he vanished down into the shadow realm with a final, muffled scream.

A few moments later I felt a surge of power the likes of which I'd never received from a single person, healing my injuries in an instant. I switched off my magic and looked down the nearby tunnel. I just hoped I could get back aboveground before whatever Abaddon and her people had planned for Shadow Falls could come to fruition.

After running down several tunnels—and spending what felt like hours of desperately wasted time—I found explosives that had been drilled into a portion of the tunnel wall. With no detonators in sight, I stepped back as far as I could and threw a tiny ball of flame at the crystal closest to the explosives. A large part of the wall vanished in a plume of smoke and dust, igniting several other crystals.

Worried that the tunnel would cave in, I wrapped myself in a shield of air and sprinted toward the hole in the tunnel wall, throwing myself through it just before another explosion sounded from inside the tunnel. Thankfully the explosions of the crystals allowed me to control my magic with relative ease.

I found myself in a corridor. But instead of the jagged stone and natural appearance of the underground tunnels, this new corridor had smooth walls. I followed it around a corner and ignored several doors until I came to some stairs, which I quickly ascended, and then I opened the door at the top.

I exited the stairs and found myself in a room with an open door in front of me, with the sights and sounds of fighting just beyond it.

I sprinted through the open door and collided with a blood elf. I quickly disarmed it, driving its own sword into its skull. I parried the blow from a second blood elf, thrusting the blade up through his throat, then pushed the body aside and killed a third and fourth, who thought they had a shot at killing me.

Dozens of blood elves lay on the floor amongst just as many of Galahad's guards. "Where am I?" I shouted to a nearby guard as the fighting in the courtyard ended. He held his arm as blood flowed out of his armor and onto the floor.

"The realm gate," he told me as a medic helped him out of his armor to tend to his wound. "The one you helped discover."

"You know who I am?"

"Nate Garrett, yes, I know you. You saved my life when we had the troubles here a few years ago."

"What's happened in the two hours since I went under the palace? I've been mostly trying to find a way out of the tunnels."

"The blood elves swarmed out of the mountain." He winced as the medic went to work.

The alchemist's own ability would heal him, but that could take hours, and frankly, when you're wounded in battle, you take all the help you can get.

"Thousands of them," the medic said. "They flooded out of the mountain like a wave. They destroyed a portion of the outer rim of the city until the guard got it under control and managed to push the majority of them over to the plains."

"Which means you guys were in the middle of a battlefield," I said.

"That about sums it up. A hundred guards were here. Now we number sixty. They hit us like a hammer. And that woman with them . . . she tore through us."

"A necromancer?" I asked.

The medic nodded.

"Abaddon. If you see her again, avoid her."

"She ran off toward the forest."

"Thanks for the info," I said. "Any chance you have a horse I can borrow?"

The guard pointed to a stable just outside the ruined portion of the fort wall. Large boulders were visible in the grassland outside of the fort, the work of alchemists. If the blood elves thought this would be an easy fight—even after an ambush—they were about to learn otherwise.

"Best wishes to you," the medic said. "There's a chestnut mare. She's the fastest, not easily spooked, either."

"Yeah, you, too." I ran out of the fort, leaving the surviving guards to their rebuilding and defense of the second realm gate. The stables weren't large, with only a dozen horses in residence, and I picked the chestnut mare as the medic suggested. He'd been right, too. She ignored the bodies that littered the ground and the sounds of battle that hung in the air as we raced back toward the city of Solomon.

CHAPTER 29

Nate Garrett

The flames could be seen well before I reached the outskirts of the town, with thick, black smoke billowing up into the sky at an alarming rate. The smell of acrid smoke and death mingled together, creating something that I had to force myself to ignore. More dead lay where they'd fallen, and I continued past them without stopping to check. There was nothing I could do except avenge them.

As I got closer to the palace, the fighting intensified, with thousands of blood elves going up against the guard, while in the distance civilians were evacuated to safer parts of the city. I really hoped that Harrison and his men would be able to stop the blood elves before too many lives were lost.

I rammed the horse into two blood elves, sending them spiraling. She kicked out, catching a third in the breastplate, sending him sprawling to the ground, unmoving. I climbed down and gave the reins to a nearby guard, whose leg was bleeding.

"Can you ride?" I asked.

She nodded and swung up onto the horse. "My king is inside. He battles many of these creatures."

"Go wherever you can get help. I assume Harrison is waist deep in blood elves."

"He fights closer to the mountain. We managed to contain most of the blood elves, but some slipped through, and others still are coming from the forest."

"There won't be any more blood elves coming up through the tunnels under the city, but we're in for a fight. Heal as best you can."

She nodded and rode off as I ran into the palace, killing two blood elves with the sword I'd taken from the elf I'd killed earlier. It stuck fast in the chest of the second elf, so I left it be and kicked the elf aside.

A guard lay against a nearby pillar; blood soaked his belly and legs. He moved slightly and groaned in pain. I ran over and knelt beside him.

"They flooded the palace so quickly," he said, spitting blood onto the floor beside him. "Never seen anything like it."

"Galahad, Leonardo, Antonio, Selene, Zamek—have you seen any of them?"

"A large number of people got caught as they were moved away from this part of the city. Selene and Zamek were helping move them. I was ordered to stay here. I'm going to die, aren't I?"

I wasn't sure what to tell him. "Your body will heal. Alchemists are made of sturdy stuff."

"I'm human."

The shock on my face must have been easy to see.

"Was in the army. Human army. I married an alchemist, and we came here."

"Rest, you can see her again."

"She died a year ago."

"I'm sorry."

"This was her dream, so I couldn't leave it. You know?" His breathing became more labored, and his skin was pale and clammy. I knew he didn't have long. "You ever love anyone so much you couldn't let go?"

I nodded. "I need to help Galahad."

He reached out and took my hand. "Please don't let me die alone like this. I want to see her again, but I'm so afraid. Do you think there's a heaven?"

I shook my head. "Sorry."

"Thanks for being honest. At least if there's nothing after this, I can know for certain that she's not in pain. That I won't be in pain." He coughed again and closed his eyes. "Being here was the best time of my life."

I held his hand as he died, before crossing his arms across his chest and tucking his sword into them. It was all I could think to do. I got back to my feet and walked with determination across the room to the nearby hallway, picking up a sword from a fallen guard on the way.

I killed the three blood elves in the hall as quickly as possible, the whole time feeling my rage fuel me, pushing me on. Lee's power flooded my body, and for a moment I thought to use it, to use my magic and end everything in my path, but I stopped myself. That would be a disaster.

I kicked open the double doors at the end of the hallway and walked into the dining room, which was empty of anyone living. I ran through, ignoring the bodies on the slick floor, moving from room to room until I reached the ballroom doors. It was the quickest way to the rear of the palace, where I could hopefully aid any guards fighting the battle closest to the forest.

Inside, Galahad was surrounded by the bodies of the blood elves who had fallen before his two blades. He moved with grace and purpose, each cut aimed to kill or maim an opponent. It was as if he were a dancer, creating a beautiful fusion of movement, grace, and death. He stabbed one blood elf in the throat and turned toward another, driving the blade into the elf's heart.

"You're busy," I said, stepping over one of the many bodies.

"I like to do my part. You okay?"

"Lee is dead. Very dead, not vampire-rise-from-the-grave dead."

"Good. Leonardo and Antonio are to the west of here. They had an idea to use the elven-rune gate in the mountain to start evacuating people to Tartarus. The place was Sky's idea, by the way. She said there's plenty of space there. Zamek and Lucifer are trying to figure out the translations for the elven runes so we can move as many people as possible."

"Will it work?" I asked.

"We don't have a lot of other ideas to get a million people out of this realm. It'll take time and effort to do it, but even if we shift ten thousand people a day, we can prepare for Avalon's arrival, and hopefully this place will be empty then. In the meantime, Abaddon ran into the woods. Care to help?"

We left the ballroom and reached the rear entrance to the palace. There had been a lot of fighting here.

"The guards are outside," Galahad said as he walked over to a nearby body and picked up a sword, motioning for me to take it. "This belonged to one of my elite guard. It's probably of better quality than the one you're currently using."

I took the sword from him just as several crystals strapped together bounced beside me, landing close to my feet. I turned in time to see Helios, in full dragon-kin form, standing in the doorway to the rear of the palace. He roared flame at us, and I was about to create a shield of air when Galahad shoved me aside, creating a shield of stone to protect us as the crystals ignited, throwing both of us across the room. I hit my head with enough force to dent the stone wall and fell to the ground, my vision swimming. I tried to get back to my feet as Helios walked over to Galahad, picked up his sword, and plunged it into his heart. Helios looked over at me and laughed before running out of the palace.

With my head still pounding, and blood running down my neck, I crawled over to Galahad, cradling him against me. The whole attack took seconds, and despite the power at my disposal, I was helpless to intervene.

"Please don't die," I whispered. "Please."

"Nate," Galahad said, placing his hand against my face. "My brother."

I shook my head as tears filled my eyes.

"You were always the best of us. You were always the one who never stopped. Never backed down. I'm proud to have been your brother. Proud to have known you. To have loved you."

"I love you, too," I said, and then as tears flowed freely, my friend, my brother, Galahad died in my arms.

I roared in pain and rage, feeling the power inside of me grow, the need for vengeance burn. I lowered Galahad to the floor and took one of his swords before standing up and raising a hand toward the palace wall. All restraint vanished in an instant as air magic exploded from my palm, tearing into the wall like it was made of straw, ripping tons of stone apart and flinging them outside the palace with ease. A hurricane of air subsided only when most of the nearby wall had been destroyed, and I walked through it, every step leaving a burning footprint as all the magic inside me lit up as glyphs along my arms.

Before me lay an army of baying blood elves. The guard had been helpless against the thousands of them. Most of Galahad's men lay dead or dying. At the thought of Galahad's murder, I let out an almighty roar, allowing my air magic to carry the noise across the sea of the blood elves, who fell silent in an instant.

I walked with methodical purpose toward the steps at the rear of the palace. A hundred feet lay between me and my enemy. At the rear of the ranks of blood elves floated Helios, smiling, hoisting aloft the sword he'd murdered my friend with. There were murmurs of laughter.

I screamed a cry of vengeance, feeling my throat burn from the noise, and I looked up as the wraith towered above me, copying my scream of rage and hate, its shadowy ropes billowing around me as its bony hands pointed at the blood elves.

Some blood elves turned, but there was nowhere to go. I walked toward them, feeling my pain and hate grow as I poured magic into my hands, into the spheres that I began spinning. Spheres of fire and air, of lightning, of shadow and matter magic. I reached the bottom of the stairs, and no one had moved.

"Kill him," Helios commanded.

"Come try!" I shouted, and unleashed hell upon those standing between me and Helios.

I plunged the spheres into the closest blood elves, and the magic tore them to pieces, ripping apart those unlucky enough to be close by as if they were made of paper. As the chaos subsided, I poured fire out of my hands, incinerating anything that came within twenty feet of me, while spreading out my shadow magic, snatching blood elves and dragging them down to use as fuel for my rage and hate.

Within a minute I'd killed a hundred blood elves, and at that point they broke, turning and trying to flee from the flames that destroyed everything, leaving me standing on cinders. The fire took hold of the forest, and trees burned to ash in seconds until I stopped it, but the damage was already done, and the fire quickly spread out of control. I didn't notice or care and slaughtered blood elves unlucky enough to get close to me. A whip of fire trailed from each hand, cleaving blood elves in half with every flick.

Lightning leapt from my fingers, and the screams of blood elves filled my ears, but still I continued, stepping over the smoking bodies to get to Helios, who stood his ground, a wicked smile on his lips.

When I was close enough, he roared flame at me, and I wrapped myself in air, allowing the superheated fire to roll over me. His smile vanished when he saw me untouched, and a moment later I was on him, driving a sphere of lightning into his chest, unleashing it and watching him driven back toward the tree line. I hadn't used too much power in the sphere; I wanted Helios to suffer.

He came at me with his talons, so I stepped aside and drove a blade of lightning into one of his wings, destroying the membrane. He dropped to his knees as blood poured from the wound. I stepped around him, took hold of his wing, and used a blade of fire to sever it, tossing the entire wing aside as he screamed in pain.

"You can't fly on one wing," I said, picking up a blood-elf sword, killing the elf who made a noise signaling he wasn't quite dead, and tossing the sword over to Helios. "Pick it up."

Helios stared at the weapon for several seconds.

"Pick it up," I said more forcefully.

Still, he hesitated.

"Pick up the fucking sword!" I screamed.

Helios did as I commanded, holding the sword in a sturdy grip before getting to his feet. I walked toward him, and he attacked with strength and precision, but I parried it, driving my blade into his second wing, severing it at the shoulder.

Helios cried out in pain and dropped back to his knees.

"Get up," I told him.

Helios sprung from the ground, charging toward me, but he was too slow and I easily avoided the attack, pushing his sword away and head-butting him. He staggered back, and I dashed forward, slashing up across his face, taking one of his ears.

He staggered back, and I maintained the offensive, taking his other ear and cutting off his sword-wielding hand. The sword fell to the ground and was soon covered in Helios's blood as it freely pumped from the stump where his hand used to be.

"Get up," I told him again.

"Just kill me," he said.

I walked toward him and kicked him in the face. "Kill you?" I asked. "Not for a long time. You took my friend, my brother. I'm going to take every single fucking piece of you until I feel like you've paid."

I stabbed the sword into his side, just under the ribs, and twisted it before pulling it out.

"Please finish it," Helios pleaded.

I cut his handless arm off at the elbow. "Fuck. You."

"Enough, Nate," Erebus said from behind me as time froze.

"It is not enough," I snapped. "How dare you stop me from extracting vengeance."

"Is this who you want to be? Killing an unarmed man in the middle of a battlefield? A man you've beaten? You're better than him, and you know it. You could have killed him a hundred times over, but you keep him alive for what, pain? You're not doing this for Galahad; you're doing it for yourself."

I spun on Erebus, feeling the anger inside begin to bubble over. "He took my friend." I felt tears sting my cheeks. "He took the best of us. He took my brother. He killed Galahad in the way of a coward. Why did Galahad push me out of the way? Why did he sacrifice himself for me? I could have saved myself. I could have used my magic."

"Galahad created a shield to stop you both being hurt, and it kept you alive. He made his choice; he chose to save your life."

"And Helios chose to finish his and not mine. Because they want me alive. They continue to taunt me, to try and break me, and I'm done with it. I'm done with it."

"Finish Helios. Clean and quick. Then go after Abaddon. But don't be this torturer. Don't be the monster the Fates said you'd become. You're better than that. You went down this road once before, and it took a lot of effort to bring you back. Are you sure you want to do it again? I don't think your friends will be able to bring you back this time, and we both know it."

Time went back to normal, and I looked down at a begging Helios. I removed his head with magical lightning wrapped around the sword that I'd taken from Galahad. Erebus was right: I was not that man anymore. A long time had passed since I'd behaved that way, and I would not rewalk the same path I had after Mary's murder. Galahad's murder would not be avenged until Abaddon and all she worked with were removed as a threat.

I sprinted into the forest away from the burning trees and, with my magic fueling me, reached the entrance to the ruins nearly an hour later. There were no blood elves or guards there, nothing to consider a threat. I walked into the ruins and followed the same path I had when I'd found Lee. Ares charged into me and punched me in the side of the head so hard I saw stars. He picked me up and flung me across the ruins as if I were nothing. I collided with the furthest wall and dropped to the floor with a thud in time to see Ares approach, anger etched on his face.

"He humiliated my son," Ares said, pointing to me. "You'll regret that."

"Good to see you again," Abaddon said from her seat on the stone throne. "I hoped we'd cross paths once more."

I got to my feet and blasted Ares with a torrent of air, smashing him through the wall, and flung a ball of flame at Abaddon, who threw herself aside. I ran out of the ruins and almost into a dozen masked men and women, all waiting for me at the mouth of the ruins.

"Which one of you is Hellequin?" I asked. "I'd like to kill him."

The sound of clapping came from behind me, and I turned so that I could watch Abaddon exit the ruins and keep an eye on the mask wearers.

"Lucifer is here, isn't he?" Abaddon asked. "I was so hoping to see him again. He needed to be punished for his transgressions."

"He's busy killing your people," I said.

Abaddon laughed. "I'm going to enjoy our time together."

"I'm not going anywhere with you," I snapped.

"Did Galahad die?" she asked me. "I left Helios to deal with him. I assume Helios is dead."

The clouds above darkened, and thunder began to rumble.

Abaddon looked at the sky for a second. "I wouldn't. You're going to need both hands if you hope to beat me."

"Just a distraction," I said. "Everyone always looks up." The shadows burst forth from the ground, wrapping themselves around Abaddon, dragging her to the ground. I felt an incredible force inside the mass of shadows as they encircled her, but in an instant they were expelled, throwing me back into the nearest tree. My air shield kept me from getting seriously hurt, but I'd never known power like what Abaddon had just done.

Before I could move, Abaddon raced forward, stabbing me through the chest with a spirit weapon in the guise of a curved sword. I collapsed to the ground as pain wracked my body, only to look up to see the Hellequin masked man standing above me. He punched me in the mouth, splitting my lip. He looked back over at an approaching Abaddon.

She nodded, and he dragged me to my feet before plunging a dagger into my side, twisting it and removing it before doing it again. The silver in the dagger burned, and I cried out in pain as he stamped on the back of my knee, forcing me to the floor.

Hellequin stood before me and removed his mask. "Hello, Nate," Deimos said. "Did you really think we were done?"

Abaddon came into view, a smile on her face. "We've got a lot to discuss, you and me. I'm going to murder everyone you ever loved, and you're going to help me." She kicked me in the face hard enough to knock me out.

CHAPTER 30

Mordred

Realm of Shadow Falls

After escaping Siberia, Mordred arrived in another cavern and saw the rest of the group looking at him as his brain rattled around. "That was not good," he said, trying to get used to the idea of his father being My Liege. "Merlin. It's always been Merlin. It's always been my father."

"Your dad is Merlin?" Remy asked. "No offense, but he's a shitty parent."

"Can't disagree with that," Mordred said.

"So, we finally know who the evil bastard behind all of this is?" Morgan said. "About time."

"Where's Elaine?"

Fiona pointed to the corner of the cavern where Elaine sat on the floor, looking up at the ceiling.

"What happened?" Mordred asked.

"She tried to remember something," Mac said.

"There was a lot of screaming," Wei said. "A lot. I don't know what they did to her, but her memory is fucked."

Mordred walked over to Elaine and crouched beside her.

"I can't remember why they took me," Elaine said. "Or who took me. Or what I was going to tell you when I saw you. I just remember pain. And Abaddon. I really don't like her."

"Join the club," Remy said as he walked over to them.

"This doesn't look like Tartarus," Mordred said as he looked around at the glowing writing on the cavern walls. "Did we land inside another mountain? And where's Nabu?"

"I'm here," Nabu said from the mouth of a nearby tunnel. "This isn't Tartarus, and you need to come with me."

Morgan helped Elaine to her feet. "You okay?" she asked Mordred.

"I'm not sure," Mordred said. He'd considered lying and saying he was fine, but faking it had never been one of his strong points. "There's been a lot to take in."

"I get the feeling we're not done yet."

They hurried to catch up with Nabu and the others and found themselves climbing some steps that led out of a hole in the ground behind a large stone sarcophagus.

"These are ruins," Diana said.

"They're old," Remy said, running a hand across a second sarcophagus.

"Yeah, ruins tend to be that way," Wei said with a smile as Remy raised a middle finger in her direction.

"I can smell smoke," Diana said, sniffing the air. "Burning flesh, wood, and a few other things. Where are we?"

"Shadow Falls," Nabu said as they reached the entrance to the ruins and walked into the forest. "I've been here before. The palace is a few miles to the south."

"Where's the smoke coming from?" Elaine asked. "That doesn't bode well."

"Few things do at the moment," Alan said. "I guess we should go look."

"You up to it?" Fiona asked him.

"I'll be fine."

"Me, too," Mac replied. "No one asked, but I'm good."

"We'll lean on one another," Morgan told him. "Everyone forgets that we were hurt."

"I'm thinking of raising the issue with HR back in Avalon," Mac told her.

"Avalon has an HR?" Remy asked. "I thought Elaine just kicked people when they annoyed her."

"It's close enough," Mac said.

"Are you done?" Nabu asked. "We should go."

Everyone stopped and watched him walk into the forest. "He is not dealing with this all that well," Mac said.

"He's not used to having so much happen in such a short time. His powers can't keep up with processing all the new information," Diana said. "Makes him grouchy."

The uninjured members of the group reached the outskirts of the forest after an hour's run. Diana had sprinted ahead, but Wei and Remy had easily caught up with her. Mordred and Nabu had joined them soon after, and they all paused at the sight of dozens of dead blood elves littering the field at the rear of the palace.

"What the hell happened here?" Wei asked Mordred.

"A battle," Remy said. "The ground is scorched. The bodies are a little on the crispy side. And some are in more pieces than I really want to count. Oh, and the trees over there are still smoking but don't appear to be aflame."

"Lightning," Diana said, pointing to several patches on the ground. "Nate did this."

Morgan and Nabu turned toward her. "You sure?" Morgan asked.

Diana nodded. "There's evidence of fire and lightning, and some of these elves are partially buried in the ground, as if something dragged them into the soil but only enough to cut them in half. Shadow magic did that. I've seen its use before. I've seen the aftermath of sorcerers cutting loose."

"I've never seen magic do this sort of devastation," Remy said. "There are a hundred bodies here. At least. Nate killed a hundred blood elves by himself?"

"Magic is stronger in Shadow Falls," Nabu said. "Unpredictable and wild. But I have to admit to being impressed."

"Something made him angry," Mordred said. "Nate isn't the kind of person to use his magic with this little regard for his surroundings. And he did that." Mordred pointed to the hole where a large part of the palace used to be. Pieces of the wall littered the field and steps leading up to where it had once been.

"My God," Elaine said as she reached the battlefield.

"That's appropriate, as it seems that Nate is a god here," Remy said. "The vengeful kind, too."

"He slaughtered these blood elves," Elaine said.

"This is why you don't piss off a sorcerer," Alan said.

"This is why people are scared of them," Fiona replied. "Especially here. And especially Nate."

Mordred walked away from the conversation, ascended the steps to the rear of the palace, and walked through the destroyed wall. He saw Galahad immediately and sprinted over to him, dropping to his knees and trying to find a pulse.

"Galahad!" Mordred shouted. "Galahad." He channeled his light magic and placed his hands against Galahad's chest. Yellow glyphs lit up over Mordred's arms, turning almost golden as he poured more and more magical power into the light magic he used to try and revive Galahad.

He didn't know how long he tried to revive his friend, but no matter how much magic he used, Galahad remained motionless. Eventually he felt a hand on his shoulder.

"Mordred, he's gone," Morgan said, crouching beside him, gently pushing his hands off Galahad.

"No, I just need to use more magic," Mordred said. "He's not gone. He can't be. I never got to say I was sorry. I never got to tell him he was a good king. I never . . . I just need to try harder."

Mordred placed his hands back on Galahad's chest and continued to use his light magic, the power spilling out all around him, barely contained inside the building.

Remy walked around to the opposite side of Galahad's body and placed one of his hands onto Mordred's. "He's gone."

Mordred stopped his magic and shook his head.

"He's gone, Mordred," Remy said again. "I'm sorry, but no magic is going to bring him back."

"He was my friend," Mordred said. "I can't lose friends. I spent so long trying to hurt them that I need to make that up to them. I need him to know how sorry I was."

"He knew," Diana said softly.

"I saw Galahad about six months ago," Mac said. "We spoke about you. He said he was proud that you'd turned everything around. That you'd fought the programming that was done to you."

Tears fell from Mordred's eyes, spilling onto Galahad's cold body. "When we grew up together, he was always the best of us. We always tried to one-up him, but we never could. Especially with weapons. It was like he was one with them. It was a thing of beauty. Whoever did this will pay."

"I think Helios did this," Remy said.

"Then I will find and kill him," Mordred replied.

"Nate beat you to it," Elaine told him. "He died hard. We found his body outside. It's not in one piece."

"Good." Mordred wiped his face. "Galahad and I fought alongside one another. We had one another's backs, but I wasn't here this time. For a thousand years we were enemies, but he was one of the first people I thought of when I regained my mind. I'd tried to kill him, but he was too good. I don't know how Helios managed it, but I'm sure there was deception involved." He leaned over and kissed Galahad on the forehead. "Goodbye, my friend."

"You need to take a minute?" Morgan asked Mordred as he got to his feet.

Mordred shook his head. "Point me at something to hurt."

A huge man appeared in the doorway, his body covered in splatted blood, one arm hanging loosely while the other held a spear. He saw Galahad's body and dropped to his knees.

"Harrison," Elaine said as the man cried out in pain and anguish for his king.

"Harrison," Morgan tried. "We know it's upsetting, but we need you to point us in the right direction. Where's Nate? Where are the rest of the people he was with?"

"Fighting," Harrison said. He exhaled and got to his feet. "You are Morgan and Mordred, yes?"

Both nodded.

"Galahad spoke fondly of you. Nate is missing, but his people continue to search for him in the city."

"What do you mean, missing?" Mordred asked.

"We can't find him," Harrison said, occasionally looking at the body of his king before looking away. "I came to the palace to see if he'd gone toward the ruins. Blood elves had come from there."

"There's nothing out there but a lot of dead blood elves," Elaine said. "So we know that Nate made it this far. What happened after that?"

Harrison shrugged. "We captured some blood elves; you can try asking them. They don't even speak any language I've ever heard of, so we're not getting anywhere fast."

The group followed Harrison through the palace as he explained the blood-elf attack on the realm. "Do you need healing?" Mordred asked him as they reached the front of the building.

"I'll be fine," Harrison said.

Mordred sped up and stepped in front of Harrison. "Arm. Don't argue."

"Your magic will cause problems," Harrison said.

"My light magic will be used to heal. If it gets out of control, I'll only be healing people I don't mean to."

Harrison reluctantly nodded, and Mordred healed his arm. Once he was done, Mordred had to concentrate to stop the magic from flowing out of him. "I remember why this place isn't good for me."

"It's not good for any of us at the moment," Harrison said.

They stepped out of the palace, and the scene of destruction that lay before him took Mordred's breath. A large part of the city closest to the palace had suffered the most fire damage. Several guards battled blazes threatening to consume more buildings.

"So, the fighting is over?" Morgan asked.

"Thousands of blood elves attacked us, and then they vanished. We found bracelets scattered around the city. Just blank copper bracelets, like the ones Zamek said he found in Tartarus. They're up at the mountain preparing an evacuation."

"Evacuation?" Elaine asked.

"We're getting the people of Solomon out of here and to Tartarus. Arthur arrived in the Earth realm, and King Galahad went to see him, but they were attacked. Arthur was kidnapped by this Hellequin. King Galahad felt that Avalon would blame us and send a war party. We're not sure how long we have, but we need to get people out of this realm."

"Merlin was behind this attack," Remy said. "He's the My Liege character everyone's been hearing about."

"Sounds about right," Harrison said. "Figures he'd be the evil bastard behind this."

"So, what happens now?" Fiona asked. "Arthur is missing, and they're going to start a war with Shadow Falls before Merlin takes full control. I worked for them; I believed in them."

"You were fired by them, too," Remy pointed out.

"First of all, I'd keep quiet about your Avalon connections," Harrison said. "People will find out about Merlin soon enough, and I figure everyone in Avalon is going to be painted with the same brush." Harrison nodded to several guards resting on the steps to get back to their jobs. "Secondly, I'm going to help people, and then we're going to figure it out. Going to Tartarus sounds good. Too easy for people to attack us now."

"Who's in charge?" Diana asked. "With Galahad dead, who's in charge?"

"Caitlin, his daughter, I guess. She's the only one of the council anyone genuinely listens to on a regular basis, and she's the only one I wouldn't pick a fight with. Or maybe him—he arrived about an hour ago."

A tall man walked toward them, his bloodred shirt and black trousers at odds with the sneakers he wore. "Elaine," he said, shaking her hand.

"Hades," Elaine said. "They have Nate."

Hades nodded. "I know. We need to talk." He looked at Mordred. "All of you. There's a lot you don't know."

"Agreed. The only thing I really want to know is, will I get to kill everyone responsible for what happened here today?" Mordred asked.

"Unfortunately it's more complicated than that. Arthur has been taken by this Hellequin character. It's believed that Merlin is My Liege."

"We know," Mordred said.

"We're thinking of just giving out cards explaining it," Remy said. "It would save time."

"In that case, come with me," Hades said. "We need to find Nate before Merlin gets what he wants."

"And what does Merlin want?" Elaine asked. "Apart from blood and death."

"All of the realms bowing before him," Hades said. "All of humanity cowering in what he believes is its rightful place."

"Oh, just that," Remy said.

"Now is not the time for jokes, Remy," Hades said. "Merlin wants to rule everything. And it appears that he wants Nate and Arthur standing beside him as his right-hand men."

CHAPTER 31

Mordred

Realm of Shadow Falls

Mordred remained calm for as long as he could, but by the time they had reached Leonardo's home, and people had said their hellos and checked that loved ones were okay, he was chomping at the bit for more information.

"You doing okay? It's been a lot to go through since you were shot," he said to Morgan, hoping to distract himself from the thought of Nate being in Merlin's hands.

"Sore, and I don't think I'll be doing a lot of hand-to-hand combat in the near future, but I'll live."

Mordred looked over at Fiona and Alan, who were at the end of Leonardo's living room, holding each other's hands. He went over to them. "How are you?" he asked Alan.

"I'm probably not going to sleep well for a while," Alan said, "but I've been in the care of people like them before. I won't let them break me."

"Good. I'm glad we got you all out of there before anything worse happened."

"They killed the rest of my team, didn't they?"

Mordred nodded. "A gang of werewolves in Moscow did it. They're mostly dead now. Or really wishing they were."

"I never thought I'd be thanking you for coming for me."

"I never thought I'd be saving your ass," Mordred said with a smile. He turned to leave but stopped when Fiona grabbed his hand.

"I'm sorry about what I said to you. I see your face, and I see the horror and fear it caused, but you're not *him* anymore, and I should have dealt with that better."

Mordred wasn't really sure what to say to that. People apologizing for thinking he was still a monster was something he still had issues getting used to. "Thank you."

"I'm sorry about Galahad," Alan said. "He was a good man."

Mordred nodded, unwilling to say anything for fear it would lead to him breaking down. Remorse and hurt would have to wait until Nate was found and Merlin stopped. "You want to explain what's happening?" he asked Hades, needing to focus on something other than his lost friend.

Hades stood as silence fell around the living room. "We have someone working within Merlin's organization. He managed to get details to me a few hours ago, and I rushed here. Unfortunately I was too late to help, and I'm sorry for that."

"Who's in his organization?" Selene asked.

"That's not something anyone other than me needs to know. He'll make contact when and if he can, but in the meantime he was only just able to contact me about this attack, and Merlin's role. Abaddon has taken Nate through one of the realm gates, although we don't know where to. We know that Merlin is working with Ares, Abaddon, Hera, and pretty much everyone who's been involved with the whole My Liege shit for the last few years."

"We just saw Merlin," Wei said. "In a Siberian mountain. Abaddon was there, too."

Hades looked over at Mordred.

"I'm good," Mordred said. "My father is the asshole I always assumed he was. Also, it looks like Gawain is helping somehow. I would assume that all of the paladins are under Merlin's control. They've worked together for a long time. I don't think that'll change anytime soon. My father and I didn't have time for a long chat."

"Wait, your father is Merlin?" Selene asked. "As in *Merlin*?"

Mordred nodded. "Real kick in the crotch, isn't it? I've known for a while now, but it's not exactly something I like to brag about. He was never much of a father."

"So, what's the plan?" Elaine asked.

Mordred reached over and placed his hand on Elaine's. "How are you holding up?"

"They took my memories," she said softly. "I must have found out something that was big enough to be a threat. But then why not just kill me? Why leave me like this?" She took a deep breath and exhaled slowly. "In the meantime, I *need* to do something. I *need* to help."

"I don't know what the plan is," Hades said. "We have several captured blood elves, although they're revealing nothing. My mole doesn't know all the details yet, so we need to wait until he can get to a place of safety. In the meantime, Lucifer, Leonardo, Antonio, and Zamek are trying to get the elven realm gate to work."

"I'll talk to the blood elves," Mordred said. "I speak the language."

"You sure?" Morgan asked. "I know you're on edge."

"I don't have a better idea," Mordred almost snapped. "Nate's in Merlin's hands. Merlin is working with Baldr and Hera and everyone else who spent a century breaking me apart. What happens if they brainwash Nate? You saw the carnage behind the palace. He did that because he was angry and in a place where his magic was superpowered. Do you want him to get that powerful on a regular basis? To start using that kind of power on Merlin's enemies? Because we all know where that's leading."

"I'll take you," Hades said.

"And what do the rest of us do?" Harrison asked.

"Help the injured," Hades said. "Check for remaining blood elves. The attack is over, but we still need to evacuate these people. Zamek,

Antonio, and Leonardo need to continue with their work. There's a city full of terrified people here, and all of them need to be reassured that they'll be safe. The blood elves came from the ruins and tunnels under the city. They've gone as quickly as they arrived. Causing panic and destruction was their aim. I've asked Caitlin if I can bring my people here to help, and she's currently working with Rebecca and your guardians to allow them through."

"We could use all the help we can get," Harrison said. "Never thought I'd be saying that."

"And getting Nate," Selene said. "They came to get him, too."

Hades nodded.

"The Fates said that Nate would become a monster," Morgan said. "Let's make sure that doesn't happen."

"Elaine said the prophecy was a fake," Mordred said. "But until she can regain her memories, I have no idea in what way."

"I tried to take a look at her mind back in the cavern," Morgan said. "But someone's put in some serious magical blocks. I shouldn't tamper with them since I don't honestly know what they do."

"I can ask around. Hopefully we'll find something."

"It's fake," Elaine said from the corner of the room. She looked over at Mordred.

"I know," Mordred said. "But we don't know how. And I don't want you to hurt yourself trying to find out."

Elaine screamed in pain and dropped to her knees, clawing at the floor in front of her as Fiona and Alan rushed to her side.

"Stop it," Fiona said. "You can't force the memories through."

"Can . . . and . . . will," Elaine almost shouted. "Ares."

She stopped screaming and looked at Mordred. "Ares and Hera. Oh, Mordred, what did you do?"

Everyone looked at Mordred.

"I have no idea," he said slowly.

"You helped create the Fates, yes?" Elaine said with a sad sigh.

Mordred nodded, his expression one of regret. "Centuries ago I helped create a new set of Fates. I didn't exactly go about it in a nice way."

"You had all of them at Mars Warfare when you worked for Ares and Hera, yes?" Elaine asked.

Mordred nodded again, wishing to be done with the conversation, but he knew he would be reminded of his past atrocities for a long time. He deserved to be reminded. "You're not exactly going through my greatest hits."

"Ares and Deimos tampered with their minds under order from Hera. I found someone who worked at Mars Warfare and had him tell me all about it. They knew you still hated Nate but also knew you hadn't spent time going after him for a while. They wanted to change that, to make you think that it was either you or him so that you'd hopefully kill each other."

"Ares and Deimos altered their visions?" Mordred asked. "That's not possible."

"Turns out it is. Enough blood magic from the sorcerers there, and you can do a lot. Unfortunately for Hera and her allies, they escaped before the work could be completed, but the vision acted like some sort of time delay. That's why they saw no future without you killing Nate. That never happens. They always see futures with different endings, but all of them ended up with you killing him to save everyone. No matter how badly you were lost, you always wanted to be thought of as the hero. You always thought you were doing the right thing to help the world."

"They set me up?" Mordred asked.

"The Fates aren't even aware. The visions might have gone by now—I don't know."

Mordred slumped into the nearest chair. "The prophecy was a lie. I spent years trying to stop it, and the whole thing was just bullshit?"

"Hera, Ares, and Deimos playing games. Hera always hated you and Nate. Always."

"Why didn't they just kill you?" Fiona asked.

Elaine paused and then screamed once again, dropping to the floor as sweat covered her face. She shook her head. "Can't . . . I just can't get through."

"You'll get there," Morgan said. "Go do what you need to do, Mordred."

Mordred and Hades left the room and walked back up into the palace and down into the dungeons. "We thought they would be safest in here," Hades said as they reached a large wooden cell door. "This is an interrogation room. They're all inside, with their hands tied behind their backs."

"We check every thirty seconds," one of the eight guards outside said. "And there are four guards in the room. They're not going anywhere, but some of the guards have tried to kill the blood elves."

"How many blood elves in total do we have?" Mordred asked.

"Five alive. Two tried to cut out their own tongues. They've been taken elsewhere to see if we can get anything from them."

"You think you can get information from them?" Hades asked. "I tried to pull the spirit from one, but it's a mess. I could have probably gotten information from it, but I suspect Abaddon had screwed around with it."

"Irkalla tried that and got snared."

"I never met Abaddon in person, although I did meet some of the other devils. Reportedly, Abaddon was powerful, cruel, and vindictive. Judging from what I've heard, I can't imagine her being someone who works well with others. I wonder how many blood elves she infected with those damn snares."

"All of them," Mordred said. "Would be my guess. She's doesn't strike me as a job-half-done kind of person." He opened the door and stepped into the cell, motioning for the four guards to leave him alone with the three blood-elf prisoners. Each of them had their hands tied behind their backs, to the chairs they were sitting on.

"This one will never get us to talk," the blood elf closest to Mordred said in their language.

"When I am free, I will have my way with his corpse. He looks tasty," the middle one continued in the blood-elf language.

"If you're going to threaten me, you should do it in a language I can't understand," Mordred said in perfect blood elvish, enjoying the shock on the faces of the prisoners. "I'll name you One, Two, and Three. One, you're the one who says I'll never get you to talk. I guess we'll see about that. And Two, you want to defile me. You'll need to buy me flowers first. I'm not against a good defiling, but I expect to be treated right."

"I'm going to eat your face," Two said.

"Raw and without condiments, or with a little salt and pepper?" Mordred asked. "I think a face should be marinated for a while. Raw face just sounds a bit bland."

The blood elf's expression showed his confusion.

"I get that you're blood elves," Mordred continued. "I get that you're used to people being scared of you, that your lives are filled with pain and suffering. That torture simply won't work on you. So, I'm not going to torture you for answers. I'm going to ask you where Merlin took Nate. And where Arthur is."

Two laughed. It was a bitter, nasty sound that made Mordred want to punch him in the face. "You're going to be nice to us? That's your plan?"

"Oh, sorry, no, you misunderstand," Mordred said. "My point here is this: you either tell me where Nate and Arthur are, or you'll die. And you'll die long and slow. No torture for answers, just for pain. I know I said your lives were full of pain and suffering, but I bet I can find a new level you've never experienced."

Two laughed again. Mordred knocked on the door, and one of the guards opened it. "Can I have a dagger, please?"

The guard looked at the three prisoners before drawing out a dagger from the sheath on his hip and passing it to Mordred.

"Thanks, I'll give it back in a minute." Mordred closed the door and went back to the prisoners. "Right, let's try again. Where are Nate and Arthur?"

Two exchanged a look with the other elves. "None of us will speak. We are servants of My Liege; we will watch his enemies burn."

"You're in charge, yes?" Mordred asked. "A higher rank, or some such."

Two nodded, pride evident in his eyes.

"Excellent." Mordred walked around the blood elf and used the blade to remove one of his fingers. The blood elf yelled in pain, and Mordred took some of the elven blood and smeared it on his hand. "Want to talk yet?" he asked as he returned to face them.

"If that is the worst you people have, we have nothing to fear," Two said.

"No, this is the worst," Mordred told him, and tendrils of blood magic shot from his hands, wrapping around Two as the elf screamed in pain. Mordred squeezed the tendrils, doing all he could to ensure that he didn't lose control of his magic, that it did no harm to the other elves. The tendrils wrapped tighter and tighter, like a constrictor, knocking the elf to the floor as his scream continued to fill the room.

"You said no torture," Three said.

"No, I said no torture to get answers," Mordred said, concentrating on his magic to remove it from the quivering mass of pain that writhed on the floor. "I don't care about answers. You have one chance, and then you die. He had his chance, and now he dies. Once you're all dead, we'll find Nate and Arthur another way. There is always another way. Now, excuse me, I have a matter to attend to, after which we'll move on to you two."

The other two elves were silent as Mordred dragged Two across the room, slamming him against the wall. "You'll be more useful dead than alive," he whispered, and plunged the dagger up into his throat, twisting the blade and pulling it free, then let the blood elf's corpse fall to the ground.

He turned to Three. "You're next. Where are Nate and Arthur?"

Three took a deep breath and tried to look as stoic in the face of danger as possible.

"Canada," One said. "I don't know the name of it. It's a compound near a place called Toronto. Abaddon has been using it as a staging area for attacks."

Mordred expected Three to berate One for saying anything, but instead he just looked relieved. "We found a lot of used bracelets around the city from those who had escaped, but you were caught without bracelets—why?"

"Not everyone was given them. Some of us came through the mountain into the tunnels under the city. We waited down there until the others arrived by using the bracelets. But not everyone who arrived here was given a bracelet to get home. We were meant to stay, cause terror for a long period until My Liege could return with Avalon approval."

"Merlin is still going to pretend he needs it?" Mordred asked, more to himself than anything else.

"My Liege is replacing people with those he trusts," Three said. "I hate you, I hate all you stand for, but we were left here to die. I love to fight, I live for it, but we're not fodder."

"How many blood elves are there?" Mordred asked. "You can't have all come from the dwarven realm."

One shook his head. "We were trapped under a mountain in Siberia. For a thousand years we lived there, underground, until My Liege came a few years ago. Most pledged their allegiance to him there and then."

"You're different from the dwarven-realm blood elves."

"We only fought amongst ourselves," Three said. "No dwarves or outsiders to lead us one way or another. No one to call an enemy. Until My Liege arrived and showed us one."

"So, how many are there?" Mordred repeated.

"Thousands," One said. "Eventually we'll take control of this realm and make it ours once again. That's what My Liege offered us."

"You'll murder innocents just to get your home back?"

"Why not?" One asked. "It's *our* home."

"Not anymore, it isn't," Mordred said. "And you both won't be there to see it become anything else."

"You're going to kill us?" Three asked.

"Not my call." Mordred left the cell, returning the blade to its owner. "One dead, two alive and chatty." He turned to Hades, who stood slightly away from the guards. "Merlin promised them this realm."

Hades nodded. "Merlin will have promised many people a lot of things he can't deliver. Despots always do."

Mordred and Hades left the prison and walked out of the palace, where Leonardo, Selene, and Diana greeted them. "Nate and Arthur are in a compound near Toronto," Mordred said. "They didn't know more than that, and yes, I believe them. Any idea how we get them out?"

"We can't," Hades said. "Not yet. We have no way of getting in and out, and no way of knowing exactly where he is or how many guard him. We have to wait for word."

"And what if that word comes too late to save them?" Selene asked.

"We'll find them," Hades said. "I promise you that. We'll get them out, but if we rush in Merlin could just kill them or kill anyone else who's there. A rescue could become a bloodbath."

"So, we wait and see?" Diana asked. "Not my favorite thing to do."

"Oh, we're not going to be doing that," Hades said. "I have a plan. Several of us will need to move to a safe location outside of this realm. I want to be ready to go in a few hours. We'll need to move fast once we find Nate and Arthur's exact location."

"Even if we know it, what's going to change?" Diana asked. "He could still be impossible to extract without a large-scale military operation."

"My man knows what to do," Hades said. "We have to have some faith in Nate's ability to withstand whatever Merlin does, and my man's ability to get both Nate and Arthur to a safe place without too much trouble. Merlin is eventually going to attack my people. They're prepared for this, but I'd rather Nate was out before it happens. Merlin's going after everyone who stood against Hera or any of his other allies over the years. He fired Olivia and moved Lucie to another job, although no one has heard from her in several days. The head of the LOA is said to be Ares."

Diana whistled. "That is incredibly bad news in a day filled with shitty news."

"Leonardo, can you change where a realm gate goes?" Mordred asked. "Can you change it so that the realm gates we already have go to Tartarus? We can start sending people there straight away."

"I've suggested that it's possible, in theory. Never tested that theory, though. People don't like me playing with the realm gates."

"Well, now you get to," Hades said. "Go check."

"So, what happens now?" Mordred asked.

"I need to leave the realm," Hades said. "I need to be ready for news about Nate, and I don't want someone to have to come find me. Anyone who wants to leave with me, come now."

"I'm with you," Selene said. "I can't leave Nate in Merlin's hands."

"Same here," Diana said.

"Me, too," Mordred replied. "We'll talk to the others and meet you at the realm gate."

Mordred, Diana, Leonardo, and Selene met up with the rest of the group and filled them in on the plan.

"I'm staying," Zamek said. "As much as Nate needs help, so do these people. And if anyone can figure out how to change the destination settings on a realm gate, it's me."

"I'll be staying, too," Nabu said. "This attack wasn't designed to kill everyone. There are a million people in this city, and it only attacked the easternmost area. The affluent area close to the palace. This was designed to make people afraid. The people who live here deserve to feel safe, and I'd like to make that happen."

"I'm with you guys," Remy told Selene. "Nate killed me, thus saving me, so I sort of owe him one."

"I don't owe anyone anything," Wei said. "But everywhere my small fox friend goes, it seems to coincide with lots of killing. I'm quite interested in seeing how this pans out."

Remy stared at Wei for several seconds. "I am actually at a loss for words. I guess we could always use more cannon fodder."

Wei stared back at Remy before smiling. "I would miss these moments if I left."

"I'm really not sure if you're just trying to wind me up, or you're a few bricks short of a wall."

Wei leaned close to Remy. "Can't it be both?"

Diana stifled a laugh as the rest of the group decided where their paths lay. Antonio, Fiona, and Alan decided to stay in Shadow Falls, while Morgan, Mac, and Elaine opted to join Hades and wait for word about Nate.

"Has anyone seen Lucifer?" Selene asked.

There was a short conversation about who Lucifer was, and why he was someone they were looking for, but no one seemed to know where he'd gone or what he was doing.

The group split up, with the half helping Hades making their way to the realm gate, where Caitlin, Harrison, and a tired-looking Lucifer greeted them.

"Find Nate," Caitlin said. "We'll hold the fort here. My father wouldn't want Nate to become Merlin's puppet."

"We'll do our damnedest," Morgan assured her. "You coming with us, Lucifer?"

Lucifer nodded. "I've been helping get people out of the realm gate. Some wanted to go to America rather than wait for Tartarus, which is understandable considering most consider Tartarus a prison realm."

"I really hadn't considered that," Selene said. "We should have considered it."

"It'll be fine," Caitlin said. "We've been spreading the word that Tartarus isn't a prison. Once we're ready to go, this place is going to see a mass evacuation."

"You sure you all have to go now?" Remy asked. "Abaddon played her hand by coming here."

"She'll be back," Harrison said. "Too many people here know the truth about what happened, about the blood elves, about Avalon's corruption. Merlin will want to silence that. We have a million people to hide. It won't be easy, but we'll manage it. Somehow."

"We'll see you soon enough," Selene said, hugging Caitlin. "We're going to need to work together to stop Merlin."

"I know," Caitlin said. "And we will."

The group went through the realm gate and was greeted by a tired-looking Rebecca Dean. "There's been no Avalon turning up to try and find Arthur. Maybe Avalon has bigger problems. Either way, Hades is outside. We'll finish up here, and then who knows what. I guess the dream of Shadow Falls is done."

"It doesn't have to be," Elaine said. "Maybe it just needs to be changed slightly."

"I hope so," Rebecca said.

Everyone found Hades outside next to one of six black SUVs while a dozen of his people looked on. "We have a long drive ahead of us," he told Elaine.

"I don't plan on resting until I find Nate," Selene said, climbing into the back of the nearest car.

"I plan on getting some sleep until we need to stop," Mordred said. "It's going to be in short supply after we get wherever Hades is taking us." He closed his eyes and, once the vehicle was moving, drifted off. He dreamed of himself as a young man with Galahad, Morgan, and Nate beside him, while the specter of death hovered unsuspected over them.

CHAPTER 32

Nate Garrett

Avalon's Wisconsin compound

After being dragged from Shadow Falls into the elven ruins, where a bracelet was placed onto my wrist, I was forced to clasp my other hand over it. I vanished from that realm and ended up on the frozen ground of somewhere else. Someone placed a sorcerer's band on my wrist, and my magic vanished. Apart from the fact that it was cold and I was in some sort of courtyard, I saw nothing before being dragged away again.

I blacked out at some point. I have no idea for how long, or what happened during that time, although I thought I heard voices around me. Eventually I opened my eyes. My arms hurt. That was the first thing that came to mind, and I looked up to see that someone had put shackles on my wrists, forcing me to hang from them. A two-foot-long chain connected the two metal shackles. There was no bracelet on either wrist that I could see, although I was still unable to access my magic. I could feel it, just out of reach, but never touch it.

Someone threw freezing water in my face, causing me to splutter and cough, but it made sure I was awake. My ribs ached, and I looked down, remembering where Deimos had stabbed me, but saw no wound. I knew I healed fast, but either I'd been out for the better part of a day, or someone had healed me.

"You're awake."

I turned my head to see Abaddon leaning against the nearby wall. She winked at me.

"You expected me to be dead?" I asked. My feet hovered three feet above the concrete floor, and they weren't shackled to anything. That was at least a little good news. I looked up at the shackles to get a more accurate impression of my predicament and found that the chain had been wrapped around a hook suspended from the ceiling. If I could get the hook, I might be able to climb it—it looked sturdy enough—releasing the chain and possibly getting down. I looked back at Abaddon. Although that wasn't going to be possible with her there.

There were three blood elves in the large room with me and Abaddon, and Ares stood in the corner by the sturdy metal door, his arms folded over his chest. Okay, so escape was going to have to wait. I glanced down and realized I wore only my jeans. Someone had taken my shoes.

"Can I at least have a chair to stand on?" I asked. "I assume if you wanted to torture me, you'd have woken me up a while ago."

"Get him a chair," Abaddon told Ares. "And tell Merlin he's awake."

Ares huffed but did as he was told, slamming the door behind him as he left.

"He really wants you dead," Abaddon told me. "Deimos, too."

I looked over at Deimos, who was leaning against the far wall, and winked. "Hey, dipshit." I turned back to Abaddon. "They both really should get in line. I think I'll be busy with every other fucker for a while yet."

"I think it'll be sooner than you'd like."

"If you can't tell, I'm shrugging."

Abaddon laughed. "I've wanted to meet you for a long time. I've lived in this realm for thousands of years, never using my abilities, keeping under the radar, but I've heard about you. I thought you were just a nobody when we met in Tartarus, but I was wrong. You're quite famous.

Heard what you're capable of. Merlin thinks you'd be a great asset in what we plan to do. I think you're going to be killed before then."

"Both excellent options. Any chance I could have a drink of water? Not water thrown at me, but an actual drink?"

Abaddon picked up a glass and jug from a table beside her and poured some of the water from the jug. She walked toward me, and paused as Ares opened the door, bringing in a metal folding chair. Abaddon took it from him, unfolded it, and placed it in front of me not close enough for me to stand on while she let me drink the cool water.

"Thanks," I said.

Abaddon laughed. "Not exactly a word I was expecting to hear from you."

"Just because I want to tear your throat out isn't exactly a reason to be rude."

Abaddon smiled and placed the chair under my feet, allowing me to take some of the strain off my arms. "See, being nice does have benefits."

"I'll show you how nice I can be," Deimos said from beside me. He punched me in the ribs hard enough for them to break, and I swung to the side, my feet slipping off the chair. It took a lot of effort to stand back on it, as the side of my torso burned with pain.

"Enough," Abaddon said. "Know your place, Deimos."

Deimos huffed again. "I'll get you soon enough," he told me before turning and leaving the room, almost walking into Gawain as they passed one another.

"He really does not like you," Gawain said, placing another chair close to me and taking a seat. "'Hates' you is probably a better word. And I don't think you were friends before you stole his wife."

I stared at the man I once called a friend, and fought the urge to kick him in the face.

"You really want to hurt me, don't you?" Gawain said with a smug grin.

"Yes," I admitted. "That would make me very happy."

"But then you wouldn't get to listen to my story."

"You're an asshole. Merlin is behind everything. You all want to rule the world and all the realms, and you're working with Hera and her clan of psychotic idiots. The thing I don't get is, why not do this when Arthur was in a coma? Why wait?"

Gawain laughed. "The last time we saw one another, Merlin really lost his temper, and he shouldn't have. But you ruined some plans, and then, well, you just pissed him off so damn much. Or pissed me off, depending on how you look at it considering Merlin isn't exactly in control of his own faculties these days."

It dawned on me. "You have mind magic. You're controlling him? How long?"

"Oh, we'll get to the hows and whys soon enough. Actually I want to offer you a job. Head of the SOA. Ares is the head of the LOA. Did you know that? I promoted him after firing Olivia. I'll track her down and her mutt of a husband and deal with them later. I don't think they're ever going to see my way of thinking."

"Good luck with that. I really don't think you understand just how much hard work it'll take to kill Olivia and Tommy. They're not pushovers."

"Everyone has a weakness, Nate," Gawain said. "Theirs is their daughter, Kasey. I know Tommy is hiding her, and a lot of her friends, too, but I'll find them eventually. Kids are such good bargaining chips. It's amazing that people in their line of work would ever have them, would ever allow themselves to create such a massive weakness that people like me could exploit."

There was little point in demanding that he leave them alone. I wasn't really a credible threat. A thought came to me, and I turned back to Gawain. "You want to offer me a job?"

"That's the plan. I don't think you're just going to agree and come work with us, if that's what you think. I think you'll need some persuasion. I've thought that maybe I could use your friends to get you on my side. I'll leave them alone if you agree to help me."

"Help you kill innocent people?"

Gawain laughed. "Oh, I fear I should start from the beginning. My plan isn't to kill innocent people—well, not long term. Short term, yes, some people will have to be eliminated, or sacrificed to the greater good, but long term, those who survive will be better off."

I stared at Gawain for several seconds. He looked like his younger brother, Mordred, but for the first time I saw the cruelty in his eyes. "What did you do with Asmodeus's soul jar?"

He laughed again. I was beginning to hate that laugh even more than I already hated him. "You think I cloned him?"

"Thought had crossed my mind."

"I know of a few people who can clone themselves. They tend to be a bit broken in the head, though."

"Because you're the very model of sanity."

Gawain's eyes grew hard. "You really should watch that mouth of yours. It'll get you into trouble. I'm trying to be nice. I'm trying to bring you into something wonderful. I'm *trying* to explain things. My brother is the broken one." With each sentence his voice got louder, until he was on his feet shouting at me. He moved his hands toward me, and a torrent of magical air smashed into my body, knocking me back, causing me to gasp for my breath.

He picked up the chair and placed me back on it. "Behave, Nate." He raised his hand toward me, showing me a bracelet that looked a lot like the ones that Tommy used. "We copied Tommy's security. You can only use your powers here if you're wearing a bracelet. They're not made for each person individually, though. I didn't really see the point."

I looked over at Abaddon and saw the bracelet on her wrist. I hadn't noticed it before, as I was too groggy. "Why are you doing this, Gawain? I once thought you were a good man. I thought you were my friend."

"Well, you were wrong on both counts," Gawain said as he retook his seat. "Asmodeus was captured by the shadow elves and executed, but his blood and spirit were kept in vessels. Vessels that Abaddon, at the time, obtained and stowed away with a few well-placed bribes."

I glanced over at Abaddon. "You used them on Arthur, didn't you?"

"I'm thirty years older than Mordred," Gawain said. "That time was spent realizing that Merlin had a wildly bad view of how the world should work. And it allowed me to try and find a way to create the tools I needed to move forward. Arthur's parents were inconsequential. They were humans who had no money, no status, and were frankly disposable. Abaddon found them in a village in northern England, living some pathetic life on a farm. They were offered a lot of money to have a baby."

"I waited for thousands of years," Abaddon said. "I had to decipher the ritual, to find out every little detail. And then I discovered that they were going to re-create us. Again. Different groups tried several times over the centuries, always with little in the way of results, but the use of the dwarven runes was a game changer. No longer would there be unpredictable results, like Pandora, or even myself. I had to use Asmodeus's blood and spirit to create the weapon we needed.

"Hera was there, as were Baldr and a few others I selected for their allegiance to Asmodeus when he lived, but I killed the dwarves who helped, to keep their secrets. From conception to birth took less than an hour. The father and mother died shortly after they finished their job of fucking, and then the spirit of Asmodeus and his blood kept Arthur alive. Kept him powerful. When we were done, I took the baby to the one man I knew would take him, the one man I knew wanted a son to carry on his name more than anything."

"Uther Pendragon," Gawain finished. "My lord and master at the time. Or the man who thought he was my lord and master."

"My birth and Mordred's must have been great irritants," I said.

"It wasn't something I was happy about," Gawain said. "Mordred's was . . . kept secret from me by my mother, much to my irritation.

Arthur was already ten by the time you were both born, you and others like you. Seven in total. We killed one at birth, and his parents, but the others fled after that. Your mother hid you until such time as it was deemed necessary to hand you to Merlin for protection. He wasn't under our control then. Arthur was strong but not strong enough when you arrived. After you survived . . . after your power manifested and saved you, it was decided you should live."

"Very kind of you," I said.

"I thought you'd make a better ally," Gawain continued, ignoring me. "You and Mordred. Despite my early misgivings. The others who were created at the same time as you remained hidden. I did love Mordred, by the way. He was my brother, but unfortunately he was not the man I'd hoped he'd become. Even more unfortunately, killing either of you would have caused issues. So I had decreed that you were to be spared unless I deemed it necessary. That's why Hera, and people like her, never tried to kill you again. At least, not before Arthur was placed in a coma. And by then I had complete control of the paladins. I wanted you by my side. I needed you by my side. You were powerful beyond what you knew, and frankly it took a lot of effort to keep Merlin in his place. To keep him feeding Arthur, and to keep Arthur's mind from breaking during the process. Turns out, Mordred making him comatose made it that much easier for me to finally break Merlin's mind.

"Mordred unfortunately had to go. He was to be king, but he was beginning to look too closely into a venture I was involved in. I couldn't risk it. My allies wanted to kill him, but then I decided to break him instead, send him back with a list of people to kill, including you. I figured having one of your best friends as a mortal enemy might push you toward Avalon, might make it easier to get you on our side when Arthur woke.

"Unfortunately Mordred wasn't as easily broken as I thought, although he still went after you, which was a nice touch. Went after Merlin, too, after I had Merlin banish him. It was another nice touch turning Merlin against his own son. I also wiped Mordred's mind. Mordred probably doesn't remember figuring out that I was one of the people who broke him time and time again while in the company of the blood elves."

"Wait, Merlin is Mordred's dad?" I asked.

"That's it? That's all you take from what I just told you?" Gawain asked.

"I knew he was sent after me. Although he doesn't remember you being a part of that. Remembers a lot of others who hurt him, though. I think maybe you created a monster you haven't quite had to deal with yet. He's going to kill a lot of your allies. That's if I don't get through them first."

"You killed Kay. I was especially fond of that man. He was loyal to a fault."

"I did. He murdered my wife."

"I know, that was my idea. Well, it was Nergal's idea; I just approved it. Merlin kept sending you away. It was his only hope to save you. I think that's why he banished Mordred. He couldn't do anything else but send you as far from me as possible." He chuckled to himself. "I was a bit annoyed about your wife. A human, that was unexpected. But I knew it would break you, that you would finally embrace everything I always knew was inside of you. Shame Tommy spoiled that party. I'll have to remember to punish him for it. I have a list of people who won't survive the coming years; he's quite near the top. Honestly, all of your friends are near the top. That's how you'll prove your loyalty to me."

"I'm not going to help you," I said. "You're evil. You're murdering innocent humans, slaughtering them for what? To make a point? And where's Arthur—is he helping you do all of this?"

"Arthur is a very helpful man. He's played his part, and the best thing is, he doesn't even know he's playing a part. It'll take a while before he's the man I need him to be. I needed to make an enemy I can vanquish. You see, I couldn't use Nate Garrett as my enemy. I want you on my side, and ruining your name would achieve nothing. But having you watch while Hellequin killed all those people . . . Well, that was always going to spur you on to find me. And then, when I have total control of Avalon, I can go to the humans and tell them that we defeated Hellequin and his allies. That they're safe now. That we saved them. Then we pass some laws putting me in charge of the security for most countries, and I go from there. I'll create a world peace force, a force that will only fight those people who wish to destroy humanity, who wish to enslave it. And when I'm done purging everyone who stands against me, I'll have control of everyone. Merlin, Arthur, Abaddon, Hera, and you by my side. No one would ever dare cross us. And when I've saved them all, people will go into the streets and sing my name. Most places are already starting."

"You're killing people so you can be their savior, and thus make it easier to control them."

"That's exactly it. All of these people will bow before us, Nate. They'll learn about Avalon, about the control we've had over the years, and about how when that control wavers awful things happen. They'll welcome us. They need us. Humanity was never meant to rule itself; it can barely go a day without starting a war or screwing up so badly that part of the planet is forever changed. They don't deserve to be in charge. They deserve to be mindless. They deserve to be food for those who need it, and playthings for those who desire it. They should be on their fucking knees worshipping us like the gods we are.

"I spoke to Deimos about being a fake Hellequin, and he jumped at the chance. When Arthur asked you to go to Shadow Falls, you were meant to jump at the chance. He doesn't know anything about what's happening right here. He didn't know about the kidnapping, or the attack. He didn't know about us using Deimos as Hellequin. At this moment he believes that we can all live in harmony."

"You're using him?"

Gawain laughed and avoided the question. "Hellequin starts to pledge his allegiance to Shadow Falls, and what a surprise, Nate is already there. But you managed to find out about Tartarus before you were meant to, and that blew the plan all to hell. Deimos was annoyed about that. He wanted to play a cat-and-mouse game with you. He wanted to murder your friends, too, but I convinced him otherwise. We both know that your friends would have taken out Deimos, and probably those I sent with him, and the long-term plan was more important than killing them. Make humans afraid of us. And damned if it didn't work like a charm."

"Yeah, it was a good plan. Glad you've thought this through and aren't just being crazy or anything."

"I had to wait for a thousand years while Arthur was in a coma to put this plan together. Arthur has charisma; he has everything you could ever want in a leader. I am not easy to get along with, and people don't always trust me. Yes, some things didn't pan out, and you managed to delay it more than once, but then Arthur finally woke up. Do you know it took nearly two thousand innocent souls to feed him? I think we finally healed him.

"When I first started to take control of Merlin's mind, he had no idea how powerful I really was. I had Abaddon put me through the Harbinger trials at the age of ten. I spent a hundred and twenty years in them. I can't begin to tell you how I wanted to try out all the awful things Abaddon had me do during my time in there. Merlin fought me at first; he didn't realize what I was until it was too late, but once he was mine, it was a joy to behold. The paladins helped. They were able to amplify my power to drown out Merlin's need to fight. They'll be rewarded for that."

I sucked down the anger I felt. "Why Lee?"

"Why not?" Gawain asked with a chuckle. "The man was an idiot. But he hated you. And he wasn't hard to find. I offered him some blood—we told him it was Asmodeus's, but it was just a vampire master's we had killed—and sent him through the trials, too. I mostly just wanted to see what would happen. And when he was ready, we sent him off to cause havoc. We just needed someone to get into Shadow Falls, into the mountain, and copy down the elven runes on the dais. Once we had those, we could break in and remove Asmodeus's body. He needed a proper burial. After that Lee's entire job was to cause problems, piss off Galahad, and get to the ruins to wait to be captured. Then once you showed up—and we knew you would—he was to escape and get into the tunnels beneath the city. He was going to help destroy some of the tunnels so the blood elves could get up into the city."

"I saw," I said. "So, how am I meant to join you?"

Gawain stood. "You've seen Mordred. You know how we broke him. I just wanted to talk to you before we started."

"Very nice of you."

Gawain shrugged. "You're going to join me. You're going to stand at my right hand. And we're going to make sure that you have total loyalty to me."

"By beating me up?"

"The process will take some time," Gawain said. "It would have worked on Mordred if he hadn't escaped."

"It took you a century. I don't think you have that long."

"No, that's true." He nodded toward Abaddon, who left the room without a word. "Your mind almost broke with Galahad's death. Your rage and grief—that's something we can use. That's a state we need to start you in."

"If you hurt anyone else, I'll kill you, Gawain."

"We'll see."

The door opened, and Abaddon dragged in a badly beaten Lucie.

"Don't do this," I said.

"Lucie, tell Nate what you told me," Gawain said, ignoring me.

"Fuck you, pretty boy," Lucie said, and spat in his face.

Gawain attacked her with a furious rage, beating her down onto the floor, as I yelled at him to stop. He grabbed Lucie by the hair and dragged her over to me.

"Tell him," Gawain snapped. "Tell him what you told me."

"I don't like Nate," Lucie said, staring at me. "I don't trust him. I don't trust anyone with that level of power."

"This is the kind of person you call a friend," Gawain said.

"Go to hell, Gawain."

Gawain passed Lucie over to Abaddon.

"Kill them all," Lucie whispered before Abaddon slit her throat and pushed her toward me. Lucie died leaning up against me, her blood drenching me from the stomach down.

"Now that's the sort of mood we need you in," Gawain said, opening the door and revealing Ares, who had a cruel smile on his face. "You know what to do."

Ares came into the room. "It will be my pleasure."

"Don't kill him," Abaddon said.

Ares pulled Lucie off me, shoving her to the floor. "Oh, he won't die," he said. "But he's going to wish he had."

Rage and hate filled me until I felt nothing else. "Bring it on."

CHAPTER 33

Nate Garrett

Ares took my rage and hate and twisted it inside my head. He didn't change any of my memories like his son had so long ago; he knew that Erebus would react negatively to his presence. He was well versed in exactly what I could and couldn't do and used it to his advantage.

He pointed my hate at the people I loved, stripping away my feelings for them, and tried to replace those feelings with something ugly, something cruel and vicious. He tried to make me believe that Gawain, Abaddon, Arthur, and Merlin were the only people I could truly trust, the only people who would allow me to achieve everything I ever wanted.

Hours turned into days, and I soon lost all track of time. Occasionally Ares would stop and beat me or have one of the elves do it. They didn't break any bones. Without my magic I wouldn't have been able to heal, but my ribs had already been busted and every bit of extra damage further hastened the mess that Ares was making out of my mind.

I hung from the ceiling for hours at a time, only occasionally allowed down when Ares decided I'd taken too much punishment, and I was allowed to sleep. But then it began again. At one point Erebus tried to step in, to get me to concentrate on him, but Ares was so powerful his empath abilities brushed Erebus aside. Ares knew what Erebus had attempted, and had anticipated it, returning to cause me more anguish as soon as he felt it safe to do so.

"Is that nightmare back yet?" Ares asked after days or weeks of not seeing Erebus.

Sweat dripped from my face, running down my bare chest to where Lucie's blood had dried on my stomach. Even after all this time, they hadn't let me wash. I looked down at where her body had been. They hadn't bothered removing it for a considerable amount of time after her murder. They'd used her to weaken me, and I'd helped them by allowing my hate to take over. My need for vengeance had been my downfall.

"No, it's just me and you," Ares said after moving my face so he could stare me in the eyes. "You're stronger than I expected. I see why Deimos was unable to break you."

"He's a coward," I said.

Ares smiled. "Yes, he is. I beat him when he came back to me after you broke his mind. I beat him over and over until he realized what a waste he was. And then he wanted to destroy your name. He thought it would elevate him in my eyes."

"I'm going to kill him when I get out of here."

"Are you trying to anger me?" Ares asked. "That's not a very good way of dealing with this. You should be angry with Tommy and Olivia, with Elaine and the rest of them. Angry that they left you here, angry that they're not going to save you. They let Lucie die. They let Galahad die. They didn't help you fight us. They've done nothing."

I nodded. "They abandoned me."

Ares smiled. "That they did. You know who's there for you, don't you?"

"Gawain. He wants me to stand beside Arthur. To make this world better. For us to have our rightful place."

"Do you want that?"

I nodded weakly. My body hurt, and I had trouble keeping my eyes open. "More than anything. I want to work for Arthur. I want to change the world in his image. Please, let me."

"I think we're not quite there yet. There was a little pause. You're still thinking you can escape from this."

I shook my head.

Ares continued with the punishment once again. Showing Tommy, Olivia dead, showing me standing over their bodies, making me feel good about it, making me feel like that was the right way to move forward. He showed me hunting down the others, skewering Elaine with a spear, decapitating Morgan, burning Zamek alive, torturing Mordred until he wept and begged to be let go. Everything I saw, Ares made me feel good about. Made me want. Made me need.

Eventually the images stopped for a second time. Ares lifted my head, which sagged against my chest. "I think we can have a break here," he said. "Keep him company. I'll be back soon."

I heard Ares walk out of the room, closing the door behind him. I watched the blood elf who had been left behind as he walked over to the chair and took a seat.

"Nate," Erebus said.

"Leave me," I said in my mind. "Now is not the time."

"Nate, you can't possibly think that your friends are people who should be killed."

"Erebus," I snapped out loud. "Leave me."

The blood elf laughed and walked over to me, standing in front of me and pushing me in the stomach so I swayed back and forth. They'd taken the chair long ago, and my arms felt sore again.

"Your nightmare trying to help you?" the blood elf said with a smile. "Ares will be pleased that you banished it. We'll break you yet, sorcerer. We'll break that nightmare and force it out of your body if need be."

"Going to have to kill me for that," I said.

"That's the plan," the blood elf said. "You don't know, do you? You don't know why Gawain has you kept alive."

"Enlighten me," I said.

"Because he knew that if you died, all of your marks would disappear. Your nightmare would take control. He told Ares about it. He wants your mind broken before you die so that when your last mark goes and your nightmare takes control, you'll be reborn loyal to whoever they need you to be loyal to."

"That's how the last mark goes? With my death?"

"Apparently so. Got to break you first, though."

"Have you ever seen *Lethal Weapon*?"

The blood elf looked confused. "What's that?"

"Oh, it's a film from the nineteen eighties. It hasn't aged that well, if I'm honest, but there was one bit in that, and if you haven't seen it, this will all be new to you."

"What will?"

I kicked the blood elf in the face, then wrapped my legs around his neck and used it as a lever to push myself up and pull the chain from the ceiling hook. I let my weight fall onto the neck and shoulders of the blood elf, and we collapsed to the floor. I broke his neck a second after, then removed his sword and decapitated him.

He didn't wear a bracelet, so I still had no access to my magic, but he did have some keys. I unlocked my shackles and dropped them to the floor next to where Lucie's body had been before putting the keys in my pocket.

Images of me murdering my friends flickered into my mind, making me feel like I needed to hunt them, to end their lives so that Arthur would accept me, would allow me to stand beside him. I pushed the thoughts away—I would deal with them later.

I left the cell and found myself in a corridor with dozens of identical doors along either side. A gate sat at one end, a stone wall at the other, which made the choice easy.

I unlocked the gate and pushed it open, making more noise than I was happy with, and paused at the bottom of a stone staircase to wait for anyone who might investigate what they'd heard. After ten seconds, and with no one seemingly interested in the sound of the gate opening, I slowly crept up the stairs, making sure to keep low. I was close to the top when I realized that the room beyond was empty.

A long table sat in the middle of the room, with several wooden chairs around it. It was littered with scraps of food and bottles of drink—it looked like they'd had a real party here. A small fireplace was close to the table, next to an ancient-looking wardrobe. A large wooden door at the far end of the room appeared to be the only exit other than the stairs to the cells, and I had no intention of going back down there.

I walked to the door and turned the massive handle, pulling it toward me, and I heard voices on the other side. I peered through the crack I'd created between the door and its frame and saw two blood elves. They were in a long hallway with dark-blue carpet and normal house doors along one side. The other side had windows overlooking the courtyard I'd been brought through when I'd first arrived. From the angle I was at, I couldn't make out much in the courtyard except for its size and the several guards that were patrolling it. One problem at a time.

One of the blood elves in the hallway was only a few feet in front of me. He was leaning up against the wall, talking to his comrade, who was looking out of the window in front of him. They spoke in blood elvish. "You think they'll break him?" the one closest to me asked.

"We've broken better," his friend said.

"You think we'll be able to get our brethren out of that horrific dwarf realm? I'd like to think that we could help Gawain destroy his enemies."

"What if we're not like them? What if we changed in different ways?"

"They're still blood elves. We were meant to be there when they slaughtered the dwarves. Instead, we got to spend a thousand years buried in a mountain. On Earth realm. Just the word 'Earth' makes me feel ill."

"Humans are worse than dwarves. At least dwarves taste nice."

I opened the door and stepped out, driving the blood elf sword I'd taken into the back of the closest elf, piercing his heart. The second elf turned toward me and was about to scream something when I charged toward him, knocking him off his feet and dumping him on his head. He tried to push me off, but I smashed my forearm into his face, breaking his cheekbone, and ripped out his throat. Rage and hate filled me again, and I forced myself to drop the lump of flesh in my hand and stagger away.

"You won't break me," I whispered, staring at the black blood on my hands. "You won't." I remained where I was until I calmed, by which point the elf with no throat was still making noise. Blood elves were hard to kill if you didn't take the head or destroy the brain or heart. I raised the elf's blade and stabbed him through the skull, pinning his head to the floor, killing him.

I fought back the anger as I searched both elves and took a belt with two sheathed daggers. For some reason it had taken me this long to realize I still had no shoes. I thought of Tommy making a joke about *Die Hard* and chuckled before the image of his death at my hands tore itself into my head.

"No," I said. "I will not kill my friends. How do I stop this?"

"Kill Ares," Erebus said from beside me. "The change he tried to implement isn't complete. You kill him, and hopefully you'll break free from his grasp."

"Kill Ares? Is there another way?"

"You find someone with mind magic and get them to fix your brain."

"Okay, so both ways suck." I looked down at the blood elf. "For now I can use this hate Ares has filled me with."

"Just make sure not to get too used to it. An empath like Ares controls people in part because he makes them believe that the emotions he forced into them, and the memories he created, are something to revel in. Something to enjoy. He'll make you think that without those memories, you are nothing but a shell of yourself."

"I'm going to kill Ares for this at some point. Gawain, Abaddon, any other fucker who happens to be involved. I'm going to pile those bastards up behind me."

"That's Ares talking."

I shook my head. "No. It really isn't."

Erebus disappeared, leaving me alone in the hallway. I decided it was best to hurry and continued along the hallway, taking a set of stairs down one level. I stopped at the bottom and took a quick glance along each direction of hallway. The left side had eight blood elves, all standing around a door. The windows on the side of the hallway gave me a clear view of the stairs and courtyard that the door led to, but being quiet and fighting eight blood elves did not go hand in hand.

I looked to my right, and apart from a set of double doors, the area was void of anyone that I could see. I crept around the corner of the stairs and ran the length of the hallway, making sure to keep on the rug to muffle my steps. I reached the double doors and pushed one of them open a fraction of an inch to look inside and, when I was satisfied the room beyond was empty, pushed the door open and slipped inside.

I'd entered a huge ballroom filled with a dozen tables, all with chairs around them, but the tables were bare. Large red-and-gold curtains hung from one side of the room. I ran over to peer behind one, but the window behind just showed a large number of blood elves running training exercises. I spotted Atlas and put the curtain back; he was close to the last person I wanted to run into.

I tried a second set of double doors at the end of the ballroom, but they were locked, and the sounds of laughter from behind me made me sigh. I placed my head against a metal strip on one of the doors and controlled my breathing before turning around to face Ares.

"You got somewhere to be?" he asked me with a slight chuckle.

"I just thought I'd come and make sure you got my food order right. I would hate to think you'd bring me something I didn't like."

"You humiliated my son all those years ago. You beat him like a drum."

I nodded. "He's a piece of shit just like you. You must be proud."

Ares shook his head. "Can't stand the sniveling little bastard. But he is *my* son."

"So, what happens now? You kill me, tell Gawain I died trying to escape?"

"I thought about it. But you know what? I think I'd prefer to just beat you into a coma and screw around with your brain some more." He removed the bracelet that allowed him to use his abilities and placed it on a nearby table. "Now you can't bitch and moan about it not being fair."

"You had an advantage with your powers. You'll really wish you'd kept it."

"I prefer to fight without my powers. I've seen people like yourself rely on them, allow them to be the best you have. I saw what you did to Helios, though—that was impressive. Pissed off Gawain a little, as Helios was in charge of murdering all those humans, although I guess you saved him the job of removing him from our organization when he eventually fucked up."

"You really don't like many people, do you?"

"I like Aphrodite, but only for about an hour at a time."

"An hour? Aren't you kind of exaggerating?"

Ares's eyes narrowed with anger. "I am all man. I should show your woman that. I should have shown her when she was married to my son.

Maybe if she'd got some, she wouldn't have betrayed us by running off with you the first chance she got."

"What a surprise, Ares is a misogynistic prick. Who could possibly have seen that coming?"

"I just know what women really want."

"You know, I should have just let you kill me instead of listening to your inane drivel."

Ares shrugged off his coat and carefully unbuttoned his dark-blue silk shirt, laying both over the back of a nearby chair.

His body looked like it had been carved out of solid granite. He rolled his shoulder and flexed his biceps, making the veins in his neck pop a little.

"You done?" I asked. "Or do you need some oil to really seal the image?"

He ignored me and removed his shoes and socks, spending time to ensure that each shoe had one sock in it.

"If you take any longer, I'm going to kill myself just for something to do," I told him.

"I don't want to hear excuses after I beat you, Nate. I want you to understand that I am the better man, that you are beneath me. You need to understand your place."

"Like Hephaestus did with you?"

"He cheated," Ares snapped. "We were to fight fair, and he used his ability to trip me. Humiliated me in front of his wife. I murdered his friend to make us even."

"Yeah, you're a real stand-up guy. In case you haven't noticed, I have no powers right now."

Ares's smile was wicked and cruel. "Oh, I know." He bounced from foot to foot while I sighed with impatience. If his game was to keep me here until Gawain arrived, he was doing a good job. I considered just starting the fight, but I needed to keep my head. Allowing my emotions to get the better of me would get me killed. Ares was too dangerous for me to think it would end any other way. I didn't even know how I was going to beat him when I didn't have any power. Several thousand extra years of experience of fighting was not something I could take lightly.

Eventually he moved toward me, keeping his hands up and bouncing from foot to foot as he moved. I moved my head from side to side and waited for him. I wasn't going to go to him; I wasn't going to give him the satisfaction of making me impatient.

When he was close enough, he threw a jab, which I knocked aside. I moved around him, either avoiding his punches or slapping them away, making him smile every time I had to back away. He feinted with a jab toward my kidney that I just managed to avoid, but I couldn't avoid the blow to my jaw that knocked me over one of the tables.

"Not so good, after all," Ares said with a laugh.

I felt like saying, "You see how good you are after someone tortures you for hours on end," but it wouldn't have made any difference. Instead, I got back to my feet and blocked a kick to my side, and then another one to my stomach. I brought my elbow down on his knee and punched him in the side. He pushed me away and began to bounce up and down again, shaking his knee as he moved.

"Nice," he said. "You've got some power in your punches. Didn't expect that."

I remained silent and breathed out slowly before placing myself in a fighting stance.

"I haven't seen that style before," Ares said. "Where did you learn it?"

I remained quiet, and his irrational hatred of being ignored got the better of him. He snapped forward with a hard punch, which I ducked under, and I smashed my elbow into his exposed ribs and slammed my palms into his stomach. He stepped back but grabbed hold of me as he did, lifting me off the ground and flinging me over his head and across the table behind him.

"Finesse is over," Ares said, throwing the table aside. I pushed up from the floor, kicking at Ares's head as I spun past him. I stood and smiled as blood trickled down his lip. He licked it and charged me. I moved aside, but he was too fast, and he grabbed my arm, using his momentum to wrench it out of its socket. He kicked me in the chest, and I staggered back against the wall. His fist slammed into the side of my head, knocking me to one knee as stars swam in front of me. I blocked a knee to the head, but he kicked me in the ribs, doing more damage to my earlier injury.

I dropped to all fours, and Ares kicked me in the ribs like he was kicking a football. More of them broke from the impact, and I rolled against the wall, gasping for breath.

Ares reached down, grabbed me by the throat, and lifted me off the ground before slamming the back of my head into the wall.

"You are not my equal!" he shouted in my face. He head-butted me and flung me across the destroyed table, where I hit a chair, gouging my forearm. Blood was soon trickling down toward my hand, and I spotted the bracelet that Ares had been wearing. It was on the floor under a nearby table. I was beaten, hurt, and had been tortured for hours. I couldn't beat Ares. It wasn't a matter of how good he was—he was fresh, and I wasn't. I wasn't even sure I'd have been able to beat him if I'd been at 100 percent, but I knew in my current state, it would only be a matter of time before he killed me or, worse, knocked me out so that he could finish the job on my mind. Sending me out to kill those people I loved the most.

"You still on the floor, little man?" Ares asked. "I can't believe how weak Helios must have been to have lost at your hands."

"I thought this was going to be equal," I said, using the table to pull myself upright before slamming my shoulder into the wall, putting the dislocated joint back in place. I cried out in pain. "You're still much stronger than me."

Ares shrugged. "Can't do much about that, now can I?"

I shrugged, too. "Guess not. So are we fighting, or are we going to drink tea and eat cake?"

Ares laughed and walked toward me. I blocked a kick and drove my knee into his stomach. I kicked out at his leg, causing it to buckle, and punched him in the jaw, knocking him to the side. As he moved he kicked out, and despite my blocking it, the power behind it lifted me off my feet and dumped me on the nearest table. I rolled over it and crashed to the floor, grabbing the bracelet and clicking it into place a second later. Power flowed through me, but I stayed where I was on the floor, allowing my magic to heal me.

Ares threw the table above me aside and kicked my newly healed ribs. "Is that it? Are you spent?"

He kicked again, and I rolled with it, throwing up shadows all around Ares that dragged him to his knees, pinning him in place.

"Cheat!" Ares screamed at me as he tried to fight against the shadows.

"Yeah, you just caught on to that?" I asked, and wrapped air around my fist, bringing it down onto his jaw and snapping his head aside with incredible force.

Blood splattered across the floor from Ares's ruined mouth, and I kicked him in the chest, using my shadows to drag him down onto his back.

"You're undeserving of calling yourself a man," Ares said.

I rained down punch after punch on his helpless body, allowing the rage and anger to fuel me, until his face was a ruined mess.

"You shouldn't have put all that hate in me," I whispered to him. "Maybe I'd have fought fair if you'd just left me alone."

I placed the tip of my finger against his temple as he muttered something.

"I hope this hurts," I said, and shot a finger width of lightning magic into his temple.

He screamed in pain and bucked against the shadows. Then I stood up, created a blade of lightning, and slammed it into Ares's neck over and over again until his head rolled along the floor. The shadows vanished, and I dropped to my knees at the sound of clapping. I turned around to see Deimos and Gawain standing in front of the now-opened door.

Deimos grinned at me. "My turn."

I motioned for him to come on over, and he drew a gun, firing at me while my shield of air kept me alive. After the fifth bullet hit the shield, I pushed it forward, smashing into Deimos and throwing him through the door to the outside of the building.

I walked past a still-smiling Gawain and wanted to smash his face in as much as I did Deimos's, but something stopped me, and I continued down the steps to the muddy courtyard outside.

Deimos was back on his feet, cracking his knuckles and rolling his head. "You murdered my father."

I nodded. "Don't be sad—you'll go see him soon."

"Even if you kill me, you don't think that it'll be over, do you? Hera will flay you for killing us."

I shrugged and threw a ball of lightning at Deimos, who flung himself aside, avoiding it. I felt pain in my side as one of Deimos's throwing daggers connected with my stomach. The pain quickly turned into burning agony as the silver from the blade went to work, forcing me to pull it out, giving Deimos time to close the gap between us and strike with another blade, slashing me across the chest. He darted away, throwing two more blades, which I managed to avoid, but a third entered my leg just above the knee, and I crashed to the muddy ground.

"You cheated against my father," Deimos said.

"We both know that after our last encounter, you're not going to be able to use your power to hurt me," I said.

Deimos nodded. "It happened so many years ago, but it still feels like only yesterday. I guess these blades will have to do."

"I don't need magic to kill you," I said, pulling out the throwing blade.

"You really do," Deimos taunted, and threw another blade, which I avoided, rolling to the side and throwing the blade I'd removed from my leg back at Deimos, who easily dodged it.

My brain swam, and I knew I wasn't in a state to fight a prolonged battle. I was exhausted, beaten, and about as close to just giving up as I'd ever been in my life, but I was not about to give Deimos the satisfaction of killing me. I pushed myself up off the ground and back to my feet.

"If you use your magic, I'll kill you," Abaddon said as she appeared out of the door with Gawain beside her.

I weighed my odds.

"Can you take us all?" Gawain asked.

The answer was no. I had no chance of killing everyone. "Why do you want this piece of shit dead?" I asked, looking at Deimos.

"I don't," Gawain called back. "But whichever one of you survives will have a place in our organization."

Deimos removed two eight-inch daggers, roared in defiance, and charged me. His two blades were a blur as he repeatedly sliced into the flesh on my arms and hands while all I could do was dodge and avoid mortal strikes.

At one point he overreached and I grabbed his arm, smashed my elbow into his nose, and snapped his wrist, grabbing the dagger from his hand. He kicked out at me, forcing me back. We were both covered in blood and mud, and the fight had gone on longer than either of us probably wanted.

Deimos raised his dagger toward me, but I didn't move. "You are the reason for my downfall!" he screamed at me.

"You murdered innocent people because you're a petulant child," I said back. "So desperate for any kind of positive attention. Thousands of years old, and all you really wanted was for your father to be proud of you. And he never was."

Deimos charged toward me, full of anger and hate. Full of emotion. I waited until the last second, then parried his blade and pushed his arm away. I used the dagger I'd taken from him to cut through the flesh around his ribs, causing him to yell out as blood quickly drenched the side of his body.

He put distance between the two of us, and I watched him without emotion. "You should never have tried to be something you're not," I told him.

"You know, after that bitch Lucie was taken, I put out the bounty on your head. I thought it was funny."

The memory of Lucie's body spurred my rage, and I had to fight to keep control. I said nothing.

"How's my wife?" he shouted.

"How's your left hand?" I asked. "I assume you married it since we last met."

Gawain laughed, and Deimos's expression darkened further.

"I'm going to kill you, Nate."

"Sure, why not, and then you're going to piss pure silver and sprout wings."

Deimos's face twitched slightly. "Once you're dead, I will claim what is mine."

"And what is that?"

"Your woman, for one. She should still be mine. She will be again, or she'll wish she was."

"She's not *my woman*, you conceited little prick. Are you so full of hate simply because you want someone who doesn't want you back? Is that it?"

"You took her from me."

"You never had her in the first place, Deimos. Not once. She has her own mind, and she's long since decided that you're a nasty piece of crap. It's something everyone appears to have figured out a long time ago."

"Well, it won't matter, will it? You'll be dead, and I can do whatever I like. I am the son of Ares, so who's going to stop me? You? Your friends?"

"You're a spoiled brat. You're one of those people who think that the world owes them something, simply because you were born to privilege. You expect everyone to behave as if you're above them. No one has that privilege, no matter how much you want it. The world is not your plaything; the people are not toys for you to destroy or discard as you wish. The fact that you've lived for thousands of years and never figured this out is pathetic. You're an evil little piece of shit, and I won't let you hurt anyone else. Your days of terrorizing people are done. Let's get this finished. You bore me."

Deimos ran toward me like I knew he would and moved quickly, but I avoided the attack and rammed my dagger into his stomach, slicing his belly open as his momentum forced him forward.

He dropped to his knees, trying to hold his stomach in as he looked down at the blood that saturated his hands and the floor around him.

I kicked the dagger he'd been holding away, then crouched before him. "You're what happens when hate wins." I drove the blade of the silver dagger up under Deimos's chin into his brain, killing him instantly.

I looked up at the sound of Gawain clapping. He grinned at me. "Now *that's* what I'm talking about."

CHAPTER 34

Nate Garrett

I was hoping you were going to kill him," Gawain said from the doorway. "You needed a push in the right direction. Why else would I have allowed you to escape from your cell? Why else would I have sent Ares to fight you? I didn't think he'd take the bracelet off, though—that was not a smart move on his part. Looks like I'll be needing a new director of the LOA. Anyone you recommend?"

I stared at Gawain for several seconds. "And Deimos?"

Gawain walked across the courtyard toward me. He patted me on the shoulder. "I just never liked the little bastard. I honestly wasn't sure you were ready, but I really hoped. How's that magic feeling? Sorry we had to threaten you so you'd kill Deimos without it, but I really needed to find out if you were capable."

I looked down at the bracelet on my hand. "It feels good."

Gawain laughed and motioned for me to join him, and we both walked back toward the compound. Abaddon nodded her head toward me as I walked past her, back through the open door.

"You're going to have to finish your training," Gawain said. "But I'll be taking over from here. Ares was such a blunt instrument, although maybe if he'd been there with Mordred it would have only taken weeks and not decades to break him. Still, he started you on the right path. I'm thinking the Harbinger trials to ensure you're completely loyal. I know you already did them, but they're a good way for you to undergo years of conditioning in only a few months."

"Mordred," I said, and feelings of anger and hate filled my heart, but they were pushed aside as quickly as they came. Killing Ares had not removed the need to hurt my friends.

"Yes, Mordred. He was a mistake to leave alive. A costly mistake, but a mistake that needed to be made. You'll kill him. Kill all of them. You'll be one of the inner circle, Nate. The man helping to rule this realm, and all others."

I stared at Ares's headless corpse.

"You should give him to your shadows," Gawain said. "It's fitting that his power would power you."

For a second that felt like an excellent idea. I stood and created a sphere in my hand, spinning it over and over again until it was a blur, and only then did I pour in other types of magic, growing the sphere three feet wide. I folded the magic over my arm, down to my forearm, like a gauntlet of spinning power. I looked over at Gawain, who was still smiling.

"You're feeling the power you have, aren't you?" he asked. "I bet it feels glorious."

I nodded and took a step toward Gawain. "Why me? Why not one of the others? Why not Mordred?"

"You had the most potential. Out of you and Mordred, you were the one I actually thought would fight alongside me. You just needed the right push."

I sprinted forward and launched myself at Gawain, driving my fist into his chest and unleashing the magic. It tore the entire wall behind Gawain apart, throwing debris all over the courtyard outside. Dust obscured my vision for a few seconds, until I cried out in pain as someone grabbed my hand, crushing it.

The dust moved aside in an instant, and Abaddon stood before me, her hand wrapped around my fist, squeezing tighter and tighter as more bones and tendons snapped. She let go of my hand and kicked me in the chest, sending me sprawling into the courtyard.

"You *dare*!" Gawain screamed at me as he got back to his feet. "After all I've done for you, you throw it back in my face?"

I got to my feet, but Abaddon struck me in the stomach, driving her knee into my face, pushing me toward the ruined wall. I flicked a whip of lightning behind me, but her necromancy power threw me back fifty feet. It felt as though a train had hit me.

"How many bones are broken?" Gawain asked as I had trouble standing. Abaddon hit me with another blast, knocking me back toward the fence, shattering bones.

Gawain walked toward me, raising a hand at a dozen blood elves, who ran over to see if he needed help. "You can't beat me. You can't beat Abaddon. And even if you could"—he pointed over to Merlin, who stood in the ruined wall—"you can't beat us all. You're weak, and hurt, and you can't have much left."

My magic went to work healing me, but Gawain was right: I had nothing to fight with. Didn't mean I was going to stop.

Shadows leapt from the ground around Gawain, who was suddenly shocked at the attack. The wraith's hand clawed out of the shadows, grabbing hold of Gawain's leg. I was about to pull him in when the breath left my body in one go, and I looked down to see a curved spirit weapon sticking out of my stomach. It vanished, and I dropped to the floor as pain flooded my body and Abaddon stepped around me, kicking me in the face and sending me to the floor.

"No," Gawain said as Abaddon was about to give the killing stroke. "Killing him will unleash the nightmare, and frankly I have more important things to do. Take him somewhere quiet, and make sure to kill that nightmare when it turns up." Gawain's face appeared in my view above me. "You could have been a god."

"Fuck you," I said.

"I'm going to make sure that no one ever remembers your name," Gawain said with as much venom and hate as I'd ever heard a person use. "I'm going to kill everyone you love, everyone you care for. Everyone who even helped you. I'm going to butcher them all so that no one would dare even whisper the name Nate Garrett."

"You promised me," Atlas bellowed from across the courtyard. "You promised he was mine to kill."

Gawain sighed. "Yes, I did, didn't I? Fine. Atlas, take some men, take him out somewhere, and kill him." Gawain bent down and removed the bracelet from my wrist, forcing my magic to vanish and more pain to wrack my body. "What a damn waste of time you became."

Atlas and five blood elves took me over to a van, opened the rear doors, and threw me inside, where several runes ensured that my magic wouldn't return. They didn't even bother tying my hands behind my back—I was beaten and broken. My body was a mess, and without my magic I couldn't even heal myself. So, I lay there on the cold metal floor of the van and pictured whatever horrific death Atlas had planned, hoping that at some point I'd get my chance to escape.

That chance came when we stopped at a petrol station and Atlas got out to fill the van. There were three blood elves in the back with me, and as I moved to sit up, I smashed my elbow into the knee of one and punched the next in the jaw. I was about to hit the third when the rear doors opened and Atlas reached in. He dragged me out by my ankles and punched me in the stomach, dumping me to the frozen ground.

"Just once don't fight," Atlas said. "I wanted to offer you dignity in death, so how about you just let that happen and we can call it a day."

Once I was outside the van, my magic returned to me, and I created a blade of air to drive up into Atlas's chest, but he grabbed my hand and hit me so hard that I saw nothing but darkness.

I woke up and found myself in the back of the van. A sorcerer's band sat on one wrist, but I was alone. I moved slightly, and my head throbbed, so I lay back down and tried to figure out how to get out of this shitty circumstance.

I'd thought of nothing when the doors opened and Atlas reached in, dragged me out, and dumped me on the snow-covered field. "You know where this is?" he asked.

I shook my head.

"Excellent. Then no one will ever find your body."

"You suck," I said as Atlas pulled me to my feet. "You suck so damn hard, Atlas. You're just a piece of shit."

He punched me in the stomach as a blood elf came over. "You're making this harder than it needs to be."

I couldn't think of a comeback that didn't contain the phrase "fuck you," so I went with that and got a punch to the face from the blood elf for my troubles.

I was semiconscious as they half carried, half dragged me through the snow before dumping me on the ground.

"Wake up, Nate," Atlas said, and slapped me across the face.

I blinked. "You again. Can't you just kill me and be done with it?"

"I think you should kneel."

"Why, is Zod around here?"

Atlas looked confused. "I don't know what that is."

I shook my head. I wasn't about to explain it to my executioner. Two blood elves forced me into a kneeling position while another passed a shotgun to Atlas. "Any last words?" he asked.

"Not really. I genuinely hope someone flays you. Is that a good last thing to say?"

Atlas looked over at a ridge a few hundred feet behind us.

"You expecting someone?" I asked.

Atlas shrugged.

I stared at him for a second before laughing. I couldn't help it.

"What's so damn funny?" he demanded to know.

I shook my head. "You won't get it."

The heads of the two elves beside me exploded in a shower of blood and bone, covering me. A second later two more elves went down, both shot in the head. The last blood elf turned its weapons toward the ridge and died a moment later.

"Atlas is fucked," I said, but remained on my knees. I had no power, so any fight between us would be over within seconds. Best to wait and see who my guardian angel was.

It took a minute for me to see Mordred, Tommy, Diana, and Selene hurry toward us. Mordred and Diana had rifles over their backs, while the other two carried no obvious weapons. Selene ran over to me.

"No," I snapped a little more forcefully than I meant to.

"What's wrong?" Selene asked as the others reached us.

"Ares fucked his head up," Atlas said. "The last month has been hard on him."

"A month?" I asked. "Fucking hell, a month."

"We tried to find you," Mordred said. "But while Merlin has a compound in Toronto, which we raided, he took you to the north of Wisconsin. We're close to Lake Superior."

"Do not take my sorcerer's band off," I said. "Ares did something to my head. He made me want to kill you all. I can feel it, the hate and need to hurt you just under my skin. It's not Merlin. Gawain is My Liege. He's manipulated everyone."

Selene grabbed Atlas and pushed him up against a tree. "You were meant to keep an eye on him."

"Wait, you're working with them?" I asked Atlas. "And the punch was for what reason?"

"I don't like you—that's reason enough." Atlas turned to Selene. "To keep an eye on him, not to get killed trying to rescue him. Gawain doesn't trust anyone, especially not people who only joined up because he hates the other guy more. That's not exactly a basis for a budding friendship."

"So, what does this mean?" Tommy asked. "You hate us?"

"It's like a voice deep inside of me telling me to hurt you," I said. "It gets louder the closer you are. I don't know how to get rid of it. Or rather, I know exactly how to get rid of it; I just don't know how to tell you."

"Mind magic?" Diana asked. "We can find someone who knows it."

"It won't work," Atlas said. "It's ingrained."

"His brain needs to be completely rebooted," Mordred said. "Like mine was."

I nodded.

"Are you suggesting we have to kill him?" Selene asked, releasing Atlas and standing between me and Mordred. "Because I'll tell you right now how that shit is going to go down."

"Selene," I said. "I want to hurt my friends. I want to feel their blood spill over my face. The only reason I haven't attacked anyone is because the sorcerer's band is keeping my power in check and at the same time appears to be keeping whatever Ares did to me in check, too. I can't live this way."

She turned to me. "We'll get you help."

I shook my head. "Mordred has to kill me. *Has to*. Not just because of this, but because he kills me in the Fates' prophecy or I murder my friends. I see why now. I see why he has to do it."

"No," Mordred said. "The prophecy was fake. Hera forced it into the Fates' heads."

I laughed. "So, I'm just going to become a murderous asshole because of reasons other than destiny?"

"I'm not seeing the funny side. So, you're just going to die?" Tommy asked. "That's not much of a cure."

"I won't die," I said. "One of the blood elves at the compound said that Gawain didn't want me dead because Erebus would take control of me. You know this, don't you, Mordred?"

Mordred nodded. "I wasn't sure it was the same for you, but that's what happened to me. You killed me; my nightmare took control and healed me. All the curse marks vanished."

"Gawain is scared that if I die my nightmare will take control and fight back. Gawain and his allies are too powerful. I barely got a scratch on him. I need those marks gone—it's the only way I get stronger. It's the only way I can stop whatever Ares did to my head."

"This is not a good idea," Tommy said. "What if you're wrong?"

"I don't know, man. I just know this has to happen. I just know that if Mordred doesn't do it, then I'll have to live with a constant need to hurt people I care about. I can't defeat Gawain, I can't stay with you all, and I won't live a prisoner in my own mind."

"Maybe we can force Ares to help," Diana said.

"Ares is dead," Atlas said. "Nate killed him. I saw the remains of his body. You don't want that level of rage aimed at any of you. Gawain wanted to use him to become the new assassin of choice for Avalon. You can't let that happen."

"I killed Deimos, too," I told Selene.

"He was an asshole. I can't just let you die," Selene said, her frustration almost boiling over.

"I'm not planning on dying for good," I told her. "I die. My nightmare takes control before irreversible damage is done, and then I get better."

"You hope," Mordred said. "It's not exactly like we're doing a scientific study here."

"No time like the present," I said with a forced smile.

"You want to do this out here?" Tommy asked.

I nodded. "You'll need to get Hades here. If my nightmare attacks, you'll need as many as you can to stop me. No offense to you, but I know you'll try and take it easy on me, and I know Hades will put me down because it's the right thing to do."

"I won't let you die," Selene said, crouching in front of me. "I'd rather never see you again than that."

"Then let Mordred kill me. It's the only way to remove the junk in my head and unlock that last mark. Isn't that right, Erebus?"

Erebus appeared on the ground beside me. He nodded. "You figured it out."

I looked at each of my friends in turn. Time hadn't frozen, and they all stared at me as I spoke to the nightmare inside my head, but none tried to interrupt. "My death unlocks the last mark," I said.

"It was never meant to. It was meant to unlock naturally like the others. Hera's meddling caused you a lot of unnecessary heartache."

"Will this be the last I see of you?"

"I honestly don't know. I assume so, but I can't tell until that mark goes."

"Then if this is the end, it was a pleasure to know you."

Erebus stood and offered me his hand. "The pleasure was mine, I assure you."

I shook Erebus's hand, and he vanished.

"If this doesn't work," Tommy said. "If this goes wrong—"

"It won't," I assured him. "Hera screwed around with the runes when the blood-curse marks were added to me. They were meant to vanish naturally over the years, but it never happened. My death is a reset. I know that for a fact. It's why Gawain made sure not to kill me. He knew that if he couldn't kill the nightmare, too, then I'd return even stronger. Same with Mordred, and others like us. Erebus, my nightmare, believes I'm right."

"So, are we all meant to say something to you?" Diana asked. "Because I'd honestly, from the bottom of my heart, like to call you a fucking lunatic."

I laughed. "Can't argue with that."

She leaned down toward me. "You best not die, Nate. I don't want to come down to the afterlife and kick your ass to get you back here."

"Noted."

Selene kissed me on the lips, and I had to force down the hate and rage that burst into my mind. Rage and hate that Ares forced me to feel about the woman I loved. I regretted a lot of things in my life, but his death wouldn't be one of them.

"I love you, Nathaniel Garrett."

"I love you, too," I told her. "More than anything or anyone I've ever loved. Tommy included."

Selene sniggered and kissed me again. "You best come back to me in one piece." She stood and walked over to Diana, who was on her phone.

"Your turn, Tommy?" I asked.

"You know what I'm going to say," he said. "You know it, and you'll say what you say and I'll cry like a baby. Damn you, Nate. Don't you dare stay dead for long, you understand?"

"I'll try my best."

He turned and took a step away before pausing and turning back to me. "I love you."

I looked up at him. "I know."

Tears fell down his face, and he smiled. "See, this is some bullshit right here. Goddamn Han Soloing me."

It was Atlas, Mordred, and me left. I turned to Atlas. "Why are you doing this?" I asked.

"I don't like you," he said. "But I'm not going to join the insane ramblings of a psychopath, either. This isn't a them-or-you situation. This is a what-side-of-history-do-I-want-to-be-on situation. Besides, Hades told me that if I helped him, he'd make sure that you and I could fight. Fairly, no powers. Gawain just promised to let me kill you. I don't want you dead, Nate. I just want to beat you."

He removed a key from his pocket and knelt beside me. "When I remove this sorcerer's band, your power, and by extension whatever shit

Ares put in your head, will flood back." He looked at Mordred. "Pick up one of the rifles here."

Mordred removed a gun from a holster against his back. "I brought one with me."

"You knew this would happen?" I asked.

"I had a good idea it would come to this, yes. I'm sorry, Nate, but when I heard that Ares and Abaddon had you, I figured they'd try the same thing on you that they did on me. I didn't want you to try and murder your friends, and I thought that maybe killing you would work the same way it worked on me. I guess this is where we find out if we're right."

I nodded. "If this goes wrong, Mordred, I want you to know it's been an honor being your friend. I know he's your brother, but kill Gawain, and burn everything he controls to the ground."

Mordred took a deep breath and nodded. "In your name, my friend. But nothing is going to go wrong. I'll see you real soon. What about Arthur?"

"I don't know. Gawain was saying things I didn't understand. It sounds like they tried to do the same to him as to us."

"I'll look into it. We'll try to find him," he promised.

I turned to Atlas. "Take it off."

He removed the band, and my magic flared up, as did the hate and rage I felt for Mordred and my friends. I growled something incomprehensible and was about to spring toward Mordred, a blade of fire on one hand, when everything went quiet, and I blinked. An instant later there was an explosion of sound, followed by another. Darkness folded over me, enveloping me in its peaceful embrace. And then nothing.

CHAPTER 35

Mordred

Wisconsin, USA

Mordred fired three times, putting two rounds into Nate's chest and one into his head. The rounds were silver and designed to create the smallest wound possible while still exiting out the back of the body. Nate fell to the snowy ground, which quickly turned red.

"What now?" Atlas asked.

Mordred turned back to Selene, Tommy, and Diana, half expecting to see anger and hate on their faces, but Selene hugged him tightly. "Are you okay?" she whispered in his ear.

Mordred dropped the gun in shock and held on to Selene as the hurt of what he'd just done threatened to overwhelm him. He pushed it down. Nate was not dead. Not for good, but things needed to be done.

"We need to bury him," Mordred said. "My nightmare didn't come out for several hours after I died. I was in a morgue when it happened. And the power I unleashed almost destroyed it."

"Burying Nate feels a lot like finishing something," Diana said. "I didn't expect to have to bury a friend today."

"Before we do that, I need to do something," Atlas said, removing the phone from his pocket and taking several pictures of Nate's body.

"What are you doing?" Diana asked.

"You need to be quiet," he told the others before making a call. "Gawain, it's done. Nate's dead. The nightmare got loose, killed the blood elves. Fought like a damn demon, but he's dead. I've taken photos for you, and I'll bury the body."

Atlas was silent for a few seconds, listening to Gawain.

"Yeah, I'll be back soon," he said before hanging up. "Right, let's get him buried."

Atlas did most of the work to create a grave before pushing Nate into the four-foot pit. Selene, Tommy, Mordred, and Diana helped to cover Nate's body with soil, just finishing as the sound of a helicopter broke the silence of their work.

The modified Black Hawk landed in a nearby clearing, and Hades hurried out before the engine had finished powering down, while several bodyguards remained at the helicopter.

"Are you sure this will work?" he asked Mordred, who nodded.

"How long has it been?" Hades asked.

"A half hour," Selene said.

Two hours passed by without anyone saying another word while they stayed at their vigil watching the freshly dug grave.

"I need to head back," Atlas said to Hades. "I've dumped the blood-elf bodies in the back of the van. I'll dispose of them somewhere away from here. If I can, I'll keep you updated on what Gawain does. Don't expect regular chats, though."

"Thanks, Atlas," Hades said, shaking the larger man's hand. "We wouldn't be here without you."

"Make sure Nate gets healed up okay. I want my match."

"You'll get it when this is all over," Hades promised.

"He's a strange one," Diana said after Atlas had left.

"That's true," Tommy said. "But we don't have many friends inside Gawain's version of Avalon."

"He'll need to remove anyone who opposes him," Hades said. "There's going to be a lot of deaths in the coming months."

"A giant purge of Avalon staff," Selene said. "That's a lot of people to kill just because they won't follow orders."

"It's already started," Hades said. "In the last month, since Nate went missing, over three thousand Avalon employees have been murdered or gone missing. And more than double that for the number of people not part of the system but friendly toward Avalon. And that's not even counting what's happening in Camelot. Word has it, a lot of people were leaving the realm before Gawain started having them killed."

"This is going to get worse, isn't it?" Diana asked.

"He wants my help tracking down people he's labeled as enemies of state," Hades finished.

"Fucking hell," Mordred said. "We're going to be the bad guys."

"I bloody well am not," Selene said.

"We are," Diana argued. "Gawain has Merlin, and after what they did to Nate, presumably Arthur on their side. They'll make it so that everyone who listens to him thinks we're the bad guys. We're the revolutionary assholes hiding away and trying to stop him from destroying the world we live in. If they do manage to turn Arthur to their side, and Arthur takes charge of Avalon, we'll be considered enemies of the state."

The ground beneath them shook, and Mordred turned toward the grave as it exploded. He raised a shield of air to stop anyone being hit by the snow, dirt, and rock that scattered all around.

"This won't be fun," Mordred said.

The group watched as Nate clawed his way out of the ground, although he no longer had the appearance of the Nate they all knew. His body was covered in thick, black, leathery skin. The nightmare ripped the tattered remains of his clothes free from his body and stared at each person in turn.

"Nate?" Selene called out. "Are you still in there?"

A low growl was the only response.

"Erebus!" Mordred shouted, and the nightmare looked his way. "You remember that name, don't you?"

The nightmare nodded slightly and took a step forward just as one of Hades's guards opened fire on him. Erebus stopped the bullets with a shield of shadow before blasting magical air toward the guard, throwing him back across the field. Erebus roared and charged the guard, swatting aside a second guard, who tried to physically stop him.

He reached the guard just as Diana, now in full werebeast form, grabbed hold of Erebus and threw him aside, putting distance between the nightmare and the guard.

"Get him out of here," Hades snapped to a third guard, who dragged the first away toward the helicopter. He turned toward the nightmare. "Don't make me have to stop you, Erebus."

Erebus snarled and charged Hades in an attempt to get at the injured guard. Hades extended his hand, and necromancy flew from it, slamming into the nightmare, who continued to try and get to the guard despite the incredible force pushing him back.

Mordred added his own air magic to what Hades was doing, and eventually the nightmare was flung back toward his grave.

"How did you stop your nightmare?" Selene asked Mordred.

"I didn't. But then I wasn't fired upon in the first ten seconds after waking."

"That's going to make things awkward," Tommy said. He'd changed into his werebeast form, too, and he and Diana moved toward Erebus from opposite sides.

The nightmare looked between Diana and Tommy over and over again until they were only a dozen feet from him, and he unleashed his matter magic, slamming his hands down into the ground and causing it to explode all around him, throwing up more dirt and allowing him to sink into the shadows he'd created.

"That's not good," Tommy said, spitting out muck.

"I didn't know he could do that," Hades said. "He doesn't have earth magic."

"Matter magic," Mordred said, scanning his surroundings.

"He destroyed those rock statues in Shadow Falls with a punch," Selene said. "Said something about seeing weaknesses in nonliving things. He's incredibly strong and fast, too."

"Great," Hades said.

"A nightmare can use a sorcerer's magic to the best of its ability. Or pretty close," Mordred said. "If Erebus is this powerful and he's only just woken up, we need to stop him. Now. On the plus side, we don't need to worry about him trying to escape."

"Why?" Diana asked.

"Nightmares see a threat, they destroy a threat," Hades said.

"So, Nate won't leave until we're dead?" Tommy asked. "Not exactly reassuring."

Mordred noticed the shadows moving beneath their feet. "Move!" he shouted, and threw himself aside, colliding with Diana as Erebus burst forth from the shadows where he'd been, slamming a fist of magical air into the ground and causing it to tear apart.

Selene darted toward Erebus, taking the nightmare off his feet and dumping him on the ground, trying to hold him in place. "Calm down!" she shouted.

Lightning streaked down from the sky above, forcing Selene to throw herself aside lest it hit her. Instead, the lightning struck Erebus, who raised a hand in Selene's direction. Selene changed into her dragon-kin form and created a shield of ice the lightning smashed into, obliterating it. She opened her mouth once more, and ice poured from it, crashing into Erebus and encasing him where he crouched, leaving only his head uncovered.

Tommy rushed forward and punched Erebus in the jaw with a blow that would have taken the head off anything human. Erebus's head snapped aside, and he growled as the ice began to crack. Mordred poured more and more magical ice toward Erebus, helping to keep him still, but the fire magic pouring out of the nightmare's hands was melting it as quickly as he and Selene could add new ice.

"Tenacious little fucker, isn't he," Diana said.

"You've met Nate before, yes?" Tommy asked.

The ice exploded, causing both Selene and Mordred to fall back. The nightmare stood still as a large sphere of air began to spin in the palm of each hand.

"Enough of this," Hades said, and a blue-and-green glow lit up across the field, leaving only the part around Erebus's feet empty. The nightmare turned toward Hades, staring with cold eyes as the glow around him intensified.

Erebus took one step, and the glow vanished as dozens of spirits lifted out of the ground to grab hold of Erebus, who swiped at them with a whip of fire to no effect.

"He can't use his necromancy!" Mordred shouted. "This is a magic-only situation."

Hades said nothing as more and more spirits took hold of the nightmare, dragging him to his knees and pinning him there.

"I wish there was another way," Hades said, creating one of his soul weapons—a bident. It almost had the appearance of a pitchfork, but there was no mistaking that the blades instead of prongs were very much meant for war. "You need to calm down."

Erebus roared in defiance, and Hades punched the soul weapon into the nightmare's chest. Erebus screamed in pain and, as soon as Hades withdrew the weapon, collapsed to the ground.

Selene was there in an instant. "Will he be okay?"

"Yes," Hades said. "I didn't use enough power to kill. And nightmares are quite capable of healing almost any wound."

Hades walked off to the helicopter and could be heard shouting at the guard who'd nearly gotten people killed, before he returned with a pair of shackles. "Zamek rune-scribed these," he said, passing them to Selene, who put them on the nightmare's wrists.

"What will they do?" Tommy asked.

"Stop him from killing everyone," Hades said matter-of-factly. "We'll deal with the rest of his treatment when we get him to a secure facility."

"I assume we'll all be staying in Greenland," Diana said with a slight sigh.

Since Nate had gone missing and Gawain's goons had started to eliminate people who would oppose his new world order, Hades had moved most of those he knew to be loyal to a secret complex in Greenland.

"You like the weather," Mordred said. "You've mentioned it several times."

Hades glanced at Mordred, who winked, causing Hades to smile.

The trip back was one of anxious anticipation. While everyone fit in the Black Hawk, no one wanted to be there when the nightmare woke from its forced slumber. Fortunately, apart from everyone being nervous, the flight was relatively uneventful, and they eventually landed on a helipad on the northwest coast of Greenland.

Hades and the medical staff at the facility unloaded Nate and took him away before anyone could say anything more to him, while the others went through the large, open hangar bay doors that signified the entrance to the complex. Most of the complex was underground, which Mordred thought was a running theme with nonhumans.

"It's been a long few weeks," Sky said, causing Mordred to turn around and hug her.

Mordred watched as Nate was wheeled onto a lift large enough to fit a tank.

"They'll take good care of him," Sky assured Mordred. "My dad isn't exactly the type of person to let something go."

"How's your mum?"

"Down there waiting for her patient."

"It took us a long time to find him. You think he'll be okay?"

"Yes, it's Nate. I can't imagine him being anything else." She passed a manila envelope to Mordred. "This is the information you asked for. I hope it helps."

Mordred didn't bother opening it. "It will. Or it'll get me killed."

"Nice extremes there."

"Yeah, I'm all about the living-dangerously kind of life."

Sky chuckled. "Be careful, okay?"

An alarm went off, and Mordred and Sky ran toward the main command center, which was situated on the top floor of the aboveground portion of the facility. The pair took the stairs two at a time and almost burst through the stairwell door before spotting several guards go for their holstered weapons in the hallway beyond.

"Whoa, guys, we're on your side," Sky said, raising her hands.

Everyone relaxed and allowed Sky and Mordred to head into the situation room.

The room had several banks of computers, and more than two dozen employees working there on a round-the-clock basis. The alarm stopped, and Hades, who stood at the front of the room beside the viewing window, turned toward them.

Irkalla, Remy, Nabu, and Elaine were all in the room, too, and Mordred was glad to see he and Sky hadn't been the only ones worried by the noise.

"What the hell happened?" Sky asked.

"Nate's magic is . . . unpredictable," Hades said.

"Meaning what?" Mordred asked.

"His lightning is striking the facility," Elaine told them.

"A lot," Remy finished. "We're essentially the epicenter of a storm. Which is a lot less pleasant than it sounds."

"It doesn't sound that great," Mordred said.

"Yeah, kind of making my point for me there."

Mordred nodded that he got what Remy was saying, although he wasn't entirely sure he did. "So, we're all stuck here until it stops?"

"You have somewhere you want to be?" Irkalla asked.

"Yes."

"I would advise against leaving the compound," Hades said. "But considering you're going to do whatever you like, I can tell you the best way out of this country would be to take one of the four-by-fours to the nearby airport and fly from there. The storm is localized directly above us."

"Just how powerful will a fully healed Nate be?" Elaine asked.

"I have no idea," Mordred said. "When I woke up from my time as a nightmare, I'd frozen the building I was in. Made it look like a palace."

"I swear if you sing one word of that fucking song, Remy, I will kill you," Sky said, forcing Remy to mime locking his mouth.

"I'm coming with you," Irkalla told Mordred.

"You don't even know where I'm going," Mordred said.

"Hades, how's Nate doing?" Irkalla asked him.

"He's stable, unconscious, and still trying to kill us all. There's no idea how long he'll be out for."

"After the initial waking up, I spent months as a nightmare," Mordred said. "We've got a long way to go yet."

"Then I'm coming with you," Irkalla said. "Wherever you go, there will be people to punch in the face. I quite like that idea at the moment."

One of the workers in the situation room walked over to Hades and whispered something to him.

"Thank you," Hades said. "I think we need to see this." He switched on a large TV screen at the far end of the room and flicked to a news channel that showed the start of a news conference of some kind.

"That's the president of the United States," Nabu said, almost absentmindedly. "Along with several other leading figures from a variety of countries—the UK, France, Germany, China, Nigeria, South Africa, Japan, and Russia. There are dozens of people there. I had no idea there was a summit going on."

Hades turned up the volume.

"These last weeks have seen some of the worst attacks on our freedom that our people have ever had to endure," the president said. "Innocents have died the world over, and we have had to change the way we work to ensure that we can protect people from further atrocities. We can now tell the people of this world that our countries have come together to stop this menace. And in doing so the United Nations has created a new worldwide organization that will help to combat these forces of evil. Forces we don't quite yet understand, but it's my hope that with thanks to this new organization's leadership we will destroy these forces. I'm proud to introduce you to the leader of this group, Arthur Pendragon."

Everyone in the situation room stared in horror as Arthur walked up to the podium and shook the president's hand before he was left alone in front of the microphone. Gawain and Abaddon stood behind him, both looking very pleased with themselves.

"Good morning to the press of the world," Arthur began. "I am over seventeen hundred years old, and I am a sorcerer. We have existed in the shadows for thousands of years. We have tried to keep ourselves to ourselves, without interfering with human lives. This changed not long ago when a man by the name of Hellequin destroyed the peace that had existed between us. And in doing so murdered hundreds of thousands of innocent people the world over in his quest for power.

"This man, this traitor to the lives we all swore to lead, has been found and killed. It was not what I wanted. I searched for a peaceful resolution to this problem, I had hoped to end this violence without further bloodshed, but he and his people would not be swayed with reason or peace."

Arthur looked appropriately sad, and Mordred felt nauseous.

"While I would like to say that these attacks are over and humanity can rest easy, this is not the case," Arthur continued. "Hellequin's followers are out there. And will need to be captured before they can strike at the heart of the freedoms that most of us take for granted. I have accepted the United Nations' gracious offer of cooperation, and I will use the new powers my people and I have been given to hunt down these monsters before they can do more harm. This organization is called Avalon. It will be the barrier between humanity and the evil that lurks in the darkness. It will protect you, and it will keep you safe.

"My kind and I have remained hidden for thousands of years. Some of you will have heard stories, or myths, about us, but these are half-truths and fairy tales. You will find the real people to be much less fantastical, and I hope in the coming weeks and months to be able to place these people around the globe in new Avalon branches to help combat this terror. You need not be afraid of these operatives. Despite their power, or appearance, they will be there for your safety. Humanity and my kind have existed for thousands of years in harmony. It's my hope that the bond between us will strengthen now that you know the truth."

Hades switched off the TV.

"Well, fuck," Sky said.

"Did he just declare war on everyone who isn't on his side?" Remy said. "It sounded like he did."

"And he outed us to the world," Nabu said. "I've spent thousands of years living, quite happily, without everyone knowing that I'm not human. This is a big change."

"This is a terrifying change," Hades said. "All of those heads of state are in Arthur's pocket. Or at least in Avalon's. I imagine a few of them will be considered unhelpful, or unpatriotic, in the coming weeks and months. More than a few will vanish."

"This was his plan all along," Diana said. "Get the humans to welcome him, to think he's their savior against a greater evil, and then slowly take over everything."

"It won't be slow," Irkalla said. "I saw the look in his eyes. Whatever remained of the Arthur we knew is gone. It looks like Gawain got his wish. Arthur wants that power as quickly as possible. In a decade there won't be a country on the planet that isn't under Avalon rule. And he'll start with the big guns."

"The gift of peace with one hand and tightening the noose with the other," Sky said. "As if I needed more reasons to hate the son of a bitch."

"I'm going with you, Mordred," Remy said. "I can't do jack and or shit here. And I don't think pissing off Sky as a hobby gives me a lengthy lifespan."

"Good guess," Sky said, although she smiled after saying it.

"Be ready in an hour," Mordred said. "We'll be a week or so." He turned to Hades. "Keep Nate safe—we'll need him more than ever now."

"It'll take a few months for Arthur and his people to get their claws firmly into everything. Until then he's going to be busy removing people who won't like where this is going. I wouldn't bank on it, but you probably have time to go do whatever you need to. Arthur thinks Nate is dead. Hopefully it'll stay that way for some time."

"Mordred, wait up," Sky said, catching up to him as he left the room. "You sure about this? What's in the envelope could get you killed; you weren't wrong about that."

Mordred opened the envelope and pulled out the photos and directions to where Viktor was being held. After he'd burned down his home for betraying so many people to the werewolf pack in Moscow, Mordred had hoped never to see the piece of crap again. "Might do. But it might also make things easier for us in the long run. I'd rather Arthur, Gawain, or whoever is in charge had as few advantages as possible. Besides, after what I just saw, I feel like pissing them all off a bit."

"Is there any point in telling you to be careful?"

Mordred shook his head. "It's not like I haven't been trying so far in life."

"Then you suck at it."

"Not arguing." Mordred paused. "In my room, second drawer on the bedside cabinet, is a USB drive. It needs decrypting, but it's Elaine's, so maybe she can help get it done. I've had a month, and it just didn't feel important considering we learned the prophecy was a lie and Elaine came back to us. But Elaine still doesn't have her memories, and we've all been so busy finding Nate that I just forgot about it. Can you decrypt it?"

Sky nodded. "We can try."

Mordred went back down to the main hangar, avoiding the dozens of people milling around, and entered one of the rooms at the far end, where a quartermaster asked him what he wanted.

Mordred handed over a list.

"You planning on fighting a war?" she asked. "Because I think Arthur just declared it."

"Just going to blow up my bit of it."

She collected the silenced Glock pistol, silenced MP5, and Accuracy International sniper rifle that were on the list, along with a stab vest, and several blocks of explosives. "This isn't like human explosives. This stuff will fuck your day up if you're anywhere near it," she said, placing it all in a satchel.

Mordred took the bag from her, putting on holsters for the pistol MP5 and picking up the bag she'd just put the sniper rifle in. "I don't plan on being near it. At all."

"These are all Avalon editions of those weapons. Silver tipped, a few modifications here and there—these aren't exactly available on websites."

"I'll bring them back. I promise."

"You'd better."

Mordred turned to find Morgan watching him. "Where are you going?"

"Bear hunting," Mordred said.

She eyed the weaponry.

"It's a bloody big bear," Mordred said, miming how big with his hands.

"Does it live in a tank?"

"It might. Bears are smart."

She crossed her arms. "What are you doing, Mordred?"

"What I can. You stay here. Please."

"Why?"

"It's dangerous, and I need to do this without worrying about you."

"And Irkalla and Remy are going because?"

"I don't mind if they get used as collateral damage."

"You're not funny."

"Fine, I don't want you to come because your head is thinking about Nate, not about what I'm going to do."

"Tommy, Olivia, Kasey, and Selene are all taking turns at holding a vigil over him. I don't think I'm wanted."

"Go find out. Morgan, you loved him once, and they will understand that. But the last few weeks, I've seen you get more and more exhausted as you push yourself. Eat, sleep, go talk to coma Nate. He can't talk back. Trust me, it's brilliant."

Morgan smiled and kissed Mordred on the cheek. "Don't die out there."

"Why do people keep telling me to be careful? It's not like I have . . ." He paused. "Yeah, I can't even finish that sentence. I'll be fine. I'll be back as soon as I can."

He walked off and met Irkalla and Remy at the front of the hangar. "You feel like telling me your plan?" she asked.

"I thought you liked being surprised," Mordred said.

"I also like knowing how crazed you are."

"We're going to kill someone," he told her.

"We figured that out," Remy said. "Who is it?"

Mordred pulled his hood up. "That envelope contains information about Viktor and Daria. Both escaped from LOA custody after Polina's team were attacked by people saying they were to take charge of the investigation. Polina and two others escaped with their lives. Sky and Olivia pulled a few favors, and I discovered that Viktor and Daria are both in a hotel in New York. Both have been a great asset to Merlin and his people, and I plan on ending that help."

CHAPTER 36

Mordred

New York City, USA

They arrived in New York, and after a day of planning and checking the target's location, Mordred, Irkalla, and Remy had finally put together a way into the twenty-story hotel that allowed them to get out again without having to jump out of a two-hundred-foot-high window.

Mordred drove the black Mercedes AMG C63 to the Stewart Hotel in Manhattan and parked in one of the few available spaces in the underground parking garage. They had a valet service, but when time is of the essence, waiting for someone to bring your car back does not make for a quick escape route.

"Are you sure you want to go in there alone?" Remy asked through the earpiece that Mordred wore.

"Yes," Mordred said as he walked through the parking lot to the lift that would take him up into the hotel lobby above. "You're the best shot, so you get to play with the rifle and cover my ass."

"And Irkalla gets to be my spotter," Remy added with some enthusiasm.

"I am not your spotter," Irkalla said tersely.

"You have binoculars—therefore you are my spotter."

"I can see why Diana is always threatening to kill you."

"Sky, too," Remy said cheerfully.

"Yes, he's a regular ladies' fox," Mordred said as the lift doors opened and he stepped inside.

"You still hear me okay?" Irkalla asked while the lift began its ascent.

"Loud and clear," Mordred confirmed. "I'll let you know when I'm heading up to the penthouse."

The doors to the lift opened, and Mordred stepped out into a bright, albeit busy, lobby. His magic switched off as he knew it would. According to Mordred's research, Avalon employees picked the hotel because it didn't allow powers during visits. The runes were built directly into the very fabric of the building.

Mordred smiled at a guard in front of a set of lift doors and walked around to the reception area of the lobby. He leaned up against a wall and pretended to look at his phone while he checked out the few dozen people milling around. Most of the crowd were dressed in suits, huddled over one of the many tables, looking at laptops, or drinking coffee and chatting to colleagues. A large sign said there was a business conference in the hotel and anyone involved should go to the lobby and check in. Mordred had put on an expensive suit for that purpose. He'd also only been able to take the silenced pistol, as the MP5 was too big to hide under a jacket, so he'd subbed it for a belt of throwing knives that sat against the small of his back. Eight knives, each one with a silver finish. If he needed more than that, he was probably already dead.

There were a few people at check-in, but he discounted them as a threat since they were clearly tourists with children. So that left four people in the lobby and check-in area who presumably worked for Avalon. The good thing about having been on the outs with Avalon for so long was that most people didn't know what Mordred looked like now. He assumed that people would be on the lookout for someone with shoulder-length dark hair, so he'd buzzed his head as close as possible without being bald, and he'd already been in the process of growing several weeks of beard, so he just left it alone. He knew it didn't exactly make him the friendliest looking person, but he also didn't care.

Mordred walked over to the reception and smiled at the woman behind the desk. "Hi, I'm here for the conference," he told her.

"Ah," she said. "The main talk has already started."

"Is it okay if I just check in and wait for the talk to finish? The person giving it gets funny about being interrupted, so I'd rather not get shouted at. Also, it gives me time to freshen up."

The receptionist smiled. "That's fine. And your name, sir?"

"Matthew Drew. I believe I asked for the Azure Suite."

She tapped a few things on the computer. "That's right, Mr. Drew. We have you here. You get to use the private elevator at the end of the hallway over there. Please be aware that we have several dignitaries staying in the penthouse, so there will be a guard traveling up and down with you in the elevator."

"How exciting," Mordred said as he passed the receptionist a credit card. "Anyone famous?"

"I'm not at liberty to say," the receptionist told him. "Sorry."

"That's okay. At least I know I'll be secure with all these guards about. Best not let Jerry get drunk at the conference, just in case he gets seen as some sort of security threat. Actually that would be funny."

"I don't advise you do that, sir."

"I'm joking. I won't really let Jerry get tazed, no matter how entertaining it would be."

The receptionist passed Mordred the keycard to his room. "Enjoy your say."

"Thanks."

Mordred went to the lift door and showed his keycard to the guard there. "I'm in the Azure. I assume you'll be going up with me?"

"Yes, sir."

"Can't have me pressing the wrong button and ending up in the penthouse."

The lift came, and both men got in. "So, who's here?" Mordred asked after showing his card to the reader on the control panel and watching as the word "Azure" flashed up above it. "See, you didn't need to come with me. This only lets me go to one place."

"It's my job, I'm afraid."

"Yeah, Gawain's a real ballbuster."

The guard took a second longer than he should have to register what Mordred said. Plenty of time for Mordred to turn and smash his elbow into the man's throat. He removed the gun from the guard and placed his knee against his throat. "No bracelet. So, what is it, you human, or they don't trust their employees not to go all crazed?"

"We use guns, not magic. No powers allowed on site—that's the rule. We can't be seen to scare the humans."

"That comes later, right?"

The doors opened, showing a hallway with only one door, and Mordred placed the gun against the man's temple. "Out. Now."

The pair of them walked out of the lift, the guard first. When they got to the door, Mordred made the man kneel and link his fingers behind his head while Mordred opened the entrance to his suite.

"In," Mordred said, helping the man to his feet and pushing him inside. "Don't fuck about. You might live."

"Who are you?" the man asked.

Mordred shot him in the head with the silenced pistol. Unlike most human silenced guns, it made no noise at all. "What a waste of ammo."

Mordred removed the keycard from the dead guard's pocket, which identified the man as William Talbot. He went back to the lift, using William's card pass to activate it. He stepped inside and placed the card against the reader, where a star flashed on the screen above. "Classy," Mordred said as the lift began to ascend.

Mordred stood to the side of the lift as the doors opened, showing a hallway identical to the one below. He stepped out and shot the two guards in the head, moving on past them toward the door.

"You ready?" he whispered.

"When you are," Irkalla said. "You've got a two-story penthouse. My necromancy says there are nine souls in there. Four upstairs, five down. Two are directly on the other side of the door, three further in. You got this?"

Mordred placed the card against the reader outside the door. "Oh yes." He opened the door and shot the first guard in the temple before he even stepped inside. He had to move around the open door to get the second, who required two shots in the chest before a third took him in the center of his forehead. He holstered his gun and drew two knives—he wanted to save as much ammo as possible.

He looked around and found himself in a long hallway with stairs to one side leading to the floor above, and a large arch in front of him. "Guard coming your way," Irkalla said.

Mordred ran to the side of the archway, out of sight of the guard, who clearly spotted his dead friends. He called out to one of them, stepped into the arch, and never breathed again, as Mordred buried one of the knives in his heart and slit his throat with the other. He pushed the guard aside, removing the blade, and threw it at a fourth guard, catching him in the head.

Mordred cursed himself as he spotted the problem of a paladin walking up the stairs to the floor above. "Shit, we have an issue here."

"What's wrong?" Remy asked.

"There's a paladin here."

"That's not great," Remy said. "Did you know?"

"It was always a possibility. He's why you're here with me," Mordred whispered. "Can you see him from above?"

"No, the windows on the top floor are covered with something."

"Guard right on the other side of the wall," Irkalla said.

Mordred stepped into the main area of the suite, grabbing the guard's arm, and forcing the gun up toward his head. Mordred pulled the trigger, shooting the guard in the throat. The noise was deafening, and as his secrecy was well and truly up, he shot the guard with his own gun twice more in the head.

Mordred dropped the gun, ran off to a kitchen area, and huddled behind the counter.

"There's a mass coming toward you," Irkalla said.

"Can you see me down here?" Mordred asked Remy.

"Yep. You want me to shoot you?"

"Does that honestly need an answer?" Mordred almost shouted.

"Just checking."

"Mordred, is that you?" the paladin asked from just outside the archway. "It can't be Nate, he's dead, but I figure you or one of your idiot friends would try something stupid. Didn't think you'd try to hit us here."

"I like to be unpredictable," Mordred said. "Shouldn't you be with my father? Or Arthur, or Gawain? I forget whose ass you're currently kissing."

A bullet smashed into the top of the kitchen counter, spraying pieces of marble all over the floor. "Your father was turned to us a long time ago. I helped."

"You're a traitorous piece of shit."

"A realist. Unlike you and Nate, I know what Avalon should be. I believe in the vision of an Avalon where the powerful rule and everyone else bows before us."

"Well, you're already a massive dick, so you're halfway there."

"You remember when you told Merlin about being experimented on? Do you remember when it drove you over the edge?"

"Well, I guess I know why he didn't listen."

"I remember Gawain telling me about it. My word, how we laughed."

A second round hit the kitchen counter just above Mordred's head. "I'll get you eventually," the paladin said. "I prefer swords, but a gun is just as good in a pinch. Actually I'd prefer my magic, but I can't have everything."

"Take the shot when you get it," Mordred said.

"Oh, I will," the paladin told him.

Mordred stood up and made sure to put part of a wall between him and the paladin, forcing the larger man to come into the room to get a shot.

"You're going to die here," the paladin said. "I might send your head back to Morgan as a gift."

"You first," Mordred said.

The first the paladin knew of the shot was when his chest exploded and he was thrown back onto the floor.

"He dead?" Remy asked.

Mordred glanced at the hole in the extra-thick glass window, and then down at the paladin. His white shirt was quickly turning dark red. Mordred walked over to the severely injured man. "I want you to tell my brother that I'm coming for him. I want you to tell him that I'm going to end everyone who stands beside him and Abaddon. If my father and Arthur are truly gone, they'll have to die, too."

Mordred took a step and turned back to the paladin. "Fuck it, they'll figure it out." He shot the paladin three times in the head.

Mordred loaded a new magazine and walked toward the staircase, keeping his gun up as he ascended. He reached the top, which consisted of a large open-plan room with two doors at the far end. He turned into the room and found it empty but noticed two more doors at the other end, where he thought the bedrooms were.

"You happen to see anyone here?" he asked Irkalla.

"Two to your left, one to your right. Who's the third target?"

"Who says there's a third target?" Mordred asked. "Okay, yeah, there is, but we'll get there in a minute." He took a step to the right and grabbed hold of the door handle just as it was pulled in, forcing Mordred to stagger forward into a punch to his jaw.

Mordred rolled to the floor, coming back to his feet in the open area of the floor as Daria appeared. But he noticed he'd dropped his gun under the nearby cupboard.

"No powers this time," Mordred said.

"Means I can take my time," Daria said with a slight snarl. She dove toward Mordred, who smashed his elbow into her face, breaking her nose and knocking her over a nearby chair.

She got back to her feet, and kicked Mordred in the knee, and he dropped to the ground, rolling away to put distance between the two of them. He got back to his feet slowly, watching Daria as she removed a long, curved dagger from behind the nearby chair. She unsheathed it and wiped her bleeding nose with the back of her hand, smearing blood over her face.

"You're not exactly right in the head, are you?" Mordred said. "And that's coming from someone who knows that look."

Daria screamed in rage and charged Mordred, who threw two of his knives at her, each one taking her in the chest, but she kept going, as if they'd done nothing. He drew another blade, parrying her strike, but she kicked him in the stomach and he fell back against the wall, unable to stop the cut that went across his stomach.

Daria darted back, and Mordred reached down, relieved to feel the attack hadn't gone through the lightweight stab vest he'd taken from Hades's quartermaster. Daria's expression darkened, and she moved toward Mordred once again, swiping with the dagger, forcing Mordred to move along the wall as he waited for an opening.

After the fifth swipe from Daria's blade, she overstepped her reach just a little, giving Mordred the moment to move to Daria's side and slam a throwing blade up into her armpit. He cut down toward her ribs before twisting the blade free, then punched a second blade up into her throat.

She swiped at him with her dagger, but it was feeble, and Mordred easily disarmed her, stabbing her in the heart with her own blade and leaving her to die on the expensive carpeted floor. He noticed the six-inch cut along his forearm for the first time and cursed himself for not being quick enough to dodge her.

"You okay?" Remy asked.

"No," Mordred said, retrieving his gun from under the wardrobe. He walked to the other side of the room and pushed open one of the doors, revealing an empty bathroom. He kicked the second door with everything he had, causing whoever was behind it to yell out in pain.

Mordred stepped into the room and kicked Viktor in the face as he lay on the floor. He looked over at Mara, who sat next to the window, staring at him with a mixture of hate and fear.

"Please don't kill me," Viktor said. "I did not know they'd come for me. I just wanted to be left alone."

"I read Polina's report. You stabbed one of her agents in the throat as you escaped. The man was forty-two years old; he had a wife and children. A wife and children you told Polina you'd kill the first chance you got."

"Not true."

"Don't care." Mordred shot him four times in the face before aiming the gun at Mara.

"You won't kill me," Mara said.

"Really? Because I'm almost certain I want to."

"Can you explain that to my daughter? You like her. You know she'd hate you if I was murdered at your hand."

"Only because I'm sure she'd like you to rot in a deep pit for the rest of your life."

Mara smiled. "You're an empty man, fighting on the wrong side of a war you can't win. You'll be running around hiding in the shadows while I stay in places like this and make bracelets for Arthur and his people to rule this realm, and then all of the others." She raised her hands. "Shoot me. I'm unarmed."

"Oh, shut up." Mordred shot her in the palm of one outstretched hand. "How quickly do witches heal?"

"You fucking bastard," Mara seethed. "I'm going to have someone cut out your fucking eyes. I'm going to heal and make bracelets just so his people can pillage those you love."

Mordred grabbed her good hand, placed it on the table next to her, and shot her three times. "Make something now, you evil piece of shit."

Mara collapsed to the floor, holding her heavily bleeding hands against her chest. "They'll kill me if I'm useless."

"Best learn to make them with your feet, then, because Gawain and his people aren't getting any more bracelets until someone else can be trained. And then I'll do the same to them, too. You're the only one they have who can make these—you said so yourself in Siberia. Now he has no one."

"This won't stop him forever!" Mara screamed as Mordred walked toward the exit.

"No, but it'll stop him until I can kill him." Mordred paused. "Damn it, you're right. I don't want to be the person who takes your life. I like your daughter, and she doesn't deserve to have a friend of hers kill you when she should have that privilege. But you're too dangerous." Mordred shot her in the head and left the room.

He made his way back downstairs and to the lift, hitting the button for the lobby. He reached the ground floor and walked across the lobby, just avoiding several armed men as they ran toward the now-empty lift.

"You've got quite a few people coming your way," Irkalla said as Mordred entered the lift to the parking garage and selected the right floor.

"I'm done here. I'll see you all back at the heliport in a few hours. I'll make sure I'm not followed. Thanks for your help."

"Our pleasure," Irkalla said. "See you soon."

Mordred removed his earpiece and exited the lift, walking through the garage to his Mercedes.

"Hello, Mordred," a woman said as she got out of a nearby red BMW M4. She was just over five feet tall, Asian, with long hair that had been dyed a multitude of colors.

"Hi," Mordred said. "And you are?"

"You can call me Ami," she said with a smile. "I believe you know my friend." She motioned toward another woman, who got out of the driver's seat of the M4.

"Cass?" Mordred asked, his happiness at seeing her again fighting against any potential threats.

"We need to talk," Cass said.

"About what?" Mordred asked.

"About fighting Arthur," Ami started, "about stopping a civil war between the Norse pantheon, and about trying to save everyone you love."

"I don't even know who you are," Mordred told them. "Cass isn't an ex-soldier."

"And Cass isn't my real name, but I needed a reason to talk to you. To find out if you were still the monster I'd heard about, or if you genuinely had changed."

"So, what's your real name?" Mordred asked.

"Not important," Cass said.

"Then goodbye," Mordred replied, unlocking the AMG.

"Amaterasu," Ami said.

Mordred blinked in surprise. "Okay, I didn't expect that."

"We need to band together if we have any hope of stopping Arthur," Amaterasu said. "We need to see Hades, and his people."

"I can arrange a meeting, but Cass needs to tell me who she is, too."

Amaterasu looked over the car roof at Cass, who continued to stare at Mordred for several seconds.

"Better hurry, exceptionally bad people are going to arrive here soon. I sort of made a mess."

"Hel," Cass said. "I'm Loki's daughter. Odin and Frigg's grand-daughter." Her appearance changed slightly, and her skin tone took on a bluish tinge.

"I know who Hel is," Mordred said. "What I don't know is why you're coming to me."

"Because we need Hades, Diana, Selene, Irkalla, and all of the others who oppose Arthur. Because we need to get into the Norse realms and defeat those opposed to Odin's rule. And we need to do it before we are overrun."

"Why me?" Mordred asked again.

"The blood elves have found a way into Asgard, and they're going after Yggdrasil. If they capture it, we will fall. And then Arthur and his minions will rule over the Norse realms."

"You need to speak to everyone else, too," Mordred said.

"That was our request," Hel said, clearly trying to keep her patience.

"And what of the other weapons like yourself?" Amaterasu asked.

"I only know of Nate," Mordred said.

"So, what of Nate?" Hel asked.

"Yeah, that's where we're going to have a problem. Nate's undergone his nightmare transformation."

"So we have one weapon, four missing, one dead, and one in a coma?" Amaterasu asked. "This is not the best news." She looked over at Hel as the sounds of shouting came from the lift area.

"Shit," Hel snapped. "You talk too much, Mordred. We've wasted time. Where is the base? Where can we find you?"

"Greenland," Mordred said as both women jumped in their car, and sped off.

Mordred got in his car and hunkered down as another car sped past him out of the garage, presumably going after Hel and Amaterasu. He waited for a few seconds to ensure there was no one else, then drove out of the garage as quickly as possible. The car that he'd seen only a few seconds ago had been hit by a bus. He had no idea whether it had been an accident or not, but it was a hell of a coincidence.

He drove away from the wreck with several thoughts on his mind. Of all the things he might have expected today, Hel and Amaterasu's appearance wasn't one, and had given him more questions than answers. And he didn't need even more things to add to the already-large pile of worry.

He wondered how long they had before Yggdrasil was breached. He realized that if the blood elves had left the dwarven world to go into the Norse realms, then that meant Baldr could be there, too. Mordred smiled. That was something to look forward to.

CHAPTER 37

Nate Garrett

Greenland

I opened my eyes and immediately wished I hadn't. The light caused them pain and forced me to close them again. I went to rub my hand over my face and found myself chained to the bed with thick manacles. There didn't appear to be any runes etched on them, so I tried to use my magic and . . . nothing. No hint of magic.

"Great, another place with runes in the walls," I said. My throat hurt, and I needed a drink. "If anyone is there, I'm awake."

The doors opened, and Hades walked in. He had several weeks' worth of beard growth and looked tired. "Nate, you're finally awake." He unlocked the manacles and placed a hand on my shoulder.

"Where am I?" I asked.

"My secret facility in Greenland. You've been in a coma for four months."

I couldn't quite process that as an answer. "What? Four months? But, I was . . . Mordred . . . He shot me. Is he okay?"

"We'll bring you up to speed with everyone in a minute. I just need to make sure you're okay. Can you sit up?"

I did as he asked.

"We're going to run some medical tests," he told me.

"Hades, I'm fine. I ache, and want a drink, but otherwise I'm good. My nightmare, Erebus, he saved me."

Hades nodded. "Let me go get you a drink, and we'll talk. Stay here."

"Hello, Nate," Erebus said from beside me.

"I thought you were going to vanish after I died."

"Apparently not. The mark on your head unlocked a lot of things, but they're all a jumble at the moment. It'll take some time to sift through it."

"Including who my father was?"

"That's in there, but it's not information I have. Your mind needs time to heal, as does your body. It's been under incredible stress. Your lack of magic will not help things along."

"My magic is gone full stop, isn't it? I remember Mordred saying something about it."

"Yes, for the next year, or thereabouts, you will have no magic. You are essentially just human."

"Anything else?"

Erebus shook his head. "Hopefully when the year is up, you will regain your power. But when you do, it would be wise to be somewhere barren."

"Why?"

I looked up as Mordred entered the room. "He'll explain," Erebus said, and vanished.

"Glad you're up and about," Mordred told me.

"I feel like I've been hit by a truck," I said.

"Yeah, it's not a fun experience. You've lost your magic, then."

"I figured that bit out. Erebus said it'll be a year before I can access it again. He also said any info unlocked by the mark will take a while to work through."

"It was the same for me. Took about fifteen months to fully understand everything in my head."

"Did you have messages from your parents in your head, too?" I asked.

Mordred shook his head. "No, I had no need. I know who they are, and I've always known who my mother was. Did Erebus say anything about when your power returns?"

"Be somewhere uninhabited."

"Make sure you do that. I didn't realize until it was too late and I'd destroyed a warehouse. When your magic returns, you'll have full use for about a day; then it dies down. You'll need to relearn some stuff. It's not a quick process."

"Untapped, incredible power, but at the cost of a year or more with nothing. Always give with one hand, take with the other with magic, isn't it?"

Mordred laughed. "You need to come with me. There are some things you need to know."

"I'm in a pair of shorts. Can I have a shower and get changed first?"

"Oh, sure. Shower's over there. I think Hades said something about clean clothes for you in the drawer."

I looked over at the door, which presumably led to the shower, and the light-blue chest of drawers. "I'll be twenty minutes."

"Take an hour. Have a long shower. You're going to need it. A lot has happened."

Mordred left me alone, and I went for a shower, making the powerful, high-pressure water as hot as I could bear.

"You feel up to a little company?" Selene asked from the doorway.

I opened the glass door to the shower. "I'm achy, but I'm sure I'll manage."

She dropped her robe to the floor, revealing that she was naked underneath, and stepped into the shower.

An hour later I was clean, dressed, and in need of something to eat. Selene had helped me with my T-shirt, as my body was still incredibly sore and stiff, but the shower and company had done wonders to lift my mood.

"Hades wants to see you," Selene said, kissing me on the lips. "I missed you. Probably not as much as Tommy, but it was a close thing."

I laughed. "I Han Soloed him. I wasn't sure he'd forgive me."

"I think it might be the proudest moment of his life that didn't involve Kasey being born."

I laughed again, and it caused me to wince. "Ribs hurt."

"You want me to kiss them better?"

"I'm not a machine."

Selene smiled. "I'm glad you're back. I was worried. We all were, except Mordred—he kept coming in here playing you his extensive list of video-game soundtracks. He said it would help, presumably because he expected you to wake up and tell him to piss off."

"So, if I start humming 'Mario,' it's his fault? Good to know."

Selene led me out of my room and down a corridor that wouldn't have looked out of place in a hospital. There was no one around, no one working in any of the rooms we walked past. It was like a clean ghost town.

"What's going on?" I asked as we entered the lift and Selene selected the floor for the main hangar above.

"For the last four months, you have had lightning strike this facility eight hundred thirty-two times. You created a storm that sat just above this facility. People know you're here. People we trust, but Hades, Mordred, and Elaine had an idea to ensure that their knowledge of you wasn't a problem."

"What idea?"

Selene sighed. "Blood-curse marks."

The lift doors opened as I was stunned into silence. I looked out across the hangar and saw hundreds of people all watching me as I exited the lift. There was a cheer and round of applause, and I sort of did this weird, uncomfortable wave thing. Because what the hell else are you meant to do when hundreds of people start clapping at you for no known reason?

"What the fuck?" I whispered.

Tommy bounded toward me and picked me up in a bear hug.

"Bones—fragile, human-powered bones," I whispered.

He put me down and grinned. "It's good to see you. Mordred said you were essentially human now. I'm sorry you've lost your magic."

"It'll come back. But it's a little weird knowing it'll be a while."

I looked beyond him to Olivia and Kasey, both of whom waved. Several other young men and women stood beside them, and I knew that they were members of Tommy's ultrasecret task force he'd put together before Arthur had taken over.

"How bad is it?" I asked Sky, who kissed me on the cheek.

"It's not good," she said.

"What's going on?" I asked Elaine as he she walked toward me with Mordred, Nabu, Irkalla, Hades, and Zamek.

"We need to talk," she told me, and motioned for me to follow her into a nearby room. She turned to Mordred as we entered. "Get it finished."

Mordred nodded and walked off.

"Get what finished?" I asked, taking a seat on the table in the middle of the room. "Selene said you were doing something with blood-curse marks."

"Everyone here has agreed to take part in a ritual," Hades said from the doorway.

"What kind of ritual?" I asked.

"The kind where we all think you're dead," Irkalla said. "Everyone but Hades, Sky, Mordred, and Elaine, yes."

"Why not those four?"

"Hades and Sky because you need a contact in case something goes wrong during your time of healing. Mordred because he was never going to agree to have anything close to a blood-curse mark put on him again, and Elaine because she used to be in charge of everything. This is the kind of thing you'll need someone keeping an eye on you for."

"And where am I going that I need to be kept an eye on?"

"A small town in Oregon," Nabu said. "It's very quaint."

"No," I replied.

"You have no powers, and Avalon thinks you're dead," Sky said. "You aren't helpful until you're healed, and if Arthur ever finds out you're alive, he will burn a country down to find you. We need to put you somewhere remote, but with people we trust. So, you're going to Clockwork, Oregon. Called that because its founder used to make clocks and was really happy about it."

"And what do I do while I'm there?"

"Read, write, learn how to whittle—I don't think it matters," Irkalla said. "Just stay safe, and don't bring attention to yourself."

"Why there?"

"I have people there I trust," Hades said. "A doctor by the name of Daniel Kuro. I met him in Korea a few decades ago. He's a good man. I've used the town a few times to send friends of mine so they can heal in peace. Or avoid detection."

"Okay, tell me more about this blood-curse ritual."

"Mordred, Nabu, and I worked together on this," Zamek said. "Essentially everyone in this facility will think you're dead. We considered just having them forget you existed, but that's too hard. Thinking you died on a field in Wisconsin is a lot easier."

"Essentially we managed to figure out a way to create the blood curse so that everyone affected will believe you dead," Nabu said. "They will believe they've grieved and have moved on. No one here will be caused any pain by your passing. That was integral to our plan. If anyone decided to dig too deep into your death, or go after Atlas for revenge, it would break the curse."

"How does the curse break normally?" I asked.

"If any of them see you once the curse has been implemented, they will immediately remember that you didn't die," Elaine explained.

"Each of them signed a document stating that they agreed to this. We couldn't do it any other way."

I walked past them all and out into the hangar, where I found Tommy, Olivia, and Selene. "You all agreed to this?" I asked. "All of you?"

"We need to keep you safe," Selene said. "This is the best way."

"Why can't you come with me?" I asked her.

"Because my father and sister would tear the world apart looking for whoever killed me. The smaller number, the better."

"They offered me and Selene a chance to not be affected," Tommy said. "But I couldn't do that to Kasey and Olivia. I couldn't lie like that to any of the people who helped get us here. I'm not a spy anymore. Deception isn't something I want to do."

"What about those who aren't already here?" I asked.

"They already think you're dead," Diana said. "It won't be hard to keep that going."

"So, it's sorted? I'll be dead to all of you. I won't be able to help you fight Gawain."

"Yeah, this is where things get messy," Elaine said.

"Okay, how do things get messier than they already are?"

"It's a long story. You up to hearing it?" she asked.

I nodded, and she told everyone to leave the room. When we were alone, she took a chair and sat down in front of me. "A few months before this all kicked off, I found out that maybe Gawain wasn't as innocent as we all thought. I was digging into the prophecy about you and Mordred and discovered that it was fake. I also discovered that while Hera and some of her people had been the ones responsible for the fake prophecy, there was evidence to suggest that Gawain was a regular visitor at Mars Warfare. I found someone who used to work there. She ran after Mars Warfare folded, but I managed to track her down and question her. She gave me information about Arthur and Merlin. And about Abaddon. And about the ritual that was used to create you and Mordred. Hera and her people were looking into ways to re-create it. It's why they were using children in the Harbinger trials."

"I remembered that well. A lot of kids had died because of those trials."

"You killed the doctor responsible."

"Can't even remember his name, but yes, I did."

"Well, my contact told me all about the meetings between Gawain, Abaddon, and Hera. She revealed that Arthur was created like you and fed Asmodeus's soul and blood."

"I know. Gawain told me."

"He didn't tell you of the horrific things that Arthur did before he was injured by Mordred. Arthur has Asmodeus's spirit inside of him, and his power level. He's not a vampire, and he doesn't have his personality, but essentially Arthur and Asmodeus are the same. Arthur wasn't an unwilling victim of Gawain; he was the one who began to turn Merlin. Arthur was the one who corrupted Merlin during his time in a coma."

"But Gawain said that Arthur needed to be changed to work with them. I saw Arthur's face when they kidnapped him—that wasn't one of happiness. He was afraid."

"You were set up to think that. Arthur is My Liege. He's been the one commanding people from his coma for centuries. He had a mind link with Gawain and Abaddon, who would deliver orders to those who needed them."

"How? Arthur came to me for help. I sensed no deception in him."

"Lucie found out. That's why they took her. She was distrustful of Arthur and started looking into him. She discovered the burial pit where a hundred people were tossed after they were used to help Gawain and Merlin place a blood curse on Arthur. A modified version of the same curse that Mordred tried to apply to you all those years ago, the one that made you lose your memory." Elaine took a USB stick from her pocket.

"This contains film of the blood-curse ritual, along with files detailing what happened and what they planned to do. She got it all from someone within Avalon who was working closely with those responsible."

"Who?"

"Hephaestus."

"Aphrodite's ex-husband?"

Elaine nodded. "He's been passing information on about Hera's activities for centuries. He's not exactly a fan, and he knew about the ritual, so he went along to check it out. He also knows that Hera records every meeting she has for blackmail purposes. He gave that information to Lucie."

I stared at the USB drive. "What was their plan?"

"Arthur's memory of his involvement with Abaddon and Gawain was wiped. And new memories were installed when he went to you for help. They couldn't risk you figuring out his involvement, or one of your friends being able to read his mind, so he had it changed. Once he was kidnapped, they changed it back. Arthur went on the news a few months ago to announce that he's going to be in charge of a task force dedicated to hunting down Hellequin's friends and allies. He's had countless people murdered since then."

I went to a nearby laptop, plugged the USB drive in, and watched the videos it contained, feeling my anger grow as they showed Arthur butchering people for their blood and spirits before the blood curse was activated. It made me feel sick that I'd been in the same room as him, called him a friend, when in reality I should have killed him.

"What happened to the woman in Mars Warfare?" I asked.

"They killed her soon after I spoke to her, and two days later I was abducted and my people killed. Arthur wanted to use his mind magic on me to twist my brain and make me forget what I knew. He tried to change my memories so that he could send me back to you with information that Galahad and Shadow Falls were behind it all, but I was too strong for him, and it didn't take as quickly as he'd have liked. That's why certain things triggered the return of my memories. When I saw him up there in front of the UN, my memories flooded back, and I fell into a coma."

I looked at her, concerned.

"I'm fine," she assured me. She opened the door, and beckoned the others back into the room.

"So, what happens now?" I asked.

"Right now we're in no position to fight him," Remy said. "Arthur has started taking control of governments the world over. He's still in the process of removing those who are against him. A lot of Avalon employees are in hiding. We're trying to help them as best we can. That's our main focus at the moment. We can't go after Arthur until we know who is and isn't working with him."

"Saving lives is the best we've got until we can organize some sort of resistance," Olivia said.

"A rebel force, if you will," Tommy said, making me laugh.

"How long have you wanted to use that one?" I asked him.

"Years," Tommy said, hugging me again. "I'm sorry this is a fleeting moment, but you need to go. You need to be safe, and when you're healed, we'll fight Arthur. But we need to find those other four weapons like yourselves. And the Norse and Japanese gods contacted Mordred, asking for help. It looks like the Norse went to the Japanese pantheon a while ago looking for allies. They agreed, but Arthur's forces have broken into Asgard through the dwarven realm."

"We're fighting a war on several fronts," Diana said. "And until we're a united force, we'll always be one step behind. We need you back, Nate."

"But at full strength, not human Nate," Remy said. "Human Nate sucks."

"Really?" I asked. "It's good that you're so supportive."

"Would you prefer if I gave you a back rub and told you you were a special little boy who just needs to try real hard?"

"That's the creepiest thing you've ever said," Tommy said.

Remy thought for a second. "Yeah, I'm going to pretend I didn't say that."

"We're all going to be doing that," Diana said.

"While you're gone, Wei told me she'll try and help me see if I have any other powers," Remy said, rapidly changing the subject. "Sounds like a plan to me."

Hades placed a hand on my shoulder. "We have to go," he said.

I said my goodbyes to everyone before kissing Selene. "When I'm healed, I'll come find you," I said.

"You'd better," she told me. "I'm going to be particularly angry otherwise. I wish I could come with you. But the fewer who know where you are, the safer you'll be."

I kissed her once again and then left the hangar with Sky, Mordred, Elaine, and Hades.

"Don't you need to perform the ritual?" I asked Mordred as we all climbed into a Black Hawk helicopter.

"Nabu and Zamek will complete it. Anyone in there is going to be affected, so it's best I'm not in there."

"What do you plan to do while I'm in the middle of nowhere?"

"What I've always done, Nate. Piss off Avalon and fuck their shit up. Only this time I'll be doing it for the good guys. I'm looking forward to the change of perspective. Just so you know, Morgan sat by your bed a lot while you were out. She was worried for you. I'm not saying she loves you or anything, but when this is all done, you two need to sit down and talk. I know you're in love with Selene, but clearing the air between you and Morgan would be good. I think there are things left unsaid, and if there's one thing I've learned, it's don't do that."

I nodded in agreement. "Yeah. I think you're right. It's something I need to do."

The rest of the journey was a chance for Hades and Elaine to explain exactly what Arthur had done since I was considered dead. Occasionally I turned to watch the ground fly by at speed far below us, wondering if Arthur's corruption had spread across the country, until eventually we landed in the middle of a forest in Clockwork, Oregon.

We all got out of the helicopter, and an elderly Asian man left a Ford Ranger truck and greeted Hades with a hug.

"This is Doctor Kuro," Hades said.

The doctor shook my hand. "You're going to be our guest here."

"I guess that's the plan, yes."

"Your house is ready. We have a beautiful town. You'll like it. It's mostly peaceful."

"Mostly?" I asked with a raised eyebrow.

"We're a small town, not a boring one," Doctor Kuro said with a smile.

I turned back to Sky, Elaine, and Mordred. "I'll be seeing you all soon," I said.

"Take care, Nate," Sky said.

"Have a nice holiday," Mordred said. "Try not to bring attention to yourself. Be a good little human."

"Piss off," I said to him, and he smiled and hugged me.

"I wish this had gone better," Elaine said. "But now we know our true enemy. We know his power and influence are great. One day soon there will be a reckoning for him."

"Our world has changed," I said. "Humans know of our existence. They know of Avalon; they know they're not the top of the evolutionary ladder. If they don't know now, they soon will, that some of Arthur's allies consider humans nothing more than food. Arthur is going to change the world, and we can't stop that. There aren't enough of us, and we're fragmented and broken. But we won't be. Not forever. We'll show Arthur the kinds of people he crossed, and we'll show him just how badly we plan on beating him and those who call him an ally."

I watched them climb back into the helicopter, leaving me alone with Hades.

"Thank you for this," I said.

"No thanks necessary," he told me. "Be safe, heal, and then we'll deal with what comes next."

"We fight back," I said with complete conviction. "That's what comes next. Rebellion."

ACKNOWLEDGEMENTS

So, here it is, the last Hellequin book. Not the last Nate book, I'll hasten to add, but this is the end of the story of Hellequin. Thank you to those who stuck with it from *Crimes Against Magic*, which feels like a lifetime ago, but it's only been a little over five years. I hope you hang around to see how I make Nate's life worse . . . sorry, better, not worse—I'd never do such a thing.

There are always lots of people to thank, starting with my wife and kids for their love and support, and in my wife's case for allowing me to use her as a sounding board for every idea I have.

To my parents, who have never wavered in their support and love, I thank you from the bottom of my heart.

My friends and family always support, nag, complain, and generally just want me to hurry up and write more. Thank you—you're part of the reason I never gave up writing, and it means a lot that so many of you still look forward to the next book.

A big thank-you goes out to my agent, Paul Lucas, for his belief, friendship, and help over the years.

And another big thank-you to my editor, Jenni Smith-Gaynor, who takes my vision and helps me mold it into something that's readable.

D. B. Reynolds and Michelle Muto are the kind of beta readers and friends that you can only wish for. Thank you for all the time and effort you've put in to help me make my work better.

As always, I need to thank 47North for their help. Emilie, Alex, Hatty, Sana, you're all awesome. And a huge thank-you to those of you who helped work on my books over the years. Whether you're still at 47North or not, you know who you are, and you should know how awesome you are.

So, this is it. The last Hellequin book. It's been a fun, exhausting, and at times difficult ride. I'd like to think I've grown as an author and as a storyteller, and I'm looking forward to what comes next.

READ AHEAD FOR THE FIRST
CHAPTER FROM STEVE
McHUGH'S UPCOMING BOOK
A GLIMMER OF HOPE

CHAPTER 1

Wisconsin, USA. One week ago.

Elias Wells had to admit to being genuinely impressed with the escaped experiment that sprinted through the snowy forest in search of her freedom. She had fled the prison she'd been in, along with two others, an hour earlier. They'd not only made it to the edge of the forest—a rare act that deserved respect—but the last of them, Liz Barnsley, managed to outpace the monsters that chased her.

Elias didn't bother running. He didn't see the point. Not only because he considered it a waste of his energy, but also because the snow beneath his leather-booted feet had begun to turn to slush. He didn't want to slip on an unseen spot of ice and make himself look like an idiot. Elias jogged at an easy pace, making sure to keep the creatures he worked with in his view but allowing them the freedom to do their jobs. Besides, it wasn't like Liz had a lot of choices when it came to an escape route.

Liz had escaped a half hour ago, and upon hearing the news Elias had been genuinely shocked. The fact that, during the years of the prison being active, she was the only one of four escapees to have lived long enough to reach the forest surprised him even more. He'd always taken her as the sort of person for whom the idea of running came a distant second to the idea of sitting. He guessed that adrenaline and the need to be free drove people to perform better than they'd ever be able to otherwise. He made a mental note of it; it was something to try on the rest of the subjects. Maybe they'd get better results.

A scream from up ahead signified that Liz wasn't as far away as she'd probably like to be. Elias didn't need to concern himself with anyone hearing it who wasn't meant to. Civilians were not an issue in the middle of nowhere. The only things likely to hear the screams and pleas for help would be the animals who lived in the forest, and he doubted that Liz was able to call the animals to her aid like Sleeping Beauty.

As he got closer to the noise of fighting, he heard the laughter of the creatures that served in the prison and the cursing from Liz. Elias began to wonder if there was a way to take her back without damaging her. He shook his head as he pushed aside a branch, letting it fly back to its position after getting past it.

Liz stood in a clearing, blood seeping down her left arm where an arrow had struck it. A second arrow protruded from just above her left ankle. She couldn't put weight on it.

"Hello, Liz," Elias said, his tone conversational and light. His English accent was still evident, even after all these years away. "Feel like coming back to the compound with me?"

"Go to hell," she snapped.

Elias glanced over at the three creatures that had accompanied him on the hunt. They were all baying for blood but would do nothing until he commanded it. "Go deal with the other corpses," he told them.

They did as they were ordered without comment and were soon lost from view in the darkness of the forest.

"I would rather you live," Elias said. "But if you're going to fight me, you might as well get it started now."

A spine, three inches in length, flew toward Elias, who easily avoided it. The next four were even faster as they left Liz's palms, and Elias had to catch one midflight to stop it in time.

"Nicely done," he commended. "Your bone mass must regenerate at an extraordinary speed." He turned the bone spines over in his hands.

"I was taught by the best," Liz said.

"Sarcasm, my dear? We've been trying to teach you to accept your new abilities."

"Abilities I never wanted! I just want to go home."

"To where, that park bench we found you on? We've given you shelter, food, and warmth. We haven't beaten you or tortured you. I think personally that we've been quite pleasant."

"You forced this onto me. You murder those who can't cope."

"Well, sometimes things don't go according to plan, but you have exceeded my expectations." He wagged his finger at her and smiled. "No one has ever made it this far. But what were you going to do next?"

Liz looked behind her at the cliff.

"You were going to jump? That's a two-hundred-foot fall into water. I'm pretty sure that even if the water was deep enough, you'd still die."

"I'd rather die than be one of your pawns."

"Fine, I'll tell you what. You try to kill me and manage it, you can enjoy your brief life as a cliff diver. You don't kill me? You'll be dead. Either way, you win."

Liz fired a half dozen spines at Elias, who moved smoothly as he dodged them, sliding under the last one and drawing out a nine-inch stiletto dagger, then plunging it up and into Liz's stomach. He twisted it and pulled the knife out, pushing Liz onto the ground. He watched her writhe for a few moments as soft cries escaped her lips. He felt nothing except relief that the job was completed. Her pain would last longer than he liked. A quick kill was important. Professional. Kills should only last a long time if you needed something from the person, and he needed Liz to suffer a little—she had escaped, after all. He'd end it soon, and then she'd be at peace.

Elias held the stiletto up to the light of the moon. A stunning piece of craftsmanship: a black handle, with silver pommel and matching cross guard. The blade itself had a percentage of silver in it and had been polished to a high sheen. As he turned the dagger over in his grasp, a drop of blood fell from the tip onto the snow below.

He looked at Liz; her already-pale face appeared ashen. She didn't have long left. The silver in the blade had made sure of it. Even so, he needed to ensure that the fight to survive was extinguished. "I realize if we take you back, you'll either escape again or kill someone. So you do get your wish."

"You should not play with your prey," a male said from behind Elias.

Elias turned to the newcomer and dropped to one knee, bowing his head. "My lord, Nergal."

Nergal was a head taller than Elias's own five-nine, with broader shoulders and dark skin. A smooth bald head and deep-brown eyes that looked almost black gave him the appearance of someone who was not to be crossed. Several thousand years earlier Nergal had been considered a god by the Mesopotamian people, and it was easy to see why—just being near him made people nervous. To Elias's knowledge, there were few people who possessed Nergal's level of power; it practically came off him in waves.

"Get up. It's cold and wet, and you've already gotten yourself filthy fighting this one." Nergal walked over to Liz and bent down, slapping her across the face to get her attention. "She's almost done. End it. We need to talk."

Elias wanted to tell him that was exactly what he'd intended to do, but there was no point in angering the man. Instead, he nodded and used his foot to push Liz over onto her front. He placed a knee on her back and pressed the tip of the dagger up against her throat. He pushed it in without comment, removed it, and stepped off her to avoid the arterial spray.

He removed the black trilby from his head and dropped it into Liz's blood, wiping the knife on his expensive suit trousers before replacing it in the sheath at his back.

"Are you quite done?" his lord asked.

"I did not know you were coming," Elias said, turning around. "We had some issues with escapees. First in a few years. She was good, too. Shame about how it ended up. Not to change the subject, but I'll have to recharge soon."

"Well, that will have to wait. We found her, Elias. I need you to go to England. To Southampton. I'll have all of the details emailed to you."

Elias didn't want to question his lord, but he'd been here before. "Are we sure she's there?" He made sure to say "we," too.

Nergal smiled. "We've been searching for so long, Elias. Yes, I'm *sure* she's there."

Elias picked up his hat from the ground; it had absorbed all of the blood that had once been inside Liz. Despite the amount of liquid it had taken, it was completely dry. To all outward appearances, the hat remained black and nothing had changed. In the few minutes since he'd killed her, Liz's corpse had turned into a mummified husk.

Elias placed the hat on his head, and a slight trickle of blood slid down his pale skin. He caught it with a finger, leaving a smear, and licked the digit clean.

"Picked it up too early," Elias said by way of explanation. "You want me to go now?"

"Yes, Elias. Take whoever you need. Just find the woman and bring her back here. Alive. And do it quickly."

"Not a problem, my lord."

Nergal turned and walked away as the three creatures arrived once more, looking hungrily at Liz's corpse.

"Make it quick. Leave no trace." Elias knew he didn't have to say that to them—they were always quick and clean—but sometimes he liked to tell them anyway. Just in case they ever forgot who was in charge.

He walked back to the compound, his mind ablaze with possibilities. He had a lot to think on, and a lot to achieve in a short time. Going back to his ancestral home would have to wait until the job was done. Find a human girl and bring her back to Nergal. Easy.

ABOUT THE AUTHOR

Steve McHugh is the author of the popular Hellequin Chronicles. He lives in Southampton, on the south coast of England, with his wife and three young daughters. When not writing or spending time with his kids, he enjoys watching movies, reading books and comics, and playing video games.

31901064759840